BIG JIM TURNER

BIG
JIM TURNER

JAMES STEVENS

Introduction by Warren L. Clare

A Zia Book

UNIVERSITY OF NEW MEXICO PRESS
Albuquerque

WITH THE EXCEPTION OF SUCH actual historical personages as William Edgar Borah, Frank Steunenberg, Charles Erskine Scott Wood, William D. Haywood, Harry Orchard, William Howard Taft, and Joe Hill, all characters appearing in this novel are creations of the imagination and any resemblance in name or appearance to any human being, living or dead, is coincidental. This story was written without partisan purpose for or against any group or cause outside individual freedom.

TO THERESA
for our own sonnets

INTRODUCTION

James Stevens was raised in the ragged sagebrush foothills of the Seven Devils on the Snake River in Idaho. All his life, the rugged quality of those mountains was deeply ingrained in his character. Stevens was a laborer, a prophet, a mule skinner, a harvest hand, and a poet. He was also the finest novelist produced by the Pacific Northwest in the first half of this century. And he brought about a significant change in Pacific Northwest literature. It wasn't easy, for, as a group, the writers of the Pacific Northwest before Stevens's time were probably as bad as any writers ever published, and yet they were tremendously influential.

When Stevens and his literary friend H. L. Davis tried to call this situation to the attention of the reading public, they couldn't even find a publisher to put their opinions into print. At their own expense they published 200 copies of a pamphlet entitled *Status Rerum: A Manifesto upon the Present Conditions of Northwestern Literature. Containing Several Near-Libelous Utterances upon Persons in the Public Eye.* This humorously virulent document attacked editors of northwestern literary magazines and professors of creative writing at the Universities of Washington and Oregon for fostering bad taste and thereby keeping the quality of northwestern literature intolerably low.

Any modern reader who examined representative stories from a periodical like the *Pacific Monthly,* one of the Northwest's most popular literary magazines at the turn of the

The editors of *Research Studies* have granted permission for the reuse of selected passages from an earlier publication discussing Stevens's canon. Some passages originally appeared in "James Stevens: The Laborer and Literature," *Research Studies* 32, no. 4 (December 1964): 355–67.

century, would agree that the region was producing very poor writing. Authors seemed to imitate the style of writers popular nearly a century earlier; plots and characters were usually stilted. By attacking such literature as "tripe," *Status Rerum* declared war on an entire literary generation. But a far better protest is the concept of literature tacitly evident in nearly all of Stevens's own fiction.

Stevens believed that the writer should write about what he knows. He should deal with the real world, here-and-now issues, and real characters. At the same time, he should be accurate in his details, depicting actual settings, and his style should be appropriate to his subject. He should also have something to say.

James Stevens started gathering things to say in 1907 at the Idaho Dairy Institute, near Weiser, Idaho. He was making butter and chewing tobacco at the same time when the principal caught him. He was prayed over and then expelled. He caught a freight, lived for a time in a hobo jungle, got a job in heavy construction, moved to Boise, and discovered the Carnegie Free Public Library. Not long afterward he discovered another hall of learning; this one had sawdust on the floor and was peopled by bartenders, as well as cowboys, loggers, miners, construction men, and prostitutes.

Stevens wintered in Boise for the next several years, spending his summers following heavy construction in Idaho, Montana, and Washington. When there wasn't a road to be built or a dam going up, he worked in the timber, felling and sawing lumber. And if he couldn't find work there, he could always get into a wheat harvest or pick fruit or just hop a freight to see what was going on in the next town. By the time he was twenty, he was lean and hard and built like a bull. He loved to fight, and, as one man who remembers him from that era says, "He was a damned tough customer."

He had another side, though, and it was so incongruously different that those who knew him in his early years scarcely believed it. He was sensitive and perceptive, articulate and intelligent. And he wrote poetry. He gave his first work away to the *Stars and Stripes,* but after he was discharged from the

American Expeditionary Force with a new scar in his scalp from a brawl in a questionable sort of café in France, he began to see himself as a writer.

In 1924, an article of his, "By a Laborer," found its way to the desk of George Horace Lorimer, the editor of the *Saturday Evening Post*. Lorimer saw a spark in Stevens's work; so did H. L. Mencken, who took a Paul Bunyan story, "The Black-Duck Dinner," for publication in the *American Mercury*. Mencken began a flurry of correspondence with Stevens that encouraged the writer to form his own literary ideas based upon his own unique experience and his knowledge of the working man. Essentially, Mencken helped him discover that he could give artistic expression to the kind of life he already knew.

While Lorimer was publishing Stevens in the *Post* and Mencken was encouraging him to write more for the *American Mercury*, Alfred Knopf invited Stevens to submit a completed manuscript dealing with the tall tales of Paul Bunyan as they were actually told around the lumber camps on the West Coast. Stevens did; the next thing he knew he was famous. Mencken and Knopf invited him to New York, where he met Sinclair Lewis and Thomas Wolfe; his friendships with these novelists were to last a lifetime.

His first novel was *Brawnyman*, a largely autobiographical story of his experiences in construction camps, published in 1926. In 1927, Knopf brought out another novel by Stevens, *Mattock*, which reflects his experiences in France during World War I. The following year, 1928, Knopf published a volume of Stevens's short stories, *Homer in the Sagebrush*. During the 1930s and 1940s Stevens confined his work primarily to short stories and articles, except for two books. In 1932 he published another volume of Paul Bunyan stories, *Saginaw Paul Bunyan*, and in 1942 he brought out *Timber*, a children's book about the way of life in lumber camps. Between these two works Stevens published hundreds of pieces in the *American Mercury, Saturday Evening Post, Frontier, Frontier and Midland*, and, as he put it, "slews more magazines."

discovers that, despite the color in the workers' lives, a threat of violence holds the working class in a special kind of slavery.

Big Jim's discovery of significance in his life parallels the discoveries made by James Stevens in his search for significant literature. A survey of Stevens's work shows that, in spite of the precepts tacitly advanced in *Status Rerum,* his early fiction tended to idealize a period in Northwest history to which he looked back with sentimental nostalgia. But *Big Jim Turner* is a mature work of fiction. The writer's protest in *Status Rerum* against the works of other Pacific Northwest authors shows that he set himself the task of giving artistic expression to what he perceived as the "real Pacific Northwest." In *Big Jim Turner* he succeeded in depicting the region's labor conflicts as a specific historical phenomenon. He wrote the novel in an idiom appropriate to his subject and dealt

In 1948 Stevens completed his finest, most mature work of creative fiction, *Big Jim Turner.* In this novel Stevens draws upon his previous literary training and blends it with his love of the Northwest. The action of *Big Jim Turner* resembles that in the earlier book *Brawnyman.* But the writer has made a good many changes in theme, attitude, and technique. Big Jim Turner is a sensitive young man with a sincere thirst for knowledge. Like young Stevens, he gets his education in the public libraries, the "poor man's universities." A minor theme of the novel is the cultural benefits bestowed upon the region by the public libraries.

Also important in *Big Jim Turner* is the presence of the Industrial Workers of the World. The Spokane "free speech fight" and excerpts from the *Little Red Song Book* combine to give color, authenticity, and a sense of immediacy to the novel.

A major point in *Big Jim Turner* is the historical explanation for the conflict between organized labor and fundamentalist Protestantism. Fundamentalists were not permitted to join any organization outside the church. Most of them were working men, day laborers and timbermen, the same men who, according to organizers, should have been involved in the labor protests of the time. Consequently the fundamen-

talists were known among the IWW as "Christers." Another
disparaging term, "dehorn," referred to a worker who refused
to join the labor agitation but moved in after the conflict to
gain the same benefits as the men who had risked their lives.
"Oh sure, sure, religion. Hah! . . . Pie in the sky. Dehorn!
Servants, knuckle down to your masters. Let the other man
risk his neck and do the dirty work of improvin' conditions for
labor, then you take a free ride. You dehorns can go to hell!"
(pp. 130–31).

Speaking comes easily to Big Jim, and he is tricked into
preaching to the workers by an employer who knows that if
he can keep the laborers happy with religion they will not
organize against him. Gradually Big Jim becomes aware of
the true nature of the labor issue. When he begins his life as a
laborer, he has romantic ideas about adventure. But he
with real issues and real people. Stevens himself gained
literary power as he gradually lost his first inclination to
idealize the past. *Big Jim Turner,* then, is the result of a
thorough reconciliation of Stevens's literary ideas and his
literary practice. As such it is one of the finest examples of
literature yet produced in the Pacific Northwest.

Warren L. Clare
Garrett Heyns Education Center
Shelton, Washington

Contents

The Silver Cap . . .

THERE WERE TWO KINDS OF CAPS IN TWIN STACKS ON
a counter of Maul's General Merchandise Store, shining on a level
with my eyes. One kind was decorated with gold braid and leaves,
and this was a McKinley cap for Republican boys. One bore deco-
rations of silver, and this cap was for the boys who stood for
William Jennings Bryan of Nebraska. Never since, never in all
my days and nights, have I dreamed of anything with such hunger as I dreamed then, in an Iowa town, of the Bryan Silver Cap.

The cost of a cap was a quarter. This was a scarce coin in
Grandma Barton's house. It would buy many a thing that was
needed by a four-year-old who had only a poor old widow woman
to look out for him.

"Nosiree, no Bryan cap for you, young man," grandma said.

I complained that the Republican boys were mocking me to
death. Even girls would squeal, "Fool fer Bryan, fool fer Bryan
—where's your Silver Cap?" It was common for grandma to say
that this or that was pitiable, and I told her my need for a Bryan
cap was as pitiable as could be. "Likely," she said.

It was really a dream of glory, not shame under mockery, that
made me hunger so for the Silver Cap. I found I could stand out of
the way in Maul's store by the hour, imagining a bookload of
wonders while I stared at the pile of blue and silver. A spirit
stirred in me, small child, poor boy; seed of the poem and the tale.

At home I lived and breathed want of a Silver Cap.

"Night on night that young un even bawled in his sleep for the
cap of his man for President," grandma would tell. "Ever' mornin' he'd wake with the same plaint. I simply had to give in to him,

headstrong as he was and so powerful of lung. It took the trade of nigh on a bushel of tomatoes to save me from the asylum."

On a Saturday afternoon I marched out of Maul's store in a silver blaze of glory.

Farmers were in town. It was a fall day of raw weather, but all was bright for me, Jim Turner, going on five, a Free Silver Democrat and able and proud to show it. I strutted from one bunch of farmers to another, yelling, "I'm Jim Turner and my grandma is from Virginia. 'Ray, 'ray for William Jennings Bryan!'"

Nobody noticed me enough to take me down a peg. The Republican boys soon mended this neglect. Long before Election Day there was nothing much left of my Silver Cap but muddy tatters.

Grandma Martha Barton was a great one for stories. Her tale of the Silver Cap grew into rigmarole, yet it kept for me the memory of the first stir and shine of poetry in myself. And I keep from it certain images. The small hand holding the Silver Cap as pure treasure. The same hand throwing it into the kitchen stove as a soiled rag. This hand——

This hand, writing. Here it rests on a yellow tablet, holding a pencil, awaiting the spirit and the word. I know this hand too well. The spread from thumb butt sidewise is over most of the tablet's eight-inch width. The palm is sheathed with calluses from teaming, logging, pitching wheat bundles, bucking sacks of wheat. There are two bulged knuckles and other marks of a fighting fist. The hand writes as the spirit moves through it, taking substance from times recalled, people remembered, books read, music heard, scenes viewed, thoughts stored, loves endured, by this one life on the American land.

So let me give testimony. I rise unasked and unknown from the midst of the congregation and testify, as in experience meeting. My tales are parables, my poems are psalms.

Here I am. Now in November, 1913, I am twenty-two years of age. I pack two hundred and twenty work-leaned pounds which stand six feet and three inches without shoes. But there are shoes on me here, oxblood button shoes with bulldog toes, size eleven, cost two dollars and a half. My suit is a blue serge that was bought for nineteen-fifty three weeks ago. Under the coat is a sixty-cent blue chambray shirt, fresh and starched, with a fifteen-cent red bow tie in its collar. My pride is a Boss Raw-Edge Stetson that set me down seven dollars and a half around six months back. Like every hard-line hobo, I wear it with no crease or dent. Now my hat is set on the table before the yellow tablet with green lines and black pencil scrawls. My shock of coaly hair is neat, as I pack a pocket comb. These days I shave my face every morning. The place wherein I am pleased to write the testimony, the story of *Big Jim Turner*, is a Free Public Library of the people. It is the only temple I know. Everywhere on the American land the Free Public Library is a temple in my sight. I do not fail to spruce up for it.

I sit at a long table that is one of a number in a room walled with books, a great room in both size and treasure. Here am I, up from the sagebrush and out of the camps, mule-breaker, worshiper of Walt Whitman, axman, poet, slave, rebel, brawler, dreamer, mystic, plowman, full mongrel American—here I presume to plant myself and write among the works of the mighty. Here for a time the Silver Cap is mine again, unworn and shining.

1. Home in Idaho

UNCLE GABE TURNER MET ME AT THE KNOX DEPOT.
He came loping up under the platform light, grabbed me for a hug,
then shoved me back and hollered in a hoarse voice, "Well, well,
well! Big fer a yearlin', ain't you? How'd you make out on the
trip? How'd you leave yore Grandma Barton? Air ye tuckered out?
Yore Aunt Sue has a sick cow to look after, Wiley is in the mountains, so meetin' you was up to me. Fine to see you, fine to see you.
Welcome, welcome. Let's have the baggage check. Think you can
fork a cayuse? That's Idyho talk. H-h-haw! Fine to see you, fine
to see you."

He was a long-coupled, stooped, rawboned, shambling man of
fifty, sandy-complected and squint-eyed. Uncle Gabe wore a red-
dish mustache that looked like rye stubble bent down over his
mouth and which he would keep parting and wiping with the back
of his hand as though it was before or after taking a drink. I soon
learned that taking a drink was something that was always on his
mind. This was why his sheephide coat and cowhand hat were
shabby from long wear and tear and why his overalls looked like
seven washings. He had a fruity smell, too.

Uncle Gabe kept on talking as I helped him lug my roped box
over to his team and wagon. "You don't show much Turner in
you, which is likely jest as well," he gabbed on. "Spittin' image
of Black Dan Barton. No tellin' when he'll show up. You'll be
proud of him, don't worry, even though he served time in the state
pen. But now it's yore Aunt Sue. Susie works her head off, and
she will your'n. Wiley, he sawmills up nigh to the Seven Devils
Mountains ever' summer, and Susie has the oldest of the Clover

girls helpin' her. Lessee—you air eleven, and Bess is a year older. Never lived in a house with a girl, did you? You can expect to be run ragged. Here's Tiresome. He's a quarter coyote, some collie, rest what-all. And these here are Frank and Cyclone, my two best bronco horses. Pile up on the spring seat, kid. I'll do the fixin's."

I knew that some of his gab was whisky, but it was mainly to make me feel to home in the Wild West and not mind that Aunt Sue and Uncle Wiley had failed to meet the train. Susie Hurd was Uncle Gabe's sister, and my pa, Lon Turner, was their brother away back yonder before he got trampled to death by steers in a dehorning pen. Uncle Gabe was known to all the relations as a man who had wasted his years in an even worse way than Pa Lon had done.

"Black Dan Barton and yore pa and me, we used to hell around the mines and in the hard-rock camps of railroad buildin'," was one thing Uncle Gabe told me, as Frank and Cyclone hauled us through the moonlighted sagebrush hills. "Then Lon went back to Ioway and was married to Tavie Barton. It come to be hell, ex-cuse me, with strikes in the silver-lead mines. Yore Uncle Dan'l Barton was black-listed as a strike leader, and that there is what fin'lly put him in the state pen. He was never a crook. Black Dan never stole a penny from nobody, and he never killed nobody who didn't need killin' bad. Don't you let Susie turn you ag'in' him. I was black-listed, too, and took to ranchin' to feed my gut. Frank, you! Up in the collar there!"

He rambled on so, until I learned more Barton and Turner family history than I'd heard through all my years in Iowa. I had nothing much to say but kept sullen, as I'd been doing mainly since the start of the trouble that had come to mean either the state re-form school in Iowa for me, or a new home in Idaho.

"You shore do keep a close mouth," Uncle Gabe said.

I said, "Yes, sir."

He remarked that it was fine with him, he appreciated it, then he hawked to clear his throat and said he felt a spell of the old asthma coming on and he'd better take some medicine against it. He stooped over, then fetched up a half-gallon jug. When he pulled the stopper I smelled rye whisky. After a tremendous snort from the jug Uncle Gabe said "Whuf!" and went on talking.

Frank and Cyclone walked at a good lick and Uncle Gabe jogged them now and then. We were close to three hours on the road from Knox to the Hurd place. Mainly it was winding along the skirts of the hills above the east bench of the valley. Under the full moon the sagebrush hills were monsters in my prairie sight. Coyote howls kept sounding down, and I kind of liked to hear them, as I did all animal sounds. A breeze was blowing up smells of wet soil and alfalfa from below the irrigation ditches. I hearkened to the rattle of wagon wheels, the clomp and clomp of hoofs in the dust of the road, the creak of hames and harness leather, the clink of trace chains, and I went to dreaming stories about Frank, Cyclone, and me. Finally I spoke up to Uncle Gabe for the first time.

"Do you expect I'll get to ride or work horses any, sir?" I said.

"Why, shore. Hell, excuse me, yes. It's a horse country."

A spot inside of me warmed up and shone a mite. But it was not for Uncle Gabe or anybody else on two legs. It was for horses. I dreamed on about them until we pulled in.

First time I saw her, Susie Hurd was a shape behind a lamp, coming down a staircase. She had a dark Indian robe on over her nightgown, yet she made a shape that was not as big as mine in the light of the little hand lamp, just as the topknot in which her hair was done did not make her so tall as me. Susie Hurd came off the last stairstep and up to where I stood, between the roped baggage box that Uncle Gabe had set down and the telescope valise that I had set down on the dining-room floor. She held the lamp high and stopped close to me. Her eyes looked up a little to mine. They were hard and glittery then. Her look switched to my coat and fastened on a big tag that Grandma Barton had wired there. She let the lamp down and peered, and she kind of mumbled what the tag read, "PLEAZ HELP THE BOY. HES LONE. THANKS KINDLY." She looked on my face again and her eyes were not so glittery. Then she kissed my face and said, "Howdy, and welcome." I said, "H'are you, Aunt Susan? Thank you, ma'am." She told me to come up and she would show me a bed and clean night things, and told Uncle Gabe to wait. I told him good night and thanked him for bringing me out, calling him sir. I felt such a relief and letdown as I went after Aunt Sue. Sleep crowded on me as we came to the staircase. I climbed a-stumbling. It was all there was to remember for that night—I followed a lamp; soft lamplight.

I wasn't much account for a week. Aunt Sue let me be, mainly. Bess Clover did not bother me whatever. I hardly said a dozen words a day. I slept long in the nights and napped mornings and afternoons. I stuffed at the table, and Aunt Sue encouraged me to.

"The dry mountain country does that to ever'body from the prairies," she said. "You go on and get acclimated. When you do, you'll be kep' busy—that there you can depend on."

She knew as well as anything it was more than a change of climate that I was getting over. But I allowed I knew more than she might ever suspicion I did on how she'd fought the project to send me here. Back in Cartwright, Iowa, I'd seen Aunt Sue's letter against me to Grandma Barton. It said she had endured a slave's life for close to twenty-five years, fetching up four boys who were their pa all over, bullheads and fantods all four, and rambunctious as mule yearlings. Now all were grown and gone, praise the Lord. Now she, who had hungered for a girl ever since the diphtheria had taken her own Cory, was at last blessed with a sweet girl to live in her home and be loving to her—in no way like a mean, ornery, stinker of a boy. It was no use for the Bartons to ask her to take and bring up another aggravating boy brat, for she'd rot if she'd do it.

Grandma had never seen the letter. I'd brought it from the Cartwright postoffice and kept it at home till grandma was out, then I steamed it open, read it, and burned it.

There was a lot back of this that needs to be told. The Rev. Pearl Yates of the Methodist Episcopal Church was to blame for my crime against the U. S. Mails. He had taken me and cornered me in the room where he wrote his hell-fire sermons, to exhort me for a solid hour that seemed like a year. He had fumed and roared to me that I was on the brink of reform school, the Old Nick surely had me there, and this was a last warning of how terrible the place would be. He made howling revival story pictures of me being chained in dark holes and lashed with bull whips when I was bad, and of killer bloodhounds chasing me if I'd try to break loose. The Rev. Yates was called "the Wabash Cannonball of Methodist

Evangelism." When he took a boy in hand to scare the Old Nick out of him, he did an almighty job, trying to make a scare that would last for life. It was dark when he let me go. I ran screaming all the way home. I screamed through half the night. Grandma told me I was a coward to let an old Methodist howler scare me. But I kept on being a coward.

Now I was here, in the Wild West, far from the Rev. Yates, Mayor Clinton Maul and the Irish Bryan Democrat, Barrick Mc-Cool, who was Satan in the sight of the preacher and the mayor. I would not be mixed in their schemes and fights any more, and I could begin to feel safe from the dark holes, bull whips and killer bloodhounds. So I let down. I slept my fool head off. And how I did stuff my belly! Back at grandma's my supper was commonly just cornbread and milk, and often this was the only breakfast, too. But Aunt Sue kept cows, chickens and hogs, she made an acre garden, even growing sweet corn, and she would pick a pile of fruit and berries every summer from places around where she was more than welcome, and put the pile up in Mason jars. She was a midwife, a prime nurse and herb doctor, and she would ever offer help in time of death. It was hard to believe she was one of the generally lazy Turners. Oh, what a table she did set!

Even while I doped around and stuffed myself I felt sore guilt with Aunt Sue Hurd. I had been forced on her. Having no word, and with her trouble over my trouble pressing her so hard, grandma had finally just packed me up, borrowed money and bought a ticket, and not only wrote a letter ahead but sent a telegraph message on the same day I was put on the Wabash train for Knox, Idaho. Both said Jim Turner was on his way, and the letter made hardly any more bones about it than the message did. Grandma's ire was up at Aunt Sue for not answering the two letters she had sent which told that I had to be shipped from Cartwright somehow, to some place, or I'd go clean to the dogs. So here she had shipped me, showing Aunt Sue.

I got up one morning at daylight. First I stirred at hearing the milk buckets banging together as Aunt Sue and Bess Clover started out on the first chore of the day, the one that came even before getting breakfast. I hearkened for a spell, coming pleasantly out of sleep. Then there were no sounds. I thought that I was alone in the big house. I didn't want to sleep any more, or be alone. I was up and dressed in no time, loping downstairs, hooking a gallon lard pail, and going out after Aunt Sue and the girl.

The morning came in fast, with one streak of light after another. It seemed I couldn't get it close enough to my skin or breathe in enough of it or turn my face up high enough to the morning. A little breeze kept following me, a kind of clean, dry little breeze that was up from the south, off the desert and over the Snake River, cool and sweet but with a mention of heat to come. It smelled with the spice of sagebrush. It whispered in the leaves of the woodyard willow as I came by, telling me I was out of the hole, I was acclimated and at home in Idaho.

Aunt Sue let me try my hand at milking one of her three Shorthorns, and I proved to her I could do well at it. After breakfast she told me to try saddling and riding old Dolly around the place, and then maybe I could fork her up to Cuddy's store to buy some truck and see if there was any mail. This was truly gladsome to hear. It was yet a black worry in my mind about what Grandma Barton and Aunt Sue Hurd might get to writing to each other.

Dolly was a white cayuse mare, aged twelve years. Some years back a Clyde stud had got her with a colt which grew so big and strong in her that he about tore her apart in his birth. But Dolly was still a tough and gingery old girl.

Dolly had a partner whose name was Dud. He was a low-slung chunk of a bay bronc who had been a powerful worker in his best day. Now in his eighteenth year, Dud was grizzled, weak-eyed, and stiff, and he had a bladder stone or some kind of kidney complaint that caused him to have a long, groaning time of it when he would make water. People don't like to hear how horses, cows and other farm stock age, ail and die miserably, just as folks do. But that's how it was with Aunt Sue's ranch horses. Uncle Wiley had four good young horses, but he had them up at the Seven Devils Mountains, snaking logs to his little sawmill.

Well, I saddled Dolly and rode her around the place to prove to Aunt Sue I'd learned to handle horses back in Iowa as well as a boy of my age could be expected to handle them. This was after breakfast and in full sunup, with the last rose of morning fading away and the little breeze coming after me with a bite of desert heat.

The slopes of a couple of fat hills gentled up from the Hurd place. There were about seventy acres of pasture, sagebrush and rimrock patches, and as many more that had been cleared for dry-land wheat. Thirty acres or so of the clearing were now green with young wheat, and its other half was summer fallow. This fallow had been plowed and disked last fall. Soon it would need harrowing, to spike out Jim Hill mustard and other weeds and crumble the topsoil to help hold moisture.

I rode Dolly up through the sagebrush. Some of it was a full six feet high, the ash soil from the old volcano times was so rich. She walked at a good lick and it was real exciting to ride a horse up such a big hill. I kept her all along the high-line fence to the gulch between the fallow and the green wheat. Eastward the gray hills rose on and on, fold after fold. Wheeling Dolly at the gulch, I hauled her up and made her stand while I looked over the lay of the land.

Between the two fat hills the gulch sloped down fairly straight until it fanned out in a gravel patch that snow and rain runoffs had washed down and spread. Below it the east bench of the valley began. The Hurd ditch snaked along there, its muddy head of water now being run by Aunt Sue over the acre of garden and the five acres of alfalfa on the northwest corner of the place. A steep-sided hill stuck out and around that corner, like a giant crooked arm and a fist. The road came along from the turn at the fist's bottom and pointed straight and close past the corrals, barn, granary, henhouse, hog shed, woodyard, smokehouse, and Uncle Wiley's private locked-up workshop. The huge house stood at the foot of the fat hill at my left. I could see the top half-floor and the cupola now. There were two more floors and a great cave of a cellar, with two-story porches around two sides and the front.

On below the road was the big ditch that watered the oldest and richest ranches of Mount Creek Valley. On them even the barns were painted. Everyone had an orchard of apple, prune, and apricot trees, with cottonwood windbreaks north and west. All had hay and feed yards, acres of corrals, alfalfa fields that would yield five tons an acre, and on each side of the mile-wide valley the old-time ranches would rise to benches, high pasture slopes, wheat hills, and ridge range for cattle and sheep. The light green of willows marked the run of the creek down the alfalfa and spud bottoms.

Over in the hills to the west there, the Clovers and other poor dry-land homesteaders were trying to make out. The hills bulged along a mile or so, then came Bob Creek Valley. It was about the same as Mount Creek, Uncle Gabe had told me. He rented on shares over there.

Both creeks emptied into the Lemolo River, which forked with the Snake at Knox.

North around the fist of a hill the road went a mile to the schoolhouse, then on past the Advent Christian church, and another mile to the Cuddy store and post office. I pointed Dolly down the gulch, to track for Aunt Sue, who was out in rubber boots and with a long-handled shovel, irrigating.

"You look like you was feelin' to home," she said, when I walked Dolly along the ditch. "Think you'd like to ride up to Cuddy's for me?"

There wasn't any word from Grandma Barton. She was still letting well enough alone weeks later, when haying time came on and Wiley Hurd was due for a trip home. The failure to hear from grandma got to hounding me on a Friday of dry, parching heat, when I was working the summer fallow, and I felt it worse and worse in the drag of deep afternoon. Somehow it led to the rise and move of the spirit in me for preaching again the wicked sermon that had been my real downfall back in Cartwright, Iowa.

It was a fever. It was the kind of fever that would possess me one time to bury myself in a story book, another time to tell monstrous lies with a straight face, another time to heat and smoke me into a daydream so deep I'd not hear a relation or a teacher speak to me until I'd find my face slapped. It was a devil out of hell in me sure, the Rev. Yates and old Mayor DeWitt Clinton Maul had agreed, and I'd been possessed by it ever since my craze at the age of four for a William Jennings Bryan cap. For more than a month here in Idaho I'd not even let myself *dream* a story, let alone get into a fever to preach, and mock the Rev. Pearl Yates again.

Along past the middle of the afternoon I was letting Dud and Dolly stand and blow a full half of the time, even though Aunt Sue wanted the summer-fallowing finished before Uncle Wiley pulled in. She had gone to Knox with Uncle Gabe to trade. Bess Clover had fixed my noon meal. As was common with us, we were as polite as you please to each other but there was no talking. After eating, I got right up from the table, went and filled my canvas waterbag, and headed up with the old horses to work again with a section of spring-tooth harrow.

Now I was back from the tall sagebrush and a sup of the water that was hung in the shade there. The water was sickeningly warm. I was sick of the slog-drag, slog-drag, the dust, the dry heat, the sweat of the slow, slow harrowing. And I was sick with being sorry for old Dud. I stopped and stood in front of him. He was simply a rotten sight. His head hung low, his eyes were shut, and they watered so he appeared to be crying. He had his hind legs spraddled. He strained and grunted. Dolly just stood, drowsing and resting.

"I wish to God, Dud, I wish to Jesus God Almighty, I truly do, that I would never have to work you again," I said. Dud paid no mind, but Dolly, who was always curious, gave me a blink. The next thing I knew, here rose the fever, and I heard myself announcing, as I'd done forty times, "My text for today, brethering and sistern, is the tenth verse of the tenth chapter of Revelation—'And I took the little book out of the angel's hand, and ate it up; and it was in my mouth sweet as honey; and as soon as I had eaten it, my belly was bitter-ah.' "

Without a hitch, I ripped right on into my good old sermon. Lordy, it seemed good, it made me forget the heat, sorrow for Dud, and the trouble that had come from the sermon in the first place. It was in me like Uncle Gabe's rye whisky in him. Back in Iowa I'd had packs of real men listen to me, at the livery stable, around the ball games, in front of the barber shop, at the square dances of the sinful Soap Crickers, on depot platforms when drummers were waiting for trains, and such like. There I'd taken up real collections, too. Here I only had two old horses for a congregation. This didn't bother me a particle. I'd read and heard of preachers and orators who practiced on the beasts of the field. Anyhow, I was so fevered. Up and on I snorted and bawled a regulation revival story.

"Oh, give me your ears and your sperits while I sponderlate a parable to show you, brethering and sistern, how the honey-sweet book of the text is even as sin on this here airth and how when it was swallered and went bitter in the belly it was even as sin when the sinner dies and goeth to his just reward in hell-ah. Now I will recimerate to you, brethering and sistern, of a man of a town that I'm not sayin' is our town but was like unto our town, and oh he was brung up to haunt the evil places-ah. From bad to worse this here man went, findin' evil companions around the barber shops and the ball games, in the livery stable and the hoss auctions-ah, and then, oh then, alas, oh alas, oh alas, alas, and I weep to tell this here sad story-ah, he got to goin', this young man did, to the square dances and to the playing of games with gamblin' cards with sinful railroad men-ah. And from there it was a short step, oh, hardly any step at all, this pore, weak young man had sunk so deep, it was hardly no step at all into the maw of a saloon hell-ah. The pity was he was now a wedded man, the father of a babe, and the father of a daughter, oh, a lovely child, a sweet child, a frail girl of tender years, only five, think of it, only five, so frail, so goldy-haired, *sech* big blue eyes, and oh so chalky in her face, for God in His wisdom had already give her the consumption, and oh God was about to take her to her immortal home-ah. But oh, God had one more work for this fair, sweet, goldy-haired child to do. One dark and stormy night He sent her out alone to the saloon hell, the licensed saloon hell, wherein her whisky-soaked, sinful father— ah——"

By this time I was truly singsonging and hollering, prancing, wheeling, pawing, jerking, slobbering, and otherwise going it like the Rev. Pearl Yates when he'd preach as an evangelist. Dolly had given me close and curious attention all through. Now, all of a sudden, she switched her head around and pricked her ears in the direction of the water cache. The fever went out in me like a doused blaze. I was shivering like a dog in winter sleet some minutes later when I got to the water bag. It was a fresh one, cold, full to the stopper. I yelled out, "W'are you, Bess Clover?" No sound came back out of the thick brush. Then I was back to feeling and being as sullen as I'd ever been in Cartwright. I took a long pull at the bag. Then I packed it over and let Dud and Dolly wet their whistles out of my hat. I put them to work and finished the land.

Bess Clover was fixing me some supper. Aunt Sue and Uncle Gabe were not back yet and Uncle Wiley had not shown up. I spoke up to Bess.

"You heard me playin' preacher, didn't you?"

She just looked hard at me, in the way Aunt Sue commonly did.

"What if I did hear you?"

"It was spyin'."

"It was not spyin'."

"It sure as hell was. It was spyin', you God-damn' right. You can tell I said that too. You can tell that, by Jesus God."

"It ain't spyin' unless I do tell, and I don't aim to tell anybody anything."

"You'd ought to let me know you was there."

"I expected to. Then I was spellbound. Then you seemed so scared."

"I was scared. I am now. I'm afraid you'll tell on me."

"I won't tell, I ain't ever told a thing on anybody. Cross my heart I won't tell." She did cross her heart. Then she said, "You rest easy in your mind, Jim Turner. Set down and eat."

2. Sage of the Seven Devils

AUNT SUE HURD AND UNCLE GABE TURNER ROLLED
in well after dark. She came flying in from the wagon, expecting to
find Wiley Hurd in the lamplighted sitting room. But there was
only Bess Clover and me. We were going it so deep on a book of
Socialist songs and poems, with Bess whanging her guitar like all
get-out, that we failed to notice Aunt Sue until she stood over us.
Then she let loose the fury.

"You been breakin' into Wiley's bookcase, young man," Aunt
Sue gave it to me. "Nobody told you to. What come over you'n's
to git so thick all of a sudden? What next, Lord, what next?" Gabe
Turner came in then, looking more sheepish than common. "Smell
the fool!" Aunt Sue turned on him. "Went and kept me waitin' a
solid two hours, then he tried to coat his whisky breath with bay
rum, sen-sen, and with news he said he'd been pryin' out——"
She slowed to a stop there, her look on me, and her fury seemed to
fizzle down. "Well, never mind. I give up. I should know by this
time that Wiley will come home when he comes. Lord knows when.
You'd better have the milkin' and the other chores done, you two,
if you know what's good for you."

She went off to the kitchen and down to the cellar to measure
the fresh crocks of milk, and we hardly stirred except for Bess to
put her guitar back in place by the Edison phonograph and to get
shed of the Socialist songbook. Uncle Gabe made ready to go. But
Aunt Sue told him to make himself at home a spell longer, after
she had come back, cooled down, and was only looking dispirited
and miserable.

"He can still git here in an hour or so, if nothin's happened to him," she said to Gabe Turner. "I want you to tell him yourself what you found out. He knows the people you talked to."

I said, "Well, the summer fallowin' is done."

Aunt Sue had set herself between Bess and me on the sofa. She gave me a pat and Bess a kiss, then she just sat and gazed at a photo of Wiley Hurd which stood with one of her on the center table that held her finest coal-oil lamp, now alight. The picture of him showed a head with hair parted on the right and combed down on a straight slant to his left eye, and with two fingers propping his face. Uncle Gabe sat out a way from us in a rocker, kind of craning his neck to look at the photo, too. Once in the quiet he said, "Yes, sir." Then just "Hmm" a couple of times. Aunt Sue went on having her suffering.

I remember the room. It was a place where some powerful things came to happen to me, as I will relate. No house on any of the old, rich ranches had a bigger sitting room. And Aunt Sue declared that not one had prettier wallpaper than her Rose of Sharon pattern or a brighter floor than hers of red-and-brown rug of thick wool nap and rag rugs of all colors on the wear spots. A baseburner that fairly sagged with nickelwork stood toward the far inside corner from our sofa. There was another sofa and more rockers and tables around. Across from us double doors opened to a sewing, weaving, and quilting room. On from it, in the far front corner, was a glass-door bookcase filled with books that were all very old, except for some Socialist ones. Across from it and on from our sofa was a secretary a full nine feet high. Its bottom parts were crammed with late copies of *The Appeal to Reason, Hoard's Dairyman, The American Lumberman, Popular Mechanics, The Scientific American, Signs of the Times,* and *The Messenger of Peace.* The last two were Primitive or Hardshell Baptist papers, taken by Aunt Sue. The others, like the books, were Wiley Hurd's. The rest of the front wall was glass door and tall windows with snowy lace curtains. The Edison phonograph was on a table over by the side wall. There was a lot more truck in the room. One item was a crayon enlargement of a photo that had been made a dozen years back of the four Hurd boys. By and by Aunt Sue got to gazing at that picture, suffering so I feared she might break down and weep.

The house had been built from the proceeds of one of Wiley Hurd's earliest and his most practical invention. It was a kind of washboard machine that could be made mighty cheap. A Chicago company bought the patent and advertised the machine as "The No-Work Washer." Wiley Hurd raised thunder and started a law-suit because he claimed the name was a mortal lie. The suit took a lot of the money that had come from the patent. But Aunt Sue did get a house out of it. A spell back Uncle Wiley had patented a machine for a small kind of sawmill bandsaw. He had sued on this, too, but enough had been saved to give the house a new set of furnishings, the phonograph and such.

"Sorrow, sorrow to my heart," Aunt Susie sighed at last, yet gazing at the crayon enlargement of the four boys. "There's Joey—I loved him so, and I favored him, and he turnt out to keep and run a low dive of a licensed saloon up in Salmon City. My Grover, named fer Cleveland, went firin' on the Oregon Short Line and was killed in a wreck. Paul run off to the Coeur d'Alenes, married him a slattern, and there he is a miser'ble miner, with two boy brats and another on the way, all millstones to hold him to the mines. And Ramon, who helled away, and I never heerd from him for so long—now Ramon, when I do hear from him——"

"You better hush, Susie," Gabe broke in on her. "Don't let go."

"I know, I know," she suffered on. "I should keep all worry and sorrow to myself. There's nothin' to be done with Wiley, the more I try the more of a bullhead it makes him. He made bullheads out of the boys. Ever' one took out as soon as he was able, and ever' one had growed so mean I was glad to see him go. But it was not, and ain't now, any lesson to Wiley Hurd. There's no reasonin' with him. He is losin' his immortal soul in Socialism and for Debs. Eugene V. Debs is more to him than I am, I tell him. He don't deny it. 'Debs is your god,' I say to Wiley Hurd, and he lets on not to hear. I tell him, 'They had yore Debs in jail. Yore Debs is a jailbird.' And he either lets on not to hear, or he will spit out some fool thing like, 'They crucified Christ, too, Susie,' and then shut right up as though that settled it, as though that was a argy-ment——"

I was hearkening there to her, and thinking she must be ready to stick a butcher knife in Wiley Hurd every minute he was around her, so no wonder he hated to be home. Then the stomping of big horses and the rumble of a wagon with a heavy load sounded in to us through the screens. That was all Susie Hurd needed to make her stop talking and fly out as she had flown in. I stood at the door and watched her run down yonder in the moonlight, looking like a girl, little and thin and in a white dress as she was, and throwing her arms around a stocky figure of a man who had swung down from a lumber load. Then I felt kind of ashamed for looking and turned back. I heard Bess in the kitchen, rustling to warm up grub.

"I aim to tell you what I learnt," Gabe Turner said, in a whisky whisper, close to me. "Some of it, anyhow. Three days back a pair of strike-leadin' miners was let out of the state pen. One was Dan'l Barton. You need to keep ready for him to show up, likely all of a sudden and on the quiet. You won't mention I warnt you?"

"I won't," I promised, all in such chills and fever from what he'd told me that I forgot to say "sir" or thank him kindly.

He didn't appear to notice. Anyhow he was still some drunk. "You run along up to bed, now," Uncle Gabe said. "You get acquainted with Wiley Hurd when he's free of women folks. Good night, good night."

Then he went out. I stood at the window, squinting out for a minute before running up to bed. I didn't see anything. I just stood as in a story, dreaming. There I stood at the window.

I remember the room. I stood at the window, watching the snow. There were only flicks of it in the big whips of late October wind that the Seven Devils were throwing down the valley. Wiley Hurd put it that way. He had caught me trying to read his old book of Shelley poems and make something out of it. He said poets were inventors, as he was, but in words. Then he turned the pages to a poem called "Ode to the West Wind," and read out loud from it—

> *"O thou,*
> *Who chariotest to their dark wintry bed*
> *The wingèd seeds, where they lie cold and low,*
> *Each like a corpse within its grave, until*
> *Thine azure sister of the Spring shall blow.*

"Now what Mr. Shelley invented there," Uncle Wiley explained, "was a notion and a picture of the west wind as a chariot, with other pictures to boot. But you stop on that chariot invention and get it into your mind. Then you might come to ponder some on how Mr. Shelley would rig up an ode on the west wind, was he here in Idaho, drilling wheat on an exposed hill, and it a blow from the mountains like this one. Blowing whips and flicking snow, he might think, inventing a picture in words. But here, if you want to get good out of Shelley, you ought to read him for the rebel he was. I'll show you another time. Now I have to go for something."

It was a Sunday, and he had been working in his shop the live-long day on an improvement which he expected to put into his sawmill next year, if the government would let him. He feared that the new system of the forest reserves might bar him out; he was determined to fight the government until he was licked.

"Theodore Roosevelt will call out the troops, even as Grover Cleveland, to shoot the poor men down," Wiley Hurd spoke defiance. "But I'll face the guns and fight till they drop me."

"I thought you believed in the gover'ment runnin' the forests and the sawmills," Aunt Sue taunted. "Where's your Socialism, Wiley?"

"Right where it always was, Susie," he said. "But while we have a system of property rights I'm fighting till I drop for my property rights. I went in and opened up that timber. I spent money and time to build in a road that lumber could be hauled out on. I sold my threshing machine and put the money in a sawmill and took the thresher engine up to run it. I've a right to the sawtimber to run the mill and the government has a right to let me have it. On that I'll face the guns."

"Oh, foof! Don't talk like a fool, Wiley."

She went on nagging at him, but he kept quiet, studying away to himself and looking a little pestered by her only now and then. That was all said at breakfast time on this Sunday morning. After it he shut himself up in his shop, leaving the barn chores to me, as he had the early milking. Aunt Sue drove Dolly on her old buggy to Hardshell meeting at the schoolhouse. Bess rode in the seat and I hung my heels over the hind end of the bed. We went to the Ant-wines' for dinner, then I hiked home, cutting across the valley fields and going over Mount Creek on a footbridge. The stream was freezing along the fringes. It was a violent dark day. I got to feeling as downhearted from it as I felt cold outside me. The mood grew worse as I went around at wood-getting, feeding and the other chores alone, and brooded about tomorrow. After getting a fire going in the kitchen range and packing in coal for the front-room baseburner, I went to messing with some of the books in the light of the front windows, along with looking out at the weather and dreaming a heap.

Wiley Hurd caught me with the old book of Shelley poems. We talked, as I've told, and he went out. I heard him rummaging upstairs, where he kept a trunk of papers and drawings. He came back down and went out to his shop. I read on in Shelley and dreamed away. The night shadows began to come, the spits of snow faded. The shadows were soft on the stubble fields, the bare orchard trees and the browning haystacks. I peered out and got to musing that I ought to hear from Dan'l Barton soon, if I was ever to hear from him. I hadn't bothered myself much up to this time about Uncle Gabe's warning. The trouble at school between a boy, name of Ollie Hicks, and me had grown into a cloud that darkened out all other worries. It was a growing thing between Bess Clover and me. I was bound to deal with it. I simply had to have it out with that Ollie Hicks.

The twilight deepened on. I could barely see old white Dolly when she came into sight, high stepping. I hustled for the lantern and the pails and bucked out into the wind to do the milking.

The next Sunday was a clear, cold one. Uncle Wiley and I were by ourselves again. He was in by the fire, reading an old book that was bound in cowhide. I kept at the front windows, looking out, my head full of Ollie Hicks. I still hadn't stood up to him. I had not dealt with my big trouble.

Wiley Hurd said from behind me, "Something is festering with Bess Clover and you. I can tell it in her. It is bothering you now. I expect you need to talk to somebody full and free about it. You can do it with me. You don't need to look around."

He was right. It was easy to talk out and not have to look at him, too. The school is fine and Bess and I get along (I told Wiley

Hurd, looking out the window lights, my back to him). The trouble is with the Hicks boy, Ollie. He took a hate to me right off, maybe because I'm as big as him and in the same grade, but two years younger. He keeps crowding me, every way he can. The more I truckle the more he bullies me. He has put a constraint on me with Bess. Ollie Hicks whispers filthy talk around about what we likely do coming to school and going home, and us not relations. Ollie Hicks demeans me in front of the others (I said) by sneering that I was sent out here to save me from reform school; but don't worry, Jim Turner, he says, Idaho has a reform school. He brags that his brother, Russ, names the sheriff in every election. I expect it's so, the Hickses are such powerful land and cattle people. Ollie Hicks has stuck his face into mine and glowered and sneered he'd see that Bess and me were both sent to the reform school if we don't quit going into the brush; and I took it.

"Go on," Wiley Hurd said. "You tell me out of your own mouth what your real trouble was back in Cartwright. You can tell *me*."

This turned me around about. I hadn't expected it. I wheeled and looked Uncle Wiley over and considered him and did some thinking.

He sat in a leather-upholstered chair between the bookcase and the heater. He was a block of a man, five feet three tall, and wonderfully wide. He bulked out on both sides of the chair, but not with fat. Wiley Hurd was simply low-slung, thick and powerful. Edison was his model, "not only because he's an inventor but also because he is a rationalist and free-thinker." Wiley Hurd was always open to a call to give his lecture on Thomas Alva Edison and free thought. He had a long piece, all written out and headed,

THE RATIONALIST OF MENLO PARK
a Lecture by
THE SAGE OF THE SEVEN DEVILS.

Wiley Hurd had given it as far away as Boise, at a state meeting of the Social Democratic party of Idaho. His life was in the like. I knew there were days at a time when I was not alive to him. But now, today, with the big house so lonesome, his spirit took me in. I felt it take me and draw forth my trust.

I said that back there in Cartwright grandma and I lived on her share in some Virginia property which amounted to eight-fifty a month and on what she could make in odd ways. When I was six I began to make pennies on small chores. That same summer I was first noticed by Barrick McCool. We lived in a shack, grandma and me, southwest of the Wabash tracks. The McCool horse-breeding farm of a thousand acres came to the road across from our yard. In the summer I was six I wandered into it and got mixed with the Morgan and Percheron mares and their colts. There was bluegrass, black walnut windbreaks, and the biggest oak tree alive out in the middle of the pasture. I got out there and the colts came smelling around, then the giant mares crowded close, but I wasn't scared until Mr. McCool rode up, swung me from the ground and said I should be scared. He took to me. He was a bachelor.

Barrick McCool was a Democrat (I went on). DeWitt Clinton Maul, the town's main storekeeper, was leader of the Grand Army of the Republic in Cartwright. He was also a leading Republican and a leading Methodist. It was ever a religious fight and a political fight between Maul and McCool.

"Vile idiocy," said Wiley Hurd. "Where did you come in?"

Barrick McCool owned the livery stable (I went on telling). He was the main support of the town's baseball and football teams. Out at his big farm place he had a kind of gymnasium, with boxing and wrestling rings. When I was seven Mr. McCool gave me choring work to do in the summer, and more when I was eight and nine. Grandma let me go, for we did need the money. There were other boys at McCool's from a dozen or so of the poorest families around the town. Mr. McCool let us mix boxing and wrestling with the work. Then I got a wild idea of preaching a sermon in the style of the Rev. Pearl Yates, who was always being mocked and mimicked, even by grown young men.

Telling on, I gave Wiley Hurd a sample of my sermon. Then I told him how it caught on, until some of the older and tougher boys began to manage me around to give the sermon where they might take up collections. That was in the summer of 1902, and Barrick McCool was running for state senator from our county, with a prime chance to get in. It began to look like his man would beat Clinton Maul for mayor of Cartwright, too. One man could count for a lot in a town of only five hundred people. But old Clinton and the Rev. Pearl Yates started a tremendous circuit of revival meetings through the county. They were not openly part of the political fight, but all the sermons were known to be aimed at Barrick McCool's ball teams, boxing matches and everything else of the kind for the poor boys of Cartwright. After the start of school I did let myself be led far astray into deep sin, by the toughest boys. I played hooky with them for days at a stretch. I let them lead me into giving my sermon around the Soap Creek Dance Hall and other places of evil. Then all of a sudden I found myself up before the mayor and the Rev. Pearl Yates together. What they wormed out of me they twisted horribly to make a pulpit example of the ruin wrought by Barrick McCool with boys. I could not tell it was mainly a lie; I had to say, yes, it is true; for the Rev. Yates and Mayor Maul could have sent me to the reform school any minute, and grandma was too sick and old to do anything——

"Stand up here and show me how much you know about boxing," Wiley Hurd said, sort of chopping in as I felt the old fever pulse and fume in me. I was already up. Wiley Hurd got up and laid off his glasses. He squared away, no taller than me. "Let's see what we can do," he said, as serious as a man could be. "We'll be kind of wrestling and chugging, then you hit my belly hard as you can."

It took several tries for me to catch on. Then I did sneak in the left hook that Mr. Barrick McCool himself had shown me how to throw, and then had made me practice over and over because, he said, "It's a pure natural, me bye, a pure natural." Now I hit Uncle Wiley so hard in his tough belly muscles that I felt it clear down in my left foot. It fetched an honest grunt out of him.

"Face the guns," he said, standing back. "It's a good invention. Come on out to the shop and we'll practice it some more."

He collared me the next evening when Bess and I moseyed in from school, stopping me away out at the barn. Bess went on. I told him.

"Well, I went and did it," I said. "This mornin' recess a scuffle got goin' with seven or so of the boys. I took hold of Ollie Hicks in it, and I sneaked the hook through when the scuffle was real hot.

He fell on his knees, and his face went white, and his eyes rolled, he could hardly catch his breath, he gagged and gagged and almost vomited. I hollered my head off I was mighty sorry, and I never meant to do it—like you said. The teacher never seemed to suspicion me. But Ollie Hicks did. He shunned me the rest of the day. He kept his dirty mouth shut about Bess and me."

"Arise, ye slaves," said the old Sage of the Seven Devils grimly.

I can never forget the big lamplighted room as it was the night Eb Cuddy rode down from his store with the telegraph message the stage driver had brought from Knox. It was an eventide of early December. We had known a number like it since the blowing of the mountain winds began the winter; with the bands of sheep and the cattle herds drifting down ahead of the snows, and the feeding from the great, fat, brown alfalfa stacks getting under way. There was real plenty in the valley for both man and beast. I'd forgotten what it was like to have only cornbread and milk for supper. Aunt Sue's cellar shelves bulged as the granaries and the hay yards did. I would look at them, feel the new, warm wool underwear on me, then go peer out from the front windows at the comfortable valley under the snow whirls, think of the pile of pine wood, the stock of coal for the baseburner, and feel snug and fine, just snug and fine.

But not Bess Clover. She knew it was different with the homesteaders all around in the dry-land hills. All were poor. Some were hungry. Aunt Sue did not dream what hate was in Bess on this account. But Bess came to show it more and more, even in singing.

We would have a singing bee almost every night. Bess was a wonder at both singing and reciting. The songs she knew best were the old and deathly ones that her pa, Johnny Clover, and his people before him had sung from away back, to help make the dark and thorny desert of their living tolerable. Aunt Sue loved to hear Bess render songs that mourned in this style—

> *"Go dig my grave both wide and deep,*
> *Place a marble stone at my head and feet,*
> *And on my breast a snow-white dove,*
> *To show to the world that I died for love."*

Aunt Sue would make Bess sing that verse over and over, as she would on this one—

> *"You see that dove in yonder grove,*
> *It's flying from pine to pine,*
> *She's mourning for her own true love—*
> *Why can't I mour-urn for mine?"*

Bess Clover would say "yonder's," "cain't," "hit's," and speak words in other ways to remind Aunt Sue of old Missouri. Uncle Wiley was reminded of Missouri by such songs too, but the reminders would gag him; for he said that Missouri was what he'd come to Idaho to get away from. But he made no real objection. He could immerse himself in a book or *The Appeal to Reason* from all singing and talk around him. For a week he'd go without saying a word to me, even at table. But ever and again he'd throw down his reading matter there in the eventides, sit up and say, "Now it's my turn. Sing some of my songs."

Bess Clover never needed any urging for that. She had learned every song in Wiley Hurd's hymnbook by heart long ago. Bess would change amazingly while rendering these songs that called for revolution all around the world. Commonly she was pale, quiet and meek, always drawing herself in to be sure to get along— something like I knew how to do, only she never made people wrathy with the notion that she was being sullen. She was really growing up and filling out here at Aunt Sue Hurd's. Now in December I had turned twelve, and Bess had come to thirteen two months earlier. The change was more than growth with her, though. She flourished in this place. I reckoned I did too, in my own way.

Well, this night she was making the old guitar more than hum, was singing like a woman grown, when Eb Cuddy rode in through the snow. I see her yet in the bright lamplight, standing against the wallpaper roses, the coal fire glowing out from the isinglass of the baseburner, Aunt Sue so tight-faced and Uncle Wiley with his head reared back as though actually facing the guns, and the song—

> *"Arise, ye prisoners of starvation!*
> *Arise, ye wretched of the earth.*
> *For justice thunders condemnation,*
> *A better world's in birth.*

No more tradition's chains shall bind us,
Arise, ye slaves; no more in thrall;
The earth shall rise on new foundations,
We have been naught, we shall be all."

The girl's voice, the guitar chords, the cry of the wind around the big house, and a stir, a mighty stir in me! The Socialist hymn sounded on. Then it was the sound of a horse coming fast, wheeling for the house, then quiet, and at the end the bad tidings.

Eb Cuddy came in without shaking off the wet snow on his cap, muffler and overcoat. While he pulled off gloves and reached inside his coat he said he was a bearer of sad news.

The stir and the light went down inside me as Mr. Cuddy spoke and as Aunt Sue sat on the sofa, held the sheet of yellow paper to the lamp, read it over and over, let it fall to her lap, and kept right on staring as though she was reading it still. She sat rod-straight on the edge of the sofa. For some time her only motion was the working in and out of her jaw muscles.

I'd let this room be home to me. So it had been for Bess Clover some minutes ago, in her singing, and for me in my listening to her. I had come along here, first in Aunt Sue's toleration, then with Wiley Hurd backing me and helping me when I was getting it in the neck from a rich old bully kid. I'd let the room grow close to me and into me, or something like it.

Then the room became changed so much all in minutes. A yellow sheet of paper in the hand of a good neighbor had torn it all away from me. It said that Paul Hurd was dead. He was one of seven killed in a mine cave-in. "Wife and three children left destitute," the telegraph said. "Please come at once." Then all in the room backed away, miles from me, and I felt worse, even more alone than I had when I came here.

"There's nothin' for it but to go," Aunt Sue said, speaking in the most matter-of-fact way. "Nothin' else but to bring Luella and her boys back with me. Jim, I expect you'll have to make out livin' with Gabe for a while." She kept looking at Bess now. "It was lovely. It was so lovely. Now it's the Lord's will. Three boys— three brats and a slattern woman in my house. And it was so right lovely."

3. The Old Judge

ON THE SUNDAY OF CHRISTMAS WEEK GABE TURNER bobsledded me over to live with him "until things are straightened out," as Aunt Sue said. Bess Clover rode along with her things as far as her home. We were both sure in our hearts that it was for good. There was room for us in the Hurd house, but Luella had hated us on sight, particularly Bess. The oldest boy, Clement, was the orneriest stutter-butt you could imagine. He was my age, but a runt. I didn't dare lay a hand on him, and as he knew more ways to be mean without showing guilt, he would get me blamed daily for his dirt. So I began to pull like sneaks on him. Aunt Sue bore just so much of it, then she told Gabe Turner he had to take me, and that was all there was to it. He said finally he would keep me until he could get in touch with my other uncle, Black Dan Barton, on my ma's side.

"I can't figger why you ain't heard from him," Gabe said, as Frank and Cyclone sledded us along. "He has a duty to you."

"Maybe I *have* heard from him," a devil said through my mouth.

"Well, now." Uncle Gabe wiped his mustache with the back of his glove, looked over his shoulder and studied me. "I'm curious on what you mean." I set my jaw. "If you want to be so close-mouthed with yore own uncle," he complained, "go ahead and be close-mouthed."

"I expect I will," I said, "until Black Dan gives the sign."

"Suit yoreself. But it ain't no way to treat a blood uncle."

"I can't betray Black Dan," I said, "not to you or nobody."

He turned his back square on me and went to talking to Bess about how long he'd known her ma and pa, what fine people they

were, even if they'd never done too well, and more of the same dull
gab.

It was all right with me. I was back in the old habit of dreaming
stories, living stories, in a kind of haze. I stood in the sled, behind
the spring wagon seat. Bess hugged her guitar between herself and
Gabe (I'd quit calling him uncle). It was an old Sears-Roebuck
instrument that Aunt Sue had given her, one that Ramon Hurd
had played a lot before he ran away from home.

"Now Pa Johnny can play again in the family singin'," Bess
said. "I sure am glad to have it. I sure am glad to."

She hugged it to her as though it was the only thing she had left
in life, and I reckoned it was just about that, as we pulled around
a hill and into the Clover place. It looked to me as though Bess
actually was puckering up and shrinking in her clothes—the new
school coat, hat and plaid dress she was wearing. The look, the
kind of fullness and brightness of a young woman, that she had
grown into lately, it was mostly gone. Her brown hair was in a big
braid, inside the coat collar so's it would not wetten in the fall of
snow. I looked at it, and at the turn of her neck each side of the
braid. I looked at the parts, wisps, waves, curlings and shines of
hair from back of her ears to the braid. I looked for the copper
threads and gold threads in the brown, and the ones a color of tall
wild grass in winter. All the way over I'd liked to look that way so
much, while making up stories of no start and no end, but of us
just wandering as we'd walked to and from the Mount Creek school,
that I came to feel I was spying. Coming to her home, I made myself look at the land.

The Clover homestead lay deep in the lonesome old hills between the valleys of Mount and Bob creeks. The three shacks, of
one floor, each built in its own time and all hooked together, were
strung along the easiest slope of the gulch. On the other side was
a poor shake of a shed barn. A half dozen cayuses with ribs showing stood around in a corral, chewing at wheat straw. A stack of
straw seemed to be the only feed they had. A plow and harrow
stood out, coated with snow. There was a pile of sagebrush wood,
with the brush dumped down in the gulch. I noted a well windlass
and watering trough above the woodyard, and a privy. On up yonder the gulch widened into four branches, and there the lay of the

land was fair for wheat. Snow covered the stubble. The sagebrush
on the hills around stood as bunches of white with gray spots and
streaks so dark they appeared to be really black. The low sky was
the color of the smoke that came out of the rusty stovepipe above
the tarpaper roofs of the shacks.

"Here y'are, sister!" Gabe Turner sung out, trying to sound
cheery. "Home again! And lookit them come! Air they glad to
see you!"

Well, they were, Pa Johnny in an old black wagon-shed hat that
spread above his scrawniness like an umbrella; Ma Essie, tall, thin,
black-eyed, shrilling in a fever of excitement; and the kids in faded
and raggy clothes, shaggy-headed, dirty-faced, and all hollering to
Bess—all except the oldest boy, Clay, the one next to him, named
Albert, and four-year-old Tack. Clay was eighteen and Albert was
a year younger. Tack was too sickly to holler and take on.

Once Bess had told me that this home gulch of hers had come
to her in a dream as the jaws of a monster trap. Now I could see it
that way over her, without using much imagination. I hated to look
at her, I couldn't do it as we left.

Gabe got away as soon as he could. He wouldn't listen when
Essie and Johnny both begged us to light down.

"Fine folks," Gabe said. "Fine as they come. But the sheep smell
of the bedclothes in them shacks would puke a cat. I don't know
how Bess is goin' to stand it, after livin' halfway decent for so long
at Susie's. Jest to think of it starts the old asthma up in me."

He hawked a couple of times and stooped for his jug of rye
whisky.

Well, Bess Clover didn't have to stand it. Aunt Sue Hurd went
and talked the widow mother of the three Hicks brothers into taking Bess in to chore for her while going on to the Mount Creek
school. I was glad enough after that to go to the poor school on
Bob Creek. It would have killed me to have seen Bess Clover come
to school every morning with Ollie Hicks and go home with him
each eventide. It just about killed me even to think of it; anyhow,
for a spell.

One morning toward the end of February I stood again in the
wagon bed and behind the spring seat of Gabe Turner's bobsled

rig, out in front of the Clover place. None of the kids came out this trip, except Tack, who was bundled up for a ride to town to see the county doctor. He was a right sick boy. I didn't need Gabe to remind me that his ma thought Tack would never come back home. She tried to chatter, laugh and carry on with us in her common way, but through it her eyes were strained and dark with plain grief. I stood back of Gabe so I could not see her while Johnny climbed up to the seat and put the bundle of sick boy between Gabe and him.

I stood and remembered how I'd got around Gabe back there this morning when he said I'd better stay by myself on the place, as he had so much business to transact in Knox that he might have to stay there overnight.

"If you leave me here alone this trip I'll get drunk and go down drunk to the Suggs ranch and stagger right in on Mrs. Suggs," I'd threatened him. "I'll chaw and spit around her, too."

I must have sounded frantic. Anyhow Gabe took me serious and stopped his hitching up to worry over me. "Where'd you get any whisky?" he asked, kind of uncertain. "Anyhow, you wouldn't dare to drink any."

"Where do I get chawin' tobacco?" I argued back at him. "I'd dare to drink whisky just like I dare to chaw. I'll get drunk, too."

He stood there, plainly faltering. Right in front of him I hauled out a twist of Honey Dip and bit off a big chaw. Then I walked around staggering.

"Hell, I don't have to drink whisky, by God, to stagger in drunk on Mrs. Suggs," I said. "I won't need to use up my whisky. I'll just sure, by God, stagger in on her if you leave me."

He didn't leave me. I was going with him. It was getting so he couldn't handle me any more than Grandma Martha Barton had been able to do. I was rightly ashamed of myself, but I'd have done worse to have kept from putting in another winter night alone on that old ranch.

I dropped back down in the hay of the bed and pulled a moldering horse blanket around me as Gabe drove on. Looking out over the tailgate, I took a glimpse of the miserable clutter of shacks, and of Essie Clover as she stood on at the barbwire gate, her head bowed and held in her hands. Then I looked up from the dark trap of a gulch to the blinding bright blue sky, then around as the land opened behind the skimming sled and trotting horses.

The road dropped down into Bob Creek Valley and back past the Hoover ranch, which Gabe Turner had rented for three years on shares. Yet seeing back over the endgate I could now look away up yonder in the shining clear air and over the frost-sparkles of the frozen snow to the Hickses' lands. They ran into twelve thousand acres that spread over fenced foothill range and the benches and bottoms of the upper reaches of the two valleys and their branches. I could see the big house, afar there, on a slope above barns, corrals and hay and feed yards; below it an orchard, hedged with cottonwoods. Of course I had to think of Bess being up there, and of how Ollie was home today, it being a Saturday. This was only misery, and I shunted to a musing on Dan'l Barton, who had disappeared as though the earth had swallowed him. I couldn't quiz Gabe on this without confessing it was a lie I'd told him, in pretending that Uncle Dan'l had come like a slave in the underground of the old days to see me. It was certainly a fine example of how a fool lie can mess you up. Now I had to admit to myself that Black Dan Barton probably didn't give a hoot about me, after all. My life was simply up to me, nobody else.

The horses kept on at a good lick, primed with oats and prodded by the sharp forks of the frosty air. I thought up that notion, remembering Percy Bysshe Shelley and William Wiley Hurd. But my mind ran restlessly on. I dreamed away some on what I could hope to make of myself on the land here, if I should manage to keep out of reform school and the pen. There were the pine forests away north yonder; the cattle and sheep range in them and below them; the mountains climbing on into the great Seven Devils range; eastward more valleys like ours, more mountains on into Montana; while to the west the River Snake plunged down and away until its canyon was a full mile and a half deep. All around up in the wild, wild country were rich veins of minerals, and spots of mining that had gone on since 'way before the Civil War. I might hope to get into the wild country with Uncle Wiley next summer. He had already snowshoed back up to his sawmill camp, the slattern and the brats in his house being too much for him to stand. Aunt Sue was long used to his leaving her, but she had never sorrowed more than she sorrowed now. Grandma Barton would have called her pitiable.

It seemed like every turn of dream and thought I could take this morning was bound to run to misery. Up on the seat Johnny Clover was droning away on his Advent Christian religion to Gabe, and most of the time there was weakly crying from poor little Tack. Once I asked would he be better off lying down here with me, but Gabe and Johnny both said the spring seat was easier riding for him. And the kid wasn't so sick but what he liked to ride high and watch the horses.

Bob Creek Valley spread away in my sight much like the valley of Mount Creek. But more of the hills were cleared, there were homestead shacks in sight all along. I looked at them, and the first thing I knew I was remembering what Wiley Hurd had told me on how the coming of men here—under the capitalist system, he said —had been the ruin of the country.

Back in the eighties, as he told it, there was no sagebrush on these Idaho hills but only bunchgrass. It grew so rich that most places a cow-critter could not bed down without crushing grass into a mat. It was a paradise through many years for such runners of cattle as the pa of the Hicks brothers. Then the sheep came. They were brought in great bands from the sagebrush deserts of Oregon and Nevada. They packed the seeds of sagebrush in their wool. They grazed out bunchgrass by the roots. The brush got a hold in the soil, then took over the dry-land hills. Yet there was kept a plenty of fair range, until the homesteaders began to pile into the foothills of the Lemolos and the Seven Devils. Wiley Hurd repeated the old saw about every homesteader betting Uncle Sam he could hold down and prove up on a hundred and sixty acres of dry land without starving to death. The brush was grubbed more or less from hill quarter sections everywhere. Then cleared soil was plowed and sowed to wheat. The grass was gone forever, it appeared. Wiley Hurd was the first of the dry-land ranchers to summer fallow—he believed he'd invented summer fallowing.

Because the homesteaders were generally so witless and shiftless, they were expected to drift out in due course. But many were like Johnny Clover, who had concluded that he could feel free on his own dry-land homestead, and that even with hunger it was healthier than a life of toil in the mine stopes. And there was his religion. In his dark, grim gulch he was far from the wickedness of the mine camps.

The way went on down past the Hoover ranch, past the Suggs eighty, through the rich Yardley ranch, which spread across a thousand acres of valley and hills, then through the dairy-breeding ranch which was one of a string owned by the mighty G. Dodd interests, and so to the last hump of hill road above the Lemolo and Snake bottoms.

There I stood up again, staring over and away at the spots of ranch buildings which reached far out there, the thick clusters of such spots, all snow-coated, which were the town of Knox, the dark streak of railroad in the snow, and the wide white ribbon of the River Snake. It was frozen and snowed over. Yonder across it was Oregon. Everywhere in sight were the high lines and low lines, the big lines and little lines, of the irrigation ditches. I'd early learned here that water was the almighty difference between the well-to-do ranchers and the people like Johnny Clover and his family. Some went in for religion, as Johnny did, some took up Socialism and the like, as Wiley Hurd did, and more turned to whisky, as Gabe Turner did—as he was dreaming of doing now, I could tell, the way he was wiping that droopy old mustache of his'n.

But all in Idaho were mainly and powerfully concerned with water. The almightiness of water was one thing there was no argument on.

We left Johnny Clover and little Tack at the county doctor's, then drove to the livery barn to put Cyclone and Frank in out of the cold. Tiresome went off on his usual independent prowl, ready for a dogfight over a bitch, or for anything else except to make friends with either boy or man. Coot's Livery was on Old Street, the pioneer part of Knox, and we stopped in the Silver Grill there for a bite to eat. Then I paddled along with Gabe to catch the man he rented from and who had him mortgaged to his ears. This man was head of the Wheat State Bank. His name was on the window in gold letters as "George B. M. Hoover, Presdt." The initials stood for "Brinton McClellan," my uncle said. We went in, and he looked more than pleased when a clerk said that Mr. Hoover was over sunning his innards and partaking of some lunch at the Old Judge Saloon.

My drunkard uncle stood back beaming, then he frowned at me, and I saw in his face it was the story that was so old to me, the story that always came to the question, "Now, let's see—what on airth can we do with this boy, Jim Turner?"

Well, I made up my mind in a sudden fume of fury, and I said right out in front of the clerk, by God, I was not going to be put to wait with the horses at the livery, I was not going to set in the back of a store by the stove, neither, and I wasn't going to go and read in the Knox Free Public Library.

"You can take me into the Old Judge Saloon and let me see it," I said. "If the saloon man makes me go out, then I'll go it. But I'll venture I can set there while you transact your business, unless you want to stay and get drunk, like you did on Aunt Sue last summer."

"Now, now," he kind of begged me. "Shush, now. Don't get excited."

I could tell I had the jump on him. So I turned sniveling, while the clerk stared on at me and Gabe plucked at the sleeve of my coat.

"It's been like this here ever since I was four," I said. "I remember the afternoon, for Grandma Barton told it so often. My pa, Lon Turner, your own blood brother, he had taken a pledge to quit whisky, settle down and give his wife and boy a home. Grandma was out with him, she'd fetched me, that day at the Coll Hill place. Ma Tavie was quittin' her hired-girl job in the county seat and was on her way to the place. My pa was helpin' to dehorn steers. A bunch of the steers went crazy from the sound of bellerin' and the scent of blood, and they trampled over him. I remember how they packed him in. He was like a rag and his face was only dirt and blood. So there went that, and ever since it has been, 'What on airth are we goin' to do with Jim Turner?' Well, I won't be poked away any more or horse-traded around any more. You leave me now, and I'll go jump a freight and hobo off to find Black Dan Barton. But go on, if you feel like it. Go ahead and leave me."

All the time he was plucking at me and trying to hush me from bawling, but the more he did the more I ranted and pawed the air, as I did when I would preach my sermon. And then I saw him looking at me kind of blubber-eyed, and the next thing he was muttering, "Doggone it all, the pore young'n, dad gum it anyhow, the pore boy, the pore boy." Then he said, "Come along, then, come along."

He started out of the bank, and as I went to go with him the clerk leaned over the counter, glowered at me, and said kind of through his teeth, "What you need is a blamed good sagebrushin'." I expected he was right, but I went on without noticing him.

"You won't blab to Susie or Mis' Suggs or any of the other church folks, will you?" Gabe asked me, at the Old Judge's swinging doors. "They'd rawhide me to the end of my days if they learnt I'd took you into a saloon hell."

"I won't tell a soul," I promised him, and we went inside.

Gabe Turner marched me over to a chair by the biggest heating stove I ever had seen. My heart was beating like sixty as he left me there. He went over to the bartender, then both looked at me as Gabe talked. In a minute the bartender nodded, then my boozy old uncle nodded at me. I was all right here. I'd had my way again.

All I'd ever known about saloons up to this time was from the sermons of the evangelists and the talk of Christian women and men. I'd seldom heard the word "saloon" alone—it was always as "saloon hell" or "licensed saloon hell." The more I'd heard of the like the crazier I'd become about seeing an awful saloon hell from the inside; most of all when the sweet little golden-haired girls were there, trying to get their sottish fathers to come home with them now, and only getting hit on their heads and falling in gore for their pains. That story was the main stab of my own sermon.

Now I was inside a saloon hell, and I simply couldn't believe it. Seven or eight men in nice store clothes were standing at a high counter, which was the bar, I guessed. They were leaning around, drinking politely out of glasses, some munching on sandwiches, some smoking cigars, all seeming to be as agreeable as you please with each other. There was no sign of shooting and stabbing, not even of simple scuffling and chugging. I didn't even hear a loud word. My uncle looked poor and shabby as he went up to one of

the men and spoke to him. But he was welcomed, and the next
thing I saw him appearing like eternal bliss, as his face shone
through the steam of a mug that held a hot drink of some kind.
I settled back some and let my gaze rove on around the insides of
the saloon hell.

A mirror back of the bar appeared as big as a barn to my sight.
It shone with wonderful soft spots of light from the ponderous
brass lamps, as huge as the spittoons, that swung from the ceiling
of rich, dark wood. At the bottom of the mirror stacks of bottles
rose and dipped like the golden stairs. The bottles had curious
shapes and labels of many colors. In front of them rows and rows
of glasses sparkled like the frost crystals of the clear winter morning. The cloth under the sparkling glasses was as the untrodden
snow. The room was so warm. The talk was soft and low. Through
it a glass would clink, or beer would purr and fizz, or liquor would
gurgle and plop from a bottle. The smells were as many as the
colors of the bottle labels, and each was a lovely one, while all of
them together were better than a bouquet, well-nigh as good as
the smells of a big farm kitchen with a dinner for the threshers
cooking. I studied the spittoons and could only think of the Bible
words, "vessels of brass." Verily, they were vessels. And I hadn't
seen such huge carved and polished pillars since the Union Depot
in Kansas City.

I fell in love with the bartender. I don't know how to say it but
that I fell in love with him. Not as with a human being but as with
a horse. His head and mustache were the handsomest I ever had
seen on a man. Under his double chin a diamond flashed, and so
did another from a finger. The bartender wore a white shirt with
red sleeveholders and a cream-colored vest all sprigged with red.
Halfway up the vest, just over the biggest part of his belly, was the
top band of a snowy-white apron. He changed it once while I was
there. But his motions were really the best thing about him. It was
like a circus to see him slide three mugs of beer all the way down
the bar, with each one stopping right in place before a customer,
then mix some drink by tossing it high and over from one tumbler
to another, and making even the simplest motion of pouring from
a bottle have a kind of ringmaster flourish to it. He was a dream.
I dreamed of the bartender as I sat and nodded in the heat from

the giant stove. I was dreaming I was him when I felt Gabe shaking me and hauling me up.

"Stand up here," he said, hauling me hard and speaking blustery. "I want you to meet and speak up yore best to Mr. Hoover here. I've been tellin' him I've turnt over a new leaf on yore account, and you are worth doin' it for. I told him how you can handle horses and be a man gener'ly on the ranch. Mr. Hoover, here he is, Jim Turner."

He certainly did spread it on thick. I tried to act up to him. Mr. George B. M. Hoover was bull-built and hog-fat; he was round, red, with a bristly stack of sandy hair under his tipped-back Derby hat; with gentle and twinkling eyes of pale blue, a kind, smiling, fat mouth, and a huge, hearty wheeze of a voice. It was easy to imagine him a-putting on a white false beard and playing Santa Claus but hard to think of him as a banker. He was shrewd enough, though, as I learned.

Mr. Hoover felt me over and looked me over now, as though I was a colt; and at the same time he made pleasant remarks and asked me what I thought of Gabe's horses; if the Bob Creek school suited me; and questions on other such things which I did not consider prying.

"You keep on like you are and do the best you know how for your uncle," Mr. Hoover said finally. "You keep on, and you might encourage me to build up the ranch some." He wheezed a laugh. "And then I think we can take care of anybody who might make trouble for you about how you left Iowa. You do right by Gabe and me, and I'll do right by you. That's clear, and it's fair, wouldn't you say?"

It was all yet a good deal of a mystery to my mind, but I was old enough to understand what it meant to have a banker pulling for me. I said I appreciated him and I'd try my best for my good old Uncle Gabe Turner.

"First thing, then," said Mr. Hoover, "you keep out of saloons after this, with him or without him." He pointed a fat, red finger at the bartender. "He's breaking the law to let you stay here. You don't want to get a good fellow into trouble, do you? It may interest you to know that Mr. Willis, the bartender there, has a sweet little golden-haired daughter. How do you think she would feel to see her daddy in jail on your account? Come on, Gabe, as long as you are here I'll buy you another one."

They went back to the bar, leaving me flustered to death. I expected the news had come out from Iowa about the stories in my sermon, and Mr. Hoover was letting me know that he was onto me. Anyhow, I did feel taken down a number of notches and properly warned. No boy could have been more meek and mild than I was with Gabe as he did his trading and on our drive home. At the ranch I hopped off to open the barbwire gate without being told, and at the barn I offered to put up the team alone while he went in to make a fire and start supper.

"You shore air a changeable boy," Gabe said. "This mornin' all I could think of to say to myself about you was, 'The stinkin' little skunk, oh, what a stinker!' Now you air actin' so handsome."

"I guess it was me seein' the inside of a saloon hell," I said. "It sure was a solemn warnin'."

"I have to thank you for actin' right to Mr. Hoover," Gabe went on, paying no attention to what I said. "After I spoke to him about you and after he looked you over, he went and renewed my note."

Johnny Clover stayed over a couple of days in Knox. The doctor kept Tack in the hospital, but it was no use. The boy was far gone with consumption, and soon he was gone for good. The Clovers were really relieved, as Tack had been so ailing and miserable for such a long time. Nobody else noticed his death. It was the third time in a winter that death had come around close to me— counting the death of the Hurd horse, old Dud, a blessing. Nobody in Idaho was pleased more than me to feel the warm smother of the first Chinook wind and to see spring break in early. Deathliness seemed to go away with the snow. I felt good to be free of school. I pitched into the ranch work harder than Mr. George B. M. Hoover could ever have hoped for. I liked the work, I seemed to be born to it; to the work with horses anyhow. Work could hold off the things that would crowd over me at the least chance. I could dream stories at work. Work for me, I said, work on the land, work with horses.

4. Inez the Strawberry Roan

AT CHRISTMAS, WHEN I WAS NEW WITH GABE TURNER
and was yet behaving in some fear of reform school, he gave me a
cayuse mare colt that was coming on two. He was generous drunk,
of course, and when he sobered up some around January the third
he tried to let on that he had no recollection of the deal. Then for
the first time since coming to Idaho, I'd ventured to throw a fit. It
was a kind of show that was common in Iowa revivals and camp
meetings. I danced and jerked, screeched and sing-songed, hollered
in the tongues, then took a glory roll on the floor and held my
breath until I swelled up and seemed to go into a trance. But it
didn't look religious to Gabe. It scared hell out of him. He knelt
by me, wrung his hands and cried—

"Don't take on so, Jim! Oh, don't take on so! I was only cod-
din', honest I was. I never dreamp you would take it so hard. Hell
'n' damnation, I meant all the time you should have her fer your'n!"

I gradually recovered, and from then on I had her. She was certainly a valuable little old cayuse; plum-dark, high-headed, a single-
footer, snap-eared, and *so* bright-eyed. She reminded me of a
black-haired girl of fourteen I'd been in love with back in Iowa
when I was nine. I named the colt Inez after her. The winter long
I gentled Inez according to the practice I'd learned from Barrick
McCool and his horseman hands. As mean as I grew to be at the
Bob Creek school and as ornery with poor old Gabe, I was yet a
dove with my sweet little strawberry roan. None of your Idaho
buckaroo breaking for me with her. From Barrick McCool I'd
learned to loathe the word, "horsebreaking." I gentled the filly
along until the first Saturday after her second birthday.

It was a Saturday deep in April. Gabe had business in Knox, and he rode Cyclone in for a quick trip, leaving me to work at cleaning the silt from the main ranch ditch, using Frank and Vernie on a slip scraper. As soon as Gabe was well gone I let the two broncs stand harnessed in the barn, and I saddled Inez and led her down to the fresh plowing on the creek bottom. The soil was a nice black loam, not mucky but too soft to encourage a colt to do much bucking.

This was all shameful, according to the rules of Idaho buckarooing. Ern Suggs, Walt Payne, Art Yardley, Ollie Hicks, and every other boy I knew would have called me a yellow coward for this kind of catering to a cayuse. I should have snubbed Inez up in a corral, blindfolded her, swung a blanket and saddle on her, cinched up, and then piled on with quirt and spurs and with big hat a-slapping, while boys and buckaroos sat around on the corral fence and hollered, "Don't pull leather! Let her buck!" Then I should have whipped her and roweled her and scared her until I could call her "broke." But here I was, sneaking her down to plowed ground, having her gentled to the saddle itself already, sneaking like a dirty little coward to fork her with nobody looking.

Well, that was how I did it, coward or not, and it worked with the cayuse just as it had worked with Barrick McCool's Morgan colts in Iowa. There was nothing to it. I rode Inez around the place for a couple of hours, then I had a notion to ride her up to the Clover homestead and show off to Bess. So off we single-footed and dogtrotted, with me forgetting that Frank and Vernie were still standing harnessed and eating their heads off in the stable. Inez stood while I opened the barbwire gate to the valley road. She made no fuss at all when I swung on her again. In the road I let her gallop for a piece, hoping Ern Suggs might be looking from up on his place. At the corner turn I let her walk again.

Oh, but it was a lovely fine morning, it sure was a goodly day! I sat up on Inez, let her single-foot me on, and I looked out over her flossy mane and lively ears at the rundown old ranch in my sight, and for one time it appeared as home, sweet home to me.

"I expect I ought to make up my mind to buckle in and help Gabe Turner to build it up," I said to Inez. "Maybe I should humble myself down and take a pledge to help him make a go of it here."

Riding on in the sweet air, I went to dreaming a story of this. I rode Inez and looked down and over the poor old place and dreamed glory on it. Yet I rode on, on for the Clovers'. I still didn't think of Vernie and Frank, standing harnessed down there in the barn, and all the silt needing to be cleaned out of the ditch before Gabe could start irrigating the alfalfa. I only dreamed.

Mr. Hoover's ranch, where I lived with Gabe Turner, was a hundred and sixty acres, with a gopher-burrowed forty in alfalfa, another forty fit for grain but pocked with sunflowers and Jim Hill mustard, a slice of bottom for spuds and garden, a three-acre apple orchard long homesteaded by bugs, worms and scale, and the rest rough pasture and sagebrush on high creek bench and bottom slope of foothills.

The house was probably thirty years old but ramshackle enough to be a hundred. Most of the windows had one or more paper patches where glass had been broken. There was an old pole barn with low-pitched roof, a tall granary made of flat-wise two-by-fours, a wagon and harness shed, a well and a privy. New posts were wanted all around the barbwire fencing. The ditch was a dirty mess, and this was the life of the ranch. It was not only piled with muck and sand but the lumber of the dam and headgate was rotted useless, so that high water was needed to get a head in the ditch. I couldn't understand how such rack and ruin could have come to be. It was a story, as Gabe Turner told it, of shiftlessness from the first, of a bank foreclosing a mortgage, somebody away off in Boise buying the mortgage and renting the place on shares, and this going on until George B. M. Hoover bought the ranch for a song and talked my drunkard uncle into trying his luck at it. Now, starting his third year of renting from Mr. Hoover, Gabe was at a point of either losing everything he owned or else building the place up into a money-maker.

Gabe owned the three bronco horses, Cyclone, Frank and Vernie, and some hard-used ranch tools—plow, harrow, disk, lumber wagon, hayrack, sled bobs, a load of forks, axes, shovels, a pick, a mattock, a posthole auger, a barbwire stretcher, two saddles, four sets of harness, carpenter tools, a sledge and a couple of hard-rock drills, and more junk. The stock and team tools were now under chattel mortgage to Mr. Hoover. The two cayuse colts were yet free.

Last night, while he was speaking of the ride he needed to make to town today, Gabe had spoken dismally to me, saying—

"I hope to ketch Mr. Hoover in the Old Jedge again and in the same meller humor he was last trip. Otherwise, the way he has me in a pinch, we are apt to leave this ranch with the cayuses, and with nothin' else. This right soon, too. Well, I might as well go fill the jug and do some drinkin' while the drinkin's good."

He claimed to have a barrel of rye stashed down around the creek where nobody could hope to find it. If they did, he said, they'd run into a beartrap or a pitfall first. I suspicioned there was a little still, to boot. But I was not fool enough to go and stick my nose into that business. I knew I could go mighty far with Gabe Turner and not set him to raging, but not that far, not into his whisky concerns.

My poor uncle was a good, hard worker, drunk or sober. He was right clean about his person and the cooking, too, and no man in the valley wore shirts and overalls more washed-out. Old Gabe was prime company in the times between supper and sleep. There was no better fiddler for miles around, and hardly a Saturday night went by but what he rode off to rosin the bow and holler the calls at a country dance. Nights at the ranch he would practice, while I huddled up to the lamp with one of the books that Wiley Hurd had made me bring along, or with a Dickens novel from the Knox Free Public Library. The young woman who conducted the library was a worshiper of Charles Dickens. Somehow she'd got the notion she could make me become the same; then one day she got after Gabe about it when he was softhearted drunk; and he promised her he'd make me read all the Dickens novels in the library or he'd kill me. So I went to reading them. I let on that it was almost as much drudgery as reading the Bible, so Gabe decided that the novels of Charles Dickens really must be good for me. I came to love them truly; and Lily Yardley, the librarian, said that now we'd be friends for life. Anyhow I read like fury, and I'd read anything that even looked like a novel.

So there it was. There was my life, as it had run along through the winter with Gabe Turner. I could mention a lot more out of it, of course. There was the school. I confess I was a pure hellion there, and it's nothing but shame on me for it. I'd even keep using, with no reason at all, the trick I'd practiced with Wiley Hurd and had worked on Ollie Hicks. After I'd roughed around with Ern Suggs, Art Yardley and even some of the bigger boys, and had plowed that left hook into their bellies while I pretended to be playing, they got to shunning me. Yet a devil in me kept me wanting to hurt them more than I wanted to do anything else. It certainly is a bad thing to tell, but that's how it was. I'd half-cry on how I'd never meant it and how miserably sorry I was, yet I got a bad name. Then I would try to tell myself that I wanted to have it; but it was a lie, I didn't want to.

There was a stampede of Clovers out through the barbwire as I pulled Inez up and let out a coyote howl. Ma Essie came in the thick of it, a faded plaid shawl over her black hair, her eyes a snapping and laughing from her thin, dark face, the pack of Clover kids clamoring and yelling around and around her. No sign of grief for Tack was left here. The cold and starvation of the winter—I knew the Clovers had come through mainly on brown beans, sourdough bread and water gravy—seemed to be forgotten in the spring weather. I guessed they had grub now. With the start of spring riding, the oldest boys, Albert and Clay, had gone to work at the Hicks ranch. But Bess was back home. I kept looking for her, while Ma Essie chattered.

Inez was prancing, snorting and sashaying from all the excitement; but I hunched low and whispered to her, took easy tugs on the hackamore rope with my left hand and rubbed her neck under the mane with my right; so she wasn't scared but was really showing off.

"Yee-hee—never rains but it pours!" Ma Essie laughed. "Winter long no compn'y, none whatever hardly, nobody stoppin' by. Now early mawnin' come Albert to make sure Pa Johnny'll be to home all forenoon, for Mr. Russ and Mr. Bud, they want to stop by to talk him some bizness. Bess thinks it's on her, Pa allows they want to buy the place, and I venture Mr. Russ wants to invite me to a dance—hee-yee-yee!"

She laughed fit to kill, then gabbed on, "Well 'n' you come 'n' shorely welcome y'are, Jim Turner; and won't you light down; oh, *do,* now, we won't take no fer an answer! You come right in. Next it's the Hickses, tomorrer it's a Hardshell baptizin'; more things comin' up and goin' down! Yee-hee! Speakin' of baptizin', Bess home, bless her sweetness, more things, you and yore spang-new saddle horse, and us, me—I wouldn't wonder iffen I was pregnun' ag'in, yee-hee, Johnny!"

That last there was for Pa Johnny's benefit as he came up and stood on the inside of the barbwire gate. It had been a rough winter on him. He looked *so* thin and little under the old wagon-shed hat with the frayed-out band and broken peak; so tattered and worn otherwise, and so starey-eyed and saintlike, too. He was letting a beard grow under his silky mustache. His hair, light-brown, with red and gold glints, was long. As Gabe had remarked, Johnny Clover was getting to look plumb Biblical.

The Clover kids, scrapping, yelling and showing off, made me go on to think of the brats who mocked Elisha, telling him, "Go up, go up, thou baldhead!" and who learned better manners when God sent bears down to rip them to pieces. They ruined the morning for me in no time. Any second, I feared, Inez would shy and run from them. Even Fave, who was fourteen, a year older than Bess, was acting the fool, straddling the handle of a busted old pitchfork and galloping up and down, bawling, "Bet my bronc can beat yore bronc in a race! Dare you to race me, Jim, dare you!" Ma Essie only yee-heed at the fool, and Pa Johnny only stood dreaming. Jen who was ten, Lester who was eleven, Net who was eight, Vannie who was seven, and Bryan who was two, raced and ranted around after the fool Fave. It took Bess to calm them down and herd them back, just when Inez had stood all that a nervous little filly could be expected to stand.

How Bess brought that bunch to taw I'll never know, but she did it without calling on bears for help, with no tearing or upbraiding. Out she came, her hair done up fresh, wearing a white-and-blue-flowered summer dress that Aunt Sue had given her, looking like a woman, looking years older than me. She spoke to

Fave and to Lester, and they led the others back through the fence and into some peace and quiet. Then:

"Now, Ma," she said, so soft and low, "you promised you wouldn't carry on. You won't forget yourself with Mr. Hicks, will you?"

"But, Bess, this ain't Mr. Hicks," Ma Essie said, all perplexed. "This here is Jim Turner. He's same as a cousin, like one of the fambly."

"He sure is," Bess said. "But that's no call to pester him to stop by if he don't want to." She came up to Inez, who stood like a lamb for her. "Hello, you pretty thing," Bess said to her. "What a shame for you to have to pack such a big, rough, tough buckaroo around! He'll get you into trouble. Fightin' trouble, pretty thing."

Well, she smiled up at me while she talked and I ate it up. She was with her family here like larkspur in the sagebrush. I loved her. I loved her then. I know this, remembering. But all I knew in myself on that morning was that we'd tried to be as sister and brother, first on Aunt Sue's account, then because we'd lived and grown into it. It had been no way spoiled by the filthy talk of Ollie Hicks or by grownup joshing. All boys and girls over ten or so had to go through and tolerate the like. I clung to Bess Clover. Aunt Sue, now, was as a woman in a cell, with Paul's slattern widow and three mean boys as stones and bars about her. She said that herself. I'd had a Christmas letter from Grandma Barton, but it was mainly about her ailments and poverty, the poor soul. The only other woman who had taken an interest in me was the one I've mentioned—the woman who ran the Knox Free Public Library. She was the oldest of the Yardley girls, Lily was, an old maid of twenty-six; yet so lovely, really beautiful, with the most golden pile of hair on her, and the deepest blue eyes. She was educated and had worked three years in the Portland, Oregon, library. I expected she only liked me because I was such a born reader. There simply wasn't anybody alive I could feel truly close to but Bess Clover. I didn't know if my Ma Tavie was among the living or not. I'd given up all but a dream now and then about Uncle Dan'l Barton. As for Gabe—well, he was all right to batch with. But there was only Bess to warm my heart.

It wasn't going right with us this morning. Bess talked away to me, but her look kept going down the road, toward the Bob Creek fork, until I thought about the expected visit of Russ and Bud Hicks. Then I thought of Ollie. I understood that Mrs. Hicks had sent Bess home when school was out on account of Ollie. The old black brooding came down through the sunlight. I bowed my neck and glowered at a patch of new grass at the roadside. I could see Ollie Hicks stretched on it, writhing and moaning, his fat hands groping at the butcher knife I'd stuck in his dirty guts and which I'd been gloating over ever since; while the green grass run red with his blood; and God damn him for a candy-fed bastard, a spoilt son of a bitch.

I looked up and over at the shacks. The shadow of the steep east hill was yet on them. I seemed to smell the sheepy bedclothes. I said right shortly, "I got to go. Ranch work's a-waitin'," and not till then did I remember Frank and Vernie. Bess stepped back, and I could tell she was relieved. I drove and wedged a grin up to my face and hacked out a halfway pleasant, "So long. Hope to see you tomorrow." Then I tipped my cap, swung Inez and let her lope free.

Down at the fork I met Russ and Bud Hicks, but no Ollie. Russ hauled me up, looked over Inez with a sharp eye, then six-gunned me with questions about her. I answered him as politely as I knew how, for he was my elder, and it was well known to be true what Ollie had bragged, that the Hickses practically named the county sheriff every election. And I just had to admire him. By gadfrey, he was one who truly tried to live up to what was expected of a western handler of horses and a king cattleman. He was yellow-headed and he looked out with an eye of blue steel from under the brim of a white Stetson sombrero that must have set him back forty dollars. He would admit, without being asked, that his palomino cost him five hundred even in the Phoenix, Arizona, market. His hand-carved and silver-mounted saddle, bridle and chaps came from the same quarter. He wore silk, a ruby stone, and boots and gauntlets made to order, and he packed a forty-five with a silver-framed butt and pearl handles.

There sat Russ Hicks, as arrogant as Satan, with the middle Hicks brother, Bud, behind him. Bud was dark and short, he was dressed like any cowhand, with Boss of the Road overalls under Montgomery Ward chaps, a broad kidney-brace belt, a buckskin-lined vest, blue wool shirt, sheephide coat thonged to the saddle, and a hat that was hardly better than Johnny Clover's. He rode a blocky buckskin. Bud ran the range, the stock and the ranch work. Russ did the business.

I was a meek and humble Christian boy to them, as I'd been to the Rev. Pearl Yates, Mayor DeWitt Clinton Maul and to other powerful people. No more than half of my answers were lies.

"All right, all right," Russ Hicks said at the end. "I'm lookin' for a cayuse like her for Ollie. I'll give you five double-eagles for her as she stands. Five twenty-dollar gold pieces. One hundred dollars."

It was in my mouth to scream and screech the filthiest curses and horriblest oaths I could imagine or remember, there was yet so much murder in me for Ollie Hicks. It was a whole lot more hell in me to think of Ollie getting Inez for his own than for his horsing around Bess Clover. Why, he could kill Inez, and nobody would bother him.

But I only said, "Thank you, Mr. Hicks, that is sure mighty kind of you, sir, but I can't do it, I just can't, because, well, I see I got to tell it on him, in the freeze Uncle Gabe fell drunk through the ice in a big hole of the crick, and I couldn't get to him only with a rope and a hook for hog-scaldin', and Ine-uh-the filly here was broke enough she came to taw and hauled, and we drug him out and saved him, and so I couldn't, and my uncle couldn't give her up, not for no money whatever, after she'd saved him from a drunken drownin'. You can understand that there, Mr. Hicks, oh, surely you can understand that; for as the prophet has said, 'Greater love has no man than he who giveth his life for a friend.' Oh, that is how it is, sir, that's how it is! Boy or man, horse or dog, drunk or sober, freezin' or drownin'—Oh, that's how it is, Oh yes, that's how it is——"

So there I was again, preaching in the old fever, rising to the old pitch of fury, lying to Russ Hicks with one of the revival stories I'd used in my sermon. I was hollering and waving until Inez began to take fright and Russ Hicks held up both hands to stop me.

"All right, all right," he said, with a grin that somehow didn't look like a grin. "I don't want her. I only wanted to see how much you thought of her."

Then he gave his palomino the spurs and came rearing by me, whopping his sombrero down on Inez's rump as he passed and letting out an Indian war cry. The little strawberry roan almost leaped out from under me, then Bud Hicks boosted her more with a hat and a holler. That all took about two seconds. In the third Inez was running wild down the road. Somehow I drove the fury out of me and put all I had into working her down, and in a half mile I had her down to a lope. She single-footed up a rise in the road. I swung in the saddle and peered back. Russ and Bud Hicks were hauled up again, watching me and the strawberry roan. I felt no pride in this. I was worried sick.

There was more trouble when Gabe came home in the middle of the afternoon and saw how little had been done on the ditch. I couldn't think of anything better than to work up a lie for him, too.

"It was Uncle Dan'l," I said. "He was mighty disappointed at not ketchin' you here. He couldn't wait. I rode around seven miles up to the mountains with him. I had to swear to him I would tell you no more, not even about how Ramon Hurd met him—oh, Lordy, there I broke my solemn oath, I never meant to, it slipped out, but I broke it, and I'll burn in hell eternal for it. Oh, can you forgive me, O Lord——"

He certainly was a soft one, after Russ Hicks. It was like taking candy from a baby. In no time Gabe was begging me not to take on so, everything was all right, and I shouldn't take on.

"It rips hell out of my nerves, Jim," he begged. "I'm tryin' *so* hard to quit the strong drink. Mr. Hoover is pleased to see us forgin' ahead, you and me. He said so. But I need fer you to help me keep my nerves steady as well as to work, Jim. Don't take on so. I'll jest *have* to go and git drunk, by God, if you do!"

So I quit taking on, and he was mighty careful after that not to quiz me about my secret doings with Black Dan Barton. That guess of mine about Ramon Hurd was the convincer, I came to learn.

But it was all folly, all was vanity. My poor uncle would back-slide into sucking at his jug at least once every six weeks. There was no rain all summer. The wheat failed and the oats did little better. The Clover family had to depend altogether on the wages brought home by Albert, Clay—and by Bess, who stopped school in the fall and became a regular hired girl when she was fourteen. I stayed out of school myself, partly because the teacher complained so about me, but mainly to help Gabe do enough work on the ranch to keep Mr. Hoover's backing. But the work wasn't quite enough.

One dark and rainy March day Gabe came home from a trip and started tearing into his jug without eating any supper. He was next to dead drunk before he could tell me what was on his mind.

"Uh needed two hun'ert," he wheezed. "Two hun'ert, or he'd hafta take ever'thing, Hoover said. Russh 'icks wash to town. Tol' him my trouble. He saysh, 'Two hunert fer strawber' roan filly, you make deal ri' now, ri' now.' Sho I make deal ri' now. Come f'r 'er 'morrow."

Then he keeled over, dead to the world, or acting mighty like it. Somehow I'd been resigned to it for most of the winter. Somehow it didn't tear me apart and set me afire so much, so long as there was nobody to hear me take on about it.

Then I did a kind of funny thing. I lit a lantern and went out to a lean-to shed at the front of the granary, where we'd fan and treat seed and sack grain, and which had an old set of scales. It weighed me at a hundred and fifty-one pounds. I had a measuring place fixed on the wall. It showed I was close to five feet and ten inches in my sock feet. I took a two-bushel sack of wheat by the ears, squatted, hefted the hundred and twenty pounds to my thighs, then heaved it to my right shoulder and stood straight with my hands on my hips. I stood there a long time, feeling good, feeling better and better under the bulk and weight, wishing there were three sacks, betting to myself I could bear three, if I get them up here on my shoulders. I went out with the lantern and dogtrotted to the shack with the sack on my shoulder, holding to one of its ears. I threw it down on the step, the gunnysack caught and tore, and I let it rip. Then I went in and peeled Gabe's duds down to his drawers and rolled the old son of a bitch into his blankets. Then I went to bed and slept like a log.

5. The Golden Heifers

THE G. DODD RANCH ON BOB CREEK WAS ONE OF seven that were located in irrigated valleys all the way between Knox and Boise. Gallatin Dodd was a Knox druggist. His father had made a pile of money as a sutler in Sherman's army, then as a U. S. Treasury agent of some kind in Mobile, Alabama, after the war. It appeared that by 1870 there were enough men thirsting for the blood of Pa Dodd to fill a regiment. So he moved to wild Idaho. Here he was shot to death, but not before he had picked up mortgages on a Knox drug business and ranches hither and yon. But it was Gallatin who made the Dodd name famous. He studied the needs of the righteous and in time cooked up a powerful mixture of fermented prune juice, with dope to give it a moral vile flavor, and advertised it as—

DR. G. DODD'S MISSION MEDICINE
for Stomach, Liver and Kidney Complaints

It sold tremendously in the godliest places from the first, and in time many sanctified Methodists and other strict sectarians came to use G. Dodd's prune bitters; Mormons too. He raised his own prunes, with a big orchard on each of his seven ranches. But in my time G. Dodd's pride and glory had come to be his dairy stock, his Golden Jerseys.

G. Dodd bred, raised and sold Jerseys in the way Barrick McCool had dealt in Percherons and Morgans back in Iowa. Mr. George B. M. Hoover said of him that no man in all Idaho had done more for good milk and less for good whisky than Gallatin Dodd. It seemed likely.

By haying time in this third summer of mine in Idaho I'd done considerable studying on the richest people around and in Knox, along the line of how I might start out on my own hook and forge ahead.

There were the Hickses. My standing was already poor in that range. There was Mr. Hoover. I was yet all right with him, but in the way of a big, strong boy who could be used in building up one of his places. Another rich party was Margaret W. Hinote, who was best known as "Big Mag," madam of the Notch, as the Knox house of ill fame was called. She owned a pile of projects, too, but I couldn't even *dream* a story of how to get a start in any one. Then there were a number of mysterious "interests," people of big money in the East and even in Europe, who owned stacks of Idaho land—mines, timber and ranches—and railroads, smelters, sawmills and such. I had no notion of how I might get in with them.

But I wasn't giving up the hope. I'd promised Gabe every cent of my wages if he'd let me go down with him and work through haying for Windy Hill, foreman of the G. Dodd ranch. I'd quizzed Wiley Hurd half crazy through a couple of Sabbath afternoons concerning what he knew about dairying and dairy stock. He'd given me a pile of his old copies of *Hoard's Dairyman* to study. Now at G. Dodd's ranch I could make the acquaintance of some of the finest Golden Jerseys in all the south of Idaho, and I might catch the eye of G. Dodd himself.

On my very first evening at the ranch a thing happened that cinched my determination to make a start in life as a dairyman.

It was sundown when I rode up the high pasture of the Dodd place, circling to go through a herd of forty-odd yearling heifers. They were as tame as kittens. The bright-bay I rode was trained to stand like a post among cow-critters. So I pulled him up amid the herd and just sat in the saddle and had me a reverie in the sundown.

The golden hair of the heifers did glow and shine as silken coats in the soft-red run of light from the rim of westerly hills. The great, dark eyes that seemed to muse up at me gave forth a gaze as gentle, kind and Christian as any eyes on earth could give. The notion came that my eyes, or any human eyes, must appear as cold stones to heifers. I leaned over from the saddle and stuck out a hand. The littlest of the golden heifers came right up, took a smell, then gave my hand a couple of sloppy licks. The bright-bay crooked his neck, stretched it, shoved out his nose, rolled his eyes till the white showed, and swapped smells with the bold heifer. Before he could pull back he was getting a couple of sloppy licks over *his* face. Then he snorted his head up, and the heifer went to licking her own chops, appearing to be monstrous pleased with herself. Her mates regarded her with the nearest expression to wonder and awe that heifers could hope to muster. It was plain that, while they might not think so much about her licking a boy's hand, they considered it a powerful big thing for a heifer to have kissed a horse.

A spell clung around me. I wanted to stay here. It was a mood I'd known concerning horses. Many the time I'd imagined a story in which I was turned into a horse, and then lived happy ever after. Now the spell gave me a want to stay on with the happy golden heifers, to abide with the herd and be shed of the torments of growing, working and studying into being a man.

But I had to look sharp and work hard at my boy's job now on the G. Dodd ranch, and please Windy Hill, if I was to catch any kind of foothold in this place for climbing upward. Windy Hill needed another man for his haying crew. He was pleased to let me ride his bright-bay saddler up to the Payne place in the hills, to see if one of the young men there would come down to help out. If none would, I was to ride on up the valley and do my best to talk Art Yardley, who was about my own age, into coming down. I had to do it all by word of mouth, for Windy Hill could not read or write.

So I rode on at my chore. Walt Payne was not able to come down in the morning, and I rode for Art Yardley. Art was willing. He packed up a horse and came along with me for the night, nagging me, as he always would do, to tell him stories, the bigger the better. Uncle Gabe was at the Yardleys' when I stopped by. He'd brought Frank, Cyclone and a hay wagon down for the Dodd haying. I was all right so far with Windy Hill.

The foreman of the Dodd ranch on Bob Creek was a sandy, warty runt of a man who had toiled up from herding sheep. Nobody on Bob Creek, or Mount, either, could put up a handsomer or more waterproof stack of alfalfa hay. Windy Hill was just as good at making every drop of water count in irrigation, and for keeping the alfalfa seeded, and for holding down the gophers. He was a broad-gauge ranch mechanic, too, being as able with ranch machines and tools as he was with livestock, and this was saying a heap. Windy also knew his prunes. In the past five years he had brought up the old orchard, not only by pruning and spraying, but by growing rye and plowing it under green, along with the scrapings from the feedyards of neighboring sheep ranches. When it was storming he would carpenter around the insides of the ranch buildings, until now they were as good as new.

Windy Hill was so apt at all these things, and at many more, he entered into them with such high spirit, and he seemed to do everything so smart-wise that I couldn't understand how he had kept his worst weaknesses for so long. He was unable to read or write. Even the mention of reading and writing would scare him, making his eyes bug and roll. Once I tried to tell Windy there was nothing in the world easier than learning to read, but he let on not to hear me and he packed off right away to "see about something." Another weakness was for Big Mag Hinote's place, the Notch. Once every couple of weeks Windy Hill would go into Knox, and then, cold sober, he would stay all night at the Notch. This was told around on him until no respectable woman would be seen in his company.

"He's a sheepherder at heart," I remembered Aunt Sue saying of him. "Once a sheepherder, always a sheepherder."

"Windy Hill simply represents a vile idiocy of the Capitalist System," Wiley Hurd automatically argued back at her.

"Foof," Aunt Sue said, also as common. "Oh, foof!"

There was nothing so big and strong about him. Windy appeared kind of scrawny in oversized clothes. He went topped by a regular haystack of a cowboy hat that was so loaded with layers of dust, old blobs of sweat, streaks of grease and what-all that you could hardly tell what the store color might have been. From under its bent-up brim Windy's eyes looked out, as gray, small and practical as two nailheads. The eyes were red-rimmed and cropped around with brows and lashes that had no more color than bleached straw. Windy Hill was so sandy-complected and weather-bitten that he appeared gritty. He smelled wonderfully of alfalfa, horse sweat, cow hair, creosote dip, sour milk, and somehow of stewed prunes. Windy would never touch strong drink, not even in the form of Mission Medicine. But he did praise prunes above any other kind of grub—prunes raw, prunes canned, stewed dry prunes, and most of all prune pie. It was a sore spot with him that Isabel Crumley would ever and always balk at baking a prune pie for him.

I was interested in Miss Crumley, too, for she and Uncle Gabe Turner had gone together at odd times in past years, and now she was letting him shine up to her again in these new sober spells of his. She was a tall, dark woman, well along in her forties, and was getting steadily gaunter, grayer, more hollow-eyed and tight-mouthed. Her pa, Luther, had been on her hands since she was sixteen or so. He had come to Idaho as a young man who had served through the Civil War in a hospital company that was kept at the battle fronts—family man with a wife and two baby sons beside the oldest child, Isabel. Gabe said it was common report that Luther Crumley's mind was affected then, from the suffering amid which he had toiled in four years of war. But the hospital corps veteran had been a good man for G. Dodd's apothecary father. So he'd been for the son until his mind grew real feeble. By this time Isabel was the only one of his family left. She had kept house ever since and taken care of her pa on Dodd's Bob Creek ranch. Old Luther was harmless; he would putter around, ever wanting to help somebody; a sweet smile never ceased to shine through his white whiskers—it would bother a body to see it on him at every look—and he was commonly pin-neat and scrub-clean. Each day he would beg to do a washing for Isabel, and she kept things fixed so there would be some for him to do. Outside washing clothes old Luther wasn't of much use. He was a mule on dishes.

Next morning I was third one up from feeding, currying and harnessing at the barn. Windy Hill and Gabe Turner were washing for breakfast on the kitchen porch. As I came along I heard Gabe ask Windy, "So you've been thinkin' it over, have you? Well, Windy, I wouldn't bother about it. It was only a thing I heard." I hauled up.

"But you heerd it from a preacher, you said." When Windy was excited his voice got a squeak in it like that of a wheel on a dry axle. So it sounded now. "You said, Gabe, that a preacher from Boise tolt you, a Baptist preacher, that his brother Baptist, Mr. John D. Rockefeller, would give a full million dollars to any man who would swap him a *strong* stummick for his *weakly* stummick. Didn't you?"

"Why, yes, shore, Windy. Still and all, I only heard it."

"But it was a preacher. Did he say how the deal could be done?"

"Well—no." Gabe had a fit of coughing and then complained of his summer asthma. "It would likely be a double operation, with resks on both sides, the preacher surmised. To be honest, Windy, I never paid too much attention. I was no way interested. My own stummick is weakly."

"Mine ain't, Gabe. Mine is exter strong. That's why I been thinkin'."

Some sloshing sounded then, and a washpan of soapy water came flying out over the porch rail. Then I heard them toweling.

"Maybe what you should do," Gabe said pretty soon, "is to write and inquire of Mr. Rockefeller hisself."

"By grab—you mean *I* could write Mr. Rockefeller a letter— *me,* who used to herd sheep?"

"Why, shore, Windy Hill! It's a free country. Thunder, you could write a letter to President Theodore R. Roosevelt, if you felt like 'er. Or to W. J. Bryan or Miss Frances E. Willard, or to jest anybody. They all git their mail. Why, you could even send Mr. Rockefeller a telegraph. All the big people like him use the telegraph."

"Well, by doggy! That's news to me. I never dreamp of it!"

Art Yardley and another hay hand came along then, and I picked up with them to go on around to the porch steps. I heard Windy Hill ask Gabe if he would be willing to fix him up a telegram to John D. Rockefeller, and Gabe say, "I reckon, if you're shore you want me to," and then the peculiar talk came to an end.

While I washed and combed and gazed into my own face in the looking glass I kept warning myself I should wheel to Windy and tell him, "Windy, it's a whizzer he's worked up on you, it's a blamed sell, Windy, and don't you bite on it, now!" But I kept a close mouth, arguing I'd tell him later on when it was just the two of us by ourselves in the stacking. But then I caught Gabe and Isabel Crumley grinning and whispering to each other at the kitchen door, and both shut up in a guilty way when I came up on them. They were so thick nowadays as to be smirking and lally-gagging around, the old fools, like a pair of young ones. I could see now that this sell was not Gabe Turner's own notion. It wasn't like him. He's been put up to it. Maybe it was from Isabel, to make a fool of Windy Hill and get even with him for something or other. But I had a feeling it was deeper than her. All this about Mr. Rockefeller's stomach, the Boise preacher, and the telegraph—I grew somehow scared of it and got a mind to back away from it.

Isabel Crumley was as nice as pie to me this morning. She asked me how I'd been, did I miss school too much, what a shame it was I had to skip a term, but I was getting a pile of reading done, now, wasn't I, and considerable help from Lily Yardley in the Knox library? Old Gabe kept fidgeting around, plucking at me a couple of times, looking as appealing as old dog Tiresome at feeding time. I humored the poor coot and was as polite to Isabel as to a preacher's wife. They were *so* pleased. It was such a pitiable small thing to please them so.

The derrick horses were four-year-old Belgian geldings, the sons of sister mares, and they were from the same stud. So I figured they were cousins and half-brothers at the same time. Art Yardley argued with me all over the place on this, and we never did agree on which kind of kinship came first with the young derrick horses. I can't begin to tell how excited I was about them. They'd done only light ranch work as three-year-olds, and now Windy figured that some training in close handling would be just right to stage them on. It would be constant going ahead, then backing up, going ahead, backing up, on the derrick. There was a risk. Let the young Belgians break and run, and they might tear down the derrick, not only raising thunder with themselves but holding up the haying.

Windy Hill was gambling on me, and, by gad, I could have hugged
and kissed him for it, his smells and all.

"I've seen you at work with horses, and I can tell that Jack and
Harry like you," Windy told me. "Drivin' derrick is commonly a
kid's job. But your'n won't be. Not with them. You will be *a-trainin'*
horses, fine young horses, at close work."

What's why I was ready to pitch in and work my head off for
Windy Hill. This morning it seemed a real true turn for good in my
life of a poor boy in Idaho had come. I gabbed my head off to Art
Yardley about Jack and Harry, and I piled out to the work, feeling as the Wabash Cannonball used to look and sound as it
smoked, roared, whistled, and belled over our Iowa prairie for old
Missouri. And yet I said no word to Windy of the sell.

There's no other hay as good as irrigated alfalfa from soil of
volcano ash—not even red clover or purple vetch. I mean for
stock feed, and I mean for good work in haying, too. On the Dodd
ranch the alfalfa made three crops each summer, and then provided
horse pasture. Cattle had to be kept out of the green stuff, though,
for uncured alfalfa would bloat them to death. Now in June we
pitched into the first and biggest of the season's crops.

The derrick, with which stacks thirty feet high could be built,
was homemade from pine timber. A great square frame, built to
sled from one setting to another, was the foundation. A mighty
mast towered up from the center of the frame's crossties and was
braced four ways. At the mast's top the derrick pole—really a log
—tapered up on a long slant, with its lower end secured by a rope
to the mast. A four-tined Jackson fork swung from the high point,
and a big rope ran back from it, down pole and mast, through
pulleys, and out over the frame to the derrick team. The driver
of a hay wagon would pull the fork down to his load with the trip
rope as I backed up the team; then he would push and stomp the
tines into the hay, give me a wave; and I'd start Jack and Harry
easy, easy, easy, letting them step right out as the forkload would lift
and swing high for the stack. There Windy would catch his pitchfork in it, I'd make the Belgians hold the load as he pushed it
where he wanted it, until he'd holler "Hi!" and the driver would
yank the trip rope. Then I'd back 'em fast.

Over and over and over, through ten hours or more. We never once had wagonloads of hay waiting on us. Often Windy had time to do a few chores around between wagons. Then I'd tie Jack and Harry and pitch in to help him, although there was no call for me to do it.

So the work went through the week, into Saturday afternoon. Yet I failed to tell Windy Hill that my old fool of an uncle was working up a sell on him, with the connivance of Isabel Crumley. I came close to it when Windy spoke right out and asked me would I write a letter to "a sartin rich man" on a matter that was shaping up as the biggest chance that had ever come to him. I kept feeling scared to tell him. All I did was squirm out of it by reminding Windy that a rich man might not think much of a business-deal letter in the handwriting of a boy. Windy said he had never thought of that, and he appreciated me thinking of it.

"You have got a good head on you, Jim," Windy said feelingly. "And yore heart is shore in the right place."

He made me feel I was a stinker, but I still kept a closed mouth. I didn't even tell Art Yardley about the sell. All I could think of or act on was to work to forge ahead here, and first of all keep out of trouble.

On the Saturday afternoon it appeared to me that good fortune was smiling my way, as it would always do finally with boys in the stories of Charles Dickens, Horatio Alger, Mark Twain and Burt L. Standish. I really felt like a boy in one of the books of these story writers when G. Dodd, Mr. Gallatin Dodd himself, drove out to the ranch in a shiny rig pulled by a span of bright-bay French Coach mares. He had Mr. Will H. Harrison, the foreman of all his ranches, along. They drove around the place, then stopped in the shade of the big barn. The foreman went to unhitching the mares, to rest and water them. We had just finished a load. No other was in sight. Mr. Dodd, a big, wild-eyed man with a bushy black beard, came kind of like a thunderstorm for the stacks. But I made so bold as to step out and speak to him. I'd dreamed and dreamed of a chance like this. I had my remarks all made up and ready. They were to show that, while I might yet be a boy, I was up to snuff on my dairying, all right.

"Oh, Mr. Dodd," I spoke real fast. "I spect you'll be havin'
the government veter'naries givin' all your Jerseys the tuberc'lin
test now, whether you like it or not."

That hauled him up, sure enough. He stomped to a stop, gave
me a gape of surprise and barked, "Test? Test? Oh, yes-yes-yes.
Uh-test—yes." Then he made as though to go on.

I spoke real fast on a second remark I'd worked out. "I see you
are runnin' all Golden Jerseys, Mr. Dodd. Have you give up
breedin' dual-purpose cows altogether? Seems the Red Shorthorns
do well for milk and beef both."

"No more dual-purpose," he barked. "No-no-no-no."

Then he streaked away for the derrick and the stack. I sure
did feel let down. I was despondent and sullen all the rest of the
day. At least five times after G. Dodd departed Windy Hill wanted
to know what in the world ailed me. I suppose if I'd broken down
and told him, and at the same time been a real friend and warned
him of the mysterious sell, he might have gone ahead and set me
straight with Mr. Dodd. But I sulled on him, and on Art Yardley,
too. I could have gone up home with Art and had a visit with Bess
Clover, who was now a Yardley hired girl, but instead I rode into
Knox with my uncle and some of the other hay hands.

It turned out to be a good choice, after all. A troupe called
"Jolly Della Pringle and Her Merry Company" was putting in a
week at the old Knox Opera House. This Saturday night the show
was *East Lynne*. I was fevered about it, and for the time I was sure
that Jolly Della Pringle, who cried and took on all through the
play, was the most beautiful woman alive. I never saw a play on a
stage but that I was crazy about it at the time, and convinced that
some woman in it was the world's most beautiful one. I can still
feel love for poor, weeping, moaning Jolly Della Pringle.

The Knox Free Public Library was open on Saturday nights,
and I got two books out of it. One was Tennyson's poems, which
Lily Yardley asked me to take. The other was the most amazing
story I'd ever peeked into; it was packed with the strangest critters
and things this side of the holy book of Revelation. It was a new
novel, *First Men in the Moon*, by H. G. Wells. What wasn't in
the moon was in England, like the lord's poems and the play, *East
Lynne*. The novel did me more good with Art Yardley. It scared

him into the horrors, yet he would read the story and read it, then ask me to tell some of it over to him after we'd gone to bed. I was glad to oblige. It was easier than making stories up for him.

There was one of the Tennyson poems that truly took hold of me, and I was proud to memorize it to show off to Lily Yardley later on. It was a poem that went, *"Tears, idle tears, I know not what they mean . . . Dear as remembered kisses after death, And sweet as those by hopeless fancy feigned On lips that are for others. Deep as love, deep as first love, and wild with all regret. O Death in life, the days that are no more! . . ."*

The Tennyson book had pleasanter rhyming in it, but this one sung all through me somehow; it spilled seed, left growth. I worked another week, not dreaming of dairying a particle more, but of such as going walking with Jolly Della Pringle and saying the poem concerning tears to her, while she wept as lovely as she had done on the stage of the Knox Opera House. I did come to speak it to Lily Yardley; and to my amaze, she had hung her head and the tears were streaming before I was half through. But it was Bess Clover who truly cried when I said the poem to her. I'd never believed a body could cry so hard until I saw her shake and shake with crying. I was kind of awe-stricken at what I'd done with just a recitation. It was soon after Mrs. Fay Yardley had given out the news that Miss Fern Yardley was engaged to marry Mr. Russell Hicks.

The haying at the Dodd ranch came to an end on the sell that Gabe Turner, Isabel Crumley, and some of the others had worked up on Windy Hill. First there was a fake telegram, like this:

DEAR SIR IF YOU CAN PASS A TEST AND MAKE AFFIDAVIT YOU DONE IT WITH THREE WITNESSES I WILL PAY YOUR FARE AND HOTEL TO CHICAGO AND BACK SO AS WE CAN MAKE A DEAL SWAPPING STOMACHS FOR WHICH I WILL PAY YOU A MILLION DOLLARS IF WE DO THE TEST IS TO EAT SEVEN FULL SIZE PRUNE PIES AT ONE MEAL IN A HOUR AS I AM SO PARTIAL TO PRUNE PIE I DONT WANT NO STOMACH THAT CANT HANDLE PRUNE PIE YOURS TRULY

JOHN D. ROCKEFELLER

A boy from Coot's Livery rode out with it after supper on the last day of the haying. Gabe Turner, Isabel, the other hands, and I didn't know who-all else had gone that far in rigging the sell on the previous Saturday night. Windy Hill passed the telegram around to be read, and he handed it to me first of all. I read it out loud and didn't say a word more. Everybody else was as solemn as an owl. Warnings to Windy kept rising up in my neck, but each time I gulped them down again. There was not a solitary snicker.

The next forenoon was given to cleaning up, writing letters and otherwise fixing for the show that would come after noon dinner. Windy ate a scant breakfast. At noon he sat at the dinner table and looked around at one and all with a trustful eye. The rest of us piled into a regular feed. But in front of Windy Hill a fat prune pie was set, along with a green pitcher of milk and a big drinking glass. He pitched in. As he forked up the first bite, and the pie stood open, there were strong inhales all around the table. I was no drunkard, but even I could tell that the prune pie into which Windy Hill was digging was well primed with something mighty like G. Dodd's Mission Medicine for stomach, liver and kidney complaints.

Windy did not seem to notice. He claimed never to have tasted strong drink. Likely he had never tasted Mission Medicine, either. And he probably did not expect much of any prune pie that Isabel Crumley would make for him. Anyhow, on he went, shoveling into one pie after another, until five were consumed. By then Windy was using gulps of milk to sluice the bites down. His face had grown brick-red. His eyes were molten inside their red rims. Gabe Turner was long up from the table, standing away back now in the kitchen with Isabel. I kept noticing them. One minute Gabe would seem to choke and double up from the joke, then he'd see that Isabel kept looking more and more troubled as she watched Windy, and he would appear solemn and worried too for a spell. It was certainly no fun for me. In my sight Windy Hill began to look like a charge of giant powder with caps set and the fuse burning. I got up and went out.

At the haystacks I rolled up my blankets and tarp. Then I moseyed around to look at the house. I gnawed off a chaw and just stood, kind of sick and disgusted and worried on things in general.

It wasn't long before all hell began to break loose. First, the hay hands stampeded out of the house and for the barnyard, with a rifle banging and bullets screeching after them. I stood on, simply paralyzed. There came Windy Hill, then, staggering out on the kitchen porch, waving a rifle and bawling, " 'Way 'round 'em, Shep! Baa-aa—baa-aa! Cougars, cougars! Sic 'em, Shep! Yaa-hoo! Koyotes, koyotes! Yah-whoo-ee! 'Way 'round 'em, Shep! Cougars, koyotes!"

He reeled, faunched and hollered on for the picket fence and gate, after the galloping hay hands. Outside the gate Windy turned for a look back at the house while he reloaded. Poor old Luther Crumley had stuck his head out of an open upstairs window. Windy fired at him seven times. Most of the bullets went high, ripping up the shingles and tearing holes in the roof. Then Windy keeled over and went to vomiting. The prunes came out of him like black blood. He fell over in the muck and lay there senseless.

Mr. Gallatin Dodd and Mr. Will H. Harrison drove in with the pay for the hay hands after Windy had been picked up and piled on the shady side of the stacks but before the excitement had cooled down. Mr. Dodd got the story, he went into Windy's room and came out with the fake telegram from Mr. Rockefeller, and he looked more like a thundercloud than ever as he began to roar through his black beard and let his big, bulging eyes flash at all of us.

"A filthy sell, a Satanic trick at the hands of fools!" he bellowed at one and all. "I suffer the most despicable, meanest and most slanderous enemies of any man alive, and one of them is at the bottom of this! I'll name him now, and he can file suit any time he feels like it. His name is George Brinton McClellan Hoover, the whisky-drinking banker! He put his hired hands up to this—you, Gabe Turner, and that overgrown Indian of a nephew of yours! I'll give both of you ten minutes to get off this property after you are paid your wages. And you, Isabel Crumley, after all I've done for you! Shame be unto you, woman; shame, shame, be unto you!"

Well, that fixed me and the golden heifers. I guessed I had it coming. Gabe knew he did, too, as he stood there, looking as sheepish and guilty as mortal man could look, wiping his mustache over and over with the back of one hand, while he tried to comfort

Isabel with the other as she cried in her apron. I tried not to feel sorry for the poor fools. They'd let George B. M. Hoover use them to work up a story that would be told all over Idaho as a tremendous joke on G. Dodd's Mission Medicine for stomach, liver and kidney complaints. And so it was. It did G. Dodd a lot of damage.

Windy Hill cornered me in Knox a week later. He was with his brother-in-law, Marshal Moss Eckert, and I couldn't talk back.

"Any man, or any half a man, or any boy, either," he said, "who would help to work a sell to show up a friend like you done to me ought to be hung up by the ears and have sand blowed in his eyes till he falls."

"Hell, he oughter be jest hung," Marshal Moss Eckert said.

6. The Murder of Frank Steunenberg

DEACON FAY YARDLEY HIMSELF BROUGHT IN THE deathly news, along with a sledload of wedding guests who had come to Knox on the night train from the east. While the folks were being taken care of by Mrs. Yardley and Fern, the deacon came into the big kitchen of the ranch house and told us that Frank Steunenberg had been murdered on this night. He had left Art to put up the horses while he came on in with his mighty news. While he told it I imagined Black Dan Barton's shape and name rising in the horror of blast and bloodshed. Fear was a fever in me then. Nobody said his name, but the people looked at me, and I could tell the one thought in all. Fay Yardley had the look too.

"They killed Frank Steunenberg with dynamite, in the town of Caldwell," said the old settler. "He was comin' home to his supper, home through the snow. He went to open the gate to his yard, this set off the blast, and that was the last of the best governor the State of Idaho ever had. Frank Steunenberg died a martyr tonight. All Knox was awake and meetin' to mourn him when we departed."

The deacon stopped and fished a cob pipe and cut plug out of a coat pocket. He looked at me while he did, and I tried to edge deeper into the shadows at the back of the range. Then the people began to fire all manner of questions. Deacon Fay shook his head at nearly every one.

"That's all I can tell, outside rumors," he said, through blue puffs of pipe smoke. "Last thing I was at the sheriff's with Russ Hicks. The sheriff had the lawmen at Caldwell on the telephone. They had not apprehended the killer. We can be sure, of course, he was one of the dastard dynamiters the Western Federation of

Miners has hired for murder. The heads of that union will be brought to book."

One of the women said, "Ain't they in Colorado?"

"They won't be for long," said Fay Yardley.

He was easy and low-spoken enough in what he said, but it was simple to tell that he wanted to say words fit to kill and that in him was nothing but a thirst for vengeance. I grew surer of this in his answers to the questions that came on at him. Once he said, "Frank Steunenberg was my old friend." I kept thinking of how Black Dan Barton was a dynamiter—and my blood uncle. And there was Socialist Wiley Hurd—and Ramon Hurd, who had been in the pen with Black Dan. And there was all my idiot gab, not only to Gabe Turner, but to Art Yardley and other boys, on how I knew where Black Dan was, all right, all right; I was seeing him! Oh, the fool! "The best detectives in the nation are on their way to work with the law and with the Redburn Protective Agency on this murder," Deacon Fay said. "The murderer will be caught, and he will be hung. The same with them who hired him. The least clue will be run down." And when he said that he looked again at me, he looked hard at me, and I wondered to God what Art Yardley might have told him, with all the imagination for stories that Art owned. The scare in me grew. But now the deacon only went on to say we were not to expect Gabe Turner home tonight. Isabel heard him and began to cry like fury. They'd been married just a month.

"He's not drunk," old Fay said. "Don't worry, Isabel. Gabe used to be in the strikes. He's helpin' the sheriff."

I chirked up some and went over to Isabel and told her I might as well hit for home, then, so as to look out for the stock in the morning. Isabel let up on her sniffles but hung to my hand for a minute. She was with Bess Clover, Lily Yardley and three other women at the round breakfast table, all sewing on a pile of wedding truck.

Bess gave me a heartening smile through the bright lamplight. It was the first time I had seen her smile since the news that Fern Yardley was to marry Russ Hicks. She'd stayed right on here. It was a good place. Clay and Albert had left home. Her pay fed the Clover family now. Lily was here just for tonight and the wedding tomorrow, and Isabel had been hired for the wedding time.

Even in the fever that seemed to smother me I noticed how Lily sat frozen, her face so set and white under her golden hair. Oh, it was a terrible thing, terrible! Many were struck to the core by it, each in a way; Deacon Fay in his, Lily in hers, and the poor boy, Jim Turner, in his. I said good night.

The huge kitchen room was quiet as I left. I gave no heed to any of the people besides Fay Yardley. He peered at me over the cob pipe as he held it out in a gnarled little hand and puffed smoke. The oldest living pioneer of the Knox country was a small man. He had a pile of white hair and bristling white whiskers. His old eyes gave me a kind gleam, or I hoped that was it, as I went by him and stopped to get my coat and cap from the back wall. The deacon was supposed to carry a bunch of certified hates around with him, but Wiley Hurd said once that it was only to help out certain people he loved.

"Em, Mrs. Yardley, takes the *Menace* paper and hates the Roman Catholics with a maniac hate. Fay don't hate Catholics himself, but he helps her. So with Socialists and labor unions. Grundy Johnson, the big capitalist who hates *them* with a maniac hate, was a young pioneer with Fay Yardley, so the deacon helps Grundy Johnson to hate labor leaders. Fay is a friend to me—and he helps me to hate the capitalists once in a while. He is simply too accommodating for his own good."

I remembered this and thought to take heart from it as I went into the snowbound night. Art Yardley was coming out of the barn with a lantern when I got there. I tried to speak offhand and say that now I couldn't stay with him tonight, as Gabe was staying in Knox and I'd have to ride on to look out for things on the ranch.

"That's too bad," Art said. Then—"Say, I bet you've already got a big story lined out on the murder of Frank Steunenberg."

"Not much," I said. "Not on the murder of Frank Steunenberg. Not me."

And on that and on just about everything else I kept good and quiet for over six months. Gabe Turner said I was worse close-mouthed than I'd been in my first month in Idaho. He was right. And I was worse scared, too. For the heads of the Western Federation of Miners were actually kidnaped out of Colorado to be

charged with murder in Idaho. The dynamiter killer, Harry Orchard, was caught, and he confessed. The Redburn detectives were
tracking suspects and witnesses down everywhere. They were after
Black Dan Barton, among many others. I lived and worked from
day to day in the expectation that they would hook me in trying
to catch him. But by the Fourth of July they still hadn't done it.
The fear fever died down.

The speaker of the day was Mr. William Edgar Borah of Boise.
He was the leading prosecutor, or was so thought of, in the case
that was being built up against the officers of the Western Federation of Miners, in particular William D. Haywood. Mr. Borah
did not mention the case in his patriotic oration. It was about the
Founding Fathers and was all in their favor. I don't remember a
word of it, but I never can forget the proud picture that William
Edgar Borah made as he stood out amid the bunting and above the
crowd in the public square; arrayed in a frock coat, McKinley
collar and Bryan tie; his jaws so strong and eyes so blazing under
a tremendous black mane; his voice sounding as a trumpet of
Joshua; his motions as mighty as Moses.

With scare down, I'd been dreaming of stories on the murder
of Frank Steunenberg for a long time, while I plugged away at the
ranch work. Now, not caring what Mr. Borah was saying, but
knowing he was a big man and liking to look at him and hear his
roar, I began to go it on a dream that Mr. Borah had his eagle eye
on me, Jim Turner, as just the young man he had been looking for
to serve as his special deputy.

Therein I did real well. At last I caught the foul bloody devil
behind the killer of Frank Steunenberg, and Mr. Borah took my
evidence and prosecuted him so powerfully he was sentenced to be
hung by the neck until dead. Mr. Borah agreed to let me do the
hanging job. So we stood on the gallows high, Mr. Borah and me,
there was a wind, and it blowed his mane of hair as the hot wind
did now, and we watched the murderer climb the thirteen steps to
his doom. He still looked real surprised. Never had he thought that
anybody would even suspect *him,* let alone catch him; and up to
now he'd been sure his pull would keep his neck from a-stretching.
Here he clumb to his doom, all in wonder, never dreaming who the

deputy was who had hooked him and who was waiting to hang him. Then he looked up to see Mr. Borah and the young man who stood ready with the noose and black cap. He well-nigh fell over. "Jim Turner!" he gasped. "You!" "Yes, Russ Hicks, it is me," I said.

There the fine story was stopped. I never got to dream of Russ Hicks a-dangling at my hand. For a real voice sounded low——

"You *have* to be Jim Turner," the voice said. "No other boy could look so much like Dan'l Barton." That quick the scare shot up in me like a match flame touching dry grass. I jerked around to look into a pair of dark eyes and a lean, tanned, handsome face, all sunned by a friendly smile. "I'm your first cousin, Ramon Hurd, and an old friend of your Uncle Dan'l."

He reached out and took my hand. It had turned limp, like all the rest of me, and was sweating cold. I let Ramon Hurd shake it and then pull me away from the crowd. Inside a couple of minutes I'd taken to him as to an old brother. He was right around thirty but he still had the appearance of a young man, and a handsome one. He had on a nice blue serge suit, and a white silk shirt with soft collar and blue bow tie. The little smile he wore had a sweetness in it, and this was in his eyes and in the singing that ever sounded in his voice. Ramon Hurd was a poet at heart, and this came to me, without the word, at my first sight of him. So he was brother to me. There was Tennessee Spanish back up the Hurd family line, and the mark of it had shown on Ramon early. So he had been given a name that suited him, and he had lived up to it. Ramon took his poetry out in singing, roving, horses, and a secret love. He told me all about himself before this Fourth of July had come to its end in a tremendous fireworks show over the River Snake. By then Ramon was calling me *compañero,* and I had vowed to throw fits at Aunt Isabel and Uncle Gabe until they would let me go freighting with him into the Lemolo and Seven Devils mountains.

"I ran away at seventeen," he said. "It was on a dream of the Spanish lands. But I never crossed the Rio Grande. I lived and worked with the Spanish-Indian people of Arizona and New Mexico. I packed, freighted, learned how to haul blastin' powder and how to shoot it in hard rock. I was there three years. There were mine strikes. I put in with the strikers. In the fightin' trouble

I met Black Dan Barton again—I'd known him around here when
I was a boy, of course. It's a story too long for now. Your uncle
saved my liberty, and my life too. We got away together to the
north, came back to here, and we went away up into the mountains,
through the Little Lemolo gorge, took up timber claims and proved
up on them between jobs as dynamiters. We bought more pine
land in the Little Lemolo basin. For a song, as they say. Nobody
else believed that the timber could ever be logged and sold, with
no way to get it out through the gorge of the Little Lemolo. But
we kept the taxes paid, or Pa Hurd did, the two years we were in
the state pen. You're sure you don't object to workin' with one
who was a convict?"

"Uncle Wiley declares you and Uncle Dan'l were railroaded," I
said. "Wasn't it all out of the strikin' miners up in the Coeur
d'Alenes bein' put in bullpens by the federal troops that Frank
Steunenberg called for when he was governor? Wasn't that it,
Ramon? Then didn't Governor Frank Steunenberg pick some of
you out and railroad you to the pen? You didn't do any crime, did
you?"

"It is hard to say," Ramon said, after a minute of thinking. "It
was real war in the Coeur d'Alene strikes. Fights. Battles with
dynamite. I was in them, side of my friend, Dan'l Barton. I guess
we were railroaded. But I'm branded for life." He gave me a close,
sober look. "I'm not sorry, though. I found religion in prison,
from a Roman Catholic priest. I made his church mine. That's
the worst sorrow to my mother. Pa despises me for it, too. What do
you think?"

I couldn't think of anything to say but "Why, I don't know—
it's your business, Ramon—I don't know about religion."

We were at Coot's Livery, where Ramon had his outfit of eight
horses, a heavy wagon and two light trailers put up. It was after
a supper he'd bought us at the Silver Grill. I'd helped him water
and brush his horses down. The little chore made us more as
brothers than ever. Ramon could spy the horse in me as I could
in him. We sat out under the livery yard oak, breathing in the cool
of the evening, watching the life of horses and men going on between barn and watering troughs. The sounds were good to hear—

gab of men, nickers and whinnies of horses, thumping of hoofs on the packed ground, water running and the horses sloshing it around the troughs. The shadows were long, the light mellow. It was a good time. I felt better than I had in ages. I knew I was going to enjoy the fireworks.

Ramon rolled and lit a cigarette, then told me more about Dan'l Barton.

"He hoped I could make it back here and look you up," Ramon said. "He is concerned about you, he knows you are him all over in your looks and that his name will be a cloud on you. I owe him a lot. I'd like to help you get your education."

"I've given it up," I said. "Isabel and Gabe don't mention it any more, and I'm stuck with them in buildin' up the Hoover ranch, with dimes doled out to me for it. I got to go hayin', and I've saved some money. Isabel and Gabe are good enough to me, but they are crazy with ambition. By God, I'd run off, like you did, only I'm scared even to throw a fit since that Steunenberg murder."

"What do you mean, 'throw a fit'?"

I told Ramon about my preaching, how I could foam at the mouth, holler in the tongues, dance with the jerks, holy-roll, and do other revival tricks in the style of the Rev. Pearl Yates.

"Devil's doin's," Ramon said. "God is love. Let me see what I can do. I'm your cousin, remember. We can make a deal that will be good for me and bring you good money. I expect to stay in Knox this winter. Would you like to go to school in town here?"

"I sure as hell want to get an education and not be a plug," I said.

"Well, let's look into it," Ramon said, sunning me with that smile of his. "I have other reasons, good reasons, to want to make a stake and settle in Knox. I don't want to be a plug, either."

He went on to speak some more about Black Dan Barton. He said that my uncle was out somewhere under another name, agitating and organizing for a new workers' union, one called the Industrial Workers of the World. I said I'd read of it in Uncle Wiley's *The Appeal to Reason*. Ramon said that the I.W.W. was not for him, as it was atheistic and revolutionary. Yet he spoke on with love about Dan'l Barton. I wondered. It was a curious thing to me to meet religion in a man without the hate that I'd learned was part of religion.

Well, we went on and on, teaming up closer and closer, as we loafed around until away late in the night, long after the fireworks were over. The wonder kept growing in me about Ramon Hurd. He had taken to me, I did believe, he really *liked* me—me, Jim Turner! He seemed to want me around him, I didn't seem to be in his road, and he wasn't just tolerating me as a duty or to get work out of me as Gabe Turner did—particularly since his becoming a cranky old abstainer. And Ramon had offered me a deal in his freighting contract which any full-grown and reliable man would have been pleased to take. I certainly did grab for it, and not only for the money but for the prospect of freighting into the high piny mountains with Ramon Hurd, a born man with horses, and one who had a song and sweetness in him. We worked it out and settled things the next day. I had to go and tell somebody. It was Lily Yardley, the librarian, I told.

"I expect to be goin' to school here by winter," I said. "Right here in Knox. I expect to go ahead and get an education."

She didn't say much, but she did a surprising thing—she got up from her desk and came around and put her hands on my shoulders, then kissed me. It was surprising, and it was a lovely thing too. I remembered and remembered it, and I always will. I never did think of fair Lily as an old maid again.

Then I rode back out to the Hoover ranch and threw fits until Isabel and Gabe both vowed they would be glad to get rid of me.

"It's for good, mind," Gabe warned me. "We've had our eye on a nice, quiet, hard-workin' boy of a Belgian fambly we can adopt. You go sky-hootin' off with Ramon Hurd, and we'll adopt him. There won't be no more room for you on this place."

Our little freighting deal worked along beautifully until that morning—that time when I heard the hoofbeats on the frozen road, drumming loud between the canyon walls. It was trouble coming. I could tell. Trouble coming with the dawn; up the wild, dark canyon, trouble out of the murder of Frank Steunenberg.

This was the morning of my fifteenth birthday, November 22, 1906. My little outfit was up ahead of Ramon's on the ground of our night camp. This was to be our last trip, and we were homeward bound. My four broncs stood two abreast and hitched to the running gears of a Bain wagon which was piled with pine lumber four feet above the bolsters. Ramon did not own this outfit, but had rented it for the season from Fay Yardley, who hired out work horses and rigs all over.

An unrelenting cold wind was booming off the Snake River breaks. The hooked-up horses, primed with oats, were fiery and snuffy and rearing to go—as it said in one of Ramon's songs. The boughs of the pines about us were fringed with frost. As the horses pawed the frozen ground and snorted and blew, puffs of steam rose from them.

It was a high time for me. I stood and thought how I had a hundred and fourteen dollars in the bank out of my freighting wages, with a new suit of clothes and a new outfit of work duds besides. Down around the warmest wool socks, and encasing the legs of herder's pants of waterproof ducking and red wool drawers legs, was a pair of high-laced boots with strap tops. My ribs were good and warm inside a heavy Canadian mackinaw, red-and-black plaid, with the name of Hudson's Bay Company inside the collar. My hands were in the biggest size of freighter's gauntlets in stock— and they were wonderful with fringing, beads and fancy stitching. The first Boss Raw Edge Stetson of my life was cocked on my black shag of hair. Inside the new duds I stood an even six feet and packed a hundred and seventy pounds of body and bones.

A fine birthday, it looked to me, fine to be fifteen and coming on. I could start in school at Knox after Christmas, Ramon said. I might keep working for wages up to then, at grain-hauling, gang-plowing and such, if hard winter did not come. Ramon had other plans for business in Knox which he had not told me about. This was all right with me. Anything Ramon wanted to do was fine with Jim Turner. I surely did love him like a brother. He seemed to bear me well.

Now I wished he'd get hooked up and going, leading out ahead of me with his eight horses and two wagonloads of lumber. Our horses had all stopped their stomping and had their heads up, with ears pricked for listening. Lord, they were pretty. There on Ramon's horses the red and blue goat-hair plumes and the little bells on the bows above the hames were bright in the daybreak. Frost crystals sparkled overhead from the black pines. The steam puffs rose.

I did not listen yet, but stood wishing and thinking. My rump really yearned for the feel of that spring wagon seat up there on the lumber; with the horses in the collars, the wheels of the Bain chunking in the frozen ruts, and the seat and me a-rocking and jolting down the mountain freight trail. Tooling the four-up, my handsome gauntlets tight on the four lines, my right booted foot cocked in the loop of the brake rope; rolling home.

So I wished, and I thought, "Come on, Ramon." I wanted to see him rolling there ahead of me; him in the saddle on the nigh wheeler, a big bay named Tard (for "tired"); the single jerkline in his hand running on to the head of Bertha, the nigh leader— the smartest horse alive, Ramon claimed, a pretty mare named for a girl in a play, a sewing-machine girl. Eight horses, two abreast, single line, jockey sticks and check straps keeping all in control under Bertha, who needed only the twitch of the line and a word from Ramon to know what to do. Bow bells jingling warnings around the bends, plumes shining in the mountain sunup, manes and tails blowing in the wind, music of hoofs and wheels from the hard road.

There could be nothing better in life. Right now I felt I wanted nothing more than to keep it up—why, I'd be glad to keep it up for thirty years, until I was a decrepit man of forty-five or older. I didn't want to be a dairyman any more, I didn't truly want to go back to school at all. This was what I wanted. But I hadn't argued on it. I was biding my time. Next spring would be time enough. There'd be black powder and giant powder and the other mining supplies to freight up to the packers, and ore concentrates and lumber to freight down. Ramon had hauled the explosives up, while I tagged him with grub and other harmless truck in my light outfit. The lumber had been for the Hicks ranch, where Russ was building a new house for his bride. It was from Wiley Hurd's sawmill and planer. Such hauling would be needed forever, it appeared. One of the outfits we'd freighted for was an engineering party with an untold purpose. Ramon hoped it was to prospect for a logging railroad route to open up the timber.

"Then we'd be fixed for life, *compañero*," he said. "Black Dan, too."

But it was only a hope.

And now I came awake to the drumming hoofs. They swept like thunder around the nearest shoulder of the canyon wall. And I stood thunderstruck at sight of the horse. It was Inez, the sweet little strawberry roan, owned now by the Hicks brothers for Ollie to ride. But it was not Ollie on her now. The rider was Lily Yardley.

It was like a play. This was the curious feeling that struck me as I stood like stone and watched Lily ride past, then pull up, light down and run to Ramon Hurd. They forgot me. Maybe I thought of leaving them be, I don't remember. What I remember is that I thought it was like a play—a play made from the famous novel, *Tempest and Sunshine,* by Mary J. Holmes, and which I had seen Jolly Della Pringle and her Merry Company put on at Knox Opera House. There was a tremendous surprise in the play's love story that left the audience simply gasping. And here it was again, right now, for me. I numbly thought, "So *this* is why Ramon really came back to Knox, is it? So *this* is what he was hopin' for this winter, hey? So *he* is the one that Lily was sent to Portland account of when she was a young girl, is he? My Lordy, and him a Roman Catholic, the worst thing on earth to the Yardleys—to Lily's ma, anyhow! This is trouble, oh, what trouble!"

Then they had pulled apart. And they went to talking, still more like Della Pringle and her main man actor, Wilton Ormand la Rue, than like the Lily Yardley and the Ramon Hurd I knew so well.

"Russ Hicks warned me of your danger," she said.

"How did he know about you and me, Lily?"

"I didn't ask, he didn't tell—there was no time. I was frightened to death just by the names Russ said—the murder of Frank Steunenberg—the Redburn detectives—Russ said he had it straight from the sheriff in Knox that they were coming after you—he said he was sure they'd caught Black Dan Barton and wanted you to help them convict him somehow——"

"That could be," Ramon broke in. "That could be pretty bad. But easy now, Lily, easy. I'm in the clear myself; be sure that I'm all in the clear on that murder. But they might use me to hurt Dan'l Barton. You were out at the Hicks ranch, you say?"

"I'd driven over with dad—to see Fern."

"Russ Hicks knew you were there?"

"Why, yes——"

"And he sent you? He gave you a horse to ride and warn me, to save me from the Redburns? That is what he told you?"

"Yes, Ramon. But there was another thing, the real thing with me—I so sorely wanted to come to you and go with you. We should have done this years go, Ramon, when I let mother send me away to Portland and you ran away to the Spanish lands!"

"Lily—now there's my church."

"I'll have it *our* church, Ramon!"

By this time I'd come back to myself enough to sidle around the wagon out of their sight. Then I stood, with Jolly Della Pringle and Wilton Ormand la Rue all out of my mind, while I sickened with the same fever of fear that had whirled and blazed in me in the Yardley kitchen on the night I first heard of the murder of Frank Steunenberg. I was surely in for it now. Even if it was a false alarm about the Redburns, as Ramon seemed to think, he and Lily would be going on, leaving me. Leaving me alone, with no home and nobody. Isabel and Gabe had adopted the Belgian in my place. There was no room for me to go back to Aunt Sue's, either. Bess Clover was with a Salvation Army family in Boise, with poor Johnny dead and gone, Ma Essie and the littlest children on the county, and the miserable homestead back into Hicks range. Nobody left for me, now. No hope in Black Dan Barton, who was likely in the hands of the Redburns and due to be hung. The last word from Grandma Barton was that she was so ailing that Ma Tavie was boarding her in an old folks' home, "a real tolerble home," she'd written. By God, I was forlorn. I felt my nose begin to run and my eyes get wet. Then I heard Ramon coming for me. I blinked down through the wet at the bulk I made in the new work duds, I thought how wonderful Ramon had been to me, and I swore at myself for a lowdown, spineless willy of a young man. "You call yourself a freighter, Jim Turner!" I said to myself. "You've got a gall, callin' yourself a freighter!"

It did me the good I needed, and it was just in time. As Ramon came around the end of the wagon I stepped up to him and spoke to him before he could speak to me.

"I heard you," I said. "You and Lily go right on. Don't you

worry about me. You've no need to. No, now—looky," I said, as
Ramon tried to speak, "I'd been wonderin' how I could tell you,
and not hurt your feelin's. Bess Clover wrote me from Boise, last
trip. The Salvation Army has a tremendous dairy school there.
Bess wrote me there was a job at the great school for me any time
I wanted it, and I could work my way through a dairy education
with no trouble. Now I'm free to go take it. Course I'll miss you
like sixty, Ramon, and Lily, too. But I can't pass up this chance
in the great Salvation Army dairy school! Don't you ask me to!
I won't do it!"

I was almost preaching, and had to choke down before I made it
too rich and fragrant. Anyhow, Lily and Ramon were both so
gloried up they were ready to believe anything that would let them
go on together in the runaway they had put off for so long. Still
a play; it was and always will be a play in my mind. And it was
like that with *everything* concerned with the murder of Frank
Steunenberg. The bloodiest kind of deed on a stage that had
smoked and roared with the worst of human violence, the evilest
passions, for many years. The deed bringing on powerful characters
—the most terrible one of all the killers of the West, the dynamite
man, Harry Orchard—then William D. Haywood, William Edgar
Borah, Clarence Darrow, Detective James McParland, the Pinker-
tons, the Redburns, Eugene V. Debs and his try at raising an army
of a million workers to march on Boise to rescue the martyrs of the
Western Federation of Miners, President Theodore Roosevelt roaring in the White House at the "undesirable citizens," and out of it
all the revolutionary Industrial Workers of the World arising! A
giant play, truly, and little plays from it.

Dynamite rode with me as I got away from Lily and Ramon and
drove on. I swiped some from what Ramon always carried to
shoot away big rocks that would slide into the narrow road. I'd
long ago learned how to shoot giant powder. And now I had a
notion.

There was a long pull up to the pass that would let the outfit
roll down to the main fork of Bob Creek. I had to blow the four
horses often on the pull. At the hump I stopped them again. I bit
off a chaw while I looked back a mile and more to a place where

the freighting road was a shelf through a shale slide, with a log bulkhead holding the slide from it. Now the shelf was gone. Back there it was a steep, straight line of slide down into the canyon gorge and up to a tall cliff. No saddle horse could cross that slide. It was a rough two-hour trip on old Indian trails around the mountain and back to the road. My charge of dynamite to blast the bulkhead logs had given Lily and Ramon that much of a start, at least, even if the Redburns should come riding for them now. Still thinking of a play, I guessed that was bringing down the curtain on the safe and happy lovers.

My back was on a thicket of bull pines. The sound of a horse stepping and breaking brush came from there. I pivoted in the wagon seat, and in the second of the move I shrunk, wilted and petered out to my natural size and was scared silly. I sat and stared.

Fay Yardley rode out of the pine clump on his high-shouldered dun. His eyes were bloodshot and his old face was gray above his white whiskers, which bristled all ways. He croaked, "Mornin', Jim Turner. I've been watchin' how handy you are with giant powder."

There was nothing in me that was able to speak back.

"You tell me what happened, young man, before you came on and blocked off the road," Fay Yardley said. He had pulled up close. His look was grim. His words were slow-spoken but they came strong and hard. "The truth, young man," he said. "In this case nothin' will be so good for you as the truth."

That was all he said, grim and hard and strong, but with no threat, no hint that he was trying to scare me or aimed to hurt me. The old man simply said what he did and gave me a plain, honest look. Then I found I was believing him. I'd never in all my life tried telling the truth to get out of a fix, and I expected I never would again, but this time I did try it. I sat there on the wagon seat, Deacon Fay Yardley sat there on his dun saddle horse, the cold wind blowing between us, and I told him the truth. I even told him I'd lied to Ramon about how he should not worry about me; saying I was not forlorn, I had a place open to me for a home and an education in the great Salvation Army dairy school at Boise; all a ripe lie.

"That there is the truth, Deacon Yardley, sir," I said, somehow feeling good inside. "But I won't confess it to the Redburns. They can burn me with cigar butts and slash me with holler-ground razors, but I won't tell *them*."

"There are no Redburn men after Ramon Hurd," the old deacon said. "Russ Hicks run a whizzer on Lily. So ease your mind. I believe what you've told me. You broke the law in blockin' that road. It slides over every winter, of course, but that's no excuse. I've got to do something about you."

"Yes, sir," I said, thinking—well it was bound to come some time; and I've done well to stave off reform school as long as I have. "Yes, sir," I said. "I am a bad egg, a right bad egg."

"You are dead right on that, Jim Turner, and I'll 'have to see about you. But right now, I want you to consider my fix. I'll tell *you* some truth." The old settler kneed his horse closer to my lumber load and his eyes searched right into mine before he spoke on. Then he said, "I expect Wiley Hurd has told you what hatred Mrs. Yardley has for the Roman Catholics and their church?"

"Yes, sir, I've heard about it," I said.

"Well, that's what I need to watch out for. She gets out of her mind on it sometimes. It would be hard enough on her, and it is on me, to know her Lily girl has run off with a man who has done time. But this other thing—the religious hate—you know what it is, and there is no need to talk about it. I can take care of it." He stopped, then fired this at me— "You don't have a place to stay now, do you?"

"No, sir," I said.

"You can stop at our place for a spell, and I'll see how you do at letting it be known that Ramon Hurd went back up into the mountains, and your not makin' mention of Lily. Leave the account of Lily to me. Can you do that?"

"Why, I think so, Deacon Yardley," I said. "It might be a story, a kindly story, sir, such as I often tell Art, and not a particle of harm done. A sort of parable, as you might say." I drew the most pious face I knew how to draw. "A soothin' sort of parable, sir."

"I allow you'll have to," sighed the old settler. "I don't see any other way out of it but to lie some now, and then make up for it with truth by easy stages. It seems right, considerin'." He looked back over the road and into the snow threat of the mountain sky.

"I hope they make it," he muttered in his bristling whiskers. "I could have caught up with her, I could have stopped her, but she has a right, she has a right. Poor Em, though, poor Em in her sick-minded hate of the Romans."

He pulled his horse around and gave me another look. He said: "You come through this to satisfy me, and I'll have a place for you at the Cumberland Institute after New Year's. Then we'll see how you live down Black Dan Barton."

He kept his part of the bargain, too. Mine was easy. You should have heard me.

7. Percy Bysshe Shelley and Joe Hill

THE CUMBERLAND INSTITUTE WAS A PRESBYTERIAN school that stood close to Knox; a place that was run to give boys and girls from back in the sagebrush a chance to work their way through high-school courses, either to go on to college or to learn trades. The school buildings were on a ranch of two thousand acres, with about half of them under irrigation; a rich spot of Idaho, truly. The Institute had a couple of hundred dairy cows, with a dairy barn like a palace, a model milkhouse, a small creamery and cheese factory, and a dairy professor who had come out straight from Ames—Ames, Iowa. I had dreamed many times of learning the dairy business in the Cumberland Institute, but never with true hope. The Presbyterian preachers who ran the school wanted poor boys and girls, but the prospectus said they must be of "unblemished moral character" to be taken. Here I was, Jim Turner, known to have a drunkard uncle, an ex-convict uncle, and an uncle by marriage who was a Socialist infidel; while back in Iowa I had grown so notorious myself that I figured the dairy professor from Ames must have heard of me. After going freighting with Ramon Hurd, I even quit dreaming about getting to be a dairy student at Cumberland Institute.

"Your sins will ever find you out, Jim Turner," I told myself, and gave up.

But you never know, not in this life. The old pioneer, Deacon Fay Yardley, was a founder trustee of the Cumberland Institute. Another trustee, a Baptist one, was the famous rich man of Montana and Idaho, Grundy Johnson. He and old Fay had been young men together in the early days of Idaho Territory. So when Fay

Yardley asked for me to be admitted to the Institute as a special
case who might well prove the power of good associations on even
the most evil of boys, I was let in.

My start was in January. And now, today, here I was, yet holding forth at the righteous Cumberland Institute, doing fine, and
getting mighty sick of it.

The day was an Idaho scorcher. The heat waves fairly jigged over
the high barns of the Cumberland Institute. In the dairy-barn corral the Jerseys snoozed where shade fell, stirring only to switch
the fly swarms. Here in the milkhouse I had just flushed the cement
floor, and the moist air had a refreshing feel and smell. Still, I was
wilted. I had been toiling with hot water and steam for ten hours.
It was now two in the afternoon. I could do what I pleased until
four, when the evening milking would be on. The first thing was
to swig a cold dipper of buttermilk. Then I stretched out on the
cream separator bench. It was in the coolest corner.

I had an old book to dream on, *The Poetical Works of Percy
Bysshe Shelley,* which Wiley Hurd had let me keep. But I was so
stripped by the heat that for a spell I could only brood morbidly
about tomorrow being another day, one of working mountains of
milk bottles through the steambrush washer, of scouring gummy
pails, cans and separator parts, and more and more of such dairy
business. But pretty soon I was reading and dreaming on this—

*At the age of seventeen, fragile in health and frame, of the purest
habits in morals, full of devoted generosity and universal kindness,
glowing with ardor to attain wisdom, resolved at every personal
sacrifice to do right, burning with a desire for affection and sympathy,—he was treated as a reprobate, cast forth as a criminal
. . . a youth of seventeen. . . .*

As they would ever do, the words raised a choke to my throat
and made my eyes wet. They were by Mrs. Shelley about Mr.
Shelley when he was a young man of seventeen and had got himself into trouble by writing an infidel poem, "Queen Mab." But
what truly moved me was my dream on her words. In the dream I
was on a street in Boise, walking with Bess Clover from the house-
work job she had with a lawyer's wife there. She was in her Salva-

tion Army rig, and we were walking to a meeting in which she would play her guitar and sing. As we walked I spoke to her the powerful poems I'd been writing back in Knox, and I told her how I'd been treated as a reprobate at the Cumberland Institute on account of the poems, being cast forth as a criminal at the age of nigh-on sixteen, e'en though I was fragile in health and frame and of the purest habits in morals. Bess stopped me to pity me, in the light of that orbed maiden with white fire laden, whom mortals call the moon. She was not a skinny, little, hungry-eyed Clover girl any more. She was beautiful in her Salvation bonnet, whilst she sighed, "Oh, poor James Birney Turner! Poor, poor mistreated James Birney Turner!"

Then Bess Clover asked me to recite the poem that had made me all the trouble. I told her, alas, it was but a fragment. Well, she said, let's have the fragment. So I recited—

BEULAH LAND
By James Birney Turner

I shall be no more forsaken
And no more desolate,
For poetry is my Beulah Land—
I see its golden gate.

Sorrow and sighing shall flee
Away, far away from me. . . .

Here on the separator bench I caught myself saying it out loud. Then I seemed to hear a kind of hoarse whisper from somewhere. I pushed up on an elbow and squinted at the screen door, but all I saw was the black mesh and sunlight glare. There came a sound that might have been the crunch of a shoe in the washed gravel of the milkhouse yard. Now I sat up and stared with sharp worry at the screen. A man's shape moved closer in the sunlight. I expected it to belong to Prof. Paul P. Stedd, the head of the dairy part of Cumberland Institute. But it was another's voice, a rich, singing voice, that came in to me, saying—

"I'm lookin' for one Jim Turner. I am Joe Hill."

"Well, I'm Jim Turner, Mr. Hill," I said, rising.

"Were you freightin' last year with Ramon Hurd?"

"Why, yes," I said, and my heart started to pound.

"I know Ramon, Jim, and I've seen him, and Mrs. Hurd too. They are in Red Rock, Montana. I can tell you about them."

By this time I was at the screen door, unhooking it with one hand and shaking high a switch of paper strips to scare back the flies. The man came inside. Joe Hill. To me at this point a shape of a man and a name, one who had come from my cousin, Ramon, older brother to me.

Joe Hill came in and I shook his hand. He stood and looked me over, and I saw him well. He stood on the wet-spotted cement floor of the milkhouse, with painted walls, scrubbed tables, shining cans, and all other kinds of bright-looking and sweet-smelling cleanness around him. He looked hard-used in it; a tall, slim, young-like man in a cheap, soiled suit of blue serge, a light-blue shirt open at its washed but unironed collar, and with a railroader's little black raw-edge hat still on. His face was tough, lean, brown, ever changing from one expression to another in features set around the biggest and most blazing eyes I had looked into since I faced the glare of the Rev. Pearl Yates. They gazed out from under the sweep of a mane of heavy hair with a center part, as he took off his hat and gave his face a mop with a red bandanna.

"I sure would like to hear about Ramon, Mr. Hill," I said. "I haven't had a word from him or about him since he left." My words seemed bound to kind of stump out on peglegs. I was dying to know about Ramon, but it was a mighty upset, this visit. Here I was on a straight-edge of good behavior. I was yet classed as one who had been placed here out of "unfortunate circumstances," as Rev. Woodman Farrier, the president of the Institute, himself had warned me. Now the fear welled up in me and I blurted it out. I said, "Joe, I work here to go to school. It is a strict place. I can be kicked out like a shot, and there's truly no place for me to go to. I'm afraid you know my uncle."

"Black Dan," said Joe Hill. "Black Dan Barton."

I put on my bowed-down look. "It's a name accursed on me," I said.

"The name is dead, Jim. For now, anyway. The mighty man who bore it is out of the mine country and in the woods under another name. There he's been since Bill Haywood was freed in the Boise trial. Dan'l Barton is workin' with Haywood to organize the Industrial Workers of the World—as I am. But he uses another name and he expects to leave you alone. It was Ramon Hurd who asked me to tell you, should I come west-bound through Knox."

"I would like to hear about Ramon, all right—and Lily," I said.

"I want to tell you, but keep it to yourself. Ramon has a freight haul out of Red Rock through the Beaverheads to Salmon City, Idaho. He has turned Christer right, his wife has a baby comin', and John Law leaves him alone. But he has done time and has a record, so keep this quiet. He said he would welcome you to live at his home, any time. You could go to school. But don't try to write him. You can't know how it might do harm. The Redburns can and will make murder out of the most innocent letter. That's all. Only, I want to be able to tell Dan'l how you look and feel and what you are up to."

Any kind of family affairs was always trouble for me to talk about. I made no answer but backed around to the icebox and got out the buttermilk can and poured Joe Hill a dipper. Then I took one and went over and sat down on the bench. I hoped we'd drink and then he'd go.

He came over, feather-footed, a hard man in his brown face and big blazers of eyes, a fighting young man in every feature and motion. Then he spied the Shelley book. A purely beautiful smile sunned his face over. He said, his voice singing-like again—

" 'Rise like lions after slumber, ye are many, they are few!' "

"Don't mistake me," I said honestly. "I cherish the poetry of Percy Bysshe Shelley, for this of his is the kind of poetry I would die, I would sell my soul, to be able to write. But I am no more one of your rebels than I am a church member."

"Well, well," said Joe Hill softly, his eyes not blazing now but shining on me. *"He* has never dreamed there was a poet in you. *That's* news for *him!"* He fell quiet and shone his eyes on me, sort of shaking his head. Then he said, "I know. That's how it was with me, Jim, how it was with me in the good time, the little fine time of my life before hell hit it. I was a poet. I dreamed on 'Queen Mab.' And on Byron's songs of revolt. And even in John Keats's 'Pot of Basil' I read hate for the merchants of greed, the 'hawks of ship-mast forests.' I was a rebel always, by God. Now I write only hymns, workers' hymns, revolution's hymns—not as poetry but only, only to arouse the slaves!"

I was afraid, afraid that Prof. Stedd or somebody would come to the door and hear him. Then, soon, I had no care or thought of this, I was caught up in the light, the fire of Joe Hill, and his voice was a bell of battle ringing through me. He talked on to me and to himself. I'd never dreamed there could be such talk. The nearest to it I'd ever known was from Wiley Hurd. But this had fire to melt me open, it had the glory of a mountain sunup, the strength of a mountain morning breeze blowing down into the festering misery of this day of mine. I began to talk up, too. It was sort of like an experience meeting, and we were swapping testimony. But this was on books, poetry, hymns, dreams, ambitions, hates, loves, and battles. Joe Hill had battled life all the way through. I never had done it. I wanted to. I wanted him to tell me, show me, how to quit being a coward and be more than willing to die fighting.

For a time, for a spell of glory, that was my high old feeling. But it couldn't last, not with me. There could never be a willingness in me to die fighting, or even just to get hurt a-fighting, not for more than a spell.

The letdown came when Joe Hill said—

"It was in Boise that I finally found out what I had to do and how to do it, Jim. I was there in the last months of the great trial which set William D. Haywood free. I laid real low and kept right quiet. I went to Salvation Army meetin's, and I studied them. Their pull is their hymns and their way of street singin'. Now my work is to write rebel hymns in words of everyday talk to the powerful tunes of salvation, hymns for workers to sing in the streets, to sing as they march to fight and die for the revolution."

I said, "There's a girl named Bess Clover in the Salvation Army at Boise. You didn't happen to know her, did you, Joe?"

Inside a second the light changed in him, and he gazed at me with suspicious eyes from a face set like hard rock. Then, even as he said, "No, No." I knew he was lying and I was sure that Bess Clover was deep in the same rebel faith that possessed Joe Hill, despite her uniform of the Salvation Army. I looked away.

No more of any account passed between us. Joe rose and said

he was with a bunch of hobos who were heading for a sawmill strike that was taking place in Portland. Could I see my way clear to provide some butter and eggs for a jungles supper. I was relieved to give him a big bag of truck from the icebox to speed him on. Joe Hill left a-whistling, and I put a dollar and a half of my own money in the cash drawer, and hoped Prof. Stedd would not ask about the big customer of the afternoon. He didn't.

As I toiled and sweated through the work of handling the evening milking I grew more and more unsettled in my mind and torn in spirit. After supper I was a body packed with unrest. It brought up the image of a girl, Ida Dorst, one I'd come to know too well, and this would not be driven away. I kept on thinking of Ida, and pretty evilly too, until finally I fixed myself up some and left for Knox.

Ida Dorst was the daughter of a section hand who lived in a part of Knox that was called Shack Row. She was a year younger than me, but big for her age, and she hoped to get married before long, as most girls in poor families would hope to do from fourteen on. Ida had German blue eyes, yellow and wavy soft hair, chubby face and hands, and plenty of pink in her complection. She had treated me as a close cousin from first acquaintance, as her step-ma was nobody but the widow of Paul Hurd, Luella. I had gone right on being a cousin with Ida. I'd learned to hold her hard to me and kiss her mouth as I'd never even tried to do with another girl. This was all right for cousins among our folks. It took considerable stretching for Ida and me to put ourselves up as cousins, but we made it.

Her pa, Ulvia Dorst, had been a section boss down in Vale, Oregon, when he met Luella Hurd. Last winter she had wound up there, after a year of catting around and leaving her brats on Aunt Sue Hurd's hands. At Vale, Luella experienced conversion in a Pentecostal Baptist revival, and at the same time Ulvia was converted. He was a widower, and soon they were wed and had moved to Knox to get Luella's boys back and bring them up with Ida as a Christian family. Clement, the oldest, had run off from Aunt Sue, and the Dorsts had to be satisfied to take the two young ones. The new family was getting along right well. Religion had really worked with Luella, it appeared. Anyhow, she had turned from a slattern into the cleanest kind of housekeeper and cook. And she was managing her two boys in a way to keep them from growing into scoundrels like Clement, their runaway older brother. But Ida was the attraction for me.

This was prayer meeting night, and I fully expected Ida would be at home, minding the boys while Luella and Ulvia were at church. But it was Luella who was at home with them. The woman who once was so well known as a slattern was at work in her kitchen, with the stove going full blast and topped with sadirons. She stood between a mountain of washed and sprinkled clothes on the kitchen table and an ironing board. Her faded Mother Hubbard had wet stains around its shoulders and sleeves, like the shirt of a harvest hand. Her eyes burned at me through straggles of wet hair. She kept right on ironing as she said, "Evenin', Jim. Find yerself a cheer." The two boys fetched some stovewood while I stumbled in the dimness and took a seat. They stood gaping and sniffling until I gave them a nickel apiece and Luella told them, "Clear out, young'n's, till I call you. Mind!" They banged out by the screen door. Luella said, "I've only trouble to tell. You won't do well to set long, unless you keer to hear troubles." She kept ironing like the Old Nick himself was prodding her.

"I can hear them and bear them," I said, having nothing else in my mind to say, but wondering where Ida might be. Then I asked. "I've had so much to do I put off comin' in to see her," I said.

"She ain't around any more, Jim. She's gone clean from Knox."

"Why, Lor-dee! I'd never heard a hint of it!"

"She left a week ago. She was ruint. A brakie ruint her. He took out when Ulvy hopped him about marryin' her. We'd knowed for a month she was ruint."

I could only flush and chill and kind of stutter, "Well, Lor-dee! Pshaw, now. Well doggone." Then stare at Luella, ironing like fury.

"Ulvy was half out of his mind afore she run off. Then he 'peared to go stark, starin' mad. He has took up with tramps. Three nights runnin' he come home drunk, jes' like Paul Hurd used to. Drunk, cursin', singin', hollerin', tellin' he's a sinner and proud of it! Last night I drove him off the place with a stick of stove-wood. I've got my church, my salvation is cinched, and I can never hope for more. I won't have it messed up by Idy Dorst or Ulvy Dorst or any other devil's Dorst! I pray for strength to hold to that there!"

She did it then. Luella prayed, ironing. She ironed a sheet by the feel of it while she prayed to her Lord, making no sound.

I sat like a wood chunk in the chair and thought on how soon I might hope to get away. Hate and loathing sat with me. They stood with Luella. I knew they were in her prayer. She opened her eyes.

"I feel better for prayin', I always do. Others are worse off, pore things. They are unsaved, and oh, I have my salvation cinched. I can hope the same for Idy. Why, I had sunk to be a chippy afore I was converted at Vale. But I hope not for him! I only want to stay shed of Ulvy Dorst and hope he comes to torment!" She spun around, swapped sadirons in a couple of snaps, and ironed fiercely again. "I have to keep arnin', excuse me, Jim. I promised to deliver this washin' afore goin' to bed. It's a dollar's worth. I won't be beholden. I won't be beholden even to the church."

I made out to stand and fix to go. "I'm mighty sorry, Luella," I said. "I'm sure mighty sorry for you in your trouble."

"You'll git over it."

She wiped her wet face with her sleeve, pushed a drip of hair off her forehead, and tried another iron. It gave off a proper hiss from her wet forefinger, and she drove back into her work. I said, "Good night," and she said, "Come again," and I went out.

In the dirt street a willow bush loomed high through the deep twilight. I stopped by it for a spell, remembering how I had held Ida close, close to me here and kissed her mouth so many times. I didn't get a mite of fever and yearning out of thinking about it. I thought of how the brakie had skipped out, and that I might be running in his shoes now, if I'd been older and more knowing. I thought of how it was the way Lon Turner had done with Ma Tavie, and even though they were man and wife, it seemed to be about the same as with Ida and the brakie. Run off and come back, until death took him. They hadn't wanted me to be born. I hadn't asked to be. It all seemed to be a kind of sell from somewhere, like the joke George B. M. Hoover had played on G. Dodd, with trouble for so many others.

Tired and low-spirited and emptied out from the heat, I stood and mused unto the conclusion that I was real glad not to be a man yet—not a man in the way Ida had been willing for me to be with her on that other night here under the willow bush.

I had half a notion to go on out the Shack Row road to the county farm and pass the time of evening with Essie Clover. I wondered what the news might be from Bess, away over there with the Salvation Army at Boise. It was wonderful how Essie was coming forth, now that she was out of that homestead trap in the gray gulch and was among people, free of the simple little dreamer of a man who had lived only to see the world end and Millenium dawn. The older boys were gone, and she never heard from them. But Essie was fixing to rent a shack and make out herself with Jen, Lester, Net and Vannie, the only children left. Jen and Lester could work out summers now. Bess might help. And Essie had learned to be a dressmaker at the county farm.

But I turned for town. The night was coming on in a smother. The sun seemed to have left the day's heat stacked all over the land for use tomorrow. No leaf stirred on bush or tree. When I'd touch a bush the dust would dribble straight down, like water, with no drift.

All was so still, even over the nearby railroad yards. A cowbell sounded from away off on the Lemolo bottoms. And then easterly, the mournful but sweet whoo-ee-whoo-o-o-o of a locomotive whistle. As it faded I caught a high-pitched strain of harmonica music from the direction of the river. I was reminded of the hobos Joe Hill had bought the butter and eggs for. They were likely at their feed over yonder, Ulvia Dorst with them.

The Shack Row road ran into a cross street that connected the depot and the newer business section of Knox. On the other side of the street ran the blocks of old Knox. I turned left, crossed the tracks and hit the road that sloped to the bridge over Snake River. In the moonlight I quit the road for a wide old path that twisted down to a strip of willows and cottonwoods along the river's brim. Soon I stood looking down at the famous old stream, so broad and smooth and gentle here as it seemed to rest between its upper canyon and its swing around Farewell Bend and into the deepest and blackest canyon the nation could boast.

Music and singing rose clearly to me. I heard—

> *"Oh the big Rock Candy Mountains*
> *Are a land that's fair and bright,*
> *Where the handouts grow on bushes,*
> *And you sleep out every night——"*

Then a voice that I knew to be the voice of Joe Hill ripped high in a fierce revival shout—

"God damn your soul to hell, Baldy, lay off that dehorn song! It's one and the same as the booze, the whores, the cards, the old religion, and the rest of the circus to make the workers forget they are wage slaves! The old dehorn! It's the stuff to disable the natural revolt in you and soften you into a dumb ox who'll toil along willin' in the yoke of the master class!"

"Hell, Joe, she's only a song, and I like her—"

"Listen, I'll give you a song you *need* to like!"

Then I heard Joe Hill singing——

> *"Halleluiah, I'm a bum!*
> *Halleluiah, bum again!*
> *Halleluiah, give us a handout*
> *To revive us again!*
>
> *"Oh, why don't you work,*
> *Like all other men do?*
> *How the hell can I work*
> *When there's no work to do?*
>
> *"Halleluiah, I'm a bum . . ."*

The words don't seem so much. But the power that Joe Hill put into them pounded up the bench slope and right on through me. As the voices of the other men came in with his, stronger and stronger, all fortified with that power too, each halleluiah line was like a shot of dynamite to me. It was over. Then I heard him singing again, Joe Hill, and this time it was rebel words to the tune of the hymn, "Beulah Land." He sang it alone, the others coming in

raggedly as though the song was new to them. I had shown him
my "Beulah Land" fragment. I wondered if he'd made the rebel
song up since. I was excited, somehow, I learned the chorus as
I hearkened—

> *"Oh, Hobo Land, sweet Hobo Land!*
> *As on a red boxcar I stand,*
> *I look away across the hills,*
> *Where toil the slaves and scissorbills.*
> *I'll work no more till men are free—*
> *A rebel hobo's life for me!"*

There in the jungles along the River Snake I heard Joe Hill
singing. I heard his voice of wrath and revolt through the heat
smother and the white moonlight. And something that took big
shape in my life came to me out of the singing of Joe Hill that
night. He was a poet, and he was a rebel born, and the commonest
parodies on poor hymns had become the one way of poetry for
him. I was a poet, I was sure of it inside me, and Joe Hill had told
me I was. But I was no rebel, I also knew. What else was I but
poet? I was asking it over and over, when suddenly the lines I'd
been trying to find for so long to finish the second verse of my
"Beulah Land" fragment came to me. I said them many times—

> *"While fear and loathing depart,*
> *And hate fades from my heart."*

They seemed so weak. Oh, I scorned them! The scorn grew tight
in my throat.

> *"Sorrow and sighing shall flee*
> *Away, far away from me,*
> *While fear and loathing depart,*
> *And hate fades from my heart."*

Nothing, nothing, nothing—nothing beside the power of Joe
Hill. I had heard him singing, and this was my one glory for tonight, what I would have to remember from this time.

The freight locomotive whistled into the yards, its snorting and
chugging broke into the heat smother and the dark, and in the
rattling and grinding over the rails the voices of Joe Hill and the

hobos were lost. Then I saw their shapes coming up the path. I backed around in the brush and out of their sight until they were well past, lining out to board the freight and hobo on. A poet led them. They followed Joe Hill.

I headed back to my place of toil and my ambitions in the dairy business all alone. I expected the night to end for me with some minutes of reading more about the sorry treatment of Percy Bysshe Shelley as a young man; and then go to sleep a-dreaming that James Birney Turner was just another pitiable case.

But I could never tell what in thunder I might do. What I did was loosen up some as I plodded back to the Cumberland Institute. I would look back in the moonlight at Snake River, then toward the Lemolos and the Seven Devils north yonder; then imagine the ranges and ranges reaching eastward to the Beaverheads—and there was Ramon Hurd, and Lily; freighting horses with bells and bright plumes on their hame bows; and Inez, the strawberry roan, who might get to be my own little cayuse mare again.

Anyhow, it was a land of horses and horsemen. All could be my country, and I didn't need to be a revolutionist or a dairyman either to have it. And I could be a poet in it too.

"Half poet and half horse," I said. "That's the man I'm goin' to be."

8. Hell-Fire

IF THERE EVER WAS SUCH A THING AS THE MALIG-
nant Old Nick on this earth, he surely was lurking for me on Old
Street that Saturday night of August 30, 1907. I'd taken it as my
last spell of freedom before the start of the new school term. A
month after the visit of Joe Hill, I was yet restless with longing
to be away over yonder with Ramon on the freighting trail from
Red Rock, Montana, and up through the Beaverheads to the valley of the Salmon. So sick and tired of the dairy business by now,
I could only look ahead to four years at the Cumberland Institute
as a Slough of Despond, with Ollie Hicks standing in the term to
come as a shape of Giant Despair. That's how he was on my mind
this night, as I tramped back from a real good family visit with
the Clover kids and Ma Essie at the county farm. The blamed
idiots were so cheery and hopeful about getting a miserable shack
of their own, in which Essie could slave at dressmaking, and the
older girls at house chores for well-to-do people out of school
hours—well, I could only marvel at them, but they did kind of
brighten me up.

But I was broody again as I stole down the shady side of Old
Street, taking the short-cut way to the Institute. Students were not
permitted to take it, as it ran so close to the Notch, the widely
known house of ill fame. But I stole along it and out nigh the
stockyards, in the light of a full moon. The pale light struck into
a feed shed for cowhands' horses. I spied three cayuses now. One
showed white spots. With Ollie Hicks on my mind, I thought it
might be his pinto, the one he'd been riding since Lily took out on

gentle Inez. I was right. The pinto nickered at me and nuzzled around for a bite of something good. That was one thing about Ollie. He had treated Inez as well as I had ever treated her. And he was a friend to this pinto. One of the other two horses belonged to Art Yardley. I guessed that the two young men were down at The Notch, probably with Walt Payne, an older young man who had been leading Ollie astray, as I'd heard.

It appeared that I'd never learn. Only trouble had ever come to me from spying and eavesdropping, yet I could seldom fight off from a temptation to do them. And now I found myself tracking back, even venturing a way down the road to the Notch, then deciding to take a peek in the Silver Bell Saloon, up and across the street from the fork of the road to the Notch. The owner, Ellis Coot, had been fined a lot of times for peddling his rotgut to minors. Finally I wound up by easing into the Silver Bell and sidling into the dim front corner away from the bar. There I gaped around.

There was electricity in Knox but the Silver Bell Saloon still had swinging coal-oil lamps. They made smoky light and rusty reflectors shed it poorly around. All inside was dim to see. There was a huge crack in the back-bar mirror. The floor was patched and it sagged against the scarred back wall. The top of the bar was rubbed down to raw wood. Around the big room were the rattiest tables and chairs, all showing haywire mendings. Along the back wall were some cases and panels of grisly lynching nooses, rusty handcuffs, old busted revolvers, boots that outlaws were claimed to have died in, Bowie and other knives black with supposed bloodstains. I'd heard all about the show a number of times, and even in the dimness it interested me so much that I almost forgot the risk I was running and what it was for. Then I spied along the considerable jam at the bar. It was a motley of harvest hands, old heads, loafers, and young men who mainly looked just a little too young to be sold drinks in any other place, unless it was the rival old rotten saloon, the Copper King. And now, among the young men, I saw Ollie Hicks.

He stood down at the lower end of the bar, between Art Yardley and Walt Payne. Even from here I could tell he was skunk-drunk.

Ellis Coot was across the bar from the three. I moved down closer.

"Git the fool outer here!" I heard Coot snarl. "Take him and pitch him into the hoss trough up to my livery. Soak him down and sober him up. Moss Eckert'll be on his rounds any minute. Hear me?"

Walt and Art looked right scared. They hauled and lifted Ollie around from the bar. He seemed to have fallen slobbery and hollering drunk all of a sudden. I was so kind of horrified and full of wonder too that I still didn't think to look out for myself, but stood and gaped.

Ollie reeled and hollered. "Me for Big Mag's!" he bawled. "No place for me but the Nosh. I'm goin' have me 'nother go at Jackie, by God, by Jesus, 'nother go at Jackie, you betcher. Come on, Jackie!"

I stood and wondered, "Why, he's yet seventeen, only two years older'n me, and he's horsin'." Then it struck me I could do it, too. I was able, surely. I had the money. A fever fired through me.

Then, for all his blear and slobber, Ollie Hicks saw me. He stiffened and heeled himself to a stop, and if any man alive ever glowered murder, he did it at me. Then the threats came.

"Don' you tell, Jim Turner! God damn you, Russ'll ruin you, if you tell and get me into trouble at the school! You tell, and you'll die like a kyote! Don't you bring grief to my ma, Jim Turner!"

I stood in a freeze. I couldn't say a word. All I could do was to think in chills of fear on what a fool I'd been to come spying.

Old Ellis Coot hobbled around the bar, on the prod.

"You limber, uncoupled minors'll put me outer business yit!" he croaked. "By doggy, I'm goin' right out after Marshal Eckert myself, so's to keep in the clear. I'll plunk all four've you in jail!"

Some of the men at the bar began to yell and curse at us, too, and I let loose and made dust out of the Silver Bell. I swung to my right and northwest, to head out of town again. But there, moseying toward me among the people on the board sidewalk, came the night marshal, Moss Eckert, on his rounds. He knew me by sight as one who had done his family dirt in the sell Mr. Hoover had cooked up to damage G. Dodd. The night marshal had looked poison at me since then, whenever we happened to pass. It had all come to be a mighty lesson to me on how some such idiocy as a practical joke could keep on in a body's life like a running sore.

I struck across the wide roadway as hard as I could go without seeming to be on the run, and dodged out of the shine of the street lamps and the moonlight into the black shadows of the cottonwoods that lined the railroad side of Old Street.

All along this side, for three of the four blocks, horses and wagons stood hitched in scatters. I swung in close to a tree trunk and hauled up. Then I peered back across the street at the Silver Bell. Walt Payne and Art Yardley were rassling with Ollie Hicks, and now Moss Eckert was coming at them. Ollie broke away, yelling again about having another go at Jackie. As he staggered into the street the marshal hooked him. Then old Ellis Coot faunched out, yelling—

"You run 'em in, Moss! I drive 'em out and drive 'em out, and still they come back, drunk; I don't. know where from; but you wave a bar rag at these here calfs, and they're slobber-drunk at a whiff, and they give my place a bad name. You run these minors in, Marshal, and see to it they stop pesterin' me!"

"You willin' to swear to charges on Russ Hicks's brother?" the marshal said. "I'll not run 'em in unless you are."

It was a turmoil then, with old Ellis yelling how innocent he was of selling rotgut to minors, Ollie straightening up and howling to be allowed to ride home in peace, Walt and Art backing him up, and Moss Eckert trying to quiet all down before a crowd should gather and force him to take Ollie to jail.

Pretty soon the marshal got things moving. It was not up the line for the jail, though. He hustled the young men down Old Street toward the stockyards and their horses. I stood in the black shadow of the tree until the excitement had settled across the street. Still talking like the most self-righteous saloonkeeper alive, Ellis Coot finally went back into the Silver Bell. I turned and tramped up Old Street to hike for the Institute by the longer way through the main business section of the Knox of 1907. I was a fool, I said, dragging along like an old man. I had never been a bigger idiot in all my days. It surely was despond ahead of me now, and Ollie Hicks stood in the night as a mightier despair than ever. I tried hard enough, but I couldn't even line out the feeblest kind of dream about killing him off with a rope or a knife or with dynamite; for in spite of myself Marshal Moss Eckert would appear in the dream, catching me red-handed and snaking me to jail.

Well, it was more prophecy than dream in me that night as I sluffed and drug along Old Street. If there *was* an Old Nick, he was there, he had taken me for a fool, he was right, and he had me.

People and locations. And money, money, money. They were in my head as a great confusion when I trudged around from Old Street, on through New Knox, and over the high road to Cumberland Institute. I should come to understand that the same kinds of powerful people and companies were what a poor boy needed to reckon with in any location of the West, not only to forge ahead but to keep out of trouble.

Right here was Old Street. Away up there were the mountains, swollen with mineral wealth. There were the streams, and the watered valley strips of the rich ranches. There were the great hill grass ranges. There was the dry-land wheat. But the most tempting wealth for men, in the land or on it, was the timber. There were a full half-million acres of mountain forest, mainly in the Federal Reserves, tributary to Knox and neighboring towns on Snake River and the Oregon Short Line Railroad. The best of the pines stood along the Lemolo River and its branches. A good deal was owned by private interests. Back in the nineties, it has been told, Dan'l Barton and Ramon Hurd had taken timber claims up there, along with some other black-listed miners. They were worthless without a railroad to haul down logs or lumber, or without the pile of money it would take to build sawmills and set up logging outfits. You could always hear talk of hopes on this in the Knox country. So it went about the hundreds of thousands of acres of basins and flats which could be made to grow anything with water—but all kinds of money were needed to build dams and ditches.

The dairy business was promising because it was such a fine country for alfalfa, the best feed going. Here again big money was needed to build creameries, cheese factories and plants for making evaporated milk. There were other concerns, such as G. Dodd's

Mission Medicine factory—or distillery, as George B. M. Hoover would always call it. There were the stores, banks and other businesses of New Knox. There were the old folks who would shake their heads dolefully at all talk of business booms and who would tell how the mining boom of old caved in when the eastern interests finally concluded that the silver, copper and iron wealth of the mountains could never be mined, smelted and shipped out at a profit.

People. There were the cowhands, sheepherders, crop stiffs and railroad boomers whose main concerns with Knox business were in the saloon hells and the Notch. They summed up to a mighty stack cf customers. Few around Knox were richer than Big Mag, old Margaret W. Hinote. She was a power in all the great goings-on of the big people of the place. Even so was the Rev. Woodman Farrier, the president of the Cumberland Institute. And Russell Hicks, Mr. Hoover, G. Dodd, the old pioneer merchant, Nathan Epstein, the grain elevator and flour mill company, the wool warehouse people, the cattle buyers, and the bankers and lawyers who had tieups with some of the country's biggest interests and richest men. And the local agents of the U. S. Forest Service, the Reclamation Bureau, the Bureau of Mines; all people of power even though they were men without money.

Locations and people had grown into my mind.

The Ames man, Prof. Paul P. Stedd, was as good as gold to me. All summer I'd bowed humbly to the fact that a man has to be willing to grind away seven days a week if he wants to be in the dairy business. Now Prof. Stedd volunteered to take my place on the last Sunday before the start of school, so that I could visit Aunt Sue and Uncle Gabe. And he let me take an Institute bronco and an old saddle and bridle.

"I've taken pains to write them both, as well as Mr. Yardley, that I have no complaint on your work," Prof. Stedd told me.

That was a heap of talk for Prof. Stedd on anything that did not concern the business of dairying and its teaching. He looked on me with such favor through his thick glasses that I felt guilt. The work had been only chores to me, and I'd dreamed the hours away over most of it. Learning the dairy business had never bothered me, either. I liked a lot about it, first of all the cows, calves and bulls. I liked the cleanness that Prof. Stedd was such a fanatic on, from cowbarn to milk bottles. The separator, the cooler, the pasteurizer, the churning room, the record keeping, the Babcock and the other tests, the kinds of feed and the ways of feeding, the points of difference between the five mighty dairy breeds, Jerseys, Guernseys, Holsteins, Ayrshires and Brown Swiss —all of this and other items of the kind were of interest to my mind. I really felt rotten guilty to have turned against it all. I could not look Prof. Stedd in the eye when I thanked him for letting me have the Sunday off and a bronco to ride. By gadfrey, here I had more of a chance than I'd ever asked or hoped for, I'd been making man's wages while a panic was on and so many had no jobs, and I could study and work right ahead and be a crackerjack cheese maker or butter maker or Jersey breeder before I should come of age. And all I could keep hungering for and dreaming of was to skulk away from it. I actually wanted to howl like a coyote when I thought of four more years of it. I guessed a lowdown riffraff of a coyote was what I was, actually. Hungering and dreaming on running away as a hobo, heading for Red Rock, Montana.

"You coyote," I blamed myself, riding the bronc up the old Bob Creek road. "What you are dreamin' of could well break poor Prof. Stedd's heart. You and your wantin' to skulk off, Jim Turner! You ought to die of shame."

But I kept on imagining the Montana freight trail, seeing the colored plumes above the horses, hearing the little bells.

The ride was through a fine dawn and sunup. I got to the Hoover ranch in time to ride along with Isabel and Gabe to services at the Advent Christian Church on Mount Creek. The Belgian boy had run away. Now they had Lester Clover with them. He was the image of his poor pa who was dead and gone; looking like a saint from his big eyes and thin face. He'd been with Isabel and Gabe all summer, and they wanted to keep him, but Ma Essie was determined to have him at home and attending school in Knox. Gabe got me off at one side and moaned around that he couldn't imagine how he might get along, so much to do, grain to haul, winter wheat to drill, third crop alfalfa coming, spuds to dig, manure to spread, brush to grub, Oh, Lordy, Lordy, and only Isabel and him to do it all, account of that Belgian sneak, and with me away from my natural home.

"We figger you orter come back to us," Gabe said, putting up his hand to part his mustache, then catching himself at it, and rolling his eyes piously toward heaven above. "We're not thinkin' of us, Jim, but for yore own good. I ain't a notion on what you done to Ollie Hicks, but I do know Russ warnt me to warn you to mind every word you say and every trick you do that concerns Ollie. Ollie is his ma's idol, and she's been havin' another spell with her heart, and *she* is the idol of Russ. You didn't beat Ollie up or nothin' at the Institute, did you?"

I said, "I never did a thing to him. At school I have to respect him. He is a senior. I don't know what you're talkin' about." I said it in the sullen way he knew would always be a stump to hang him up with me.

"I know you demeaned him many's the time out here, knockin' him around and purtendin' it was only fun. One time, Russ said, Ollie's ma took him in to see the doctor, his rib was so sore she was worried it was broken."

That was news to me. I brightened up at it, I couldn't help myself. "Well, by golly!" I said. "When was that there, Gabe?"

"One of them there times in a scuffle," Gabe said.

He was lying, I was sure, because it was such a mighty concern to Isabel and him that the Hickses might come into ownership of this ranch and crowd them out. But it was a cheery notion to me, anyhow. A story started going in my mind right away. There was a bunch of the boys at the Bob Creek school, the story went; or after Advent church, or in the yard of Coot's Livery at Knox; a scuffle starting, and Ollie in it with me because he couldn't help himself. Then I sneaked the old left hook in on him. He grinned and bore it until he got alone with his ma; then the unweaned blubber-gut bawled and took on about how I'd broken a rib for him; and then Russ had to hitch up to the surrey and take them to the doctor. In my story every rib Ollie owned was caved in. It was beautiful to imagine.

"How in thunder did you 'n' Ollie git into it, anyhow?" Gabe whined on, taking heart, I reckoned, from my cheery face.

"He was so rotten dirty with Bess Clover," I said. "First with us at school, then when she went to work for Mrs. Hicks. You know why she had to leave. You know it as well as I do."

"I hadn't heerd that. You didn't speak of it," Gabe said. "I had the notion from Johnny that Mrs. Hicks got rid of her because she was makin' such a fool of herself around Russ. Why, Bess was only thirteen, and Russ nigh thirty, yet she got fit to kill herself because he never noticed her. You knew that, didn't you?"

He asked it, I guess, because I'd been so thunderstruck at what he said. Then I felt ready to die. I stood shaking, shaking inside anyhow. It was true, now that I'd heard it. Yes, now I knew it was true. Bess Clover was wild in her heart with love for Russ Hicks. I could remember a hundred things that showed it, now that I had the cue. And I knew I couldn't go on to church with Isabel and Gabe. Russ Hicks generally attended with his ma. I wouldn't try to do anything to him, but I knew I'd sit and watch him and murder him a thousand times over while the services were being held.

"Sure, I knew it all along," I lied to Gabe. "Bess told me. I promised her I wouldn't say anything. It was why she was so crazy to go to Boise after Russ married Fern Yardley. Sure, I knew it."

Then I lied some more, telling him I'd promised Aunt Sue I'd come to Primitive Baptist meeting when possible, and I rode off without even a word of parting for Isabel. I was ornery to do it, no matter if it was all hell-fire inside me. Hell-fire, hell-fire; I didn't know why; I was still somehow unable to think straight out that it was wild love in me for Bess Clover; I just knew I hated Russ Hicks.

There were plenty of sources for the spread of gossip about Ollie Hicks's sinning at the Notch and drinking rotgut in the Silver Bell. It came to the Institute, it reached the Rev. Woodman Farrier. I was sure of it after Ollie Hicks, now the senior over the milkers, warned me that awful things would happen to me and all my folks if I was to be a fink on him. I cowered to him. Somehow it seemed that the fiercer the hate burned in me for the Hickses the more it made me play humble and act the coward. In the roughhousing and scuffles I let Ollie strictly alone. He got so that he

began to sneak over punches, kicks and digs on me as I'd done on
him. He was worse at this after a day on which I was called up
to Rev. Farrier's office to be quizzed on Ollie. I didn't tell anything, I swore to Ollie that I hadn't, and after some days with nothing happening to him he decided I'd spoken the truth and was
afraid of him.

Then, in the middle of December, I was told by Prof. Stedd to
come along with him to the president's office. I did, and I stepped
through the door to face Mrs. Hicks, Russ, Bud and Ollie, as well
as the big man of the Cumberland Institute. Principal Everett O.
Kirdle was there, too, and I knew that the case of Ollie Hicks had
become mighty, mighty serious.

The Rev. Farrier didn't look like a teacher or a preacher, as he
sat there behind his desk, with the others half-circled in chairs,
facing him over the desk's left-hand corner. I was stood over at
the right of the desk, so that Rev. Farrier had to make a quarter
turn in his chair to eye me, while I faced the glowering Hickses.
He eyed me kindly. He was a roundy, browny little button kind of
man with snapping eyes, chubby cheeks, a most agreeable expression, and a voice that said, "Business, business," in every
word. And he did make every word sound honest and convincing.

The Rev. Woodman Farrier sat there and turned me inside out
on what he called rumors that Oliver Hicks had been frequenting
evil resorts on or in the vicinity of Old Street during the summer.

"Oliver is a fatherless boy," Rev. Farrier said. "All of his living
relations are here to defend him. He claims, and they believe, that
you are the spreader of the rumors. Now, then. Have you done so?
If you have, what are the facts? If you have not, we are all willing
to be convinced." He stared sternly at the Hickses. "If the least of
the rumors is proved to be a fact, Oliver will be summarily expelled," he said, "Expelled." He thumped the desk. "Summarily."

I was an old hand at this kind of thing, although I'd never been
hauled up just like this since the Rev. Pearl Yates and Mayor Clinton Maul had tried to send me to reform school back in Cartwright, Iowa.

"Why, Rev. Farrier, sir," I said, so honestly, "I've never heard
Ollie Hicks say even a byword. I don't know just what you mean
by an 'evil resort,' but if it is a saloon or even a pool hall, I'm sure

and certain Ollie Hicks would sooner spend his time with sheep in a sheep pen. Why, Rev. Farrier, sir, Ollie Hicks is my fav'rit' senior, like he is of so many of us freshmen boys, partick'ly the milkers. He is an example to us. I would be horrified even to *dream* of the rumors you speak of, Rev. Farrier, sir, let alone listen to 'em—and I would have to be clear out of my mind, Rev. Farrier, sir, to go and *tell* such rumors. Oh, what a shame and a scandal 'tis for this fine family, that rumors should be peddled in the highways and byways and among the hedges, oh, *what* a scandal, and oh, *what* a shame, that it should be told hither and yon that a boy I love like I would my own brother, if it was to come to pass I had a brother, that it should be told of him, *good* Ollie Hicks, he was free-a-quentin' evil resorts——"

There I pulled up some, knowing all of a sudden that I had swung into the old rant of my sermon as I had not even thought of doing for a year and more. The knowing came in the sight of my own hands waving before me and beside me, in the sight of the bugging eyes and slack jaws of Ollie and his ma, in the hearing of the singsong that I'd learned from the Rev. Pearl Yates, and in the feeling of the spirit a-possessing me and taking me over; the Old Nick, the hell-fire.

But I couldn't halt now. I ranted on again—

"Why, Rev. Farrier, sir, you can look on the pure face of that fine young man, there, Ollie Hicks, and you can read there he is pure of heart and clean of mind. Oh, it is not with him as it was with one of whom I seen once upon a time, a young man no older'n Ollie here, but oh, the sin had et into him, Rev. Farrier, sir, this young man of seventeen, till it had grayed his hair on the sides and balded it on the top, and sin had given this young man —I don't know I should tell you his name, but I will, for he was a Borah, one of the black-sheep Borahs, Johnny Borah—and oh, he sinned till the bags growed big and black under his eyes, which was bloodshot and mattery from sin, and the pimples and blackheads of sin were on his face from the free-a-quentin' of evil resorts, and sin grooved his face, Oh, he was lantern-jawed from the evil of the resorts, his breath stunk, he belched from rye whisky and he coughed from the vile cigarettes——"

It was in me now to glory-shout, or to fall down rolling and talking in the tongues, or just to leap into a fit of the jerks—then through the hell-fire haze I realized that the Rev. Woodman Farrier was standing up and shaking a finger at me and ordering me to shut up. Then I did, even before Prof. Stedd had grabbed me from behind and clamped a hand over my mouth. That quick I came down out of it and broke into a cold sweat. There before me I saw Ollie Hicks and his ma hanging together and crying fit to kill and the eyes of Russ Hicks staring at me like points of blue steel, of steel frosted. Bud Hicks just sat there stolid, looking amazed. And now I heard the Rev. Woodman Farrier saying—

"Get the boy out of here. He's scared, scared to the point of hysteria. And I'm convinced it's a fear that covers up the knowledge that Oliver is guilty—that a certain story told me by Ellis Coot is the truth! Stedd, you see to the boy."

That's how it was, that's how it went, as truly as I'm able to tell it over from what actually happened. That's how I played a part in Ollie Hicks's being expelled in shame and disgrace from the Cumberland Institute. And I was let to stay. Maybe Deacon Fay Yardley was standing on by me. It could have been George B. M. Hoover, too. Or maybe it was something in the Rev. Woodman Farrier that caused him to be charitable to a poor boy with convicts and infidels in his relations, while being stern with a rich, spoiled and unweaned boy.

Saved though I was, the rest of the winter was as miserable a time as I can ever know, I still truly believe. And I am not going to tell about it. The work was all right, no kick on the work or on anything else about the life of the Cumberland Institute, except chapel and prayers. I milked my best with my string of Jerseys for the five hours of time a day that was needed to pay for board and tuition. I studied hard for the other hours that were left from meals and sleep. I tried to live up to the faith of the Rev. Farrier, Principal Kirdle and Prof. Stedd in me, but it was no use. Inside I was dead to all of it. Inside I was bound to pull out for Red Rock, Montana, at the end of the school term.

One evening in the last week of April, word was sent me from the principal's office that my uncle, Gabe Turner, had telephoned out for me to meet him on something important at the Atkins Restaurant in Knox. I was told I must be reported back in at ten o'clock. I was full of wonder from the start. Atkins Restaurant was a small place on a side street, and was considered respectable, yet it stood close to the alley that ran behind the Copper King Saloon and other places of the second block of Old Street. But I'd never known Gabe to eat there. I expected he was drunk again. Maybe Isabel had left him. Or it could be that Russ Hicks had grabbed off the Hoover ranch and had kicked the Turners out first shot. Curiosity took me into Knox with such strength that I dog-trotted the whole two miles.

It was the dark of the moon. No street lights shone on this side street and no building was lighted except the little restaurant. Its front windows made shining oblongs and cast a glow out on the board sidewalk. I pulled up at the door, then sidled over to peer through a window, as a feeling that things were wrong chilled through me. Even as I stooped over to push my face against the glass, quick steps sounded from the nigh alley, the loop of a lariat swished down over my head and shoulders, and my arms were caught hard and fast. I tried to holler, but my throat was a mess of knots. Then it felt like a gun muzzle in the small of my back. Russ Hicks snarled low—

"Keep quiet. Do what else I tell you to do, or you'll be hurt worse than you may expect. Turn right, into the alley there."

I kept quiet, I walked and turned into the alley, with Russ prodding, and Bud and Ollie closing in both sides of me. They herded me on in the blackness, then turned me to a door. Bud opened it and I was pushed on into a dimly lit hall. Away on yonder was a big barroom, of the Copper King Saloon, I guessed, wondering what might happen now, and surely I wouldn't be murdered in cold blood, not with all those people so close. Then I was hauled up and around again and shoved through a door in the side wall. The door closed at my back. I heard it slam and a lock click while a match flame shone up. Then Bud Hicks was lighting a lantern that was hung high on a wall. The lantern shone around a small square room that was empty except for us four and the lantern.

Russ Hicks flipped the rope free of me, then stepped around to my front. "This room is for grudge fights," he said. "The same is now a-goin' to take place. Hollerin' will do you no help. Abe

Melroy trusts me. Ollie has a grudge on you. You've bullied him around for years with your pug tricks. You put on that crazy preachin' show a-purpose before Rev. Farrier to make him think what he did. You are here and now goin' to be put in your place with the Hicks family."

His way of saying it was as easy and slow as you can imagine. But it sounded to me like the slow and easy whets of a skinning knife on a stone. Russ Hicks stood there in the lantern light, as tall as me; he let his look run level into mine, and it was a blue-steel look; it was cold hate in his eyes, arrogant hate. I failed to hold up to it, I could not. Ollie stood behind him. Bud stood under the lantern. Fire whipped and whirled through me. Inside me it was like the blow of a blazing summer wind. It took my strength, it emptied me out. Oh, God, I felt so pitiable! I looked low and fell to crying.

It was a fair fight, Russ Hicks kept claiming, when he pulled Ollie off me and kneeled down beside me as I lay dying; half-dead, anyhow; I *knew* I was at least half-dead. Maybe it was fair. But all the *fight* there was to it was Ollie a-swinging haymakers on me that could never have come near to touching me another time. I took a beating, I deliberately took it, standing up as long as I could in the hope that if I was beaten hard, then Russ would let me go. I didn't make a real try at fighting back. I didn't throw one hook with my left. I was scared, I was a long way more scared than I was when I broke into a frenzy of preaching before Rev. Farrier. I was a coward. I ought to have fought till I died fighting. But I went on to let Ollie Hicks give me a bloody beating.

"A fair fight," Russ Hicks said again. "Ollie beat hell out of you in a fair fight. That'll show you. That'll learn you, you slick-ear bastard of a Barton! Now you'll keep your place, I reckon."

My eyes were swelled shut, and I wasn't trying to hold them open to see him. So I didn't know that Russ Hicks was pouring whisky into me until the neck of a bottle was rammed between my teeth and it came flooding into my throat. Still I made no try at fighting back. I swallowed and swallowed until I began to burn and choke. I heard Bud Hicks—

"God'n'b'Jesus, Russ! He's dreened off half a pint!"

The bottle was pulled away and I was hauled to my feet. I could only see through slits of my bunged eyes as I was prodded and hauled out into the hall and up it to the barroom. Then a powerful heave drove me on. The whisky fumes were hell in me now; hell-fire, hell-fire, hell-fire. The lights of the barroom wheeled and sloped, faces and bodies swung and slanted with them, then all began to spin, and I scarcely knew it when I hit the barroom floor. Then I heard a tremendous bawl—

"Hey, Marshal Eckert! Here's another one of Ellis Coot's drunken minors run in on me! Eckert, you come and do your duty! You git this young feller off to jail!"

9. The Escape

AT FIRST IT SEEMED TO ME THAT I WAS IN A DREAM out of a novel by Charles Dickens. But too soon it was real life; miserable, dark, lonesome, and thorny with pain. I came wide awake but lay on in a frozen kind of panic on a hard bunk in the Knox jail. That's how I was located when Russ Hicks, Moss Eckert and Muley Madden—a deputy sheriff who had once been a Hicks hand—came into the cell and looked me over. I'd heard the midnight bell before they entered. Then I'd begun to feel some glad to be living and sobering and able to hear it. The visit soon blighted that feeling.

I lay still and pretended to be sodden drunk. Actually the whisky had died out of me and I was in no way sick, except that my face seemed as big as a hay bale and was hurting as though stuck and burning with barley beards all over it. A rib hurt from a kick that Ollie had got in when I fell a-yelling, "Enough! Enough!" But this was the least of my bothers now as I lay like a frozen corpse; not wanting to cry or curse or anything else, and not trying to. I didn't twitch a muscle when Russ Hicks and the other two came in and held a lantern over me, not even when Russ said——

"He'll keep. See that he does, now. A couple of Redburn agents will be here on the noon train tomorrow. They want to look into his brags that he's in touch with Black Dan Barton. Don't either of you tell anybody that you have Jim Turner here, don't you let a soul see him. Is that clear?"

"Yes, sir, Mr. Hicks," the marshal said. "Yes, *sir!*"

They went out with the light. I heard a door slam soon. Then came sounds of dishes rattling, and I guessed Marshal Eckert was fixing himself a snack. I thought of the other two cells in the jail and how they were empty. Now well after midnight, there was nobody in this place but the two of us, Moss Eckert and Jim Turner. There were other things to think about that were all hooked around this one main thing. A freight had whistled into Knox. It was switching down yonder in the yards. I could hear the Mogul snort and chug. A word began to sound with its exhaust, a book word. "Escape—escape—escape." Then my heart pounded with the word. I was ready. It was the time now. I let out a sound of retching, then I groaned horribly and hollered, "Water, oh, water! oh, my belly! It's poison! Water—water—water!"

Moss Eckert came a-stomping, banging a lantern against the cell door and calling, "What in thunder ails ye?" As the lantern light swam through the bars I stiffened on my back, hooked my hands like claws at my belly, stuck my tongue out its limit, and acted a death agony so truly I did well-nigh strangle myself. It must have been a pretty horrible sight to old Eckert; him with a guilty conscience, too. I had blots of blood all over me, and my face was bungs and bruises. Anyhow, I surely did scare the hell out of him. He got a pitcher of water and a glass. He unlocked my cell and came in. He set the lantern on a stool. Then he stood close, at my right as I lay; and when I did that turn and hooked my left fist, it sunk into him low in the belly, dead center *under* his cartridge belt.

He buckled, the pitcher and glass crashing, and then he keeled over, groaning more horribly than I'd managed to do, gasping for breath, grabbing where I'd hit him. In the lantern light I saw the marshal's head hit the corner of the bunk. Then he pitched over on his back and lay there, with blood spreading from a crooked cut that slanted from his bald head to his left eye. He'd raked a nail head with his forehead, I guessed. Anyhow, it was no worse than a gashed scalp. He was yet among the living.

I knew what I was doing. It didn't seem to me that I was wild with fear and panic, as Jim Turner should have been. I went right to work knotting the marshal's wrists together with a shirtsleeve, after I'd ripped it off him, and gagging him with his bandanna. Then I took his keys and locked him in the cell; went on to his front office room and opened the closet in which I'd seen him put my valuables; got the pocket book with its four dollars and some cents, my jackknife, the sheets I'd cut from the Shelley book to memorize; and then I blew the lantern out and went into the empty dark street.

Later it shaped up in my memory as a story I'd dreamed. Back there in the jailhouse I'd acted as I could so easily dream of myself acting in a story. All that happened was unreal in my mind, and I was unreal to myself, as I struck down fast for the railroad yards. I didn't get back to feeling my own proper, lowdown, fearful, miserable, hungry, sorry being of a Jim Turner until I'd ridden at least thirty miles through the night; all on the six truss rods of a furniture freight car; rolling east in the dark to meet an Idaho April dawn; and figuring I'd probably done just about what Russ Hicks had hoped and planned I would do.

On through the next three days and nights I was the real old Jim Turner so much that I can't more than begin to tell it; I've never been able to tell it. It was one trouble and misery after another. At Nampa, the first division point, I ran afoul of Nampa Larry, the roughest railroad bull on hobos in seven states. He got in two licks on my tailbone, and then I outran him. I hid out daytimes, hiked the ties at night, hooked on freights and was kicked off, and so on like that, until I reached Shoshone at last on a nice April night. Blackened up from hours in a car of coal, I kept out of town and found an old haystack for the night. I was up and feeling fairly pert at milking time. Then I spent my last four bits for a breakfast of ham, eggs and hot cakes and for three mighty sandwiches of ham and beef; and off I tramped for the great lava and sagebrush desert to the southeast. I was thankful to be free, so thankful that my last threats of numbness raveled away. The freeze went out entirely and the waves of fear rolled in. I kept looking back. It naturally seemed to me that I'd likely only broken jail by assault and battery and then struggled on for a couple of hundred miles and more, just to suffer the mockery of being captured by a posse. But I made it on. Five miles, now, judging by the rise of the sun. Gray road winding yonder through gray brush and gray outcroppings, and the same to be seen back yonder. It sure was a desert. So dry for April. The dust of volcanic ash and alkali soil was in the hard breeze, and I could make out nothing of the hoof and wagontire tracks of yesterday.

I tracked on, feeling easier, even dreaming a little story now and then. I plodded and trudged away, a speck of life alone in a great desert land. Hope rose, even, as the sun rose over the gray. Over there, southerly, I knew, was the Snake River Canyon, a monster crack in the desert, hundreds of feet deep. I'd heard tell of it many times, how sixty years ago and more the people of the covered wagons had crawled over this desert here, sorely athirst, while the river mocked them from the canyon deeps. I could imagine it. I could imagine me back in that time, galloping up to a wagon train; Jim Turner, the famous young scout, trapper and Indian fighter; up to tell the people of a way, secret to all but the Shoshones and me, down the canyon wall to river water. Well, they were grateful. Most grateful of all was the Clover family, the folks of a beautiful girl named Bess.

I sure did wish I could have gone from Nampa up to Boise to see her. But I couldn't. I'd had to fly on from the vengeful law.

So it had gone, until the sun looked to be high noon. By then I had to break down and admit that I was on the wrong road. I'd taken directions from the restaurant man on the way to get to the line of construction camps for a reclamation project. I was afraid of him, as of everybody, and I'd listened and struck out in a fearful hurry without being entirely sure of my tracks. By this time, or a lot sooner, I should have come to the first of the pumping stations for the camps.

Why I kept on instead of turning back I don't know. It was fear that drove me, I reckon, and the hope that a road which had been used a lot at some time or another was bound to come to some place with water before long. Anyhow I did keep on, not trying to eat the dried-out sandwiches, not wanting to eat until I could have water.

But it was past sundown before I had it. I'd walked over forty miles without a sup when the old road took me down from the plateau to the bench of a little valley. By this time I didn't know what I was doing except to pick a foot up, shove it ahead somehow, and set it down. Then I heard a gurgle of water from an irrigation headgate. I was able to run for it. I bellied down on the ditch slope, and drank the dirty, lukewarm water until I was fit to bust. Then I hunkered up in my sheepskin coat and slept into the sunup. I still had the three huge sandwiches. They were brick-dry by this time, but I soon downed them, with more ditchwater. I didn't seem to feel worse. When I stood up to get my bearings I spied a camp across the little valley, up on the plateau there. It turned out to be the last one on the line of seven Bolt & Company ditch-grading camps. I reached it in a half hour or so, just as the teamsters were hooking up for work. One of them directed me to Burly Hughes, the walking boss. I was given a flunkying job. There I stayed without trouble for better than two months, until the camp closed down for the Fourth of July.

Then I figured I had money enough to go to Ramon Hurd in Montana.

The flunky work was not so bad; simply dull and tiresome. The belly burglar, as the crew called the cook, got up at four, and the three flunkies at five. Breakfast was on the table at six. Then the cook would beat a triangle made from a steel drill, using a steel bar, ding-donging the men in to eat grub that was plentiful and clean enough but always weak or bad in some way to taste. The triangle and bar were called a gut-hammer. There was a pile more interesting names and rigs in the cookhouse. I learned considerable from the belly burglar in the two months, mostly how not to cook good plain grub to spoil it. By gad, the way the fool would boil and boil the life out of cabbage, which was our only greens at first! But I didn't try to tell him anything. I only worked my hardest, and would say nothing but "Yes, sir" and "No, sir" and "Thanky, sir" to the cook and the other two flunkies, who were grown men. When I was quizzed I would sob—

"There was only ma and me left on the homestead, the house took fire from the leaky flue one night, and the chimney fell on me when I was tryin' to get ma out. The bricks like to killed me, and the burns killed ma—oh, my poor ma—oh, *don't* make me tell no more!"

And they wouldn't. Even Burly Hughes, the walking boss, gave me a poke in the ribs for sympathy and let me alone. I gave him the

name of "James Birney" for the time book, but it was such a bother
and a kind of shame on me all the time that I vowed to be "Jim
Turner" after this, even if I went to the pen for it.

There was spud peeling and dishwashing and clothes washing.
Dull and tiresome. Dull and tiresome. And that was how it was
with the company of the cook and flunkies. Five in the morning
till eight at night, with some time off morning and afternoon.

The teaming work was no attraction, either. After mid-May the
hot winds blew dust day after day over that sagebrush desert land.
On the works the team hands plodded behind their mules, four
abreast on Fresno scrapers, in clouds of dust. No trees were in
sight except for a trickle of green in the tiny spring-fed creek of
the valley. The land spread away and away in waves on all sides,
all gray in brush but for the breaks of lava rock. When the North
Side project was done a hundred thousand acres of this land would
be watered into some of the finest farming country on earth. But
now it was grim desert.

The men of this camp were pretty much trash. Some were here
after starving out on homesteads. Others were broken-down cowhands or castoff sheepherders who had been working on projects
of this kind ever since the Milmer Dam was started on Snake River
in 1903. A number of the men were hobo team hands, but they
were the lowest grade I was ever to meet. Plainly they'd all had
miserable lives ever since they were born—and even before it, in the
wombs of their sorry mothers. Their talk was mainly lying brags
on all the vile items of life in cities they called Chi, Cincy, K.C.,
Los and Frisco. Even when they talked of good things like meals
and horses they made all seem evil.

There was a kind of grand beauty on the gray desert; but here
were men, here were men.

On the third of July I pulled into Pocatello—"Pocaloo," as the
hobos called it. I had some new duds and more than fifty dollars
left out of the seventy dollars clear that I'd made at the Bolt camp.
I fully expected to take a passenger train in the morning on the
Oregon Short Line branch that ran to Butte, Montana, and then
spend the Fourth on a trip to Red Rock and Ramon Hurd. But
Burly Hughes was also in Pocaloo, and he was roaring drunk. He

hooked on me and trapped me in a bunch of the riffraff who ran with him. I was weak enough to have some snorts of bar rye, and then I tracked along with them to the "Hell's Half Acre" of cribs.

The place was walled with a high board fence. Inside were little streets. The cribs were little houses out against the sidewalks. The whores would sit in brightly lighted windows, fixed up every which way, from doll dresses to next thing to naked. Or they'd stand in doorways, inviting customers inside, and a few would parade along the walks.

I was reeling along with Burly Hughes and his gang when I spied Ida Dorst about four doors down. She was in the simplest kind of a girl's dress, a blue-checked gingham it seemed to be, as I came closer to her, coming just below her knees, such as a twelve-year-old would wear. Her thick blond hair was in two pigtails. I hauled up. The gang went hollering on, not seeming to miss me. I wanted them to go on. The fumes of the old bar rye were fire running through me now. I looked on Ida Dorst and wanted her.

Then a pair of policemen loomed. It appeared to me that they were looking at me, for me, coming for me. I dodged back, but knew better than to break into a run—and then I was being pulled into a crib. The woman shut the door and locked it and snapped down the shade. Then she drew herself close to me and began to work her hands all over me. I was still drunk, but now I was in a freeze again, as I'd been back there on the hard bunk in the black cell, that April night in the old Knox jailhouse. I tried to act as I expected a man with a woman should act, but it was no use.

"First time, baby?" I heard the woman say. "Don't worry."

She gave me a drink. It was mighty powerful stuff. The woman set me on her bed with her and went on fooling around me, but I could only be afraid. She knew it. Finally she said—

"I know what's eatin' you. It ain't poon-tang you want, kid, it's to skin away from the bulls. Well, I like you and I'll show you. There's a back way out of here and through the big fence."

And there was. In a minute I was heading up to town as fast as I could walk it and not appear to be running from anything. I was inside my two-bit room before I found that my money was gone. I'd sewed the fifty dollars in a packet of gold pieces under the left arm of my undershirt. It had been slit away with something as sharp as a razor. I had a dollar and thirty-five cents to my name.

Now I'd have to start all over again in the making of a stake that would let me go to Ramon Hurd as a man who could take care of himself, as one who had come to visit a friend and not seeking favors. And now it would be winter in Montana by the time I had a new stake. Winter in Montana, was all I could think. Winter in Montana.

The Stone River dam-and-ditch irrigation project was up toward the Sawtooth Mountains. As winter came on I was working in the fifth camp along the line. Each camp was run by a small contractor who was subbing from the big company that had the whole project. Ours was the Dew & Bird outfit, with the famous George Gallerty as its walking boss. It was from the South, having moved up for the building of the Milwaukee railroad, and had many southern team hands. But Jack Hard, or John Navarre, was of French and Irish descent and his home state was Michigan. We all got along just fine.

A week before Thanksgiving a storm stopped the work. The team hands turned to draw poker; joker wild, jackpot ante. Three tables of seven players each were set to be run in a special tent. The top hands were gambling fools. A special tent and arrangements for draw poker made one of Dew & Bird's standard attractions for dirt-moving men.

On Thanksgiving Day I earned seven dollars at washing clothes for gamblers—washing handsomely in the ways I'd learned from Aunt Sue Hurd and Prof. Stedd. I was paid in chips. After supper I sat in at the pony game. I won a little there, and I ventured to take out a fifteen-dollar stack in the middle game. In two hours I won fifty dollars and some cents. When there was an opening in the big game, I made a bid for the seat. A couple of the players kicked, one saying it would be like taking candy from a baby; and let me keep my place, they said.

But a main gambler of the camp, one who was now a big winner, said, "By God, let the gazoony play. Here's where friendship ceases. His money is as good as anybody's to me." He was an

Indian-featured team hand who bore the moniker of "Black Hawk." His job was shaking plow on the grading machine. Jack Hard got along with him by ever giving him a soft answer and by speaking to him as "Black Hawk, sir," every so often. I understood the system. I used it myself.

Now Jack Hard dealt me into the big game, with no more argument about it. If Black Hawk had figured to bluff me out of my fifty dollars in no time, then he was fooled. I had bull luck a-running. By midnight I was a hundred and seventeen dollars to the good. A spell later the deal came to Jack Hard again.

As in every deal, I tucked my chin down in the collar of my red-and-black-plaid shirt and tried to keep a hardpan look on the wheel of red-backed cards that was turned from Jack Hard's hands. But inside me it was endless stormy excitement from the game. It was a mood to match the weather that beat on the canvas of the poker tent. I liked to hear it, and to see the shake of the lanterns that hung from the tent's ridgepole. The light of the lanterns kept moving over the colored chips and the green blanket and the faces and hands of the men. There was hardly any talk, least of all from the two dozen or more men who were playing rubbers. Some would leave, others would come in, and changes had likewise been going on at the tables. There was a feeling all through and around of high life, of life high-strung and feverish. This was the main attraction, the fever of the gambling game.

A pitch pocket blasted loud from a pine knot in the heating stove. The chips clicked, as the players fooled with them, watching the deal. Then it was done.

I found three hearts in the hand I picked up from the blanket. With them was the four of clubs and the joker. The hearts were the seven, eight and ten. I had a four-card straight flush.

Black Hawk opened the jackpot. Jack Hard stayed. Three dropped their hands. Lord Baltimore, the cook of the camp, put in. Then it was my hunch to raise the opener by two blue and two red chips, or by two dollars and a half. Black Hawk raised me five. Jack Hard threw down his cards. So did Lord Baltimore. I had a hunch to call, and then as the two of us drew cards I tried to do some figuring on the deal and how to play it. Black Hawk took one card, as I did, on the draw. I judged he was bluffing, and I figured he probably thought I was drawing to two pair, or at most to a low set of threes and a kicker. *He* might be trying this last, or bobtailing or fourflushing. I could only imagine.

Black Hawk's Indian eyes arrowed into my face as I picked up my cards. I slid the new card into the old four and shuffled without looking. Then I only showed myself the corners of the cards. The new card was the ace of hearts.

I had me a double-ace-header flush, a hand that only a full house, a set of fours or a straight flush could beat.

Black Hawk bet ten dollars. I raised him ten. He raised me twenty. I had a right only to call. But even though I was sitting like a smoked rock, doing my best to look like one, the furor in me was as great as it had ever been when I'd torn loose shouting and jerking and foaming in my sermon. And I was as much carried away.

"I tap myself," I said, the powerful spirit moving me.

Into the pot I shoved one hundred and eleven dollars and thirty cents, in white, blue and red chips, commissary vouchers and three double-eagles; shining gold in the lantern light. If Black Hawk was to call, it would be what even the big gamblers called a sensational. He fixed himself to study me, to stare me into a breakdown of expression that might tell him to call or to lay down his hand. Black Hawk was known as a star player on a call. I was yet a young man, and in this camp I'd not even been trusted with a team, I was still waterboy and wagon greaser. But I was an old hand at sitting smoky-faced and rock-sullen, thinking to myself, dreaming stories, amid the gab and goings-on of others. So I faced Black Hawk now, not letting his eyes shoot into mine, but staring at a spot between his eyes—a trick Ramon Hurd had shown me. By the rules Black Hawk had thirty minutes in which to make up his mind. I listened to the wind shaking the tent. Inside me I struggled again to keep my face a rock, to remember, to dream, to think outside this circle of life here. I looked up from the chips and cards and tried to look through the faces. I thought how the main thing I wanted now was not to lose before them. These men here were up to the land, a credit to it, and I could look up to them, even to such hellions as Black Hawk. The difference between them and the riffraff of the

Bolt camp was the difference between George Gallerty and Burly Hughes. Each as a walking boss was like the chief of a tribe. Men such as John Joseph Navarre, Jack Hard, a proud ex-Marine, would never work under a Burly Hughes, or go for cheap boozing and whoring with him in the towns. The king dynos of the hard-rock tribe and the star teamhands followed Gallerty.

I'd hoboed to the Stone River line from Pocaloo and worked in three camps before getting a chance as combination waterboy and wagon greaser at the Dew & Bird outfit. Next to Lord Baltimore's flunkies and Hughey Dowd, the boy who worked as hay tumbler for the stable dog, I was the lowest of all in the camp. My ranch experience with horses counted for next to nothing with George Gallerty. I'd have to prove myself as a Gallerty man somehow before he'd put me on a dump-wagon three-up as a hard-line team hand.

Now I spied Gallerty's face among the faces above the poker table. He was a runt of a man and his face was lean and small, a great red mustache covering most of its lower part. I saw past him. I saw the great Gallerty as I had on many a clear, frosty desert morning of late fall, standing out on a knoll in the trampled camp yard.

The Sawtooths sharp in the daybreak, telling that the sun was on its rising way behind them, the light spreading up the sky. Here in the yard the men in mackinaws and sheepskins plain to see as they tramped out of the bunk tents and from the tarpaper-covered cookhouse. Every breath a puff of frost-fog. The boss of all the men with a green-plaid mackinaw hanging all loose from his freckled neck, his iron pants and high boots looking too big for him, a raw-edge Stetson with undented crown set level on his red head but with the brim in front bowed up from his eyes. Then his piping kind of voice pitching an "All out! All out!" It was a pipe, but it never failed to start things moving fast. Out of the tents the men would stream, out for labor, the big, tough teamsters, and the even tougher dynos who lived by drilling and blasting in the hard rock. George Gallerty standing on there, maybe parting his big mustache, as the shod hoofs of the Dew & Bird mules would come clomping on the packed and frozen ground, men hollering and cussing to each other, trace chains jangling, then the hitching up and the rolling to the works well before the sun was reddening the Sawtooths.

There would come a morning, oh, surely there would come a morning, when George Gallerty would notice me, notice too that he was a team hand short today, and he'd tell me to step in and come on! Come on!

It was a sight to imagine, it was a dream to wrap myself in—now here, with the great George Gallerty's face in the faces there. I was lost in the sight, in the dream, then I was out of it, seeing all the faces in the lantern light, the light swaying from the beat of the storm on the tent roof and the sway of the ridgepole, hearing the wind, and hearing Black Hawk say—

"I call."

He shoved in the stack of double-eagles and chips that he had been hauling back and forth through the half hour, and let them go.

"Show your hand," Jack Hard said to me.

I spread out the double-ace-header heart flush.

Black Hawk said no word. He took his five cards in his two hands and deliberately tore them into tiny bits. Then he picked up the rest of the deck and tore it in half, ten or so cards at a time.

Jack Hard shoved the pot my way. I reached and began to rake it in, and as I did my heart began to pound my ribs and into my throat. Then, in the high-pitched but powerful pipe of George Gallerty, I heard—

"Well set under the gun! Well set, son. You are a team hand now. You can team for me any time. And you've earnt a moniker. Another *Big Jim* has come up, for my book. What say, you savages?" The great George Gallerty let his look swing and hammer among the forty top team hands in the poker tent. "Is his moniker *Big Jim Turner?*"

There was no argument. There never was with George Gallerty in this man's outfit. Later on Jack Hard let me know that the walking boss had come into the poker tent when he was told of the sensational pot, for the real purpose of easing the strain for Black Hawk, should he lose the showdown. Plenty more of the old heads were to bolster him and take me down by informing me that I was the biggest fool for luck ever heard of on that stormy night. Well, it was time for a change of fortune. Here it was. A high time. Glory be. In its heat and shine I forgot Ramon, my friend Ramon. I was Big Jim Turner in this almighty moment—a monikered team hand—a *Gallerty* team hand!

10. Preacher Boy

FREE IN MONTANA! THE WORDS SUNG THROUGH ME
as I stood early in the April morning and rocked the heels of my
hobnails on the fresh pine planks of the freight-shed platform. I
let the big wind from the Beaverheads slap hard on my face and
lift the brim of my Indian hat up and against its band of rattlesnake skin. I felt wonderfully full of hot breakfast, a prime chaw
bulged the hide of my left cheek, and I was ready to shoulder
my roped balloon of tarp, blankets and duds, and plow away
through mud, sleet and wind to the Navarre & Hurd camp, twenty-
two miles up the construction line.

John J. Navarre (Jack Hard), and Ramon Hurd were together.
I was the line of connection on the start of this partnership, and
this was one of the reasons I was feeling so cocky and proud on
this third day of April, 1909, a Saturday morning. There were
other reasons; fool-bright and hollow dreams, I was to learn too
soon, but strong in me now.

In the breaking daylight I stood and looked the Montana land
over, and then this speck of it, the headquarters for the building
of a railroad over ninety rough miles to Salmon City in Idaho. It
was this for me, I expected, for months to come.

This surely was wild, cold country. I'd never seen bigger foothills. Snow still capped them. Below that white the red, wet earth
of the slopes and ridges, only stubbled with sagebrush, looked savage. The sky was roiled with dirty gray clouds that threw squalls
of sleet.

Close by, spreading out from the railroad tracks, were acres of
wagons, scrapers, dump cars, grading machines, steam shovels,

lumber piles, and other construction rigs and materials. Mountains of baled hay bulged under canvas, flanked with hills of sacked
oats and barley under sheets of corrugated iron that were wired
and timbered down against the wind. Up the tracks were feedyards
in which horses and mules were gathered for the starting of the big
job. The smell of fresh pine lumber was all over the place. Already
in the breaking day hammers drummed and saws droned from
everywhere. The place swarmed with the life of horses, wagons
and freighters. Twenty-horse teams slogged out for the old freighting trail up the valley, the hoofs and wagon tires churning mud
through the new surface of gravel. They were jerkline outfits, with
the freighter riding his nigh wheeler or down alongside his string
in the mud, with a blacksnake popping. Two or three covered
wagons rolled after each team. It would be slow going. I'd travel
two times as fast on my hikers.

But there they rolled. Wheels rattled, whips cracked, hollers
and barks rode the wind, and the big job was beginning to open
up. Soon, now, the dirt would be moving, and the steel drills and
giant powder would be tearing into the hard rock from here to
the three-mile tunnel at the summit. It all made a powerful stir in
me. I was up to it, by God, I said. The great George Gallerty himself had told me I was one born to handle horses, yes, and mules.
And I had more strength than I'd yet needed to call on. I inched
well over six feet in these hobs, I tipped the beam at a hundred
and ninety-five pounds.

Free in Montana, free to be a man among men and then some.
Big Jim Turner—that was me, half poet and half horse. But the
poetry was down at this time, deep away under a darkening door.
I had come on among men, I was coming on here, coming with
bells, and I could see nothing but a clear way. Young stud, fool-
proud, a cocky young stud. God damn.

Over town yonder the Floradora Dance Hall hogged half a
block, with a second story of cribs and rooms, and already boast-
ing two murders. I'd been around there last night. I knew how to
handle myself now, how to take care of myself, how to play the
man-fool. And I swelled and flushed with a fool's pride, remembering.

Part of the big job, always part of the big job in the West, men and women being made as they are (Jack Hard had said, warning me—then the ex-Marine telling me how to take care of myself if I was *bound* to be a man-fool. "Take due care, and use your head. Take care." And I did. I was a fool but I guess I had to be one.) Last night the saloons were packed. Men waited four deep for their rotgut. They said a new bar would open for business even before the inside shiplap was on the studding. Big job in the West. Head-quarters town, full of hell and booming.

Brig Hanford and Joe Beal came out of the office of Grundy Johnson, Inc. They had come in while I was inquiring about getting out to the Navarre & Hurd camp—a Johnson sub-contract. Hearing me inquire, Joe Beal introduced himself and his partner and said they were headed that way, too, and would be glad to have my company. Joe was a little old coal-black man who had been a jockey. Brig Hanford was a Texas man who packed two hundred and fifty pounds of raw bone and muscle. Both were members of the Holy Hope Mission Way, of which Mr. Grundy Johnson himself was the founder. Jack Hard had hired them at the Holy Hope Mission in Spokane; Joe for stable boss and Brig as plow shaker for the grading machine. I didn't know any of this, of course, when we started. Over in Idaho I'd been dressing and trying to act like a young Indian man, on a notion of Jack Hard's that this might fool any lawman who had a description of me. Joe Beal thought I was a Blackfeet who wouldn't mind *his* color. Anyhow I didn't. But I went on humoring him and had a pile of fun being an Indian all through the mud and dirty weather of the hike to camp.

"I'm not a Blackfeet but a Saginaw," I told them. "I'm a Michigan Injun. I'm out in Montana tryin' to track down my ma. It was a Blackfeet she run away with—she met him when he came into the Saginaw country with the Buffalo Bill Circus. Ma was always weak-willed, and this Blackfeet wooed and won her with no trouble. Now I've got to work and save some money to go and hunt my ma."

Well, the big Texan and the little old black man lavished so much sympathy on me that I began to worry on how I could worm out of my big story without making them appear to be fools. But then I got the proper cue. As we slogged along in the mud and stopped for blows they told me their stories of past sins, all to point up what a miracle it was that they had found salvation and were bound for glory eternal. Joe Beal had hair-raising tales about the life of racetrack people in Chicago, California and such places, and Brig Hanford had really horrifying ones about the lynchings he'd taken part in as a young man in his Texas home. It was a prime article of the Holy Hope creed, I learned, for its converts to give testimony every day of the week on their sins of old.

"Testimony is water for the green tree of repentance in the desert of this world," Joe Beal said. "Repent and testify, Injun boy."

Well, at the end of the day I told him he made a powerful impression on me and I knew he was surely right. Then I said I was repentant for lying to him and Brig about being a Saginaw Indian, for I was no Indian at all but a blood cousin of Mr. Hurd's.

"I lied to you fine men," I said. "I repent it, and I testify."

It worked, too. They agreed I had taken the first big step on salvation's trail, they forgave me, and they would help me on.

Well, there I was, lying again; lying to get out of a lie.

It was muddy old going, sleety and blowy and cold all the way. Yet we talked the time so well that the trip did not seem long and hard. We passed a number of freighting outfits, some stuck in the mud, most of them crawling along. We caught up with three other bunches of men in the morning. One was a parcel of drunks who had swigged so much whisky in the first miles they could hardly keep their feet. The two others were bunches of hard-rock men. They were members of the Western Federation of Miners and the Industrial Workers of the World, and each bunch started agitating with us as soon as we'd caught up. I kept my hat brim low in front and the wide woolly collar of my sheephide up, for fear one might spy the image of Black Dan Barton in my features and ask me about him. Joe and Brig were as polite as you please in each case, telling that their religion did not allow them to join any kind of organization, labor or another kind. One of the rebel workers slammed back at them—

"Oh, sure, sure, religion. Hah! You've been snared in the Grundy Johnson flytrap. Pie in the sky. Dehorn! Servants, knuckle down to your masters. Let the other man risk his neck and do the dirty work of improvin' conditions for labor, then you take a free ride. You dehorns can go to hell!"

"Peace, brother," said Joe Beal kindly. "Peace be unto you."

And Brig Hanford, pale eyebrows bristling, pale gray eyes murderous, and muscles working like fury in his bull neck, said, "Peace-uh-peace."

And now I knew, without more telling, one reason why Jack Hard had been hiring men from the Holy Hope missions. He likewise wanted peace—on the job.

We went on. The valley narrowed and the hills rose higher as we made miles after a noon meal at a gyppo camp. Then we met freighting outfits and camp wagons on the way down, empty and moving fast. Yet the country seemed savager and lonesomer every minute. I got to telling, before I thought much about it, how a culvert trickle would run down and into the Missouri and the Mississippi rivers, and finally into the Gulf of Mexico; while up there on the other side of the Beaverheads a trickle would run into the Lemhi, the Salmon, the Snake, the Columbia, and finally into the Pacific Ocean. I said the Lewis and Clark expedition had come up this trail and over the Continental Divide. I told them Brigham Young had sent a colony up the same trail to settle the Lemhi in an early day. Then it was a mining boom. I remembered Ramon's accounts of the country that lay from the Wallowas in Oregon to the Beaverheads here. I told them, saying it was a country that stood on end. One range after another with peaks ten thousand feet high and only deep valley strips and canyon wedges in between. Not much of it was known. This railroad ought to open a wealth of minerals and forest.

"Spread Idaho out and the state would stretch to the Mississippi," I said.

"How'd you learn all that back on the old Saginaw?" asked Joe Beal.

Well, there I was, he sure did have me. So that was when I took the cue and told him I'd lied and I was repentant, and he said it was all right. So did Brig, but he looked unpleasant about it. I could well imagine how he'd burned the colored brothers down there, as he testified he had.

Anyhow, I was forgiven, and we slogged on into the stormy dusk. It was black nightfall when we spied the lights of the first stage and freighting station. The down stage was changing horses when we stopped by. We rested and watched the fresh six-up being hooked on, under lantern lights. It was the first six-horse Concord I'd ever seen. A guard with a gun sat with the driver on the high seat as the rig rolled away. With the lights on, it seemed like a circus act. A freighter told us it was the last fast express stage line in the nation.

We went on for three miles, and here was the camp. Then we were in the warm and bright kitchen tent; and here was Lily in the lamplight of the doorway crying, "Well, if it isn't Jim Turner! How-dee! Welcome, prodigal!" And Ramon, giving me an old-time "Hi, *compañero,*" and hugging me in. In back of me I half-heard the rich bass voice of Joe Beal saying—

"You see, Brig? He testified true on this. They are his folks."

It was hard telling, but I did try to tell Lily and Ramon the straight of what had happened since that morning of more than two years ago. When I'd come to what I didn't want to tell the truth on, or a lie either, I'd jump it. I said right off I guessed I'd turned out to be a pretty bad egg, and it was sorrow in me on account of Deacon Fay Yardley, Lily's fine old pa, and the folks at Cumberland Institute who had been real good to me on his recommendation.

"I had a chance," I said, pious and humble, "and I fell down on it. Ever since I've been a hobo. Once I even got drunk. Another time I fell into the sin of gamblin' with playin' cards. But now, Lily and Ramon, I aim to do better."

This talking with Lily and Ramon was all after some grub had been set out for Joe, Brig and me in the cook tent and we'd been shown places in one of the new bunk tents. Ramon had then walked me around by the corral and stable layout and showed me that Inez was still alive and kicking and as gentle an Inez as she'd ever been. She didn't know me, of course, she was simply sweet and nuzzly and nickery to me as to anybody who would speak right and smell good to her. Ramon reminded me they'd kept her as small return for the wagons left behind with the Hicks lumber.

Back in the winter, when Deacon Fay had come with Jack Hard by train to Red Rock, the title to the strawberry roan had been settled, along with the other business. Lily was going to have another baby and by summer wouldn't be riding Inez so much. If I wanted to buy the cayuse any time, *muy bien,* Ramon said.

"I'll think it over," I said, "I'll look into it." By God, I was dying to close the deal right there, weary as I was, but of course you simply don't deal on horses like that. "Yes, I'll consider it, Ramon, old-timer," I said.

He did not seem so happy, as we walked back to the housekeeping tent in which Lily was making a kind of home for him and Francis, their fifteen-month-old boy. I knew he'd never been ambitious to be more than a jerkline freighter, with good horses and wagons on a fair-paying route. But here the railroad would kill off the wagon trains. And here a chance had come to him to go into partnership with Jack Hard, with the mighty backing and outfitting of Mr. Grundy Johnson, one of the richest old men in Montana and Idaho together.

So here he was, with a Grundy Johnson camp outfit, a Grundy Johnson mule corral, a Grundy Johnson elevating grader and round of dump wagons, a Grundy Johnson sub-contract—all Grundy Johnson except for Ramon Hurd's twenty-eight horses and John J. Navarre's chip-in of thirty-five hundred dollars.

And it wasn't just this contract. Grundy Johnson was also a great power in the rising timber development of the Idaho Lemolo country. The high mountain sections owned by Ramon and Dan'l Barton were some kind of key in that. It was all a promise of big doings and riches for Ramon, but he seemed downhearted about it anyhow.

Well, we got into the tent, and it was like home. Lily was lovelier than I'd ever seen her, there in the moving lamplight. The glow was rosy on the tent roof and was alive in the shake of the Montana wind, the wind from the Beaverheads, the Great Divide.

The baby was awake, I went to calling him Frank right off, he liked it, and it was plain we'd get along well. Frank was a regular colt—I could tell he had horse in him. Ramon hauled out his Spanish guitar and he and Lily sang Frank to sleep with old songs— "Hear the Winds Blow," and other sweet ones.

Then it was more talking, low-spoken on account of the sleeping baby. I recited the move of the Dew & Bird camp down from the Stone River high-line to a winter job on the warmer Snake River plain, and bragged on how I'd worked a four-mule outfit on the move. I told that the snow of late November had turned into a rainstorm the third day of the move, mucking the road and sticking us in a miserable temporary camp on the Snake. That was when I grew to be a close friend of Jack Hard's—Mr. Navarre (I said). I confessed that probably I'd gabbed more to him than I should have about my first cousin, Ramon Hurd, of Red Rock, Montana, but I hoped no ill would come of it. Ramon said no, that Jack Hard was proving to be just the partner he needed; a strong, able and ambitious man. It was a relief to hear that.

Well (I went on to say), finally we made winter camp, and Mr. Navarre had left to visit authorities in Boise and Mr. Yardley and others in Knox, to get Ramon's record cleared up. I confessed I'd told him how Lily's pa and the famous rich man, Grundy Johnson, were old, old friends, and that both were Cumberland Institute trustees. That was how this deal here had all started, far as I knew. (I still hadn't said anything about my Knox jailbreak.)

They hearkened kindly and did not quiz me. I was made to feel so welcome. The soft lamplight shone on their faces and in my heart. Lily asked me with warm feeling about my reading and what I hoped to do for an education. I wasn't truthful in reply. It was easy to tell that she had gone far with Ramon in his religion. The tent room was barely furnished, but it had saintly pictures and figures. I looked at them and at Lily, appearing so saintly herself in the move of the lamp glow with the wind, and I failed to tell her of my interest in Shelley and how much I'd mixed Shelley in my dreams. And I did not tell about the new poetry book, all new to me, that I'd packed along in my blanket roll—Walt Whitman's *Leaves of Grass*.

To please her I said, "I haven't looked in a novel by Charles Dickens for a long time. I hope to this summer."

It pleased her. She smiled, and my heart swelled into my throat with love of her as I looked at her smiling. Yet we seemed so far away, far from each other. And Ramon. He sat there a-brooding, strumming at his guitar but making no sounds, saying no word, looking at us, smiling too, but not as in the night camps of the freighting trails. Pretty soon I rose up and we said the kindest good nights that cousins might say to each other. But I felt forlorn, going out into the night and the wind.

In my blankets I made a dream. I was back again in their home tent, the poor, bare, warm, glowing place with Lily and Ramon. I was Frank's big brother. I was thirteen, I was eleven, I was seven, setting on a stool with my golden hair and blue eyes, Lily's little boy, Ramon's Little Boy Blue, no tromped-on, bloodied-up Pa Lon Turner to remember, no Rev. Pearl Yates, no Mayor Maul, and their "That Turner boy is headed for hangin' and hell-fire shore! That Jim Turner needs puttin' away!" No trouble by me on the heads of poor old Grandma Barton and Aunt Sue Hurd. No trouble on my own head, no hoboing, gambling, drinking rye whisky and lying in with cathouse women. Little Boy Blue, rock him too. Five years, three years, fit to hold and rock and lullaby. Hear the winds blow, love, hear the winds blow, hold me close to thee, hear the winds blow. Bess Clover sung it. Feel my heartache, hold me close to thee, end my heartbreak. Poor Bess, so lorn for him. Mr. Russ Hicks, a fine son of a bitch. Sleep, sink. Sleep, sink. It's that time, time on edge of Snake River Canyon in a red, red winter sundown. Dark down. Down dark seven hundred feet and, why, there's the Phantom of blue Ontario's shore, come to life from old Walt Whitman's poem. What the hell you doin' in Snake River Canyon, Phantom? Can't be lookin' for no poet there. Look, kid, me no Phantom, he say. Oleman Nick me. Blackfeet Oleman Nick. Oleman Blackfeet Joe. You want to be poet, you say. You want to set on high seat and drive twelve horses. You'd sell yore sole to drive twelve horses. Oleman Blackfeet Nick he buy yore soul. Yassuh, Yassuh, Yassuh. He buy, boy, he buy.

Then I floated down into the canyon, blacker and blacker, until the Sunday morning dingdong woke me and I was ravening, as usual.

We were halfway through June, and over. I worried some about it as we worked into the heat of the late afternoon. It was a Saturday. Two weeks from tomorrow would be the Fourth of July. What I worried about was how the camp might hold together and how much longer Navarre & Hurd could keep Grundy Johnson's backing. The hard-rock gang was the trouble. Ramon ran the work, all right. He knew just where to drill and just how to spring the holes with dynamite and shoot with black powder. But he could not handle the rambunctious rebels, the old Western Federation men who'd been black-listed in the mines and were now Industrial Workers of the World. They came and they went, always agitating. They raised so much hell with the peaceful dirt movers, the Holy Hopers, that this side of the contract was failing too. Their peace faith was not working.

I was sorry for it. The work was wonderful to me. On days like this I could wish that there was nothing in the world but work with horses, or even with mules. We were grading a third of the way down a cut that would be forty feet deep on the finished grade. I drove six of Ramon's twenty-four horses. They were abreast, three on each side of a pusher beam. The front end of the beam was swiveled into the rear end of the grading machine's frame. A pushcart held up the hind end and the hookup of six whiffletrees. I sat up between the wheels, not only driving, but handling a steering rig.

On from my horses Brig Hanford stood spraddled at the wheels that controlled the beam of the machine's plow and the belt rig that slanted up through the machine's frame and jutted at the right to spill the plowings into one moving dump wagon after another. At the front of the frame the high seat of the machine skinner set him above Brig Hanford's head. He drove twelve horses, six abreast. The skinner was the walking boss, John J. Navarre, gambling man, ex-Marine, Jack Hard. He knew well he needed to be all over the works, particularly out with Ramon, and he knew well I was dying to set on that high seat and handle twelve horses.

Yet there he stayed. It saved a man's wages. Brig got along without an elevator tender, and this saved a man's wages. Ramon was boss and powder man both in the hard-rock. Phil Burns did the blacksmithing without a helper. Lily was timekeeper and she looked out for Charlotte and Jeanne, the Catholic Indian women who did the cooking and flunkying. Jockey Joe Beal was barn boss and hay tumbler too. That was how it had to be, Jack Hard said. That was

how the Mormon camps kept going. Surely the Holy Hopers would
see to it that a Gentile camp was kept going as well.

They would have, surely, except for the rebel dynos. Many of
the thirty Holy Hope men would be going to Butte over the Fourth
of July. Not all would come back, maybe not half of them. And
the story would likely go to Grundy Johnson that the camp was
not nearly so Christian as it ought to be. Anyhow, it would take
a powerful drive, and winter holding off to boot, to get the work
of the contract all done this year.

It was no worry for me, and I tried not to worry. I liked the
work, even from the pushcart. From the punching of the tunnel
through the rim of the Beaverheads down to the Pocatello-Butte
railroad blasting was to be heard any time of the day and was fre-
quent at night. Steam shovels rammed, kicked, gouged and snorted
at the cracked-up rock; dinkies and dumpcars wheeled the diggings
away on their little tracks. Yes, sir, she was building. Dirt was moving on most of the crooked miles that snaked between the grade
stakes up through the big red hills and the pinnacles. Mainly this
was by elevating grader and dump wagon, just as we were moving
it here.

But for me the times to remember in the work were the ones in
which Jack Hard would be called off the high seat. Then he would
have a dump-wagon teamster pull out of line and take the pushcart, while I had a whirl at the twelve-horse team. Once there had
been a whole half day. I'd made out all right. Even Brig Hanford
said so. I was born to horses, I had the strength and the judgment
—but a young man of seventeen had to be kept in his place in the
eyes of the older men he worked with. So I drove pushcart, doing
the work right and dreaming, and trying not to worry on how
things were slipping downhill with Navarre & Hurd.

The sun nodded nigh to the pinnacles and the moving shadows
of men, mules, horses and wagons at work longed out. A half hour
before quitting time Jack Hard took a dump wagon and drove off
for the hard-rock work, putting me up to handle twelve horses
again. And again it was glory, it was pride. They were sweet horses,
wonderfully gentled by Ramon, and I'd been trained myself to

handle horses as he did. A minute back I'd been flabby and yawning on the pushcart. Now I was as fresh as a son of morning. It almost cried aloud from me, "Oh, what could be so good as work in the earth, plowing work, with horses!" I settled into the side of the high seat. I gathered in the four thick, inch-and-a-quarter-wide lines, the fine-feeling leather. The two right lines ran between the middle finger and the two each side of it. The left line from the wheel horses ran under the little finger of my left hand, the lead line ran over the next finger, then both turned up and over my thumb. I hauled the lines tight and steady, leaning over a little. I said, "Yay!" hard, sharp, as steel bites steel. Then it was an even strain. I could feel the muscles of the horses up through the leather, a fire through me. Under me I felt the swing of the pushcart six back there on the machine. I pushed on the lines, and said one more time, "Yay!" and the twelve horses hit their collars as one horse hitting one collar. We rolled. The dirt moved. The big old plow ripped through the red dirt. I watched the left front wheel of the machine along the furrow line. I watched the three mules of the dump wagon in position alongside my off wheelers. In the lines I felt a lag from the nigh side. I said, "Ben, *you!* Even 'er!" Ben evened. Brig Hanford hollered, "Hi!" The machine team stopped on tightened lines, without a "Whoa" from me. The wagon team wheeled at a right angle, and an empty slipped in. "Yay," I said, sharp and hard. We rolled. The dirt moved.

Up the hump, twelve horses tramping in heavy harness, as one horse. Trace chains clinking. Tromp-tromp. A snort. A nicker. Jockey sticks clacking against hames. The smell of horse sweat. A halt while a dolliper drops and it's a sound that makes the old barrelhouse stiffs remember the beer. Red sundown on the big red hill. Dirt and rock moving for ninety miles of railroad. The country's opening up. The country is a-building. Takes men who can handle horses to build her. Me, Big Jim Turner, I can handle 'em.

Brig Hanford called, "Quittin' time!" away too soon for me.

After supper but before dark I was saddling Inez to ride for a night at the Floradora. Jack Hard came along and asked me to go a piece with him. I said, "All right," and we went on past the hay pile at the far end of the manger. There, still under the canvas roof, was a kind of pulpit that the Holy Hope men had made of split pine fence posts and old two by fours. Here on Sunday mornings they'd form a congregation on hay bales and hold experience meetings.

"Tomorrow morning," said Jack Hard, with the deadliest determination any man could ever put into words, "you are going to stand at the pulpit and announce you have experienced a call to preach. And you are going to preach your sermon just like you played that poker hand against Black Hawk. It's like that. A showdown play. Ramon and me, we've trapped ourselves. We've got to build up as a Christian camp or nothing with Grundy Johnson. A sensational is our one hope. You are it. If the play wins, you have that high-seat job for yourself—for keeps!"

I simply stood and hung on to the fence-post pulpit with both hands, stared at Jack Hard, saw he meant it, and nearly died.

Jack had heard me preach, and the way of this was certainly another lesson to me not to get drunk enough to show off; or just not to get drunk. For it was in that night camp on the Snake, when I was beginning to rise out of my horror and scare of being a hunted criminal, that I'd ventured to get drunk. Some rye whisky was brought to camp. I sneaked some snorts, and the next thing I was preaching the sermon that Barrick McCool had trained me in back in Iowa for the mockery of the Rev. Pearl Yates. The team hands gaped at me with wonder at first, then they got interested in the revival stories of sin and damnation I was hollering. One story had struck a case-hardened sinner to the core on that drunken night, because the moral, as he said, hit him right where he lived. He was sobered on the spot, he repented through the night, and the next day he quit and went to Pocatello. There he'd found his peace, in the Holy Hope Mission. A few days back he'd come to the Christian camp of Navarre & Hurd. His name was Luther Owen, once known as Overland Slim.

"You preach that same story," Jack Hard said. "Old Slim will rise and testify for you. I'll prime him and start him."

"He'll tell I was drunk," I said.

"You've repented, haven't you, like the rest of them?"

Jack Hard bore on me with all his power. I saw he really meant this as a showdown play, and that I'd either have to make a stab at going through it for him, or he'd be through with me. I was nigh broke. Last winter I'd kept piddling away my big winning until I decided it had been just a lucky fluke, and quit poker for keeps. After making a deal with Ramon for Inez I had nothing left. And I'd been catting away my wages. It appeared that I was stuck. Once more I had to preach my sermon, I guessed, and this trip preach it like I meant it, preach it sober.

Ramon had heard me preach it. I'd let loose with pieces of the sermon every so often in our freighting-trail camps, although he'd never encouraged me to. This Sunday he and Lily were up at four to drive to Red Rock for their own church. They would not say anything on Jack Hard's play but left it up to me.

Well, I attended the gathering for the experience meeting, and when Joe Beal had led in prayer and song and then asked for testimony, I arose in the congregation of around twenty. I arose from among the men who were so piously and earnestly sitting on the hay bales, and I said I knew I was a young man to have it, but I had surely experienced a call to preach.

"You come and try, then," Joe Beal said. "Come right up, Jim Turner."

I went up to the fence-post pulpit in a cold sweat and with watery knees, but as soon as I turned and faced the people I was sure of the power in me. As I spoke my text from Revelation X: 10 I felt the preaching flame of old burn. In no time I was again even as the Rev. Pearl Yates, evangelical preacher of the Methodist Episcopal Church in Cartwright, Iowa. I said the text, then looked over the people. The shade of the tent roof was on them, yet I saw a light there. On beyond the hay bales the heads of the horses and mules were lifted from hay mangers and grain boxes, looking and pricking ears to me. They hearkened as I raised a voice. I brought it forth so slow, like the chug———chug———chug of a Mogul locomotive starting a heavy haul. And, like the Rev. Pearl Yates would do, I said—

"Yea, let me be a locomotive of the Lord this day here!"

That was how I always tried to make myself feel, preaching, as the Rev. Yates used to tell that he would do. I was a locomotive, steam up, rolling on the main line to save sinners. The Main Line of the Lord!

I went on first with the story about the golden-haired little girl who came to take her drunken pa home from the saloon hell.

Then, with Jack Hard standing by over there, nigh to Luther Owen, I preached on. Through the smoke and sun of the preaching fire I could see him; rock-faced, dark-blue eyes like the points of drills ready for the hammers. Others were standing. All the camp had come down at the news that Big Jim Turner had answered a call to preach.

I preached away. " 'The shapes arise,' " I said, using words from a Walt Whitman poem. "Yea, the shapes of hell in the sins of men. What pictures of warnin' they do make, oh, brethurn, what direful and calamatatious pictures do arise to warn of what happens to the sinner from his sin, yea, even on this earth of the fleshpots and the lutes and the wine that is a mocker and the Babylonian dance-ah!"

Now I reared back and let 'er rant—

"Oh, let them take a warnin' and have a care who chaw and relish on the book when it is in the mouth and sweet as honey unto the tongue, oh, let them remember that there will come a time if they keep on, oh, a direful and calamatatious time, when the book is swallered and hell-fire comes engulfin' forevermore-ah! Yea, the pitcher goeth too often to the well, and is broken, and the silvern cord is broken, and the book is swallered, and this is death, oh, take warnin', brethering, I say unto you! Oh, see the shapes arise! Oh, see that shape arise, brother, ere it is too late-ah! The shape I wouldst show you now as the Lord God's own warnin' is that of a gamblin' man. It is no made-up story I'm tellin' you of, but it happened, oh, it truly happened, to a poor sinner, a lost soul-ah, a gamblin' man of Tyrone, Ioway."

Well, I let 'er rip for about ten minutes, taking the gambling man around to saloon hells, racetracks, dice and card games and houses of ill fame. I'd really improved on this part, with my experience and all that I'd heard, from what I'd preached at the age of ten. It's no good to put down the words, as it never is of any sermon; for the power was in the swing and heave and storm of it; the boil and fury and lather in the preacher; the voice and the words carrying the steam and fever out to the congregation. Finally I came to the point that told of the gambler being in rags and yet lost in his gambling sin. There at the card table he hung his head, while the Old Nick hovered over him, tempting him to make the one last bet, tempting him to draw his dead mother's ring from his finger—

"Oh, can't you see him now, can't you see him there, that sorry, that ragged, that stricken, that scornified, that perditionated gamblin' man! Oh, can't you see him and suffer with him and pray for him not to yield—oh, dear brother, don't you yield—oh, don't you do it—but he has gone too far, he has sunk so low—and he does—oh, he draws that keepsake from his finger, that one bond and token of a mother's love and care that is left to him, oh, he draws his dead mother's ring from his finger—and he bets it on a gamblin' game-ah! Oh, brethering, can't you see that picture now? Can't you see the glarin' lights in that gamblin' hell? Can't you see the shine of the hell lights on the cards as they are dealt from the devil hands of the gamblin' devil who runs the gamblin' hell-ah? Oh, look there, look on the poor boy, the ruined young man, the lost soul, as he hangs his head! He hangs his head in shame there, while the cards are dealt on, while the cards fall. His head is hung while he loses the play, his head is hung as his dead mother's ring is raked in. Oh, his head lays low! And oh, the deathliest hush and silence and quietudeness is on that place! Not a breath is drawed, not an eye blinks while the hellions of the gamblin' hell reach over with their pasty faces and their quakin' devils' hands and raise that poor head-ah—from which the tears do fall no more—and from which they nevermore can fall-ah. For, oh my brethuren, oh, that pore gamblin' boy—he is dead!"

Then, just as though he'd been waiting for that one word, old Overland Slim reared up from his hay bale and raised a glory shout.

"It air the God's truth!" he hollered. "It was even so with me, Luther Owen! Only it was a gold watch my ma left for a lone keepsake, and I lost it in a gamblin' hell! But I never died. I was allowed to live and repent and be saved to see my dear old mother up above!"

Well, there it was. I'd made it. I expected I could go on making it, if this was what Jack Hard wanted and needed to hold the backing of Grundy Johnson. I mopped my face with a blue bandanna, I looked out and up to the big red hill where the grading machine stood idle in the cut, then I looked back to where the twelve high-seat machine horses stood at the mangers, and I went on preaching.

Oleman Blackfeet Nick, he buy your soul. Yassuh, boy, he buy.

II. "Lilac, with a Branch of Pine"

THIS IS TO TELL OF A DAY. I HIKED UP THE VALLEY road from Boise in the break of the day, early in November. On the road I shouldered into a wind that jumped the peaks and carried on the cold of the Sawtooth Mountains. It was gray daylight in a sharp spit of snow when I drew nigh to Mother Morgan's place. There was one more bend to turn. It was a side-cut around the rimrock shoulder of a hill.

First I heard the slow march on the rock of the road. Brank—brank—brank, with brunch-a-brunch-as in between from feet out of step. Slow, heavy feet. I should have thought right away, for I knew that the state pen was up the road yonder, but I did not. It was a surprise to me when the man with the rifle swung into sight.

In the deep of my mind I was going over and over the poem I'd tried to write for the poetry scraps I hoped to show Bess Clover—

> Here is a black and a bitter mood,
>   Humor of hate and fear,
> A barrel of hell, a thimble of good,
>   For a life I have known is here.
>
> A life that pressed as a sackcloth pall,
>   Till I knew not seasons or skies;
> But now I love and treasure it all,
>   For 'twas lived to be read by your eyes.

To me it read well, it sounded good, and it was best of all in the deep of my mind, a light, a singing. For a week and more it had been my one consolation to get down in the deep there with the lyric and argue with myself on whether it was more like Shelley or more like Byron. That was only one fancy. There were others on the other scraps that I had in a buckskin wallet in the pocket of my sheephide coat. Since Montana I had turned to poetry with a vengeance.

But poetry was forgotten now. There came the man with the rifle slung in his left arm, his head up and eyes glittering hard at me from under the scoop brim of his black hat, the stormy sky so dusky gray above him—then the men of the heavy-footed march. They came on in stripes, prison stripes.

"One side, there, you!" the rifleman yelled. "One side!"

I slid and scrambled as fast as I could make it to the line fence below the road. Then I backed against a post and peered up. The convicts did not turn a head my way. Two more riflemen were on this flank of the march and another two tailed it. I saw the faces. Some were old, some were young, more were of middle age. They were faces of men in my sight, just men. I remembered Ramon. I thought of my uncle Black Dan Barton. For many months they had worn the stripes the heavy-footed marchers were wearing. Ramon's name had been cleared of the charges that put him there.

But not Dan'l Barton's. He had served his time, he was free, but his name had not been cleared. He was an ex-convict, with only an old con's rights. If he was alive, it was under another name. And now, as the penitentiary prisoners made that dragging march on to their day's hard labor, I felt fit to die. I stood listening to the dwindling sounds of the brank—brank-brank, with the brunch-as mixed in, and I mourned.

I was to find Black Dan Barton if he was among the living. That was why I had run the risk of coming to Boise, and the further risk of coming on out here to see Mother Morgan. If anybody could tell me where and how to find Black Dan, she was the one. I hated to do this, I loathed being here, I had all along. Only the poetry had helped me to come on through with it.

The trouble was about Ramon. He was in a Butte hospital, lying there between life and death somewhere, as he'd been since early in October. It was a black-powder blast. When the earth began to freeze there in the Beaverheads Ramon would have to thaw out the dynamite sticks of mornings. So a fire would be kept going under a tub of water, and the giant powder would be kept in the water for a slow thaw. Some black-cat bastard, some sabotager son of a bitch, had dropped coals in a sprung hole before Ramon poured in the black powder. He'd heard the burn start, and he wheeled. But a shot rock just about tore the back of his head off. If he lived, he'd not be good for much. John Navarre, his partner, was more than ready to carry him along in a deal they'd worked up with old Grundy Johnson on a timber development in the Lemolo Mountains. Ramon's wife, who was Lily Yardley, was for it. But Dan'l Barton was an owner with Ramon of a couple of sections of timber that would have to be part of the deal. The name of Black Dan was among the missing. But all hands were sure the man himself was alive and kicking.

I went on downhearted, around the bend and to the mailbox that had the name of "Mother Morgan" on it, as I'd been told it would have. Her place was seven or so acres above the main valley ditch. The acres were spring-irrigated. A little prune orchard was blowing bare in the November wind. Away over on the other side of the valley the gray hills sort of crawled up in easy rises to the cloud packs. Down midway a ragged ribbon of trees marked the course of the river. There were squares and strips of fields on all the valley floor; dark fall plowings, brown and yellow stubble, orchard blocks, rows of cottonwood windbreaks; clumps of houses, barns and other buildings. From the barbwire gate here by the mailbox a narrow graveled road went down a piece to a low, un-painted house with a shed porch and walls of boards and battens. A few cottonwoods and a woodyard stood between house and poultry sheds and runs. There was a little ramshackle barn with a toolshed roof stuck to it. In the woodyard a tall old woman and a thin young woman were on a crosscut saw, ripping into a pine log. They were in worn and heavy clothes.

I crawled through the gate, hiked down, and was real close before my steps in the gravel were heard. Then Bess Clover straight-ened around, she stared, then put her cotton-gloved hands up in a kind of X on her mouth, and the next thing she was laughing and crying both while I held her.

It struck me that I hadn't felt so fine, so wonderful, so good and alive since that end of the workday last June, when I'd last handled

the twelve horses of the Navarre & Bird machine as a free young
man. For seconds I felt good, never cocky and proud, just good,
and then I remembered I was not free now, and likely I wouldn't
be.

"I'm Mother Morgan," said the tall woman. "I'd know you in a
million. You're lookin' for your Uncle Dan'l, I bet. Come on in."

First I told Bess alone why I was running this risk, told her in a
hurry. Mother Morgan had left us after chunking wood in the
long-stove and opening the lower draft and saying she had a couple
of roupy hens to look out for. She had taken hold of me at first
sight, reminding me of Grandma Barton, then of the Indian people. A straight, strong woman in her late sixties, Spanish-dark,
gaunt and lined in her face, some gray in her hair, fiery-eyed as
any girl of twenty, or man either. I'd heard of her from away back,
even from grandma, but not much except on how she'd had the
name of being a wicked anarchist agitator since 1870 and earlier.
But here she'd bid me welcome and made me comfortable, then
gone out to take care of her hens, just as my Baptist Aunt Sue
Hurd might have done.

Then I told Bess why I'd come here from Montana. "I reckon
Mother Morgan has a right not to tell you what she knows," Bess
said. "She does know where he is, and I can guess. Once a week,
anyhow, somebody comes out to ask about him. I can tell you he's
alive and well—or was lately. That's all we ever tell anybody—
even his old miner friends."

"The Redburns are after him, along with Haywood, Debs, and
anybody else like that they can get," I said. "It's hell on me. I
seem to grow his build and his face more all the time. If he'll come
back in on this deal, he can get the name of Black Dan Barton
cleared and free, as Ramon did. Then I might live it down."

It was like the touch of a match to dry leaves, the way Bess
Clover flared at that. I'd kept standing by the long-stove, and so
had she. She stood close to me. Her face was drawn tight in white
anger. Her gray-blue eyes grew dark and big in her face.

"There's nothing to live down, Jim Turner!" she cried out, up
into my face. "Not by you—for him, Dan Barton, who has fought,
bled, starved, given his freedom and name, and risked life twenty

times over for the enslaved and oppressed! You are a bobcat to
a lion alongside him, Jim Turner! I tell you he's glory to me, a
saint's name, my kind of saint——"

She was close, close and afire. So was I close to her, and it was
fire in me, knowing I loved her; knowing it through these days
when I was sure I'd see her; knowing it since I'd brought my poems
into the light again. Well, now I'd been around, I knew what to do,
and I took her and held her and kissed her seven ways from Sunday. I held her, soft and crying. Then this was *my* mood and humor, mine, too; for she was so thin in my hard arms; and more
than that I could feel she had little strength of life apart from her
spirit. I looked and looked on her face, hungeringly, but I did not
kiss her again. She opened her eyes. Tears spilled out. It was pain
in me as though the tears had been twisted and wrung out of my
own heart. Love was in her eyes. Not first love, not the true love.
Cousin love, no, sister love. Well, little sister. Sister Bess. Yea, sister. Well, good enough for a slick-ear like Big Jim Turner; fair
enough for him, a hypocrite of a Holy Hope preacher boy. She
stirred and turned a little from me, toward the windowlight. White,
thin face in the light, tear-washed. Brown hair with threads of red
and gold catching the light. Halo on her. Outside it was snowing.

"You're right, Bess, and I'm sorry," I said. "Here, I've some
poems to show you. None finished, all just tries. I thought of you
in about all of them. One is for you; the latest. Can we set for a
spell over by the window?"

It snowed on into the noon hour. Up on the road the outside
grading gangs of state prisoners were marched out of the storm.

"They are well treated," Mother Morgan said. "It's as fine a
state pen as any in the country, the boys tell me, outside of maybe
Deer Lodge, Montana."

She tramped up through the snow whirls to the gate, then stood
there so the convicts could see her as they marched past, as convicts had been seeing her here since there was a pen. They could
not wave or call out, but even from this far I could tell that all
were giving their best to Mother Morgan, famous rebel fighter for
the downtrodden. Chins lifted against the wind and snow, shoulders came back, knees rose higher. Bess claimed it, anyhow, and

I saw it with her. Yet it was a sight of the Slough of Despond for me, and icy tremors to think that I could be there. Oh, I could be there, in the prison march!

We went on making stovewood. Bess told me what she had learned about how I stood in Knox. On a trip home Bess had learned that old Moss Eckert was scarred for life on his forehead from that fall he'd taken on my breakaway. The marshal hushed the matter up, but to his cronies he'd swore that I'd pulled a knife on him and down his face to make that forehead scar—he swore it was an armed jailbreak by Jim Turner and that I'd be put in the pen for it. I hadn't heard that much from John Navarre, but Bess declared that it was my danger and told me to shun Knox.

Anyhow, we stood out by the woodpile and watched the stripers and the rifle-packing guards go by and fade away on in the snow; and in spite of being with Bess, all I wanted was to be going away from here. But Mother Morgan hadn't volunteered to tell me yet where and how to find Black Dan Barton. And Bess had cautioned me to let her bide her time on the question. I was willing to wait, but I said I did hope to get out of Boise tonight. The place was too well settled and had too many officers of the law in it to suit me. But here we were. I picked up the double-bitted ax and whacked off some more splits from a pine block. Bess packed them over to a rick on the front porch. Mother Morgan came back from the gate, and we went inside and had a prime chicken-soup dinner.

I liked the way she fussed with Bess and made her eat hearty. Bess had the lung weakness of Johnny and most of the other Clover children, and now she was getting over a siege of grippe that had run close to pneumonia. She had made herself acquainted with Mother Morgan on her first coming to Boise, knowing about her from talk of the Hurds, and others, and from pieces in *The Appeal to Reason,* just as I had known. A year ago, when she was free for it, a young woman of eighteen, Bess had quit the Salvation Army and come into the open to agitate and organize for the Industrial Workers of the World and the revolution of her dreams and hopes.

Mother Morgan got to talking after we finished eating and went into the front room, leaving the table. She told about Bess and herself, leading up to a hope she had of me.

"Bess could fare forth right now and be another Gurley Flynn, if she had the strength for it," said Mother Morgan. "But she does not have it. You do, Jim Turner, livin' image of Dan'l Barton. How do you account for your dirty work in Montana?"

"What work was that there?" I said, knowing, of course.

She said I knew what she meant. "Grundy Johnson's dirty work, to be sure. No man alive has more blood of labor on his hands. No man alive, not even Sandy Andy or John D., works harder at coverin' murder with the robe of the rebel Jesus."

"You may be right," I said, so humbly. "But I was told there was more to him. There in Montana Grundy Johnson set Ramon Hurd and another poor man named John Navarre up in business. It looked to me as though his Holy Hope missions had helped quite a few men. There was a man in camp who had been a brute lyncher in Texas. There was a man in camp who had been sunk deep in sin by racetrack gamblin', a black man. In the Holy Hope the white lyncher and black gambler had grown to be Christian friends. But you may be right."

"You are no Holy Hoper in your heart, Jim Turner!"

"No, ma'am," I said.

"But you preached your head off every Sunday on it. You did your level best week after week to fill the wage slaves full of holy hop—Bess! that's a good one, and don't you forget it—holy *hop,* I said, to make them forget they *were* wage slaves."

"I was a bastard to do it, ma'am. A no-good bastard."

"Don't talk like that to me! I won't hear anybody who is the picture of Dan'l Barton, that great old rebel fighter, talk like a Uriah Heep to *my* face. You know what I mean?"

I said, humbly still, "I've read the novels of Charles Dickens, ma'am."

"You're actin', actin', puttin' on!" she fairly snarled at me. "No wonder your grandma and your Aunt Sue were driven so crazy by you!" Then she bit her lip and calmed down some. "Forgive a cranky old woman," she said. "You somehow irked me so I forgot that you are also a victim of the System. You truly are an irksome kind."

I sat and looked as bowed down and sorrowful as I knew how to look. I'd rolled a cigarette and lit it up, but now I let it go out and held the cold stub in my fingers. I leaned low, propped an elbow on a knee, and stared as pitiably as I knew how at the cold stub.

"Well, pore boy," Mother Morgan said.

"He's a poet," Bess ventured to put in. "He's written some fine pieces of poetry for a young man of seventeen."

I was glad to pull out the buckskin wallet and hand all that was in it to Mother Morgan. I'd kept some of the lines from *Leaves of Grass* which I'd written down as Jack Hard said them from memory before I was able to get the book itself.

I stood up and recited in my deepest preaching voice—

> *I listened to the Phantom by Ontario's shore,*
> *I heard the voice arising, demanding bards, . . .*
> *Of all races and eras these States with veins full*
> *of poetical stuff most need poets, and are*
> *to have the greatest, and use them the greatest.*

"Bess says I'm a poet," I said. "I don't know. Nobody will know for years, even if I get a chance to work at it. Last summer all I could think of was that I'd sell my soul to drive twelve horses on a big machine. Now, and for the past two weeks, I've been ready to sell my soul to be a poet. That's me, Big Jim Turner."

I went on thinking to myself that it was always a burning hell in me for one thing or another. There was the helling around. There was the preaching. By God, I'd got myself more drunk on my own preaching there Sunday morning after Sunday morning than I could have on rye whisky. And my sermons certainly had brought on, built up and kept a working Christian camp. I could still want to preach.

They went on reading, murmuring, whispering. I lit the cold stub of cigarette and stepped over to the window. The snow seemed to be letting up, but flakes yet swarmed, blew and fell. I brooded—

> *Who are you indeed who would talk or sing to America?*
> *Have you studied out the land, its idioms and men? . . .*
> *What is this you bring my America?*
> *Is it uniform with my country?*

Is it not something that has been better told or
   done before?
Have you not imported this or the spirit of it in some ship?
Is it not a mere tale? a rhyme? a prettiness?—is the good
   old cause in it?

This was not stuff of dreams but of work for a poet. Much of *Leaves of Grass* was Greek to me, or as Revelation; the great visions, the big-word images and symbols; and my own poetry tries were yet patterned on rhymes by Shelley, Tennyson and Byron, with some Poe. But John J. Navarre had opened me a trail into Whitman, as a way for a son of poverty and labor in this land. Inside him it seemed I'd find something to live by, keeping on looking; to live by and for, and not having to ask for license from either the old religion or the new revolution. Meantime, I had to work to eat, and work hard. And I was an outlaw, and on this a coward, a coward in my heart.

Sometimes it only seemed a fancy, a dream, that trouble. But not now, with what I'd seen and heard marching on the road up yonder. Ramon Hurd—poor Ramon, still laid low in that hospital over in Butte—had been a lot more innocent than I was, and he had been railroaded into the pen. Many another, many a one.

It snowed on. The wind creaked around the old house. I went over and put some wood in the heater. The women were through with the poems, for the minute, anyhow. Bess looked up at me. A smile sunned her thin face and tore my heart. Mother Morgan had a clay pipe going. She drew hard on the stem, sucking deep hollows in her gaunt, wrinkled cheeks. Her look was as piercing as a look could be through smoke.

A dream took hold, even before I moseyed back to the window. Bits of the things that Mrs. Shelley had written about Mr. Shelley, and which I'd learned by heart to dream on while I worked, rose to mind. I wondered could Bess ever say this like of me—

. . . *he loved truth with a martyr's love, he was ready to sacrifice station and fortune, and his dearest affections, at its shrine. The sacrifice was demanded from, and made by, a youth of seventeen.*

I would not be eighteen until the twenty-second of November, so the dream was still good. I said it over, trying "eighteen" instead of "seventeen," but somehow it was not as touching. I mused on, remembering—

Born in a position, which, to his inexperienced mind, afforded the greatest facilities to practice the tenets he espoused, he boldly declared the use he would make of fortune and station, and enjoyed the belief that he should materially benefit his fellow-creatures by his actions; while, conscious of surpassing powers of reason and imagination, it is not strange that he should, even while so young, have believed that his written thoughts would tend to disseminate opinions, which he believed conducive to the happiness of the human race.

Usually I wasn't above throwing in a few words of my own here and there, such as "the *bastardly, blowhard* human race." But I had no heart for such improvements now. Never yet in this life had I felt so sorry and forlorn. Thinking of me as one dead, I turned away from the window and to look on Bess Clover. She was leaning on the right arm of Mother Morgan's huge cane chair. The little sheaf of poetry fragments was on the chair arm, too. Bess Clover's head was bowed over them. It was a prime picture for my deep dream. There she was, Mrs. James Birney Turner, mourning over the poems of her husband who was dead and gone, just as Mrs. Percy Bysshe Shelley had mourned. There she was, studying, getting ready to write about her particular poet as Mrs. Shelley had written on hers.

They both caught me. The next thing I knew they were staring, and Bess was asking me what in the world I was looking so stricken for. I stood feeling like a fool, as I would always do when caught full depth in a dream or a story. And now the tears were tumbling down my face.

"You beat me," said Mother Morgan. "You surely beat me."

The gaunt old woman sat there in the big cane chair, shaking her head at me, holding her pipe from her mouth. I wanted to tell her, well, she beat me, too; an anarchist woman who had raised hell and gone to jail all over the West since 1870; and here she was, raising chickens, setting around and acting like any other farm woman I'd ever known; and irked and upset by me, as every woman I'd ever known, except Lily Hurd, had always been. But I kept a shut mouth, only to say, "Yes, Ma'am."

"Sweet little Jesus boy," said Mother Morgan. "Preacher babe. Sucklin' poet. But a gift, maybe. You beat me. Well." She gave her bony shoulders a shake. "He *is* the only one who can handle you, and I know he wants to," she said. "You get to Spokane. Inquire at the I. W. W. hall for Ben Sweet. *Ben Sweet*. He's there, or will be soon."

That was the day for me, although there was something more to it.

It was miserable misfortune, and I hate to tag it on the story of what was a fine day to remember, take it all in all. I'll only tell that on my way back from Mother Morgan's to the two-bit flop-house where I'd been staying, I was waylaid, knocked out and robbed. There were two men. Maybe they were Redburns. Anyhow, they not only slugged me and took my money belt, but they piled me on a freight. When I came to myself I was half frozen in a boxcar and rolling west. That was the real end of the day for me. But the day I remember is what I've mainly told.

12. Wobbly Elder

THE FREIGHT TRAIN SIDETRACKED IN UMATILLA. IT was past midnight. A freezing wind cut through the yards. Six shivering hobos swung stiff legs down from a boxcar half full of coal. Four had blanket rolls. All stood in a miserable huddle, staring around through the dark at the red and green switch lamps. I was one of the six.

We straggled on, each numb and hungry wayfarer stamping as he stepped. A switch engine chugged past, showering sparks and shedding heat. Two snakes waved lanterns from the tender's rear end. One let out a Wobbly meouw. Then a lantern was jigged.

"Sandhouse sign," said Ty Collins. "Follow me."

He had taken the lead over us when we had bunched back at Huntington for rough travel. His partner called Ty Collins "Wingy." He was a wiry runt, he had a bad limp beside the loss of his left arm, but he owned power to move out in front of a gang of hard men and rowdy boys. His way of speech told that he was from the South.

Wingy Ty Collins, limping, led us on. The packed and frozen snow was glassy under our soles and hobnails. We skidded and stumbled as we bowed our necks against the windy darkness.

The one-armed hobo knew the Umatilla yards. He brought us without a hobble to the sandhouse.

The place was as a warm cave. The wind slammed in with us and swooshed into a flame that burned from a nest of oily waste on the dry sand. Smoky waves of light crawled over two men who were sitting crosslegged back yonder, peering out of shadow and over flame at us. Their hats were low-pulled and they kept their chins deep in the upturned collars of logger mackinaws.

Ty Collins nosed ahead of us, saying, "Men, howdy."

The biggest of the two swung up a huge hand shape, offering Ty something. He took what it was and held it down in the poor light. It was an unfired match. On the road this meant, "Declare yourselves or light out!" Wingy Ty Collins knew the sign. He spoke up agreeably.

"We air dirt movers," he said. "We aim no trouble for any man who is good work stock and no john. We aim to please, sirs."

"Then welcome," the biggest of the two men said. "Welcome to this palace of the damned. We are timber beasts."

My heart seemed to skip a beat, then it jackhammered my ribs, and my bowels swum. It was furor in me, yet I stood as a pillar of stone, while Ty and the four others crowded around the pitiful fire and flopped on the warm, dry sand. Oh, that voice!

Yes, that well-deep and atrembling voice of the preacher born and called was of a nature I might never miss. I had heard generations of Bartons in every tone of it. God, I was shaking. If ever leaf trembled on aspen tree, then so did every part of me now, while I let myself down on the sand behind Bush Brown and Rough Rider Bliss. Pretty soon I had a grip again and quit shaking.

Pipes and cigarettes were lit. Talk began to range around the circle. I started to roll a smoke, then I put the bag of Durham away and took a chaw. I'd never had a good old chaw do me more good. I nursed it along, felt the restful ease of it flow through me, and began to hearken with more calm and to think straighter on the circumstance I'd entered here. It took a more certain shape when the biggest of the two timber beasts said, "We can swap monikers before we try to get some sleep. I am known as Ben Sweet. My friend is Joe Hill."

A rise in the smoky flow of light had told me that Joe Hill was here, even before Ben Sweet spoke the name. I held the grip. If ever in my life I needed to take care, now was the time. My misfortune back there in Boise was a cloud of warning still. The Redburn devils wanted me, had tracked me in the tracking down of the vanished name of Black Dan Barton. And had let me off only because they'd robbed me. Any one of this gang could be a Redburn fink. This was in *his* mind surely. Ben Sweet went on asking each hobo to have his say, to tell what he would about himself.

Ty Collins said that he and his partner, Fitty Bill, had been arrested and tried for vagrancy while they were hoboing through Mississippi. It took two years of slave labor to bring freedom.

"We wore leg shackles together all that time," the one-armed hobo said. "Billy was born to epilepsy. Them air bastards of guards would beat him up whenever he throwed a fit. His face was knocked out of shape so that he cain't work his jaws to speak. We've been two more years gittin' into a free country, and I lost me an arm. But now I can take keer of Billy. And now I can fight back some at them air kind of bastards who live off the same old slavery."

Bush Brown was my own age, he'd told me, and had run away from an orphans' home in southern Indiana. He was freckled, blue-eyed and red-haired, and he appeared to be at least two years younger than me, although he was as tall, and actually a year older. On that night I did not yet know that Bush was a black boy and that he had hoboed to the West to turn white. But I learned it later. He had finally become sick and tired of being called a nigger and treated niggerly by his brother and sister orphans and other Posey County folks. And for a long time he had dreamed of growing up to be a cowboy, only to learn that there wasn't much chance for any kind of boy but a white boy in the cowboy's trade. A red boy, Bush told me, could expect to go farther in it than a yellow boy or a black boy, but the best-known cowboys were white boys purely. He had made a deep study of the whole matter.

Tonight, though, all I knew about Bush Brown was his pink and freckled face, blue eyes and red hair, and I did not dream a black boy was inside.

On a sidetrack in Knox we had picked up a drunken hobo who called himself Rough Rider Al Bliss, and an old dyno who would give no name for himself but "Mike." Like Wingy Ty Collins and Fitty Bill, old Mike was California bound.

"I hope for a job in sunshine, if it's only muckin' rock," Mike said. "Won't worry me what the work is, jest so's I can work in sunshine the rest of my days. Sunny Cal! Sunny Cal for me!"

Wingy said, "I'm a-hopin' the sun will help Billy's trouble."

Fitty Bill only croaked something. What it meant nobody could tell, not even his partner.

Nobody else said much. I put down the temptation to tell a big one and only said I was a team hand from Montana.

The Rough Rider took no part in the talk. He looked sick and acted sick, huddling up in his blankets, back to the poor fire.

Marshal Moss Eckert had put him and Mike on the train back there in Knox, telling them, "Make 'er out, you damn' bums, or you'll be givin' us a start on a new chain gang here. Make 'er out!" I fully expected him to search the boxcar and hook me, for I was so sunken in misfortune that it seemed nothing good could ever happen in my life again, but he had kept to the snowy ground. We all made 'er out. Then we'd rolled free into Oregon. A night and a day. Another night, and we were here.

Yes, here, and I'd found *him*. It was a big time in my life, sure to be one of the biggest to remember. I squinted and peered through the smoky light at "Ben Sweet," who was yet sitting up, while Joe Hill had sprawled down with the rest of us. I could make out features that had been clubbed much and hard, with no resemblance to mine left to speak of. I reckoned that when people said I was his living image they were remembering Black Dan Barton as he was before the labor wars of the 1890s. The light made a little flare over his eyes. Their look brooded from circling lumps and ridges of beaten flesh, black-browed. It was the brooding of the wild. I could see the fight, the fierceness there. Inside me it was drump—drump—drump at my ribs again. I wanted to go over to him and take hold of his hand. Then the flare ebbed down. I thought of what I'd have to tell, to confess. Oh, that preaching of mine! The rebel hard-rock miners must have spread the story all among the Industrial Workers of the World. *He* must have heard of the preacher boy on the Salmon City line in Montana. Surely it would make me despised in his sight, for I was so in my own. I'd sold my soul to drive twelve horses. It was for that, I knew in my heart, and not to help my friends Lily and Ramon and Jack Hard. Oh, what a shameful sell! *He* would surely rip me up one side and down the other for it. By God, I could never drive a team of horses again, I could never have the heart for it. Agonizing that way, I fell asleep in the warm sand, not knowing I was falling.

The sleep was torn from me like raw flesh. Fitty Bill was having him a spell, and a bad one. I awoke to his croaks, gasps, hollers in the clutch of a convulsion. I thought of the sounds made by a hog a-scenting slaughter, or by a steer in the dehorning pen. The other hobos were all sitting up, staring, muttering.

Wingy was tending to his friend. He warned us to stay back.

"Jest kindly bear with him, please sirs," Wingy said, like one in prayer. "I do hope you can feel it in you to bear with Billy and me. Only thing can be done is to see he don't harm hisself till the convulsions air through with him. I'll give him a pill to ease him some when he is able to swaller it.

It was an hour of nightmare before Fitty Bill quieted down, until his inhuman bawls were no more than blubberings. Through it the men sat up, fed the fire, smoked, chawed and tried to talk. Nothing helped much. The going had been too hard on the winter road, the night was yet so cold in this miserable shelter, and the old hunger was a devil gnawing in every hobo's belly.

Ben Sweet did not speak in that time. He sat with his knees drawn high, arms on them, fingers laced mostly, now and then dangling one hand while resting his chin on the other. His hat was off then, showing to my sight a shaggy dark mat of Barton hair. That shag and his forehead reminded me of a Lincoln picture. Dan'l Barton would be fifty-five now, I reckoned. He'd been organizing labor in one way or another since the railroad strikes of 1877, and fighting for labor. The story was in his face.

"A saint," Ramon Hurd had said, telling of Black Dan Barton to Jack Hard and me. "A fightin' hellion, a dynamitin' devil who grew into a saintly kind of man. Jailed for it. Nearly killed for it."

"He went out looking for trouble," Jack Hard said. "He got what he asked for, didn't he? What's the kick on that?"

I sat up amid the torment of inhuman sound from Fitty Bill and wondered at *him,* that blood uncle of mine. Now and then he would bow his head low and press fingers through his shag of hair, as though he was trying to press away pain.

Beside Ben Sweet, but more back in the shadows, Joe Hill would raise himself up only to rest on an elbow for a spell, saying nothing.

Every so often there was a flare from the greasy smoke, stink and dull flame of the doped shreds of cotton. In the rises of light I would look around at eyes blinking from red rims and coal-smeared, cinder-pitted faces all a-strain. In the last half hour or so of it nobody spoke a word. Right then there was nothing so much that any of us wanted in life as quiet. We would watch Wingy Ty Collins sort of nurse Fitty Bill through a convulsion, not holding to him, but wiping off the poor face and speaking lowly to it. Then we'd hope it was the last fit of torment. And then it did end.

"It warn't sech a bad one," Wingy said. "I surely do thank you all kindly for bearin' with him. I surely do, sirs."

There was the soft crying then, the whimpers, the blubbering. I heard the wind again, blowing around the sandhouse walls. There were other natural sounds as all settled for sleep. I could hear Bush Brown, a year older than me but looking and acting so much younger, sobbing to himself, close to my face. I wanted to touch him, but I did not, as I expected crying was what the poor boy needed and wanted. I felt so sweet-Jesus sad in my own self, but more than anything I wanted sleep. It came on. I heard—

"Joe, the drums! I can hear the drums, Joe Hill!"

"Rest, comrade, rest."

"The drums, Joe Hill, the drums. They are beating 'round the camps, ten thousand camps where wage slaves sleep tonight. Solidarity's drums. Slaves rousing up, slaves marching on! I can hear the drums!"

Then I heard, or dreamed I heard Joe Hill singing to him, deep and low. Dream or not, I heard Joe Hill singing on that winter night.

The rest was a dream, and no doubt about it. I heard drums in the dream and saw men marching. They came up to me and marched all around and past me, like a stream around a stone. I dreamed of Old Street in Knox town. I saw miners in shackles being marched past, while crowds stood and watched from in front of the Copper King and Silver Bell saloons. In a wink the miners were convicts in stripes, and Old Street had become the road past Mother Morgan's chicken farm. I was in it. Then I was heaving a dynamite bomb and breaking loose. I sailed through the air from the blast, and when I came down I was at a table in Boise's Free Public Library, with Andrew Carnegie and Grundy Johnson sitting across from me, talking, just talking. Joe Hill came up, stood behind them and began to sing. There was a howling big wind. Pages of newspapers and books sailed and whirled like flakes in a blizzard, many with big red letters on them, as on a front page of *The Appeal to Reason.* I just sat there in the storm, trying to write a poem, read Walt Whitman, listen to Joe Hill sing, and hear what Grundy Johnson and Andrew Carnegie were talking about. A pretty library girl, the image of Lily but a lot younger, came up as if to bring me a book, but it proved to be a bottle of whisky and a jigger glass. Andrew Carnegie reached over and took the whisky, then the library girl and I went over to sweet Inez, who was bridled and saddled and tied to a table. The pretty girl helped me untie the strawberry roan, then we got on her and rode out into the red hills of Montana.

On and on the dream went, real fine and interesting for the most of its parts. I could remember a pile more to tell, for there was enough in all the dream to make the start of a brand-new sect. Then the dream left me in the dark, and it was only sleep until Ben Sweet rousted me out with the others as daylight broke.

Down in the rimrock ledges of the riverbank Joe Hill had a fire going in a kind of cave. The walls shoved away the wind and nursed the heat of the fire. A gallon can of coffee was boiling, and stacks of what the hobos called lumps were on a table made of cull crossties. The lumps were meat and cheese sandwiches, as thick as your wrist, slabbed with homemade bread and lavish with butter. And there was a paper bag of raw onions.

"Ingerns keep the old scurvy down," said Joe Hill. "You'll likely catch something else, though, from the meat lumps. I bummed them at the whorehouse. A priest's housekeeper gave the cheese. The coffee I stole, and I killed a farmer for the ingerns."

"That's a pure story," said Ben Sweet. "It could be the truth that a work train is in the yards and that the cook for the gandy-dancers is a red-card rebel. This grub is his donation to you fellow workers."

Joe Hill smiled. He had looked at me first this morning with a face like the winter itself. But now his face was sunned over for a moment and a poet's eyes looked forth, as they had on that afternoon so long ago in Idaho. Then he spoke up, for all the world like William Edgar Borah.

"Gentlemen," he said, "the real giver of this breakfast is Mr. Edward H. Harriman, boss of this railroad and seventeen more. The work-train cook was only the humble agent of his generosity. Come and get it while it's hot."

We gathered around the fire and the steaming coffee with the small tomato cans that had been left clean in the jungles by the last pack of hobos. Then we went to wolfing down the sandwiches, with a scalding gulp of coffee for each powerful bite.

Ben Sweet and Joe Hill had been fed in the extra-gang's kitchen car. They left us eating while they moved out a good way from the fire and then stood talking. Now I was able to study the man I had left Montana to track down. In daylight I knew this was *him*. As I tore into the three chunks of sandwiches which were my share I looked on that giant of a man, and I remembered all I'd ever heard about him.

A preacher, he had started as a Primitive Baptist elder when he was hardly older than I was now. There was no pay for preaching in that denomination. The young elder made his living as a railroad man. In 1877 he was a freight brakeman on the Illinois Central. The strike made a labor agitator of him and brought him before Gene Debs. Black-listed on the railroads and his religion lost, young Dan'l Barton had gone west to the mines. There he came by his hellion's name.

Ramon Hurd had warned me not to believe a tenth of the stories told about Black Dan Barton. Many were on how he always packed one or more sticks of dynamite, on the hip or in a side pocket. One stick might carry the threat of short fuse and fulminating cap, others were unprimed sticks for assorted fighting uses. Ramon said that Black Dan had once stood off a mob of mine guards and scabs with a bunch of the yellow sticks in each fist. That was in the mine troubles of 1892. Ramon guessed that had started all the big stories. Then Black Dan had gone to the Southwest, and, back up here, over to the timber coast to turn logger. He was back to the mines in the strikes of '98 and '99. When one gang of strikers set a boxcar of dynamite loose on a railroad grade and switched it into a mining company's mill for a mile-high blast, Black Dan Barton was charged with inciting the men to the violence. The charge was never proved on him, but he was thrown into the bullpens with Ramon Hurd and hundreds more when the federal troops were called in by Governor Frank Steunenberg. And other charges were brought up which put Black Dan and Ramon both in the pen.

I sat in the cold, ate down the rough but mighty good breakfast, looked on Dan'l Barton, and remembered a lot more stories about him. Then I thought some about Joe Hill. Bess Clover came to mind with him. I had a good idea that Joe Hill had been at Mother Morgan's too. I wondered why Bess had not seen fit to mention his name. It *was* a wonder that she hadn't, even if Dan'l Barton had been there alone. And then it was wonder in me at myself, for all of a sudden feeling so tormented by this thing; a fool thing surely. Look up!

Dan'l Barton, excuse me, Ben Sweet, was preaching. The hobos had licked up the last crumbs, the last coffee drops had trickled down. I turned and I heard the gospel of the Industrial Workers of the World. The preacher took shape to my eyes in a frazzle-edged and faded mackinaw of black and green checks. His trees of legs stood in blue wool breeches inside faded blue overalls, cuffs turned to the tops of ten-inch logging boots with calks in the soles. A shapeless dab of a hat sat back on his head. The beaten-up face, Indian dark and lean, cheekbones high, was clean-shaved, and the Barton hair was combed back under the little old hat. Ben Sweet (I made myself call him that) stood straight by the fire, left fist on his hip and the right one up and waggling a finger for quiet.

Joe Hill stood back a way, saintly eyes big and bright under a low hat brim, face as hard and cold as an ice-coated stone.

"I beg your leave to tell you a true story," said Ben Sweet. "It is a story of twenty men and their journey. They were workers, and their journey was for freedom. I was one of the twenty men."

That was what he said. He talked on, just talking, except that every word seemed to come from deep within him, from the spirit. I saw him there, I saw Joe Hill, and the hobos, Fitty Bill so sick-faced, the fire of the cave, the ice and snow on the rocks, and I heard the river giant and her winds.

I stood away from it, looking and hearkening. No more for me the conversion, the mourners' bench, the faith, and the testimony on the faith. No revive us again for Big Jim Turner! But this was a story, one for a Black Dan to tell, a chief's recitation to his tribe. So I saw him there, speaking. I saw pictures. Twenty big, tough, determined men of the woods and the mines, such as Ben Sweet, hoboing, east-bound, an overalls brigade vowed to drive the labor skates, the politicians and the Socialist drivelers out of the One Big Union for the masses of toilers, the Industrial Workers of the World. Twenty men singing Joe Hill hymns and giving testimony on Big Bill Haywood at street meetings all along the line, then passing the hat for bread money. Twenty men of the West's work camps in Chicago, sleeping in the parks, free-lunching in the dehorn dives. Twenty hobo brigadiers shouldering and hauling their ways around the national convention hall of the I. W. W., the ways of men with ax and saw, with hammer and drill, with horses and dynamite, the ways of building dams, tunneling mountains, clearing forests, digging mines. Twenty working men in working duds making William D. Haywood general secretary of the Industrial Workers of the World, then hoboing home to agitate and organize. One Big Union. Solidarity Is Our Shield.

"Now the big job is to march and stand for Free Speech in Spokane," Ben Sweet said. "Come with us. Come with me. Come with Joe Hill."

Fitty Bill was the first to go forward. He was yet under the sickness of the night, but he went for Ben Sweet, holding out a scrawny hand, his crippled jaws working hard to speak. Wingy Ty Collins was right in the little man's tracks. Old Mike, the dyno, came after them. His shoulders were up as though they had thrown off ten years and fire was in his weathered and grizzled face. He saw big doings, mighty goings-on; and to hell with rheumatism and Sunny Cal, for he was going to take one more whirl at the old life! Bush Brown was a worried boy and his look appealed to me. Rough Rider stood back, hostile and grim, and bothering none to hide the fact.

I shook my shoulders in answer to Bush and moved forward. Revive us again. I looked at Joe Hill and remembered the piece of poetry I'd been toiling on when I met him on that hot afternoon in Idaho—

> *Sorrow and sighing shall flee*
> *Away, far away from me,*
> *While fear and loathing depart*
> *And hate fades from my heart.*

Poetry was as far from me now as then, I reckoned, and fear, loathing and hate were no farther from me. Then I looked on *his* face. We shook hands. A light came on. I was afraid, but I could not help myself. I loved this man and would follow him. He saw the light and he smiled. It would be tough to imagine an uglier smile, for the teeth that were out of it, for the scarred and beaten flesh that was in it. But the smile came out and circled me and took me in. I whispered I'd been looking for him and was glad to have found him. He said, "Likewise." Bush Brown nudged close and spoke over my shoulder, "You'd better know right now I'm a nigger." That smile looped around him, with the words, "Welcome, fellow worker. Welcome, comrade. Welcome home."

Rough Rider Al Bliss still stood back.

"Count me out," he said. "I'm an old soldier. I was with Teddy in Cuba, and I'm no more for the I. W. W. than he is. You are a bunch of undesirable citizens to me. By Jesus, I'm patriotic. There's no red card goin' to be packed around in my pants—not while I'm wearin' 'em!" His say said, he pulled out his plug and bit off a chaw.

Joe Hill cat-footed over to him and said, "Where bound?"

Rough Rider took a big spit. "No business of your'n!"

"You could find the goin' hard," Joe Hill said, sort of chopping out each word. No saint looked from his eyes. "I mean, without a red card," he said. "The road has changed, comrade."

"I'll risk it. And don't you 'comrade' me."

"You could fink on us. You'll join for Spokane."

"The hell I will!"

With the last word the gun was swinging. It was a big, blue, mean revolver. I was looking right at the two men, but my eyes had failed to catch the motion of Joe Hill's draw. There was the word, then his hand, and the gun barrel swinging. The muzzle, sight down, banged the Rough Rider's left temple, then it jerked down the side of his face. The gunsight left a spreading streak of blood. Bliss swore, slapped a hand to his jaw, then stared at the blood on his fingers.

"All right," he said, eyes steady on Joe Hill. "I'm no fink, and I don't stool. I'll ride along till I've proved it." He shook a thumb at his raked face. "This is to be settled," he said. "I'll ride along till we settle it."

"Fair enough," said Joe Hill.

He put up his gun. We faced for Spokane.

The freight train stopped on a jerkwater siding just over the county line. Special deputies were waiting for the hobo invaders. Some were caught, but most of us—numbering thirty or more by this time—scattered and escaped. I dogged the tracks of Ben Sweet. Snow was falling. We ran through it to the car sheds of a grain elevator and feed outfit. There was shelter for the time, our first time away from the others. I said, "Let me tell you about Ramon. I need to get the news of his hurt to you. It's mighty bad." He told me to go ahead and talk fast while he watched for a high sign from the head brakeman, an I. W. W.

It was in Montana (I said). Rock work on the Salmon City railroad. Ramon poured black powder into hot holes. One blew. A rock kicked him over and cracked the back of his skull. Two weeks back he was still alive but out of his head. He had married Lily Yardley. Two babies now. Ramon's partner was willing to keep on for both. All had been organized for a contract on building a logging railroad up the Little Lemolo River gorge. Then it would be a timber deal. You have got to be there and in on it (I told *him*). You know the land, the rock, the river and all like a book. You can blast through that gorge like nobody else can do it. And you are partner with Ramon in two sections of pine timber up there.

"Sorry news," he said. "I am sorry to have to hear it, me, Ben Sweet, organizer for the Industrial Workers of the World. You are speaking about one who is rigged to be railroaded back to prison. The Redburn Protective Agency has it all set." He was as bleak-faced as the weather, his voice was as mournful as the wind. "Poor Ramon. Has he stayed in the Roman church?"

I said he had and that Lily was with him there.

Ben Sweet raised a hand and pressed hard on his head. "I have work to do," he said. "The work of my life. I don't know."

A minute or two, and that was all the talk we had. I did not get to brag to him then that I'd handled twelve horses on a big machine through the summer and fall, or to confess how I'd risen to such a proud place among team hands at my age. I did not even tell of my misfortune in Boise. There was no time to speak of our folks, or of poetry, or of any of the things I'd dreamed over and over of talking to *him* about. That signal came from the head brakeman, we ran through the snowfall for an empty gondola near the tender, joining the others who had dodged the deputies. Then again we rode for Spokane to stand and march for Free Speech.

We marched in the Spokane snow, two hundred or more. The snow fell on. The white flakes glistened in slants and whirls through the glow of each street-corner lamp and in the casts of light from the saloon windows and the slave markets on Front Street. Calked boots and hobnailed brogans crunched the packed snow. Men in mackinaws, sheephides, copper-riveted overalls, Boss of the Road breeches, tin pants, pinetop shirts, balbriggan underwear and raw-edge hats formed the march.

Ben Sweet and Joe Hill were yonder in the lead. I bowed my neck and hunched my shoulders in a mean humor, back a way with Bush Brown. Wingy Ty Collins and Fitty Bill were up ahead of us. The Rough Rider was still farther up front, marching like a fighting man.

Other men in mackinaws and overalls stood on the sidewalks. Some raised jeers and catcalls. Yet more looked with some wonder and a little hope. It was still a marvel to see hobo workers joined in a fighting spirit, marching as to war up a city street, instead of hiding out and skulking around single or in small bunches, fearful of the bulls at every turn. And it was even more of a marvel that here was a union that was out in battle, not for bigger wages or such, but simply and only for the right of free speech. Full-blood American, too, from Haywood down. Socialism was foreign, the Wobblies said, and they called the craft unionists Cockney-led.

The marchers took up a song, a new one by Joe Hill which ridiculed the workers who stood by while others fought for them—

> *"Please give me your attention, I'll introduce to you*
> *A man that is a credit to 'Our Red, White and Blue';*
> *His head is made of lumber, as solid as a rock;*
> *He is a common worker and his name is Mr. Block.*
> > *And Block he thinks he may*
> > *Be President some day.*

> *"Oh, Mr. Block, you were born by mistake,*
> > *You take the cake,*
> > *You make me ache.*
> *Tie a rock to your block and then jump in the lake—*
> > *For Liberty's sake!"*

Another spoke with more solemn strength—

> *"There is power, there is power*
> *In a band of working men,*
> *When they stand hand in hand,*
> *That's a power, that's a power*
> *That must rule in every land——"*

The voice of Joe Hill rose above all the rest. This far down the line I could hear it pealing Bess Clover's hymn—

> *"Arise, ye prisoners of starvation,*
> *Arise, ye wretched of the earth——"*

I heard Joe Hill singing on this winter night, I heard him surely. Poet Joe Hill. Joe Hill, the hellion. But I was cold to him, and to Ben Sweet.

Ben Sweet stopped to preach at a corner where street meetings had been held without trouble for fifty years. His soapbox was a hardware packing case. Close by the Salvation Army was already preaching its gospel of keeping humble on the earth and hoping for pie in the sky. The I. W. W. chief was caught in the ragged edge of white light from Salvation's carbide flares. In it he appeared to be even bigger, blacker and grimmer than he was in common sight. He pulled off his hat, and the black but gray-streaked Barton mane was whipped by snow whirls and light rays. He spoke free.

Ben Sweet's voice shook through Salvation's testimony and preaching. Yet he only talked, as he had in the Umatilla jungles. He told the story of the hobo workers of the West. He pictured them making the grades of the Union Pacific, he told of them singing, "Drill, Ye Terriers, Drill." He pictured armies of workers in hundreds of camps building the Northern Pacific, the Great Northern, the Southern Pacific, and the others. He told of their moving dirt, driving tunnels, laying steel. He said these men who were kept to the skidroads and the slave markets in the towns had done the hard work and the dirty work of this land since the covered wagons. They had sunk the mine shafts, dropped the timber and raised the dams; they had sailed the ships, netted the fish, shocked the wheat, baled the hay, picked the prunes, knocked the apples and dug the clams; they had punched the cattle, wrangled the horses and herded the sheep. Then Ben Sweet made the blackest pictures of raghouse camps in alkali deserts, filthy crop camps on the ranches, starved and beaten strikers in bullpens, old men being poisoned in county hospitals, and more grief, more grief and wrongs.

Such were the conditions, he said, at which the Preamble of the Industrial Workers of the World was directed—

The working class and the employing class have nothing in common. There can be no peace so long as hunger and want are found among millions of the working people and the few, who make up the employing class, have all the good things of life.

Between these two classes a struggle must go on until the workers of the world unite as a class, take possession of the earth and the machinery of production and abolish the wage system.

The police had started in, whistles squealing, as the preamble was begun. They were clubbing him when he was halfway through.

He bore the blows. He did not strike back. He cried out the words.

The bulls beat and dragged him off the packing case. They shoved and hauled him my way. Now it was another of the times for me. I'd been sure I was a man to stand up and fight and go through anything. By God, I was a man to handle twelve horses. I'd had women. But here was the coward of the boy's life, loosening my knees and making panic pluck at me all around. I would have run, but they crowded nigh, his bloodied head shook there above the helmets of the bulls, shook as tree boughs shake in a storm, and his eyes looked agony into mine.

A club struck the shaggy head from behind. He stumbled. Two clubs prodded and beat him on. He staggered sidewise, swaying closer.

The other officers of the law of the land were going after the other free speakers. One speaker would mount the packing case and be clubbed down before he could speak a dozen words. Instantly another I. W. W. would take his place. I looked desperately for Joe Hill. Rough Rider Bliss was up there, in a yelling and fighting fury. Then it was a battle around Ben Sweet again. Joe Hill leaped from the sidewalk crowd, swinging a pickhandle. He was tripped, then struck from behind. The bulls swung around, hands off Ben Sweet, up and ready to fight. It was a prime chance for me. Yet I stood. I must testify to it. Even tonight I may awaken in a sweat of shame for standing, waiting, while Joe Hill was kicked and clubbed in the slushy gutter of the street. I stood until Bush Brown struck in and clubs hit him twice. I saw his blood start.

That much I saw in the street, in the lights, against the bodies of the watchers, the unblinking eyes and slack jaws of the faces, the craned necks and loose lips of the faces, the faces red and wet from the melting touch of snowflakes.

Then it was blast and heat and smoke in me. I don't know. I don't know what happened, or how it happened. When I came out of it I was with Ben Sweet and Bush Brown in a side alley and a man was prodding us in a hurry through a dark doorway.

He was a barrelhouse bartender off shift, no Wobbly but a sympathizer. He hid us in a cellar washroom. And before midnight the bartender had us fixed with two rebel boxcar brakies for a ride to Seattle.

"I know who Ben Sweet is," the bartender said. "I knew at first sight, even though his features have been worked out of the shape they used to own. The bulls knew him too. Spokane is too close to the old Coeur d'Alenes for his health. If he stays here he'll be killed or railroaded. Take him out—on out of Seattle, too."

Black Dan Barton was still on his feet but he had only a dim notion of what was going on. He let us start him for the train.

My left hand was a solid ache, all swelled and bleeding. The two middle fingers would not move on their bulging knuckle joints. I had dropped the two bulls with just two left hooks, the bartender told me. He spoke with the mightiest respect.

"Just one for each, only one hook per bull," the bartender said, well-nigh reverent. "You might be a hope of the white race."

The year to come was 1910.

13. Winds of the Rain Forest

NOW IT WAS MARCH ON THE HUMPTULIPS, THE DOSE-wallips, the Duckabush and other places with like names around the nation's northwest corner. The weather was powerful. For three days and more a giant blow roared down from the ice of the North Pacific and the Bering Sea. It kept columns of rain clouds running like rivers across the sky. The giant tore away branches of Douglas firs nigh on three hundred feet tall and scattered them like leaves of corn fodder. The winds slammed into trees with trunks ten feet through and tipped them over. It was death to go into the big woods while they blowed. Even in the slack of this March morning I was worried. There were monster snags that stood teetering. Others had half fallen on small trees or boughs that might break any minute. Broken branches dangled high in the standing timber. They could drop at any time. The loggers of the rain forest called them "widder makers."

Yet it all did me good, right where I lived. Through the winter there'd been only spells of *big* winds. Generally they lazed along down the wilderness coast, pushing fat clouds that would rain gently and with no hard cold. I liked the toil with trees. Never had I dreamed that I could be as stirred by trees as I'd been by horses in the day's work. But it was a thing in my nature, as it was with the old-timers in this outfit who must work in the woods or die. Black Dan Barton had it. And now I could remember the tree talk of Jack Hard with understanding. I could chant old Walt's "Song of the Broad-Axe" and "Song of the Redwood-Tree" while I toiled at timber falling with Rud Neal in the round stuff of the Chittum Creek benches.

From these men I'd learned the timber coast—the big-woods wilderness that began, south end, in the place of Walt Whitman's song—

Along the northern coast,
Just back from the rock-bound shore and the caves,
In the saline air from the sea in the Mendocino country,
With the surge for base and accompaniment low and hoarse,
With crackling blows of axes sounding musically driven by strong
*   arms,*
Riven deep by the sharp tongues of the axes, there in the redwood
*   forest dense,*
I heard the mighty tree in its death-chant chanting.

There were men in this camp who could talk with such poetry of feeling, for all their rough words, about the forests of the Oregon coast, the Columbia River, Grays Harbor, Puget Sound, Vancouver Island and the Queen Charlottes. It was Rud Neal who told me of the Queen Charlottes, the islands of big spruce. He was a Canuck, the son of an old soldier of the Crown who had known in India the story writer and poet, Rudyard Kipling. My falling partner's full name was Rudyard Kipling Neal. He felt pretty much bound to live up to it.

"But not enough to go for the soldier's life in peace, as my old man did," he said. "I could, easy, mind. If Canada was to go to war—or even the States, I reckon—it would be no use for me to try to keep out."

Rud would seldom say more than that many words at one time. But once in a while he would talk up about the northern waterways among the great forested islands, of the sealing, the whaling, the salmon fishing, and of the Indians there. "The Haidas of the Queen Charlottes," he would say, then daydream. We were a team in this. We were a pair of sootheads, black-hided, smoky hell in us, both bigger than any man had business to be, natural axmen and each able by nature with his fists. We were akin, Rud and me. He shook his black head at Walt Whitman, though. Rud liked poetry that singsonged with rhymes and measures. Naturally his favorite was Kipling, with Byron next, and then a couple of poets I hadn't run into before—Algernon Charles Swinburne and Ernest Dowson. The Dowson love poems haunted him. Rud Neal had run from love, as I had run from other fates. It was an Indian girl, with some of his family raising hell, until at last he had sailed away on a coasting schooner. In Grays Harbor he had been left ashore drunk. Sobered up, he discovered that he had joined the I.W.W. And as a Wobbly he had come out to this haywire outfit, which was able to get loggers only by giving the rebels of the woods a refuge.

For three months Rud Neal and I had faced off on springboards set up in notches of giant Douglas firs, above the root spreads. There we would swing five-pound, double-bitted, timber-falling axes and pull seven-foot saws, working as a team to fall the round stuff. We worked in quiet, mainly. For hours at a stretch we would have no more to say than the gentle rains and winds of the rain forests.

It was an overaged bunkhouse, the main building of a camp in which two outfits had gone broke. The layout had stood idle and rotting for years in the times between loggings. The shakes, rafters, walls, double-barreled bunks and calk-pitted floor planks of the bunkhouse held the smells of many winters of steam from drying clothes and of many summers of sweating bodies. Smells of tobacco smoke and snoose juice were permanent fixtures. Old scents of death were here, too. Men had been taken mortally sick in this place. Men smashed in the woods had been brought here dead, or here to die, or to wait for a while on the way to death. Men without homes, lost to their people.

But human life at its lustiest had left its spirit here, also. To-night, in the hour or two between supper and sleep, the shapes arose. The talk of the old-timers brought them forth, in the names and the stories of mighty axmen and fighters who had worked here in other days. The shapes arose around the real body and name of Black Dan Barton. The stories roared. Once Jerney Sanders, the old Michigan man, rendered a couple of stanzas of the ballad about Young Munro. Then another Lakes Stater ventured a few remarks on Paul Bunyan. Young Munro, Paul Bunyan and Black Dan Barton lived here, with other mightiest of the woods, in the rotting bunkhouse of a haywire camp.

Wire swung the coal-oil lamps and their reflectors from the cedar ridgepole. Wire lines held the mackinaws, shirts, socks and drawers nigh the roof to catch the ballooning heat from the pot-bellied heating stove. The loggers sat on benches along the bunk rows and at tables which stood in place of bunks nigh the heater. Some had candles or their own small coal-oil lamps in their bunks, to read, write and study by. Rud, Bush Brown and I were among these. So was Black Dan Barton, who had been made boss of the outfit, bull of the woods, two weeks after we arrived here by Wobbly underground from Seattle—under his own name on the timber coast. He had balked at moving over to a room in the commissary building. Usually Uncle Dan'l would spend a deal of his evening time with Bush and me, with Rud Neal sometimes coming into the circle just to listen and have company.

Tonight he was late. An hour and a half after supper Black Dan was still absent. There was casual talk that the gasoline speeder had brought Thorwald Cohen, the banker who was backing the outfit, and another man in while we were at supper. Bush had gone to the commissary and come back with some mail and the news that Black Dan was having a big confab of some kind in the back room of the office. He didn't know what it was, and he didn't care, for he had his mail. Bush read through this mail, then he called Rud and me over, looked at us with the solemnest face, and said: "Friends, I can't wait any longer on Uncle Dan'l before I tell the news. I met you and I came here a *black* young man, as I had been brought up to be. But now I know my relations in these parts are all *white* folks, and, friends, when I leave here to see 'em I'm a white young man. I'm tellin' you honest, and then I ask—are you willin', friends, to help me turn white? I'll need help. It won't be easy."

Rud said, "Yes, Yes, Bush."

But that wasn't enough for me. I still didn't have it all straight.

"Let's get this here straight, Bush," I said. "You are redheaded, freckled and pale-faced. I'm black-complected and soot-headed, like Rud. Why in the world have you stewed, fretted, fussed, argued, written letters and laid awake nights about you bein' *black* and me bein' white? Why didn't you just go ahead and *be* white, and no bother?"

"I've told you over and over," Bush said. "I was brought up black. Bein' black got to be my nature before I could walk. It's as natural for me to be black as it is to have blue eyes and red hair."

"I've considered that," I said. "Of course bein' white is *my* nature, just like my coaly hair, black eyes, swart hide and burnt-stubble beard. But I'd as soon as not quit bein' white and start bein' black, if circumstances called for it."

"No you wouldn't, Big Jim. You wouldn't seem like yourself to yourself. I won't either, not for a long time, anyhow. And I won't stick to it for sure until I see how my relations make out at it."

"I still don't see it straight," I said.

"Well, doggone, and you couldn't unless you'd had it pounded and licked, snapped and snarled, preached and teached into you all your days that you were white. That's how I was made black, by hurt and fear. You can't take that off like you do your shoes."

"I reckon not, Bush," I admitted. "Well, let's not argue. Only, I do want to say again it beats hell out of me why you are goin' to make this change, if it's such trouble inside you—and it all just to be a cowboy. Why in the world should anybody, black or white, want to be a cowboy? It's a life only a notch above herdin' sheep."

"There's no argument on that," Bush said stubbornly. "I've always dreamed of bein' a cowboy, I hoboed West to be a cowboy, a man has got to be white to be any kind of a cowboy, so I'm turnin' myself from black into white to be a cowboy—and I don't give a damn how I suffer!"

Rud asked him if he minded telling us about the letter that had determined him finally, and Bush said we could read it. So we did, and it was so interesting I'll tell what I can remember from it. The letter bid Bush welcome and asked him to come and pay a visit. Then it told a little story about a wagon train of pioneers called the Simmons party. They had come out to Oregon Territory in 1846, but were barred from it because of a Negro family in the train. The white families were loyal to their black neighbors, and so all had wagoned north into Hudson's Bay Company territory, to become the first party of settlers in what was today Washington state. The Negro family's name was Bush. The father and mother were light-complected, and their nine children were yet lighter. All were greatly loved and respected, and nobody among the settlers raised any word against their marrying all around. The letter said that it appeared that Bush Brown's Indiana grandpa, William Bush, was a brother of George Bush, the loved and respected head of the Negro family in the Simmons party. The letter told Bush kindly that out here he must learn to be a white young man. I remember the last words. "In Rome do as the Romans do," it said.

He took the letter back and studied it; dreaming, I knew, of the cowboy's life he hoped to win. Rud Neal sat on the bench there, elbows on knees, big swarthy hands hooked around a briar pipe— which he'd suck on now and again; musing, dreaming in smoke. I could have sat there by him, hunkered and dreaming too, rolling, licking and dragging on a cig or ruminating with a chaw, and made it fine company. Through the storm I'd been scrawling around at an ode that was patterned on Byron and Kipling mixed, mainly to please my falling partner, the overgrown, black-knot son of a soldier of the Crown. I wanted to set around with him and mull the ode now. But it was uneasy hell in me. I could smell trouble concerning Uncle Dan'l. I reached for my mackinaw and hat, said, "Breath uh air," and moseyed down past the bellying stove, under the steaming duds, through lamplight, smoke, chesty talk, man smells, ghost smells, all rough, mean and some foul, yet good to me. It was a place of work, and work was good. It was a place of peace, and peace was good. I feared it was ending. I expected hell.

"The Old Nick again," I said, going out of the bunkhouse and into the rain-forest night. "He'll be around, sayin', 'Pay me.' "

There was something to it, for Jack Hard was in camp.

He was making a play. God damn him, I knew it the second I spied through the commissary window and saw him going to it, while the others stood back with eyes bugging at him, mouths open, ears jackassing. Even Uncle Dan'l appeared bemused. But what struck me was the light on the face of the banker, Thorwald Cohen, of Grays Harbor. I'd never before seen him out here in the outfit that was kept going by his bank's money but that he appeared ready to drop dead from despair. But now Jack Hard had hold of him. A big gamble was rolling, I knew, and the banker was on it. His light was hope.

I stood back on the plank porch of the commissary, away from the ragged blur of lamplight that seeped from the small window into the blackness. There was a heavy pole railing. I leaned against it, bit off a chaw, hauled my hat brim down against the drizzly wind surges, folded arms and spied on Jack Hard's play.

It was nothing to me, I told myself. Nobody in there was more to me than a rabbit, I said, excepting Uncle Dan'l. He was a warm soul to me, about me, but for his faith.

It was Black Dan there who had sent the word to Jack Hard of our whereabouts, I surmised, for I had sent none. He'd come, here he was, so it was likely that the Grundy Johnson deal had gone through to the point of a move from Montana to Idaho and the pine woods of the Lemolos, and that Black Dan Barton was more needed than ever on the land deal and on the rock work for the logging railroad. I could feel little hope about Ramon. If well, he'd have come for his old friend. But why had anybody needed to come here for my uncle? Probably he'd asked it on account of the Norblads.

There they were, standing back, old Cap'n Andy and his tall, golden-haired daughter, Anna, watching the fool-looking play of Jack Hard's. For years Andrew Norblad had been owner and captain of a timber-coast steam schooner. Now Norblad's last nickel was in this layout where two other operators had failed, and which was in deep mortgage to the Tidewater State Bank, Thorwald Cohen, President. Over half of the timber on the Chittum Creek benches was over-aged, in dead snags or butt-rotted. They were giant trees. There were ranges of snags that the winds of the rain forest had blown down. The simple job of getting out the good timber and skidding it through that dead and dying forest was one for the Paul Bunyan and Blue Ox that Jerney Sanders and the other Lake Staters talked about.

"Paul would've fed his ox and him to the brim on ingerns and beans, then they'd've belched skid trails through that rot," Jerney said. "But us, *we* got to try to do it with weakly dynamite. I allow we're licked."

That was the mood of everybody in the rotting old camp about the prospects. There was prime timber and a slope for good logging above the creekside. Up there a fire had killed all the old stuff around a hundred and fifty years ago, after starting along the high side of the benches. The new growth was now as big as sawtimber needed to be, and it was alive, sound, clean all over the slopes. But the benches had to be logged, plowed through first.

We all knew the picture by this time. And I knew it was on the maps and in the ledgers that were spread around on the tables and the high desks of the commissary office. For some reason, Jack Hard had been given a look-in. And now the hellion was highrolling.

There stood Black Dan Barton, legs spraddled, shoulders in a dark mackinaw jutting like fir boughs, the overhead lamplight bringing out the gray in his mane, his eyes alive to each move by Jack Hard.

Thorwald Cohen was as big as Dan'l Barton and as Swede-looking as the Norblads. But he appeared as a banker should, too, with his hair oiled, mustache trimmed, middle bulging, wing collar on his neck and a huge gold watch chain across his vest.

Cap'n Andy was a little old man with a red, weathered face, white hair, and a hatchet of white chin whiskers. His blue eyes were as bright and interested-looking as a baby's while they followed Jack Hard's play. He was a fine old man, a good soul. His Anna reminded me some of Lily Hurd, but she was taller and even blonder, and cold-seeming, while Lily was so warmhearted. Anna was said to be thirty—young enough for the old men, anyhow, to get fevered about. But it was told that none ever had.

"Figurehead," said Rud Neal once. "Really. She might have been the model for the one on a schooner named the *Hulda*. You'll see."

But Anna Norblad had no cold eye for business now. She was paying little attention to Jack Hard's moves. Her eyes were on his face. I thought, what's he up to, how'd he come to be like this here?

The son of the Navarres of Michigan went on with his queer doings. He was a wonder to watch, truly—just as he'd been when banking a poker game, or handling twelve horses, or handling me as a tool in his great gamble on the Salmon City line. The burly bastard. Damn him, there he was, low-slung, stocky-shouldered and stud-necked, black hair in little piles and tumbles of curls, a couple batting around over eyes that could be blue steel, blue lightning, blue smoke, but always making you think there could be no bluer eyes on the face of the earth. There was his lean, tough, blocky face, always with little muscles playing through it, and with that hook of a smile that would sucker you in even while you hated yourself as a fool for letting it. The devil, oh, the devil!

There he was, making fools out of even a bank president. Jack Hard had sticks of stovewood, a pile of it in scatters on the floor within the circle of watchers. There were single sticks and sticks in tangles and stacks. A number of short chunks seemed to be nailed or somehow stuck to the floor. For, when Jack Hard stood back and went to pulling a stick through the litter and chunks, these last would hold fast. He pulled the stick with a long cord, while he stopped, keeping the cord close to the floor. The end of the stick would hang fast on the chunks, and Jack had a time pulling it through the loose stick piles. Then he rigged back for another pull. But this time he threw the cord over a crossbeam, a pole, just overhead, where the loose boards of the ceiling were separated. He pulled the stick through the mess again. Now the slanting cord made a lifting pull on the stick of stovewood that up-swung and sledded it over chunks and piles when it was pulled to them.

That was all. It appeared idiotic in my sight, but I was not such a big fool myself as to think it really was. I was full of wonder and curiosity on the business, but nobody was going to make it mine. I had an ode to mull, and that was what I was going to turn in and do until slumber's chains had bound me.

And I did, after cat-footing off the porch and slogging back through the muddy camp yard to the bunkhouse. The lamps were out, the heater fire failing. I groped to my bunk and was soon in the blankets. And then I mulled her, seeing in my shut eyes an image of the words and lines—

AN ODE TO TOIL
By James Birney Turner

O Toil! My cold and bitter wife,
  Who feeds me stones at day's dark end,
And gives me shackles, ills and strife,
  Without one hope or joy to lend:
I have you on our marriage bed,
  And so I'll have you till I'm dead.

With mouth of iron and breast of thorn,
  Embrace of sinew, sweat and grime,
You serve the urge of the unborn
  And make me too a slave of time.
Your whip by day and chain by night—
  My one redemption, lone delight.

That was as far as I'd gone. The more I mused the lines the more I saw their holes and patches. I figured on ten more verses. It was surely slow, mean work, and dull, too, for I could hardly keep awake on it. Rud had tried to tell me that my trouble was the "grief" I'd cooked into the ode. Rud argued that actually I liked toil, as anybody could tell, seeing me fall timber. I said this was outside the matter. What I was seeking in the ode was the form and spirit of a mood, of despair, swamp colors, and the like, and then a way to be true to the mood. He only said, "Well, go to it," and quit arguing. Uncle Dan'l said the tortured lines showed that deep in me it was a rebellion against shackling myself to the old-time rhymes and singsongs, after imbuing my soul with Walt Whitman's freeborn chants. Well, I didn't know. I only knew I was mightily discouraged.

Uncle Dan'l came in just as I gave up the fight against sleep and was drowsing off. As he would do every so often, he stopped by and stooped over to take me by the shoulders, kiss my face, and whisper, "Good night, dear son." Tonight it surely was comforting.

It rained on in the morning, but softly now, spring breathing. The young bloods rose fiery and snuffy with the first dingdonging of the gut-hammer. This was before daybreak. Rud and Bush and I washed, toweled, combed and gabbed around together as we commonly did. Then the three of us horsed out for the cookhouse, bragging on the weather as we tramped, mauling and chugging and yanking each other along just for the hell of it. I'd hit this rough-housing pretty hard with Rud, for he was bigger and tougher than Bush. We'd had a set of pillow gloves during the last six weeks and I'd never known such a real good time out of anything in games as I'd get from putting them on with Rud. He could box, jabbing and crossing me all over the place; but when I landed that left hook he was stopped, pillow mit or not. It was sure good, the feel of fist driving into a strong, moving, quick-muscled body; with ribs springing or guts giving from the throw and thud of a fist; the force of the drive and its back-kick felt all through arm, shoulder, body, leg, foot by me. I likewise relished the blows I took; the riding back with a punch, the feel of power in holding up to it; the hammer of bodies coming into a hard clinch, tug and shove, close jolting; nigh glitter of eyes, pant and snarl, teeth and tongue of a face at mine, furiously panting; butting of heads, the wild urge to bite.

This morning was no time for the gloves, but we chugged and hauled considerably with spring's touch pricking us. In a tussle I heard, sharp and tough—

"Big Jim! Yay-o! Front 'n' center!"

I wheeled to the voice, and there was Jack Hard, swinging off the commissary porch. Before I thought of it, I was going for him, calling his name, and then, "How's Ramon?"

We pulled up at the open shed between the commissary and the cookhouse, and hooked hands. Rud and Bush kept their distance, waiting. There were others, straggling in the drizzly dawn light for the cookhouse. I noticed Uncle Dan'l.

"Ramon's alive and kicking," Jack Hard said. "But he has a long way to go. The outfit's in Idaho, up the Little Lemolo now. Big Jim, why didn't I hear from you?"

The first minute, and here he was, cornering me, throwing out that power of his and looping me to him. As it pulled I fought it by instinct, like a colt suddenly caught in barbwire. Then I got a grip on what I'd thought to tell him.

"You heard from Black Dan himself, didn't you?" I said.

"Of course. How else could I have found him—and you? But you were both in Spokane, and in Seattle, and you sent no word from there. Nor from here. Was that shooting square on our deal, Big Jim?"

It was not. I had to look away from his face to my feet in the mud, then aside to the fine, soft rain, to the ramshackle old bunkhouse, the leafless dripping bush of the old cutovers, the mountains high yonder, green-piled with forest. As if to answer my look, the winds surged, the rain-forest winds from the north, from Rud Neal's country, the Queen Charlottes.

"Come on, Big Jim. What do you say?"

For a minute I looked at him, thinking to tell him of what had befallen me that night in Boise as I came back in the snow from Mother Morgan's. But there would be no pity from Jack Hard on it, there would be only some disgust with me for letting myself be slugged and for talking excuses now.

The dawn winds of the rain forest heaved harder on me and their force helped me to make up my mind. I took a breath that went to my bowels; a breath of timber smells and the northern ocean. I looked around to see Bush Brown and Rud Neal away back—and now Black Dan Barton, great and dark, was coming. He would hear what I said. Well, I'd say it for anybody to hear—

"Mr. Navarre, sir," I said, as to one at Sunday meeting, "I'm pleased to see you here and to have your good news on Ramon Hurd. I wish you well in your business, I surely do. On this I claim we are even, and so it's a good time to quit." His eyes hammered at me, but I stood up. Somehow I recollected William Edgar Borah's manner of speaking, and I took it on. "Mr. Navarre, sir," I said, "I have no excuses to make to you or any other man, by the Lord Harry. I want only to say to you, sir, that I like this country, I've learned to be a timber faller in it, I've got me the best partner a faller might hope for; and when spring comes on apace, sir, I'm goin' north with my partner to do some hand loggin' in the big spruce of the Queen Charlottes." There I stopped, glowered into the hot blue of his eyes, then said, lowdown, "To

hell with you, sir—muck you, Buckley, and your Christian camps!"
Then I swung to face Uncle Dan'l and to say to him more than
loud enough for Rud to hear, "North for me! With Rud Neal.
What do *you* say to that?"

"Why, all right," he said. "All right, son." His beaten face smiled.

I let loose a wave of my left paw at Jack Hard, then tramped
past Black Dan and up to Rud Neal. I gave him one hell of a
jolt in the ribs with an elbow, he passed part of it on to Bush,
and then we all went in to breakfast.

14. Notes for a Long Poem

ONCE UPON A TIME THERE WAS A FREE MAN. HIS name was James Birney Turner and people called him Big Jim. From the spring of 1910, when he was age eighteen, to the fall of 1911 he was as free as man born of woman may be. In that time he voyaged on the waterways that flood inland from the North Pacific, he toiled on tugboats, he rafted logs, he felled trees on steep shores, he screw-jacked timber down to tidewater, he took love and gave love, he had a friend, he roved free coastwise and southerly to Walt Whitman's redwood trees, he trailed back northward by land into the reach upon reach of the virgin forests of the Willamette, and he came to the Columbia, to books again, to an old love and freedom's end. Enough, more than enough for a book of poems, a Walt Whitman book. No sweetness, no light, not much of dreams. These poems, or this long poem, will tell of hard labor and tough traveling. The poem will sing rough and harsh and profane of terror, dread, guilt, despair, sickness, flesh and devil. The poem will not sing high-flown of man triumphant. The poem will sing Freedom, and only man as the instrument of Freedom. The first line is written here, and for many a day there will be no other—"Once upon a time there was a free man."

This is how we worked, Rud and me. It might be a Douglas fir or a Sitka spruce six foot through, more or less. I chopped from the left, Rud from the right. The first thing on a big stick was to notch for the springboards, our working foot rests. Sometimes we were up ten feet before setting in above the pitch pockets and the spread of the trunk to the roots. Then each planted his calk-booted feet far apart, sprung his knees, bowed his back, and swung from the hips with the ax. Shunk-shink! Shunk-shink! Shunk-shink! Rud led, I followed. On then, swing and swing, the thudding clang of the axes a powerful beat, boot-size bark chips flying; then a richer ring in the ax beats, with soft, white sapwood chips fist-big a-sailing; and then the cut into the true tree, the gold and red heartwood—if it was a king fir. At summer's end on the island of spruce I could have notched a big tree blindfolded. Any tree it was a deep notch to guide the fall. Then we set the springboards to the other side of the tree and began to saw timber. The prime thing was timing for the sawing team. Rud Neal and I were one man in the pull and ride of hands on the saw handles, in the turns of teeth and rakers from one position to another in the kerf, in the feel of just when to stop and slush coal oil in at binding pitch, in the time to wedge against the bind, in the sense of the tree's death shudder before crackling groan and fall notchward—the signal to yell, "Timber-r-r!" and jump from the springboards for shelter from limbs broken and flying.

Well nigh a year of it with Rud Neal, in one spot and another of the big-timber coast. I might have kept it up with him for fifty more years, as many pairs of friends have done. But then it was love for him, love of a girl, return of his lost love, a kid coming, and Rud turned marrying man. I stood up with them, gave them a blanket, kissed them both, and shipped down for Vancouver on a twenty-section raft of spruce logs. So long, friends, swart Rud Neal and red girl, lovely Haida of the Queen Charlottes.

Uncle Dan'l told me, a-walking one night. Grandma and Grandpa Barton were brought together as young folks because they were both for unlimited freedom of the Negro. Her pa and his pa were neighboring slaveowners in Virginia. Grandma had been brought up by a black woman who had come to be all to her that a mother could be to anybody. When Martha King and Whitfield Barton were wed they set forth to agitate for freedom of the slaves. Finally they were disowned, and they emigrated to the Missouri country, then to southern Iowa. Before the great war they were able to buy Mrs. Julia Bloodgood, the black woman who was as a mother to grandma. It hadn't worked out too well. Mrs. Bloodgood had grown so strict in her religion that she made it a misery to everybody in the family. Uncle Dan'l and the other children, even my shy, scared mother, left home as soon as they were able, to escape Mrs. Bloodgood's old Jealous Jehovah brand of piety. I guessed that was why Grandma Barton had never told me about Mrs. Bloodgood, who was dead and gone before I could remember anything.

When Rud Neal went in with me to Grays Harbor on a Sunday to see Bush Brown make his start at changing his life from that of a black young man into a white young man, I told them both about Mrs. Julia Bloodgood, my pious and cantankerous old black great-grandma.

"You won't have any trouble, Bush," I said. "Grandma Bloodgood really was black, but she came to Iowa to live as a mother-in-law to a white family, and she went right to work to be as a white mother-in-law would be, and she did it. What she did you can do."

But Bush Brown only looked scared and worried. He had hardly a hope that he could make it in turning white, and only his crazy want to be a cowboy held him up and drove him. We promised to write to him, and he said he would to us. Actually deathly pale around his freckles and under his red hair, the poor black boy shook our hands, gulped and shivered, then turned and climbed the steps of a railroad passenger car as though he was mounting a gallows. But he climbed them.

Timber town saloon night. Paddy's Day was a Thursday. Some camps shut down for the rest of the week. Men by the hundreds piled into Grays Harbor from the timber, the lumber and shingle mills, and the ships on Saturday. In the Saginaw Saloon four aproned bartenders rushed and sweated between spigots, bar, backbar bottles and till. Big Al, who'd made "square" the word for the Saginaw all through the woods, cashed check after check, and banked gold coin for many of the loggers. By midnight Saturday his safe, I heard, held more than twenty thousand dollars. By that time men, loggers mainly, were six deep before the bar. Bottles and glasses slid without end through splashes of beer and furrows of foam. The bartenders picked up wet dollars and half dollars and the loggers picked up wet quarters and dimes of change. Hour by hour the smoke had thickened inside as the fog had outside. Hour by hour the vast barroom scene got a richer glow. The splattered and foamy top of the bar seemed fair to see. The faces of the drinkers in the back-bar mirror grew bright and became the faces of handsome and intelligent men. The rumble of talk and clink of glasses swelled into music, the shouted jokes and bawls of laughter got to be killingly enjoyable, the wildest and roughest kind of men smiled around and loved each other and everybody. Every few minutes you'd hear a double-eagle smacked on the bar, then a voice booming something like this—

"Set up the whisky! All you timber beasts drink on a Michigan man!"

Midnight, and yet well enough for the old stiffs. But for Rud Neal and me, the old evil crawling hot within us, helling out on Heron Street, going for the girls.

All "dehorn" to Black Dan Barton and the other Wobblies. They were mates with the members of the Jehovah's Pilots sect on this proposition. Dance-hall, saloon and gambling hells stood between Men and Religion, and between Men and the Revolution.

Jack Hard and Anna Norblad. He was three weeks in camp. Black Dan had written him, at my telling, about the business that held him to the Norblad outfit. It was to help Cap'n Andy win through on the Chittum Creek spread, and then go on keeping his camp as a kind of Wobbly harbor. Of course Uncle Dan'l didn't write the reason, but he did write at length about the circumstances, then said he was obligated to work out ways of overcoming them. With winter still deep in the Idaho mountains, Jack Hard had come on the scent of a deal to the Humptulips country. The first play he sighted for himself was through the sect that Anna Norblad had joined. It had been started in Grays Harbor as a seamen's misson named Jehovah's Pilots. Now numbers of Scandinavians of all trades belonged. Anna played the organ and sang old-country hymns, and she preached a little. On the second Sunday Jack Hard was here, Anna appeared before the Jehovah's Pilots' congregation in a white robe and with her hair fixed somewhat as a golden crown above her cold, white brow. She preached that an angel had appeared unto her and commanded her to dress thus and to stand forth to the congregation as a prophetess. The angel had anointed her head with oil, she said, and named her "Pastor Joanna." That was how she printed it, but the Swedes called her "Yo-*hahn*na." Jack Hard told me he'd figured on that and said he also had something about Joan of Arc in his mind. He even tried to talk me into turning into a Jehovah's Pilots preacher, promising me riches, the bastard.

The faith of John Navarre, Jack Hard. He despised man as a species on the earth; for man had done nothing to improve the earth itself but had raped its soil and polluted its waters all over. A couple of times he talked to me as himself, not Jack Hard, but John Joseph Navarre. Then he said that the truest thing ever written on mankind was by a preacher named Swift, who called the species a pestilential race of little odious vermin. "I'd say 'murderous vermin,'" said John Navarre. "The man who preaches love in human life gets crucified for it, always. Walt Whitman lived love and he sang love and preached, 'Love one another, love enemy, love neighbor.' He labored as a saint of love through years of war. And in a way he was crucified for it.

"I have faith in and love for one family of life on the earth," said John Navarre. "This is the tree. Not the great, imposing, aged, decaying, dying tree, but the tree in fresh, young growth. I'll tell you of the Navarre place in Michigan, lived on by Navarres and Lennanes mixed since 1850. It was in the path of the big clearing made by the shanty boys. There was a white-pine forest on three thousand acres. The trees were kept from the ax. Then, in the summer of '71—the summer of the Chicago and Peshtigo fires— fire hit the Navarre forest, and left it a black land of dead trees. Land speculators brought settlers into the cutovers all around us. The fools fired the land to clear it, year after year. New growth on the Navarre burn didn't have a chance. I grew up hating the black desert of snags around our home, and despising the men whose clearing and pasture fires killed young trees year after year. I ran off and did a hitch with the Marines. Then I saw this country, a tree country, a rain forest, land too rough and stumps too big for the worst idiot of a settler to tackle, climate too wet for bad

fires. Here's where I set in, here's where I get into the timber for
good. My business will be to log off the old trees in the way of a
harvest and grow new crops of trees on the tree land. And now you
know me, Big Jim—half tree and half man, with the tree my good
half and the man half no worse than the run of its species."

I've bunched it on him, but it's about how he talked.

High-lead logging. It was an invention that meant as much in the
big timber as the reaper did in the wheat. There was that senile
stand of fir a-breaking good Cap'n Andy Norblad, as it had broken
other men. His regular donkey engines had main-line cables strung
along the ground; and when they hauled, it was on a stump-level
pull. Snipe the ends of the big butts, and still they would hang up
on stump, snag or blowdowns. It took a lot of men for chasers on
a skidding side to keep a ground-lead donkey roading or yarding.
And still they'd hang, rigging would break and the output would
fall.

Jack Hard had mulled that problem ever since his service in the
Marines had brought him to the big-timber coast. When he heard
from Black Dan Barton the answer was waiting in his head. He
opened up and gave it out free to the Norblads—but he'd come
to an understanding with Thorwald Cohen before their coming to
camp. Then it needed only the mechanical and logging and dyna-
miting savvy of Black Dan Barton to set the invention in motion.

He did it on a Saturday at the end of March. It was a sunny
morning. Black Dan, Jack Hard, the Norblads, and Banker Thorwald Cohen, too, were out at daybreak, to take advantage of all
the time possible before the usual midmorning rise of wind.

Black Dan Barton harnessed himself in gear like that of a line-
man, only it was heavier, and the climbing irons on his boots were
long enough to drive through thick bark into tough wood. He went
to a big fir by the new railroad landing, and he climbed. A stout
rope circled the tree from the two sides of his big belt. At his back
light lines were tied, to swing a one-man crosscut saw and a falling
ax, and a roll of cord to unreel for a passline at the top. It was a
new rig for the timber, but Black Dan had already worked out its
use. He climbed the eighty feet to the first boughs. He sawed them
off, then climbed, chopped and limbed upward sixty more feet.

Then some forty feet more of the trunk tapered up into heavy bush and crown. This had to be topped. Black Dan's way was to saw and chop a shelf around the tree, then to bring sticks of giant powder up by passline and secure them in the shelf. He primed one with a detonator, lit a fifteen-minute fuse, and swung down the trimmed tree, using the strength of a bear on spurs and rope.

The top blew free, cut clean by the blast. A mighty mast remained. Then an old sailor and rigger took over the job of guying the mast and mounting blocks and cables at its top, after Black Dan Barton had made one more climb and secured a light block and line for a bosun's chair. Gideon Putonen, the sailor, then had only a safe and simple job to do.

He did it, and the donkey engine brought in a log. It came just as Jack Hard had planned it and as Dan'l Barton had worked it out in the machine shop and in the woods. The main line ran from its spool in blocks or pulleys up the tree, through a high head-block, then down on a slant to the felled timber. On the haul its pull lifted the logs over stumps and windfalls, where the ground pull had rooted logs into them.

It was as simple as all that—just as Jack Hard had demonstrated in the commissary on his first night in camp, using sticks of stovewood and a rope slung over a ceiling pole.

"This system should double board-foot log production per man," was what Banker Thorwald Cohen said about it. "You win, Cap'n Andy."

A year later the Jehovah's Pilots had a temple booming in Portland. Its tracts all told of miracles of faith and vision among loggers, sailormen and fishermen. One tract told this story, which I put in with my packet of notes—

It came to pass that the Holy Ghost visited our revered Pastor Joanna and gave her to see in a Vision the Convert Gideon Putonen, high on a Large Tree that had been pruned of its Branches and its Crown severed, and thereupon he was Reeling Logs to the tree by Power of hand and rope. The Vision being interpreted meant to Our Pastor that God wouldst have her contrive and put into being that Mortal Invention which men have come to call high-lead logging. The mortal Work was done by Bro. Gideon Putonen

*and his woodsmen Members of the Mother Mission of Jehovah's
Pilots. However, as Pastor Joanna hath said, "The true Creator of
high-lead logging, as of all things, is Jesus God and the Holy Ghost,
with Jehovah's sanction." And so when Our Pastor first beheld the
high-lead logging operation she Involuntarily Ejaculated, "What
hath God Wrought!" Selah.*

And that was how much good poor Uncle Dan'l's toil and trouble
did for the Industrial Workers of the World and the Revolution.
In time Jehovah's Pilots held all the good jobs in the Norblad outfit. I'd expected some outcome of the kind. Again it was Jack Hard,
the hellion.

North with Homer. I love and praise Dan'l Barton for making
no try at binding me to his faith. He was for the poetry in me and
for all that might serve to bring it forth. So he had been with Bush
Brown, encouraging him to seek out his western white folks who
had descended from the pioneer black people. Uncle Dan'l wished
me well on my journey with Rud Neal to the Queen Charlottes.
He'd sent to Seattle for a package of books to be taken along. One
was by the dreamer, Thoreau, on his days and nights by Walden
pond. But the one I took to my heart at first sight was Homer's
Odyssey as rendered in English by A. Lang, M.A., Hon. LL.D.
I poked into this volume first as the old steam schooner, *Hulda,*
rode out over the Grays Harbor bar and into mighty ocean. I read
it up around Cape Flattery, down Juan de Fuca Strait, and I nosed
into little other reading until the stinking and creaking old wallower
of a *Hulda* rolled to a Vancouver dock and brought me on a
foreign shore.

I'll tell you that I liked A. Lang, M.A., Hon. LL.D.'s own sonnet as well as anything in the *Odyssey* itself. I learned that sonnet
by heart, as I had done with many other sonnets, starting on
Shelley's ever singing "Ozymandias," with which I'd think and say
over, " 'The lone and level sands stretch far away'—'boundless and
bare,' 'the lone and level sands'—'far away'—'boundless and
bare'—"; roving back and forth, around and through this fine, fair
shape among the works of men.

And so I lived this voyage with a sonnet new to me—

As one that for a weary space has lain
  Lulled by the song of Circe and her wine
  In gardens near the pale of Proserpine,
Where that Aegean isle forgets the main,
And only the low lutes of love complain,
  And only shadows of wan lovers pine,
  As such an one were glad to know the brine
Salt on his lips, and the large air again,
So gladly, from the songs of modern speech
  Men turn, and see the stars, and feel the free
    Shrill wind beyond the close of heavy flowers
    And through the music of the languid hours,
  They hear like ocean on a western beach
    The surge and thunder of the Odyssey.

This I heard, reading, "This song it was the famous minstrel sang," and the golden rest, bells clanging from the days of old. I felt the free shrill winds.

As the *Hulda* hobbled and groaned through the blue, white-foaming swells, passing one forest-piled headland after another, I truly rejoiced. Old life was lost behind. Its people were left forever, I vowed. Vacant waters between us, vacant waters widening. I had a friend today and for the life of tomorrow. I had Homer to read, a sonnet new to me to dream on, while sailing for a land where struggle and terror and guilt might be forgotten. I had a packet of poetry scraps of mine own; good, fair enough for a young man of eighteen, said Rud Neal; and I also packed notes for more poetry or fragments thereof.

The *Hulda* heaved and snorted on, around Cape Flattery and for Vancouver Island. So I went free into the northern mists.

15. Little Pretty and the Seven Bulls

THE SAD OCTOBER DAYS HAD COME TO THE TIMBER coast and its lumber rivers. This was a morning of gray drizzle and no wind. I toiled through it comfortably enough on the green-chain of the Copenhagen sawmill, shielded by a shed roof. Most days there was no harder work to be found in Portland, a city of hard work that stood amid valleys of hard work. Seven of us were strung along two sides of a waist-high platform a dozen feet wide and a hundred long, on which conveyor chains crawled with fresh, green lumber from the old sawmill. There were four stations on one side, three on the other, with a row of two-wheeled trucks along each station. Every truck was for a particular size and grade of green lumber. A chainman's job was to watch the crawl of lumber for grade marks and sizes, then pull off and load the items that belonged in his station. No work could have been simpler. So I liked it, for it left me free to muse and dream. No work was heavier. This bothered me none. Soon I'd be twenty. I was a bull. We were seven. You had to be a bull to hold 'er down anywhere on the Copenhagen green-chain.

The weather drizzled gently on through the morning—"Oregon mist," the old Portland Webfooters called it. I liked it fine. It was a prime morning. They were small logs today, out there in the river booms; and small logs riding up the slip, the jack-ladder, in grip of creeping bullchain to log deck and bandsaw headrig. This meant a smaller cut than common for the day, and easy going for the men with weak heads and strong backs who took care of the cut on green-chain and timber chute. So I jogged along with my share of the slugs of rough-green; sorting and hauling; bunching pieces and swinging each bunch into a slide through my mulehide mittens and over thighs aproned with belting leather, to its proper truck.

Like that, over and over; taking it as it came with no rush or worry; musing on why and how I had returned to my native shore; dreaming of the books.

I was free. A free man still.

The quitting whistle blew through the gentle gray weather; the cool, soft air, the sweet rain; so fine and good for the life of hard work with trees and lumber in the Oregon outdoors.

We headed with our lunch buckets for the fire room of the mill's power plant. Sawdust was the fuel, fed in from towering bins the size of railroad water tanks. It was clean heat, a good-smelling place. I liked the noon hour here, not only because of the pleasure of stuffing a hungry gut, but for the company, the talk, the arguments, the stories; all serving to pull me out of myself and back into the world of men. An hour of it was enough. But it was a good change.

One of the chainmen, one English-born and with the name of Cecil Hurst, was openly a member of the Industrial Workers of the World. Today he brought along a new copy of the weekly paper, *Direct Action*. Cecil passed it around. Each bull gave it a polite look, a wise nod or two, then passed the paper to the next man. I was about to do the same when the face of a girl in a picture on the front page reached out and fairly took hold of my eyes. It was a little picture above a poem. The poem was called "Rebel Girl." It was by Elizabeth Clover.

I looked in her face and read her true name again and again, and between my looks her printed poem—

REBEL GIRL
By Elizabeth Clover

I am a rebel for reason:
I would hear young mothers singing
As only the secure and hopeful sing.

I would see their cupboards full
Of everything,
And the young fathers bringing
More, more, more.

I am a rebel from hearing
The bitter cry of the children
And the young mothers' crying;
From seeing the young fathers,
The strong, the good young men,
Seeing them despair
Over their dying.

The lines lost me from the present. The paper was taken from my hand and voices sounded, but for me the barrier I'd built against the old life was broken and I was far through it, backwashed.

My memory saw her stand and sing, a pale, scrawny kid in faded dress and wrinkled stockings in Aunt Sue's front room, a kid escaped from that trap of a homestead place in the sagebrush hills —singing "Arise, ye prisoners of starvation," to the pleasure of Wiley Hurd, to the disgust of Aunt Sue and to my wonder. As plain as life I could see the back of her head again as it had been on the snowy day Uncle Gabe drove us on a bobsled through the hills; Bess up on the spring seat, me standing behind her, seeing her ears, neck, and silks of hair so close; with my first faint scent and sight of girl touching on woman. Then the day, the moment of holding her to me in Mother Morgan's place. What I'd kept of that was a note in mind, "Poetry is made of moments." Sweetness and wonder, delight and glory. Then the sight of her paleness, and the feel of her thinness in my arms and to my hands. Sorrow, sorrow to my heart, hold me close to thee, as the tears start. Tears from the depths of. Deep as love, deep as first love and wild with all regret, Oh, God damn, damn, damn. Back now where I started from. Ocean, mountains, forests, foreign land—all a barrier blown away as the mists are blown.

It was a blast. It knocked the wits out of me. I caught myself saying aloud, "I love her. I love her." Then—

"V'at the hal you talkin', Big Yim? You mean you love Emma Goldman?"

I swung the heel of my hand up against the side of my head and batted out the haze. The chainmen, and four or five others too, were gaping at me. It was Shot Gunderson, the boss of the green-chain, who had spoken.

"No, Shot," I said, trying to sound offhand-like. "Not Emma. The girl who wrote the poem there—Elizabeth Clover. We were kids together in Idaho, and I've known her since."

"Oh," Shot grunted. He peered at the Wobbly paper again. "Bay Yeesus," he said. "Vell, v'at you know! V'y, the little pretty! Look at her har, noo! Big Yim's girl—v'y, the little pretty!"

All hands shoved around and craned over to look again. The big pictures and headlines on the front page were of Emma Goldman, and of Mother Morgan and Joe Hill, with a story on how they were all coming to Portland to fight for free speech in a week of meetings at Millwrights Hall. The Wobblies, anarchists and Socialists were joining for the fight. Another part of the page had a headline that read, "COL. CHARLES ERSKINE SCOTT WOOD LENDS SUPPORT." I knew of him as an old Indian fighter and a famous Socialist poet. What he said in the story was—

"We have free speech in Portland, and free speech is here to stay."

Bess Clover's picture was a little one, with her poem, down in the left lower corner of the page. But it said she was to take part in the free-speech meetings. And so for me there was no more peace.

The talk roared on around me. I half heard what was said. It appeared that the fight to come had been boiled up mainly by the local I. W. W. on one side and the also rowdy Jehovah's Pilots on the other. During my four months in Portland I had taken great pains to keep clear of both camps, even in my mind. But I'd heard that the old American Protective Association, once powerful in Portland through the organizing of hate against the Roman Catholics, was thriving here again by doing the same against the labor rebels. First, the A.P.A. leaders had raised a great uproar to stop the well-known anarchist and free-love woman, Miss Emma Goldman, from giving lectures in Portland. Now Miss Goldman was coming, with the famous old-time labor agitator of the West, Mother Morgan, and the Wobbly organizer, Joe Hill, to back her. It appeared that Bess was an I. W. W. too. She was to appear as a singer of Joe Hill's rebel songs. It burned in me that Joe was a man like Russ Hicks and that Bess would be drawn to him, and was with him. It burned, I say, it was a live coal eating in me. The talk went on with me half hearing. But I was well-posted. The Grand Army of the Republic and the Spanish War Veterans had been the first to threaten the meetings. Then Pastor Joanna of Jehovah's Pilots had made a special trip up from Grays Harbor and raised the loudest outcry of all against free speech for Emma Goldman, Mother Morgan and Joe Hill. At the present point she had put the A.P.A. and the G.A.R. deep in the shade. Pastor Joanna had plainly preached that blood would flow in the streets around Millwrights Hall if Emma Goldman tried to lecture there.

"V'er the hal is this har Millwrights Hall?" Shot Gunderson wanted to know. "Vat street is goin' to run vit' blood?"

"It's the old Knights of Labor hall on Front," a mill man said. "It's across the street from the river dock where we take the sawdust scows and tie them up for use by the Eastway power plant."

Shot Gunderson nodded that he knew the place. He stared at me while he nodded, his Swede eyes lighting into a wild blue glitter. His face split in a fearsome grin.

"Bay Yeesus," breathed Shot. "Them Yehovah's Pilots think they goin' stop Little Pretty from her free speech, hey? Vell, ve see about that—the Seven Bulls see about it, you bat you! Plenty room for a gude fight, yesiree—and sawdust to bury the bodies, bay the holy ol' mackinaw! Coom on, you Yehovah's Pilots! Moor lumber!"

The mill whistle had blown, and we stood up to go back to work. I was busy for a minute, talking Cecil Hurst into giving me his copy of *Direct Action*. Then, heading out into the soft rain, I began to remember some of the bughouse stories on Shot Gunderson that were circulated up and down the Columbia River. They worried me all the afternoon. There were no more dreams. I was no longer a free man.

Shot Gunderson was the smallest of the Seven Bulls of the Copenhagen sawmill. A wiry runt of forty years, with straw hair, pale eyes and a peaked chin, Shot owned more muscle power and whizzbang per pound than any man and a half I'd ever known. For ten years he had bossed this green-chain, and for twice ten years he had boiled his innards in *aqua vit'* weekly from Saturday night until midnight Sunday. In all the time he'd never needed to take a day off for drunkenness, sickness, broken bones, love or death. He commonly consumed at least a quart of tomatoes with each meal. The sawdust savages of the Columbia River mills wondered little at Shot's consumption of firewater, but they did marvel at how he downed the canned tomatoes. When a savage was at a table and wanted a helping of this dish, he was apt to say, "Please pass the Gundersons." The saying spread.

Every new "squarehead Swede" story that came along was hung on Shot Gunderson. Years back some bard had set going a string of tales about Shot and his crew, calling them the Seven Bulls. The name caught on with the sawdust savages of the Columbia River mills. In the stories they passed along, the Seven Bulls were ever the same—in their way like the eternal Seven Axmen of Paul Bunyan's logging camp. But Andy Jonken and Mike Hrbacek were the only two who had worked with Shot long enough to be considered as home guards. The others would change, come and go, but Shot would hire none who was not a young bull of a man; large, powerful and full of steam. He himself was always the runt of his crew; standing five feet, seven inches, and weighing no more than a hundred and seventy-five pounds. But no man could beat him at handling lumber.

Andy and Mike were each heavier and taller than me, and I was now nudging past six feet, two inches, and two hundred and ten pounds in socks. The other three go-abouts who were now in the Seven Bulls—Turk Manique, Mart MacHagg and Sailor Cecil Hurst—were my size and more. By October we'd all become a really solid crew that had known no change for three months. Now we knew just how and when to gang up on the rushes of lumber that would pile down on the crawling chains for a single station. Shot Gunderson would go a whole shift very often without calling an order.

It was just the place, just the job I needed, to keep on in my way of lone freedom after return to my native shore. There was a warm

comradeship of work around the green-chain, without much time
or want for talking. Of course every place of work has its reader
and argufier, and the one here was Cecil Hurst. He had read the
philosophers, and what he'd read seemed to be sort of mired in his
mind—he just couldn't run it out straight in his talk. But the Sailor
did give me names and make me curious enough to look through
the ponderous and heavy jaws of the books of Buckle, Kant, Spi-
noza, Marx, Spencer and Huxley in the Free Public Library. Sample
plowings in the works of the philosophers only made the reading
and study of Walt Whitman seem easier to me. The *Leaves* and the
Lang *Odyssey* were the only book gifts of Uncle Dan'l that I'd
kept. I had found good for my soul in Walt Whitman at every turn.
Now nearly all his poems were printed on my mind and heart. So
I could read them and say them by the hour on the work of the
sawmill green-chain. Walt Whitman made Big Jim Turner feel so
welcome I never wearied of reciting—

The youngest mechanic is closest to me, he knows me well,
The woodman that takes his axe and jug with him shall take me
     with him all day,
The farm boy ploughing in the field feels good at the sound of my
     voice,
In vessels that sail my words sail, I go with fishermen and seamen
     and love them.

He told me to let my soul stand cool and composed before a
million universes. He said to me there is no trade or employment
but the young man following it may become a hero.

Among all the poets, storytellers and philosophers I'd read, Walt
Whitman was the one who walked, worked, sat, stood with me as
living face and voice, living arm on my shoulders, living hand
clasping my hand. Truly his poems were a man to me. I gazed into
the face of his poems and said, "Father," sometimes with tears.

No sadness, though, in the poems or the work. Good days, good
days still. Looking out under the eave of the shed's roof and over
the truckloads of green lumber and the piles on the cargo dock, I
saw a broad river. Yonder flowed the Willamette, sister of the
Salmon and the Snake, soon to join them in the Columbia, the Old

Whale. From this place I had seen ocean ships of all the maritime nations pass.

Coastwise schooners, stern-wheelers, tugs, ferries, fishing boats, sailing craft, sawdust barges, rowboats, log rafts, boys' rafts, liners, whalers and battleships passed my place of labor.

On many days freighters were moored at the dock yonder to load lumber. Black sides, red trim, white superstructure, brown or yellow booms, emblems of many colors on smokestacks, various flags astern.

There was a green ribbon of island nigh the far bank. The bank lifted in a bluff that would brush the blue sky, or the fleecy sky, or the wet, gray sky, with evergreens.

Eventides and Sundays there was the Free Public Library, the rooms walled with books, long tables, chairs, welcome, kind people.

Ellen Crady was so lovely, golden and fragile I could fear that a strong look of mine might hurt her. But she was at ease with me and kept me at ease. I'd grown into the habit of looking up tough references with her, some of them real, some invented. Looking, we'd speak of other things. Ellen liked to tell me of young men who had caught aspiration in the deeps of poverty and ignorance to write books of poetry or tales. She talked me into a study of the novel, *Martin Eden,* although I'd come to believe that Jack London was one who had sold his talent for gold and then used Socialism as a hidey-hole for his shame.

"Look for the good," said Ellen. "There is good in all things."

I said, "You might be right," a remark I'd come to use as a standard reply to moralizing. "You know, Ellen, you may be right," I said. "I'll take a prowl through *Martin Eden,* lookin' for good."

Mrs. Mary Wink was Ellen's boss, chubby, black-eyed, always full of business, sharp but kind to Ellen and the other library girls, and the same to me. I met her in the way of going up to her on my first visit to the Free Public Library and speaking to her about Lily Hurd, who had worked in the Portland library years back, when she was Lily Yardley. Mrs. Wink had loved Lily. I told her what I knew she would like to hear; most of all on how I had first met Lily when she was Knox librarian. I told that I'd been a ragged, diseased boy who was being egged into a life of crime by a drunkard uncle. I had started to drink rye whisky myself, and was on the point of rustling cattle, I told Mrs. Wink, when Lily Yardley the same as took me by the hand and led me into reading *Oliver Twist* and other novels by Charles Dickens.

"It was to improve my morals," I said, "and it did."

Well, it was like drawing four aces in poker when I had the notion of kind of spreading it on with that story. Mrs. Wink was almost rabid on Charles Dickens.

"Indeed," she said, her black eyes shining, "and it was I, young man, who led Lily as a young girl into appreciation of Charles Dickens; so I am going to claim a mite of credit for your juvenile regeneration!"

Mrs. Wink fairly sang the fine words. I'd gone right on playing up to her for four months, and she was as good as any woman alive could have been to me, except for being strict with Ellen when I was around. I didn't really mind the strictness. Ellen was engaged to a college man. But he wouldn't graduate for a year; and so in her kind of fragile, saintly way she would get, well, cousinly with me; and I expected she would with other poets.

A free place of free books in a free land, the Portland Free Public Library had grown in my sight as an American glory. There I lived with books. The Library was Poor Poets' Home for me. I walked with books read to its doors, and I walked with books unread from its doors to my place. Thereby I was a rich young man.

My place was a basement room that was just about big enough for me to turn around in without stepping on my own feet. It was furnished for what was called light housekeeping. The room was really a hole in the ground, with two little street-level windows that looked down from under a ceiling of beaded boards with well-smoked gray paint on them.

Above the outside door dampness had seeped through the concrete wall to make a blot on the painted surface. The blot had taken on the shape of a fat face with a mighty mustache and three chins. At first I called it my bust of Pallas just above my chamber door. Then it struck me that the blot looked more like an image of the face of President William Howard Taft than anything else.

I was always having such notions. The like was needed to make the cheap room a tolerable habitation.

Now, at October's end, this basement room had been my home for four months. The rent for it furnished was an even seven dollars a month. On the average, light and gas put another dollar and a half a month on the rent. My natural big appetite and the hard work made the grub come high. Breakfast was commonly ham, eggs, hot cakes, or maybe oven biscuits, with hot beans for extra hunger, and three or four bakery doughnuts and a quart of coffee to top off. I'd pack a plain lunch of a loaf of bread cut into slices fit for man-sized sandwiches of meat, cheese, fried egg and jelly. No pie or cake for me at a lunch, as I was careful for my digestion and would eat plenty of canned tomatoes; not as many as Shot Gunderson did, but plenty. Evenings I'd whack off a shave, pull on my blue serge, a real nice suit that had cost me seventeen dollars and some cents, stick a readymade bow tie in the neck of a fresh shirt, give my button shoes a polish, then go eat a steak or pork chops in style at a restaurant; never less than a quarter meal, sometimes a splurge for thirty-five cents. Then and then only in any day I would indulge myself to a hunk of cake or a quarter of pie, as this would go with the meal. I would not take a chaw after the evening meal but only a cigarette. Then, as genteel as anybody, I'd hustle for the Free Public Library. Some nights, of course, I'd hole up in my basement home to read or to work on poetry notions. I resisted evil.

We got four bits a day above common wages on the Copenhagen green-chain. The big pay was why Shot Gunderson could be so choosy in his hiring. I made twenty-seven and a half cents an hour, two dollars and seventy-five cents each ten-hour day, sixteen dollars and fifty cents every sixty-hour week, and seventy-one dollars and fifty cents any twenty-six-day month. It was good money, however you looked at it. Old Einar Skjalgsson's system was to pay high for good men, and then treat 'em right. He'd grown rich at it and all his hands were his friends to boot.

I've set all this down here to give simple facts on how poetry can be studied and written out here in the West by a young man with no schooling, if he is strong, willing and sincere. Simple facts on a simple thing. Many were doing it in ways more or less like my way. A hobo circus worker, a boy sailor, an immigrant logging-camp blacksmith, a milk-wagon teamster—many and many young men at the same time were forgetting the poverty of their lives and their lack of schooling; and were finding their ways to pure art, to the eternal peaks of poetry, through the Free Public Library of America.

In my basement room I wrote poems for Bess Clover. One was a sonnet—

Again, again light fails in swamp of thought
   That life is murk for me; the toil and fears
   The bondboy knew, his hunger and his tears—
From these my shapes of beauty must be wrought.
Hope beds with others as each day is caught
   In net of night to feed the bestial years.
   Sleep scorns me then, and sullen fancy leers,
Yet Poesy I praise; O love long sought!
   O bearer of my only wanted fire
      And light! Come lie with me; so that my dreams
   May fertile prove, and grow in this desire
      My life's pure light; glow-warmth to thread the seams
   Of dismal workdays closed in grime and mire.
      No sun I seek, only meek candle gleams.

Rough work; and nobody could tell the spike knots, checks, conk and wane better than I could in a glance at any line. But I was bound to keep at it. I hoped to write a pure yet fiery sonnet by the age of thirty. If I didn't I'd yet keep on. My last lick in life, I vowed, would be a try at a sonnet. Did I drown, like Martin Eden, that horse's rosette, my last struggle would be to write a sonnet line on water. That's what I bragged to Ellen Crady.

With that sonnet in the rough and kindred rhymes, I fared forth for Bess on the night of battle.

Men and women were coming along the old street and turning regularly under the canopy and lights of the wide entrance and stairway to Millwrights Hall. I had no more than arrived and inquired if Miss Clover had come yet (which she hadn't) than a parade appeared. It marched on the planks of an open dock of the river front, across the street from the hall. Twenty or so men were stringing along like labor pickets. Each wore the kind of pilot's cap that marked a member of Pastor Joanna's new sect. Each man packed a big sign, home-painted. The signs read like this—

GOD HATES FREE LOVE . . .

AMERICANS HATE ANARCHISTS . . .

SHAME, SHAME, EMMA GOLDMAN . . .

PROTECT PORTLAND'S PURITY . . .

STAND BY THE FLAG . . .

Somewhere up the street yonder, in the rainy shadows and post lights, Shot Gunderson, Cecil Hurst, Andy Jonken, Mike Hrbacek, Turk Manique and Mart MacHagg would be waiting for me. We had all met down here the afternoon and night before (Sunday, with no one around) and practiced out the plan that Shot had rigged up for the Seven Bulls to follow in the fight for Little Pretty. Then it had looked to be the damnedest foolishness, with us all simply begging to be beaten up by a mob, then ending in jail. But now the prospect was not so bad. Many had joined Charles Erskine Scott against the "enemies of American free speech," and the mighty newspaper, the *Oregonian,* was standing for free speech, too. But what had really made the A.P.A. and the G. A. R. back up was the Jehovah's Pilots.

Pastor Joanna got her picture in the papers, robes and all, along with a new threat to fetch an army of Christian loggers up from Grays Harbor "to take care of the Anarchists and Free Lovers, the Devil's Own." The *Oregonian* thundered a warning against sham saints and said it would be a mistake to make a martyr of Emma Goldman. The proud Protestants and Old Soldiers were keeping quiet. Now, it appeared that the Jehovah's Pilots were all that the Seven Bulls would have to worry about in the protection of Little Pretty.

I hustled on to join them. Then—

"Jim!" I heard. "Jim Turner!"

I plowed to a stop and wheeled about. Bess Clover ran from ahead of a bunch of people who had come into the hall's entrance behind me. I fairly lunged toward her, and she stopped in the fringe of the canopy lamps. I saw her face, her hands reaching, light between us, and fine slanting lines of rain in the light—and then the shape of a man swung around her and shouldered in between us, and that voice like steel pounding steel drove at me.

"Get back to your Christers, Big Jim!"

It was Joe Hill, all right, Joe Hill with his gun under his coat and his right hand ready to flash for it. The eyes that could look at you like the eyes from a picture of Jesus Christ were deathly in their glittering stare. I saw murder in them and in every line of his frozen face. I saw it and realized it in seconds; in a split of a second. And with it I remembered the face of Rough Rider Al Bliss, the crooked long scratch, the blood spreading. And with it I felt the natural cocking of my left fist for the snap of the hook that I could throw as fast as Joe Hill or anybody else might pull and shoot a gun. There was no time to think. I did not think. These things were in me, images of instinct, light-fast.

But I flinched, and this was in me too, without thought, I flinched backward, from Joe Hill and then from Bess Clover, as she caught at Joe Hill's right arm in both hands and gripped it to her.

I saw her face again. It was stricken, her eyes accused me.

"Yellow fink Christer," Joe Hill chopped out the words. "Scissorbill fink and stool! I know and Bess knows and Black Dan Barton knows you for a grayback bastard dehorn, a traitor to your fellow workers! What you did in Montana you will always do. Now get back to your gang over there in a three-count or I'll gun you!"

Preacher boy in Montana—and they believed I was at it here—even Bess believed it. I tried to ask, "You don't, do you?" but there was a lock on my throat.

Then the voice of Shot Gunderson sawed down the street—

"Hey, you bulls! Look noo! Big Yim and Little Pretty!"

Hobnails hammered on the cobblestones.

What I might have done I'll never know, had I been given the three seconds, Joe Hill's three-count. Surely I'd have hooked him, as I later imagined it over and over in my mind. But with the roars of the Seven Bulls the people who were with Bess and Joe grabbed

them and hauled them for the stairway hall and I was driven to
join Shot Gunderson and my other mates in their charge on the
parade of Jehovah's Pilots.

What had just happened was as slag inside me. I swung around
like a machine and ran over for the dock with the bulls, then lined
out as we had practiced the battle plan last night. I was wildly alive,
yet numb, frozen.

Shot Gunderson, with a war cry so blood-curdling it would have
done credit to an old-time Modoc, charged. His charge was over
the river dock planking for the straggle-parade of Jehovah's Pilots
and their banners as it turned at one end of the dock. He charged
low-crouched and leaping, like a cougar, or as he would lunge
after a large timber on the green-chain of the Copenhagen sawmill.
Right as he had planned it, Shot Gunderson hooked the head
parader of the Jehovah's Pilots, hoisted him, swung him, heaved
him, let him sail; all with the neck-and-butt grips of the bum's
rush. Then Shot swung and charged for Number Two, yowling—

"Moor lumber! She's rollin' from the old sawmill!"

It was a nightmare in my sight and in my mind. You couldn't
believe the like was going on even when you were in the thick of it.
And I was frozen, all slagged inside from taking what I'd taken
from Joe Hill. I piled into my place with Cecil Hurst, but there
were not just the two of us—the Old Nick was hooked to me,
also; grinning through the rainy lights, snorting in the wind, "Now
you pay me, Big Jim Turner!" Oh, the mess, the mire!

The wild, crazy play went on, to make another big story of Shot
Gunderson and the Seven Bulls for the river sawmills, then to
grow in another shape as lore of the fighting Wobblies of the West.

Actually it was no more than a roughhouse. On from Shot
Gunderson the first Jehovah's Pilot was caught before he spread-
eagled by Mart MacHagg, who hooked and slung him on to Turk
Manique. Then he was rushed and lofted away to Andy Jonken,
who green-chained him down the line to Mike Hrbacek. Then it
was up to Cecil and me to unload the man.

We stood nigh the end of the dock which was used as a well
mooring for the sawdust barges that were collected for power-plant
fuel here. About ten feet down in the shadows bulged the top

of a load of sawdust from a Copenhagen sawmill barge. Shot Gunderson had used his influence to make sure it was here tonight. It was our target.

Cecil and I were used to teaming up to pull timbers off the green-chain. He was such a Wobbly it was simply fun for him to hook that first Pilot as the man came flying at us from Mike Hrbacek's paws, and to swing him high with me and let him fly on over the dockside. The poor fool of a Pilot let out the most pitiful howl and wildest plea as he sailed; being sure and certain that he was on his way to the black water of the deep river; never dreaming he was aimed for a pile of soft sawdust. Cecil was laughing his head off by the time the second Pilot came at us, whooping and flopping. In any other circumstance I'd have died a-laughing, too, but not now, not with the Old Nick here.

We swung and heaved the second man over, with him praying lickety-split in groans of despair.

Up the dock Shot Gunderson kept unloosing his Modoc yells, cougar screams, with green-chain calls in between—

"V'at's wrong in the old sawmill? Ve vant moor lumber har! Coom on vit' the lumber! T'ree cheers foor Little Pretty, bay Yeesus!"

All inside of a couple of minutes Shot Gunderson's lumber-slugging paws closed on the duds and flesh of one Jehovah's Pilot after another. Some fought free of his hooks. Others bunched on him to try to beat him down and take him apart. All of the signs were flat on the dock planks, I could see, up there in rain-glimmered rays from the lights at the entrance of the hall across the street. Shot had been beaten seven ways with the banner standards. Out of the melee he would plunge regularly, hooking and swinging and rushing a Pilot, while he let out a cougar squawl. Then—

"Fire, fire! The old sawmill's burnin' down! The roof's fallin' in! Ay don' give a gude damn! Moor lumber! Keep lumber comin' har!"

In the couple of minutes or so we heaved a dozen of the Jehovah's Pilots overside. Then the police came charging two ways along the street. The paraders who were not already running lit out now. But the Seven Bulls stayed, all for Shot Gunderson.

He stood in the thick of broken and fallen banners, legs spraddled over one that read, "PROTECT PORTLAND'S PURITY." He hauled a pint of *aqua vit'* from his hip pocket, broke it open, reared back and drank the bottle dry, then threw it toward the howls that came as from the deep, dark river.

The police were nigh on us. I stood by with the others, feeling a fool, low, lost, and not caring a hoot. Peering through the wet light I saw a blob of people under the canopy of the hall entrance. Surely one of the faces was Bess Clover's. She had seen, she must know now that I hadn't been here against her or to keep Emma Goldman from giving her lecture.

"Whuf!" said Shot Gunderson. "Nothin' like a gude little snort after gude vork." He faced the squad of police. "Vell, men," he said, "now ve got to yail and have fine sleep. Don' vorry. Old Einar is primed to bail us out in time for vork tomorrow. The old Copenhagen sawmill got to keep sawin' lumber, you bat you!"

And so for the second time in my life I went off to jail, while the Portland Fire Department rescued the Jehovah's Pilots from the sawdust barge, and Emma Goldman went on in freedom to deliver her lecture of the evening on "The Social Significance of the Modern Drama"—and all of it for the sweet sake of Little Pretty.

16. Horatio Alger Boy

BUSH BROWN HAD BEEN IN PORTLAND FOR A COUPLE of weeks at the time of the foray of the Seven Bulls. He was looking all the while for pointers on where to go for a winter job to start his life career as a cowboy; talking to experts in the Portland offices of the United States Department of Agriculture; visiting the stockyards; hunting up retired cattlemen and quizzing them dry. Bush kept right at it; he hated like sin to fare forth alone to make his start in the cattle business.

He was making ready for it, though, on the morning he saw the newspaper picture of me among the bailed-out Seven Bulls. Bush struck out on my trail as soon as he saw the jailhouse picture in the paper and read the fool piece that went with it. This more than ran on to tell how the Seven Bulls "had stormed down the river dock like plumed knights of old to defend fair ladies and free speech." I could spy the mockery in it, but most people read it as sober statement, and so came to make it the biggest of all the Shot Gunderson whoppers. The writer hadn't talked to any of the Copenhagen men but Shot, after Einar Skjalgsson got us out on bail. And by that time Shot had dug up and consumed another pint of *aqua vit'*. He kept calling Emma Goldman Little Pretty to the newspaper writer and gave him—anyhow the piece said he did—the most garbled mess of gush on how Cecil Hurst "vas sveet on Emma Goldman, you bat you, sveet on Little Pretty Emma, yesiree!" It was sickening. Well, Bush Brown tracked me by it, anyhow. And then I didn't need much urging to pull out of Portland with him, leaving more than enough pay due at the Copenhagen sawmill for my bail.

All I wanted was to go. I was sure in my heart that now I was worse than dead to Bess Clover; a dehorn and fink in her sight, else she'd have looked me up as Bush had. I told him all about her, going away on back to the old life, bringing up Russ Hicks, reminding Bush about Joe Hill and how he'd put the gunsight brand on Rough Rider Al Bliss at Umatilla. I brooded and muttered around on how Joe had made me look a polecat·coward in front of Bess Clover, which likely I was, else I'd go back, by God, to Knox and have me a showdown with the Hickses.

"You're a poor boy and won't have a chance," Bush said. "People will hate you for bringin' up old scandal. But I'll go with you."

"I'm beat," I said. "I've no guts for it."

"I like to hear you say that," Bush said. "I have no guts, either. Maybe we could help each other along."

"I won't do you any good, Bush. I'd bring a cloud on you."

"I've got me one, bud."

"Excuse me, Bush, I'd forgot about it."

"I wouldn't coax you, Jim. Maybe you'd be better off to go back up to Fort Fox and hole up away from trouble with Rud Neal again."

"No. He's happy like he is. He wrote me so. I'll let Rud alone with his Haida wife, his baby, his old stump farm, and his folks at the army post."

"Well, only other thing I can think of is us in a two-man winter feed camp in the Wallowas. Deep, warm valleys there, with little snow."

It kind of appealed to me right off. Bush warmed up and gabbed away about the Grande Ronde region in general, and the Wallowa and Imnaha valleys in particular, all in such a bright and cheery style you'd never dream it was mainly out of government bulletins. I brightened myself, I couldn't help it with the boy. (Bush was a year older than me, but I kept thinking of him as a boy.) And that was our start for a winter feed camp on the Evangeline.

Two young men, one hopeful, cheery and bright, and one morbid, broody and glum, met Mr. C. K. Burry at a noon of early November. Mr. Burry was an old man, a *mean* old man; one who owned so much meanness that there was scarcely room in him for anything else. The young men, of course, were Bush Brown and Jim Turner.

We'd eaten a bite in Wallowa's Occidental Hotel and had gone into the warm barroom to spy around on what Bush would keep enthusing about as "the true life of the cattle country, the real quill." By now I'd given up arguing with him on his cowboy dreams. Never before had I been prodded so regularly with the need of looking out for somebody else as I was with Bush Brown. I wouldn't let him take anything stronger than lemon pop at the bar of the Occidental, and that was what I drank myself. It didn't appear to harm me any.

The barroom was about empty when we came back to it. But pretty soon the bartender, a wheezy old lard-neck known as Bulgy Pete Pod, came and leaned close to us, pointed with a fat thumb, and spoke low—

"There comes the number one cattleman of all the Grande Ronde country. You wouldn't think it to look at him, but here comes the ramrod of 'em all; yes, sir, boys! Owns seven ranches, and as many thousand head of baldfaces. Retired, mainly, but he keeps his hand in with a prime little spread up in the fine scenery of the Imnaha country. Evangeline Valley—named it hisself, C. K. Burry did. A true lover of nacher, Mr. Burry says he is, and he is. A great sheriff he was, too, back in the seventies and early eighties." The bartender leaned closer, breathed harder, then went on in the stagiest whisper you ever did hear, "Yes, sir, boys, you are lookin' at the man there who *wrapped the cold clay around Hank Vaughan!*"

All through old Pete Pod's gab we'd stared around to watch a lean and little man of grizzled years stub on in saddle boots for one of the rawhide-bottomed chairs that stood along the back wall. He sat himself down with motions quick and sharp, no crick of age. His scrawny body appeared to be as hard and tough as a strip of wire rope. He sat, then whipped a foot to a knee and jerked the boot off that foot. A small chunk dropped out. He caught it before it could hit the floor. He held it up and looked our way. Pete stopped his big whispering.

"Arrerhead," the ancient party said. "Little Avery snuk it into my boot. I got the dam'est grandkids." He pulled the boot back on. "Must say I'm glad to see 'em off for Californy."

"Rusty's stayin' though, ain't she, Mr. Burry?" the bulgy bartender said.

"Sure—I didn't mean her—dynamite couldn't pry Rusty from her old grandpa." He was up and coming for the bar now. "And who are these here fine-lookin' young men?"

I smelled a big old rat, a couple of them. Mr. Burry could not keep his voice from sounding like the grind of hobnail boots on gravel, and he could not soften the granite in his lone eye. He gave me the shivers in no time. His left eyelid hung over an empty socket like a wrinkled leaf. Between the limp eyelid and the granite orb was a sawtooth nose, and under this a gray mustache and goatee which bristled like three bunches of trimmed haywire. Coming close, these features moved around and reset themselves in a strained style that we were expected to take for a smile of friendship, I guessed.

The bartender gave Mr. Burry our names and said we'd been inquiring around Wallowa about winter jobs on a cattle ranch.

"I'd jest mentioned to them what a fine little spread you still run person'lly on the Evangeline," he said. "What fine scenery, and all."

"Bulgy, old hoss, you've tetched my weakest spot, onless it's Rusty," Mr. Burry said. "I don't like to brag on her, or on my Evangeline place, neither. But I will relate a true story on the scenery. It concerns a United States senator; and it is not for me to speak his name in a public place; but he took a quiet campin' trip up to there this last summer; and he said to me after it, he said—

" 'Mr. Burry, I envy the cowboy who is privileged to work and abide in sech scenery of the gods. If I was forty year younger, Mr. Burry,' the United States senator said, 'why, I'd hire out to you for my board and overalls and socks; and I'd settle down here in this scenery of the gods for the rest of my days; and to hell with the United States Senate!'

"Well, there was more to it," Mr. Burry went on. "The senator had taken a stack of pictures of the Evangeline Valley. And so his last word to me was a promise he was goin' right into the White House office of the Honerble William Howard Taft and spread the pictures in front of him, let him look his fill, and then tell him, 'Jest think, Honerble William Howard Taft, that *you are President of all that!*"

"Oh, Lordy!" Bush breathed, pale as any corpse from excitement, his blue eyes so wide. "I wonder if he done it!"

"I expect, son, I expect."

The bartender sidled away to wait on a couple of customers. Bush Brown looked on at C. K. Burry like a young quail hypnotized by a rattlesnake.

"Mr. Burry, sir," he said, just breathing out the words again. "Pete said you wrapped the cold clay around Hank Vaughan. Did you, sir?"

"I can't make no bones about it, son. I done it as my sworn duty. He was the deathliest outlaw ever heard of in Oregon. I shot him stone dead in a fair, square fight, then pungled up to give him a proud funeral. Yes, I got to admit I nailed the mahogany on Hank Vaughan and in the cold clay sunk him."

Bush was a goner, and me with him. There was nothing I could do about it. I couldn't walk off and leave Bush alone in what I smelled that Evangeline feed camp to be. So we both went for it.

The memory of how things had gone to smash with me in Portland was as heavy and jagged a pile of misery as my soul had ever been made to bear. Yet it was a help to me. With all that grief riding me, the kind of cowboy's life that I was aiding Bush Brown to learn dwindled into the shape of something tolerable. But it was hell, it surely was.

Evangeline Creek and its valley were a wild, forsaken and forlorn branch of the Imnaha—a riproaring white-water river that rampaged through the Wallowa Mountains into the mile-deep canyon of Snake River. Mr. Burry had grown irrigated wild hay in the valley for many a year. He had a twisted pride in the fact that the place had served him so well without many improvements. We had close to four hundred head of mountain-bred steers and a band of cayuse crips to haul hay for and to water. The troughs were not much better than washtubs. They had to be filled by hand power with a pump that I named "Old Leak" right off, and by windlass and bucket from the log bridge over the creek's thirty-foot crevasse

nigh the camp. The work would take a dozen hours any day—
more with the cooking and cleaning. The tent was pure raghouse,
and it was furnished with a stove that had as many cracks in it as
C. K. Burry's own mean face.

But Bush Brown kept in glory with it all, week after week.

"It's what I've dreamed of since away back in Indiana, Jim,"
he'd tell, even in the worst of the grief. "It's what I trained myself
for with my folks over on the Nisqually. The stock there was milk
cows, but they grazed on rough range and had some real wild
calves. There I learned to ride, rope, pack, make bobwire fence,
brand and such. Now, I'm in a famous cow country, learnin' on to
be a cowboy while bein' paid wages by the country's leadin' cow-
man!"

Bush had along a pile of books and bulletins put out by the
United States Department of Agriculture on cattle and cattle
ranching. He pored over them in most of his scant spare time. He
really seemed to get fun out of the dry reading matter. Bush Brown
simply packed around the most cheerfulness and friendliness and
natural joy in life that was ever bunched in one human parcel.
The interest he took in such a dismal aggravation as Old Leak was
something that seemed to put character into the pump, that primed
it with his faith. Here was a pump that only needed to be treated
with kindness and respect to be reformed, was Bush's attitude. And
that was exactly the attitude he kept toward C. K. Burry, only this
was really worshipful.

At the end of our first month on the Evangeline Mr. Burry had
worked off on Bush a decrepit Mex saddle, a pair of moth-eaten
wool chaps, a Smith & Wesson thirty-eight with a pitted bore, and
some other junk that had been left by a cowhand who'd cut his
throat in a Burry feed camp last winter. Could I tell Bush that
Burry was robbing him? Not much! End of the next month Bush
was more than pleased to take a pinto three-year-old for his wages,
even though I warned him that the poor critter had plainly been
spoiled by some quirt-and-spur buckaroo bastard. Bush only smiled
and chuckled.

Then, by the end of March, it beat me, it was hard to believe,
but the gear was fixed up and slickered into tolerable shape, and
the pinto was gentled into a fine riding horse—anyhow, for Bush

and me. I did the main work on all this, I can say without bragging, even while I called myself a fool for doing it. I knew how,
and I was willing to do it for Bush. I was somewhat paid when
C. K. Burry looked at Bush with a real glint of respect in his eye
and said—

"Dah-gone, but you come out all right on these here deals. I've
got to admit you come out all right, son. All right, yes, sir."

As for Bush, he was fairly exalted for a week by such praise
from a man he'd come to look up to more than to any other alive.

There was no good word for me, though, from the old range
wolf or from Rusty Lark or anybody else. I was an object of suspicion. As I said, it beat me at all turns.

"Grandpa says your partner looks like a Modoc renegade,"
Rusty told Bush, as he finally confessed to me. "He's black-
featured and high-boned enough in his ugly face," she said. "Bush,
you watch out he don't turn treacherous and knife you in your
bunk."

That was just a joke to Bush, but I was hard put to push out a
single short laugh on it. I'd worked all winter to case-harden myself against hurts from others, but it pronged me to be looked on
that way by Rusty Lark. She was a carrot-top, light-complected
under a lot of freckles, like Bush; a kid of sixteen who cared for
nothing but to ride a fiery sorrel around this wild country; and
who wouldn't stay with her folks in California or go to school anywhere after she was through the eighth grade. Her pa, Dr. Jabez
Lark, was a surgeon, and none too bright, it appeared. In his practice here at his start a couple of Tarheel Hardshells had perished
under his knife, with the result that his country trips began to be
made exciting by stray bullets. Dr. Lark could not stand excitement. So he had moved his family to California, where bad luck
in surgery was not so risky. The family would come back to the
Wallowas for the summer. When Rusty elected to stay with old
Burry it was a crown on her in his sight.

Every ten days or two weeks Rusty would ride out with her
grandpa and some pack horses on camp-tending trips. Rusty had
taken to Bush right off and grown confidential with him. She told
him all about her Uncle Harmon Burry, who ran the Burry ranches
and herds, with a couple of partners.

"That's how it's been for a dozen years," she confided in Bush Brown. "It was when grandpa began to slip back into the kind of stingy ways he got his start by, before the Civil War. This is his old pet place, so he is let to keep it; and he works it cheap, then crows over Uncle Harmon on how much more profit a beef he can still make than uncle and the partners can. I feel sorry now that a nice boy like you should get stuck this way, but if you can hold through maybe you won't be so bad off in the spring."

Bush told me that, then he said, "But I'll go on home with you, Jim, like we started out from Portland to do. I'll go on to Idaho with you, boy, and help you face your music."

I thanked him kindly, but I knew I could never let him leave a place and a life which had come to mean all that success in this world could ever mean to him. It was a Horatio Alger story for Bush Brown, and he simply had to see it through to a happy end. He must not spoil the book.

One mid-January day I remember well in its light of a visit by Rusty and her grandpa. Its start was like another, Sunday or not. It was my turn to rise by lantern light and fight the stove into a heat for baking sourdough biscuits and cooking coffee and sow-bosom, and for warming water in its reservoir to use in dishwashing and to prime Old Leak. All went pretty well, with use of a peck of fine pitchy shavings. As the biscuits baked I went out for a look around. The big old black-and-tan shepherd dog, name of "Shep" like seventeen thousand others, came up to wag and paw me a howdy; and we both stood and looked out at the moon so bright in the sparkles of frost crystals, and the black rims of the Wallowas a-leaping up so high—so high all around that it made a small, a kind of toy sky. I had a turn at feeling crowded over. William Howard Taft could have the scenery, for all of me. I took a big spit at it, then went back into the warm tent, breathed the breakfast smells and felt better.

While we ate from rusty tin dishes on a split-log table Bush gabbed as he commonly did about the good work of cattle watering and haying ahead for the day, and on what improvements might be furthered if we could squeeze in time for them. I was no way interested, but it pleased me to listen to him and to look at him and to know that one soul in this dark and thorny desert of a life could be both so satisfied and contented on little or nothing.

We ate and then cleaned up the place as though it was a dairy barn and not just a hole for a pair of ranch hands. Then Bush bundled up and pranced away for his pet, Old Leak, while I harnessed the crowbait span of camp horses and hitched them to what was surely the oldest hayrack rig on the whole Grande Ronde. The team was the pick of a dozen cull horses, castoffs from the main ranches, which Mr. Burry would not allow to be shot. He kept them for trading purposes. When he'd foist one on somebody, as he'd put the pinto over on Bush, the old coyote of a cattleman would seem a year younger.

It was a mystery to him how we'd built the two hauling horses up into good shape, in spite of their age. What I'd done in the first bitter cold was to borrow—as I called it to Bush—some woolsacks from a cache in a winter-closed sheep camp down on the Imnaha. In the stable shed, or whenever they'd stand at work, we'd cover old Em and Boo (nobody knew where he got that name) with layers of borrowed woolsacks. Mr. Burry never happened to catch us at it. With his old-time Western buckaroo notions, he'd have been horrified, not at the borrowing, but at showing mercy to horses, even though it paid.

In the first weeks Bush and I had worked our heads off at odd times to patch up the pole fences of the feed corrals, which we needed to use for feeding and watering the beef in bunches. Each pen had a pole manger. After the fences were patched, Bush had worked out a pattern from some diagrams in one of his government bulletins, and we began to put up a slatted V-shaped feeder, around seven feet high, with the bottom of the V in the bed of a manger. The steers had to stretch necks over a manger side and chaw hay from the slots or gaps between the poles of the V feeder. The rig kept them from horning hay out and wasting it underfoot, as they would do in manger feeding.

Now we had five of the rigs up, as Mr. Burry had admitted that he was not opposed to them. "Go ahead and have yore fun," he told us.

So we started plugging through another day of hauling hay and watering, hauling hay and watering, doing chores between, and looking ahead to improvement work in the late afternoon. But well before noon Mr. Burry and Rusty came riding up in the fine sunny weather.

We had just topped off a jag of hay fit for Em and Boo to pull and had taken off their blankets in the warming sun. Rusty wanted to ride out with Bush and help with the feeding, and I stayed back, as I always would at such times. I stood on the part of the hay-stack we were taking down and proceeded to ask Mr. Burry to get us a new hayknife.

"A new hayknife," he said, sounding like a man who'd just had a pitchfork stuck into him. "A *new* hayknife. You must be jokin'."

"Well, sir, watch," I said.

Each big haystack had been built to shed rain and snow. We'd slice it down to make feed, as with a loaf of bread, and a hayknife was a sort of breadknife three feet long. The life had been whetted out of this one long ago. Bush could do nothing with it. I was break-ing my back pumping the junk. I pumped now, saying no more, and it surely was as plain as day to Mr. Burry that I needed a new hay-knife.

"Well, it could be better," he was bound to say. But then he went to whining his old tune. "I've told you young men over and over how I've never been more land-poor, cattle-burdened and tax-robbed. Here I am in my old age, not knowin' which way to turn. How I'm goin' to keep on payin' Bush and you the prime wages I do, same time keep feedin' you so good—why, we brung a whole case of can' tomaters in the packs—and same time keep my head above water until I can sell some beef in the spring, I don't know. I hate to bring my troubles up and complain," he blatted on, "but you forced me to it, young man, by tryin' to impose on me to throw away a good hayknife jest so's you can have a slick and shiny one with red paint on the handles. Why, I was only about to tell you I need to make some more dickers with Bush and you on yore wages. How you fixed for readin' matter?"

I had to lean all my weight on the hayknife to keep from throw-in' it at him. Last fall I'd asked for some fresh reading matter, and Rusty had brought out *Man's Place in Nature,* by Thomas Henry Huxley. It was an old book but its pages had never been cut. Her pa had left a set of Huxley books with others in his doctor's library when he moved to California. Rusty had brought me the one book with some notion of a joke. She was thunderstruck when Bush told her that I'd not only read the book but told him a heap out of it. At this news, Mr. Burry had proceeded to take two dollars out of my wages for the book.

"We got eight more in the set," Mr. Burry said now. "You can have 'em for a dollar apiece, if you'll take all. You want to go on with your education, don't you?"

All I could do was glower like a Modoc and shake my head.

"Well, say eighty cents apiece, then."

He came down to a quarter and gave up. But he appeared chipper and bright as he went to unloading the packsaddles. He'd played poor to a hired hand again and had staved me off on the hayknife subject.

Pretty soon hoofs clomped on the frozen ground and the wheels of the hauling rig rattled back from the feed yard. I straightened from my knife-pumping and peered over the pile of hay I'd sliced and forked out for loading, to see Rusty and Bush on the empty hayrack. Their laughter rung to me. They surely were a natural pair. I looked over at old Burry. Sidewise I saw a kind of softness in that one eye of his, something like the point of an icicle that's begun to melt. Maybe he was thinking how much like sister and brother the two carrot-tops and freckle-faces appeared there, while he wished that one of the grandkids now in California could have been more as Bush was now. Certainly no boy of his own blood could have looked at him with more worship and spoken to him with more respect than Bush Brown did.

Well, the day toiled on. Rusty and her grandpa ate noon dinner with us, both acting as though sourdough bread, belly bacon, brown beans and canned tomatoes were a banquet. Rusty helped Bush with the work while Mr. Burry inspected the beef, the horses and the layout. Midafternoon the girl and the old man started back for Joseph town. Bush and I worked away, feeding and fixing, taking care of the horses and getting in wood, cooking and cleaning again, reading, studying and gabbing some, then rolling in to rest for another day.

This night I slept without dreams. Such nights grew more and

more common as winter labored on. Hardest life, but what I
needed. I bulled on with it until grass time, real spring on the
Evangeline.

There's little more that asks to be told about that particular
time. Here was Bush, here to stay, working and growing in the
way he wanted, while the old life would let him. For me, it was a
thinking out and settling down to *my* business in life. The job was
inside me. The first thing, the main thing I had to take hold of and
handle was this fact. Next November I'd come of age. By that
birthday I should be ready to start Big Jim Turner's real, own
plowing, seeding, harvest. It would be for books, for books of
poetry, with the poems of Walt Whitman as flags for the line furrow of the first plowing. Away back in that night camp on Snake
River Jack Hard had hammered at me to think and work on nothing but the way of life that I was made for, the way of the book.
I could go out now, go it alone, go look around and live easy outside myself, while getting set inside me for my first plowing.

Now for me the open road, the spring ramble.

March went out like a lamb. Rusty Lark and C. K. Burry rode
to the Evangeline on a day when big clouds were riding high in the
spring blue. Bush Brown squared up to the old man and did the
talking for me, just as he had said he would do; telling what I'd
rigged up for him to tell, so that I might quit without getting in
trouble and being beaten out of my wages.

"Mr. Burry, sir," Bush said, "it 'pears like you've been enter-
tainin' an angel unawares, as the preacher says. Last night Mr.
Turner here—oh, you'll soon catch on why I call him Mr. Turner
—he told me that the reason he was so much at home with that
Huxley book is—Mr. Huxley is his uncle! His own grand-uncle,
Mr. Burry!"

Bush stopped on that, rolled his eyes at me, looked pale, and
gave a mighty swallow. Rusty and Mr. Burry gazed from him to
me with the bewilderment of sheep. Well, I was ready for their
looks and more. I stood out proud before them in the style I'd ad-
mired in the soldiers as they stood sometimes on the parade ground
of the Fort Fox post up in Canada. It was called a "rest" position.
Now I held it, my head reared back, right leg stiff, left knee bent

and foot set out in front of me, hands crossed and resting behind me, in the small of my back. A stud colt never looked prouder.

"Mr. Turner told me," Bush gulped again and chattered on, "that for two years he has been hoboin' around the West on the quiet to pick up matter for a book, like so many writer folks do —like the United States senator done here last summer." Now Bush was going smoother. He was remembering right on my coaching. And Rusty and her grandpa were looking more impressed and less bewildered. "You will be pleased to hear, Mr. Burry, sir," Bush gabbed on, "that Mr. Turner expects to make a fine chapter in his book about the Evangeline and the leadin' cattleman of the Grande Ronde country—he told me. That's your angel unawares, Mr. Burry."

There was the play. I stood on like a soldier at rest on parade, my heart hammering my ribs while I wondered would we win or lose. The first move was Rusty's. It was not for me but to Bush Brown. She just went to him and stood with him. Old Burry's granite eye shot its stare from me to them. I had a notion on what he was thinking. It was that my story through Bush might be true. And if it wasn't, what was to be lost by acting as though he believed it? Mr. Burry knew nothing about books and writers. But he was yet sharp enough to figure me out as one who could be careless with the truth. It was his brag that once his mind was made up nothing could change it.

Mr. Burry made up his mind. He came to me, his right hand up. It was his gun hand too. I yet held myself reared back like a Fort Fox soldier, but my gaze was slanted without a wink to that hand. Then the fingers forked to me, while Mr. Burry's voice of hobnails on gravel grated over his outstretched arm and hand.

"I kinder suspected it, Mr. Turner," he said, the barefaced old liar. "I suspected it and appreciated it. Which is why I kept eggin' them Huckley books on you. We appreciate havin' you with us, we hope you will think of us kindly when you write your book, and remember us kindly to yore Uncle Tom Huckley. Yore fine old Uncle Tom." It was a kind of coyote sneer in his voice when he said that. Then he went on, friendlier. "Well, son, let's shake on it." A wind of pure relief wheezed out of me. I was never so glad to take a hand in mine or to give a grin into another face. "Well, that's fine, finer'n frog hair," Mr. Burry said. "I do hope you won't fergit my name is favor'bly known to President William Howard Taft. And I won't no way mind it bein' writ up who he was that drawed the coffin lid over the bullet-ridded corpse of Hank Vaughan!"

Bush let me have his pinto to ride to the railroad. Soon I was on my way. My last look back saw Bush and Rusty laughing with each other, then waving to me. And then old Burry. Maybe he'd seen Buffalo Bill do it in a show. Anyhow he waved up his range hat in his left hand, high on a straight arm, while his right hand pointed his Colt forty-four with the hogleg handle up toward the mountain peaks, the tall sailing clouds and the spring blue. He fired five times.

Two great wide cloud shadows sped down on the three. I was glad to see the shadows miss Rusty and Bush, flanking them, leaving the sun shine on them. It seemed a sort of promise. The pinto loped on. Free again.

17. Daylight in the Swamp

NOW IT WAS EASIER TELLING. OVER THERE IN THE light of a barn lantern I'd looked in his face and confessed to my preaching in Montana. I'd made a picture of the rainy night on the Portland river front and how Joe Hill had poured molten words into me and abased me before Bess Clover. Then I said I was sorry to have been such a shame to him. I said it, looking right into his face; into that flesh knotted and ridged and scarred from the many beatings; into the dark eyes which were so ever agonized now because the drums (he told me) would nevermore cease their beating back in his head.

"Son, son," he said, through the lantern glow. "I knew it all along. Yes, there in the rain forest. Each to his lights. Yours are *in* you; none without. Why brood about Joe Hill? You don't wish you'd killed him, do you? Come on out here and tell us something good about yourself."

"God is love," said Ramon Hurd. "Resist not evil."

"Just nod and smile when he speaks," Black Dan Barton said, blowing the lantern out. "It will only bother him if you try to talk to him."

We went out, after I'd taken a final peak at Montan, my big red horse, and at Inez, gentle old mare, a grandma now. Moving in the dark of the mountain night with Uncle Dan'l and Ramon, I felt wonderfully that the coming here and the telling had already proved to be the right thing for Big Jim Turner. Back there in the barn I'd scoured off and shed away a crust of shame, it seemed. It was one thing done. This had come out well. Now there were the poems. I needed to settle it with him, and with Lily Hurd, about the thick packet of poems in my saddlebag. Then, by God, I was riding down to the roundup camp on upper Bob Creek to see about Mr. Russ Hicks. And there was a little matter to straighten out with Bess Clover, who was now back living in Knox.

"Then," I told Black Dan Barton, "it will be the jailhouse, if not sooner. Maybe the pen. I give a damn. This is a cleanup."

"After which?"

"I've got to line out my life and start plowin', Uncle Dan'l. God a'mighty, here I am, long of age—I'll be twenty-two in November —on November 22, 1913, a couple of months from now. I'm gettin' on, I must get busy. In poetry, if I'm fit for it. I expect you'll know."

The three of us had set ourselves on the baled hay pile of the Hurd logging camp, facing a black sweep of piny mountain slope and the moonrise. Frost was nipping but there was no wind. I started telling him and, as I said, now it was easier. Uncle Dan'l kept quiet. Ramon did too, except to speak a word on the love of God now and then. The roar of the Little Lemolo kept rising to us from far down in its canyon. I breathed the rousing pine smells. Back yonder was shine of windowlights in the camp houses. Close by the horses chomped at their hay. One would snort now and then, or another would paw. Stable sounds, so good to hear, always. A horse-logging camp in a Western pinery. There was no better place of work, no better life of work on all the green earth, I said to Uncle Dan'l. He nodded. Ramon sighed, "Show mercy and compassion, every man to his brother." I wondered how much Lily might blame me for what that black-cat blast in the Beaverheads had done to him. "Compassion," he whispered.

There is a place of peace and a way of freedom (I said from my hay bale). I breathed its air and learned its way for a year, and coming back to my own land I kept on as a free young man for a long time. Freedom is a brave thing, but it is a lonesome thing. Like the moon yonder.

The moon rising was something less than a half one. It was a rich autumn gold. It rose rocking on a ridge that struck me as having the shape of a horse's back. The moon is a saddle tonight (I said). Saddle moon, lovely and lone, like freedom.

I told them of my rovings with Rud Neal and our labors as free men in a wilderness country and how we were a team; big black brothers as axmen, sawyers and all-'round hand loggers. Rud knew the right places. Rud was drawn back into the life of his soldier family and among a lot of soldier friends, enough to sort of leave me drifting. Then, when we'd headed on north to make ready for the spring, an old love took him in. A Haida girl, an Indian of the Queen Charlottes. I drifted.

The pull back never lets up (I said). Every three months or so Rud writes me letters that take me as a strong wind does a sail. I've missed them since last winter at Orofino, with all my roving, but they'll catch up. Last word, Rud and his wife and kid had a farm pretty close to Fort Fox, yet back in the timber, above a wilderness shore. I nearly headed for there after that slice of hell with Joe Hill in Portland. And then at my leave of Bush Brown in the Grande Ronde. And I don't know how many times up in the Idaho panhandle I felt myself blown Seattle-wise—and a Canadian boat —and another season of hand logging with Rud Neal on waterways of freedom, in mists of peace.

"Blessed are the peacemakers," said Ramon, so sweet and low. "Love one another. Love, love, Jesus love, peace love. My head hurts." Uncle Dan'l put an arm around him.

That's the good, that's about all the good I have to tell about myself. I've been going at random these months (I went on). I struck into the Idaho panhandle, after leaving the Grande Ronde. By winter I'd been around the woods and mills and people of Coeur d'Alene, St. Marie's, Sand Point, Bonner's Ferry, and the white-pine logging town of Orofino. All the time I was working with myself to get lined out and geared for plowing. I mean (I said) the plowing, seeding and cropping of Big Jim Turner's particular field of life. Well, in Orofino it seemed to begin to come to me. There I wrote a long poem in one short day. It was my twenty-first birthday. The poem concerned my search, Jim Turner's quest. I wrote it and put it in my buckskin pack of poems and fragments of poems, and in my memory—where all are kept, too—and then I walked out in the streets of Orofino and got me a job tending bar.

It was a strange thing, Uncle Dan'l (I told), but I would never have dreamed of trying for such a job before I wrote the poem.

It was tending bar in Orofino's toughest joint. My size and cattiness got me the job, and my punch made it easy to hold. I was a hellion right for a spell. Why, I still wonder. You'd think I'd have gone on writing more poems. But instead, I turned brute mean. I ended by putting in with a carnival actorine. We went to Spokane and caught on with a wagon circus that was headed for Montana. I drove a six-up and played a fake act with a sideshow prizefighter all through the Missoula Valley.

In Butte (I went on testifying) I got a chance to go on a fight card with a cowpuncher White Hope. It was for a preliminary four-rounder. The cowpoke had a horse, a big dark sorrel with a yellow mane, a horse that turned me to mush with love of him at first sight. Well, I won the horse, after tapping myself to put up gold against him for a bet on the fight. I took this three-year-old sorrel gelding and his gear; introduced the carnival actorine and the licked cowpoke to each other; started on a ride that was to take me through the Beaverheads to Salmon City; then through the West's wildest country to the Snake River plains; on through harvest jobs to the headwaters of the Payette; and at last to this place on the Little Lemolo.

It was a running away, always a runaway with me (I confessed); but now it was a seeking, too. I didn't know. Too often it seemed to be the Old Nick prodding me again. Such times I longed to go back to Rud Neal. But freedom and peace were not my great want now. What I wanted was what I'd found on my birthday in Orofino, a power to work in poetry, life to me. But a year had gone by, and there'd been no other such day. Sure, I had written more poems to their ends, and more fragments. But in all the vision was dim and the strength was poor. Even the one poem might be a mockery. I didn't know (I said again).

A reason for the ride by way of Salmon City was to call on Albert Clover. I'd learned in Butte that he was a partner in Joe Hurd's saloon—Joe, the son who was such a shame to Aunt Sue Hurd. Neither Albert nor Joe would talk to me—about home and the home folks, that is. I sermonized Albert about his sisters but he only snarled back. All that I picked up in their saloon was a trail partner who turned out to be the filthiest and foulest-mouthed old buzzard I'd ever sat at a meal with. His name was Len Hyde, he was hairy, leathery and lean, and a tremendous walrus mustache bulged from his face, its ends hanging in spikes formed by the juice of Granger Twist. He wore waist overalls on suspenders that let the overalls sag far from the bottom of a vest that was spotted with everything from fried egg to mashed horsefly. I met Len Hyde in the dimness of the saloon at night, I was oary-eyed from rye whisky, or I'd never have dickered with him. But we made a deal and started out at daylight. Then it was foul. At one meal after another Len Hyde would cackle his head off when he could gag me with filthy remarks. At night, when the stars were aswarm over peaks that stood two miles high, and with mountain rivers singing a chorus to the gods, the old lecher would snort and snicker by the hour about the low women he had known and cheated and caught doses from. He sang all along the trails. He had one song, and of it he knew two lines—

Thar was Cocaine Alice and Cocaine Nell—
All the cats in the alley give the cocaine hell!

Well, I needed it. Len Hyde was a mighty moral lesson to me, Uncle Dan'l. Day after day and night after night I looked on Len Hyde and told myself that there I'd go thirty years from now, if I was to keep on dissipating my health away, ruining my stomach and risking doses. I had to admit that many a poet had appeared to profit by living, acting and talking as Len Hyde did; and I conceded that if a poet wanted to do it and if his health would stand it, he had a right to go to it in this free country. But not for me. At least once a month, now, I'd find a meal disagreeing with me, and even oftener there'd be a night when it would take me an hour to get to sleep. I didn't need a doctor to tell me these were signs of failing health. The marks of dissipation were getting pretty plain on my face. I could see them in the looking glass, and more than once I'd stood off and preached my boy's sermon to myself; not more than half joking, either.

Anyhow, at last we hit Ketchum by way of Roaring Hell and Yellow Belly lakes. My last sight and sound of Len Hyde was from the doors of a saloon, with him up asking the bartender—

"Whar's the house of ill fame, son?"

And then I headed off without a handshake, marveling at how the human race could bring forth two such different men as Len Hyde and Rud Neal. Or, for a bigger gap, Len Hyde and Thomas Henry Huxley.

"There's a field for you," Dan'l Barton said. "There's all kinds of good lands between the Hydes of this world and the Huxleys—for you between the Rev. Pearl Yates in his swamp of sectarian superstitions and the great Jesus-soul, Walt Whitman. What about going up to the house now and reading your poems?"

"That's what I want. I'll get them right away from the saddle-bag," I said. "I can't tell you how much good all this gab has done me. I've been so damned lonesome. Lonesome in my belly. Lonesome to my marrow. I feel a lot better. If my poems are trash, all right. Like you say, the fields are many."

"Sow not among thorns," said Ramon. "Reap in mercy."

"Right you are, Ramon," Uncle Dan'l said. "Let's be moving."

It was a pleasant room. I hadn't seen its like in a month of Sundays. Pine chunks snapped and blazed in a lava rock fireplace. The camp had electric lights. Two were on, well-shaded over a reading table that stood back from the fireplace. Chairs stood around. One was a rocking chair so solid and roomy it could belong only to Black Dan Barton. Indian rugs made wonderful color all over the floor. There were pictures on the log walls, curtains at the windows, but most of all there was Lily Hurd, lovelier than she'd ever been in my sight. She was as slim as when she'd come back from Portland to take over the Knox Free Public Library, a long ten years ago. She seemed taller, for her yellow hair was piled so high. At the door she took time to give me another welcoming smile, then she turned to Ramon. I watched her while I hung up my hat and coat. There it was on her face, the love fire, not a flush but a sort of shine from inside that glowed out through her paleness; her eyes not burning but shining from deep lights. I can't tell it. She looked at him, and it was peace on his face and the mist lightened from his eyes. Lily led Ramon over to a couch with an Indian blanket and pillows. She fixed him with his head on the pillows. He turned his face to us.

"He gets better, then slips back," Uncle Dan'l said, low to me as he closed the door. "I expect to see him through, as he did me a couple of times. He and Lily are squared up with Jack Hard. In time we'll get a deal through so Lily can be free of business, then take him to Portland and the treatment he needs. He's a long way from hopeless."

I thought, Ramon seems so happy being out of the world as he is; why bring him back into it? I remembered that idiot war of the religious fanatics and the revolutionary fanatics that had made a hypocrite preacher boy out of me and which had led the losing rebel hard-rock men to try to destroy Ramon Hurd with a black-powder blast.

Dan'l Barton went on to put a couple of pine chunks on the fire. I stood a way inside the door. Lily called over for me to find myself a chair, while she went to the kitchen for some coffee and apple-cake that she'd been fixing. I'd refused supper when I showed up at the back door around two hours ago, as I'd eaten down at Le-molo Lumber Company headquarters camp. But now I was good and hungry again. I sat in the chair, then recollected the poems. I got up and went over to my mackinaw coat, where I'd hung it by the door, and pulled the buckskin-wrapped packet from a pocket. It made a double handful. I tossed it casual-like at Uncle Dan'l. Then I sat down again and got out the makings, leaned toward the fire, propped forearms on my knees and slicked up a cigarette. I'll never forget the place, the scene. I'll always remember every little item, all the motions there in the glow of the shaded electric lamps and the firelight.

I sat there smoking, musing, wondering, hoping, despairing; seeing pictures in the big fire; knowing that all I might ever do and be could be decided here tonight by Lily Hurd and Black Dan Barton.

He put the packet by the rocker, then went into the kitchen. I heard low-spoken words, dishes clattering some, and smelled coffee. Ramon stirred up, looked to the kitchen, then turned his head back and saw the guitar case that stood against the wall at the end of the couch. He put a hand on its top, then let it fall away. I heard a little of what Lily and Uncle Dan'l were saying. It was about reading my poems. I was bound to have it done tonight, he told her, even as I was determined to leave early in the morning before the camp was astir. Pretty soon they came in with coffee and plates and a pile of apple cake that hit me right where I lived when I got squared off at it. I ate half the pile all by myself before I was through.

Nothing could have been more quieting to me than this, with Lily talking along as though we were back as we'd been so many eventides in Montana. Uncle Dan'l only looked and listened, musing at me, picking up my bunch of poems a couple of times and giving me looks that said, "We'll get to them. Settle down. Let's take our time." Lily got me to telling her about the Portland Free Public Library, where she'd worked three years after she was out of high school, and the next thing I knew I was gabbing away about her old boss, Mary Wink, and of Ellen Crady, and on the beauty spots of Portland, even on the Copenhagen sawmill, good old Einar Skjalgsson, Shot Gunderson and the Seven Bulls. I got to feeling good all through from the cake, the coffee, the talking from deep inside me, and the love that shone to me from Lily Hurd. I'd never seen the like for me on the face of any other woman. I remembered the half-dream of that first night in the Beaverheads camp. Me sitting on a stool with Lily and Ramon in their tent home; me getting littler and littler, getting goldy-haired too; and at last too little to set and having to be picked up and held. Yet I'd gone on from evil to evil. She knew it, looking at me now. She was as a saint. She had patterned her present life on the saints of her church. There in a back room slept her two children. Here was her Ramon, as a child. That way was her love. This love shone on me. It was a new thing on me, for what I'd shed in facing Uncle Dan'l and telling him. It was good. I made another cigarette and looked through the smoke at Uncle Dan'l as he went to stir up the fire again. The poems had been put back in my mind. A boy's cry sounded. Lily got up to answer it. I looked around and saw that Ramon was half up from his couch. Then I went over, pulled a chair with me, sat down, and took his hand. Ramon looked long into my eyes, then sank back, resting. I sat on, his hand tight on mine.

When Lily returned Dan'l Barton was reading the poems. She had a couple of newspaper pages with her, and she handed them to me without saying anything before going on to her chair. I held the paper to the light with my free hand. The pages were from the *Sunday Oregonian*. They were filled with descriptions and pictures of the new building for the Portland Free Public Library that had just been dedicated and opened. Print on rough paper and blurry pictures. But memory and imagination were awakened in me with power and light to fill them in with colors of my faith. Books. Poetry. Rooms walled with books. A table, a chair, a blank page, a pencil in hand, words in my head; and a certain power of the spirit to open the inner headgate and start the words flowing in order through my hand to the desert page; flowing in order by means of a form perfected by poets through thousands of years in all nations: Poesy, Poesy. Life there, too. The library people, who lived with and for books. One picture showed the people of the new library. Mary Wink. And one was Ellen Crady. So there she was, unmarried. I dreamed a little.

It was not of Ellen then, but of the way of the writer at his work. The hand resting on a blank page, a pencil or pen in the hand. On walls the books from this way of writing. Books of writing older than the redwood tree, and living books still; the oldest living things on the earth of life.

Free for me, Big Jim Turner. Full welcome for me to seek and labor on my aspiration; free welcome for me there in the new temple of books by the great forest river and in the arms of green hills.

They were reading on, Lily Hurd and Uncle Dan'l, not speaking. The old anxiety rose in me again as I put the paper down and watched them. They had read deep into the pack. The early scraps had been on top. They were all stacked aside on the reading table. Now Uncle Dan'l passed on to Lily the pages of one of the longer poems. I knew it at sight of the pages. On this one I'd sweated blood. I couldn't tell by his look what he thought of it. Still holding to Ramon's hand, I watched Lily, I remembered—

THREE EXERCISES ON AN ANCIENT THEME

It was a pretty high-flown title for a hobo poet to apply to one of his notions, but there it was, that was how I'd written it. The images of the words were as clear as day in my memory—

I

Forest Sunrise

I have seen a thousand suns rise
On forests and forest rivers;
Sunups on the white pine of the Clearwater, on the Missoula
    tamarack, on the fir, cedar, hemlock and spruce of the Tilla-
    mook, the Hoh and the Skagit, on the Klamath's sugar pine,
    on the Humboldt's redwood tree, and on the yellow pine of the
    Okanogan and the Deschutes.
All saying the beauty of morning is the best beauty.
Let me not sleep past any rising of yours on forest rivers,
O sun!
Even through the thundercloud I see you there,
With faith for my eyesight.

II

Sunup Hangover

I am in temper to strike at anyone or anything.
Self-hate and self-loathing are alive in me, too,
Crawling and whining.
Right now nothing could exult me more than a blow on my cheek,
A bruising, bloodying, rocking, dazing blow.
By Jesus, I would exult to it,
Turning the other cheek;
Heart pounding, blood engorging my eyes, hands lusting to tear
    my brother.

Words obscene and profane gall into my mouth,
Now I can curse what I cherish,
Now I can kill the thing I love.
Swamp dawn.
Gray, sullen, humid, smothering dawn.
Blood lightning in the east,
And thunder.
Not lusty, stirring giant thunder ringing:
Devil's thunder, Old Nick a-growling.

Let hell yammer.
I give a damn, I give a damn for nothing,
Not even for dying.
My testimony is for red hell this morning,
This sunup.

III

Daylight in the Swamp

Roll out, you savages, roll out or roll up!
Pull on your rags, you timber beasts,
You hair-pounders.
She's time to cuff and leather up the hay-burners.
Mind that dingdong—
Rise and shine!

DAYLIGHT IN THE SWAMP!

COME AND GET IT WHILE IT'S HOT,
COME AND GET IT WHILE IT'S HOT!
KEEP A-COMIN',
KEEP A-COMIN',
DON'T STOP,
DON'T STOP!

Some call, sizzler!
Can't cook, can't even make a rhyme—
Christ, what a gut-burglar!

DAYLIGHT IN THE SWAMP!

The stomach-robber makes that gut-hammer ring:
Ding-a-dong-a—ding-a-dong-a—ding-a-dong-a—ding!
Rise up a-roarin', and sing, bullies, sing!
Come all ye scratchy pinetops, so lank around the middle,
Grunts and cackleberries and slabs are on the griddle.
Tim-BER! Smell 'em, smell 'em with the pine,
Come a-horsin' and a-hoggin' to the cookhouse line!
The big-wheels want for rollin'
Where the ridge wind blows,

So pack your guts
And hit the ruts
As the sky
Turns rose.

DAYLIGHT IN THE SWAMP!

They read on, giving me no sign. The light dimmed inside me and the words, my tries at poetry words, faded. I looked to the fire. It was sinking some, but Dan'l Barton did not stir to tend it. The ticking of a clock grew loud to me. I looked back at Ramon. His face was turned from the lamps and he slept. I put his hand over to him and he let it rest beside him on the couch blanket. Then I made a cigarette. I noticed that Lily was reading through a page that held a sonnet. Writing a sonnet was going to church for me. I wrote sonnets on my knees, feeling myself before the spirits of the godlike sonneteers. Work, prayerful work, a sonnet, even this poor thing—

SLOUGH OF DESPOND

Years, years so lost and yet so closely held
In this the grave of being which is mine,
How can I see my love's pure beauty shine,
While hearing dirges, still so harshly knelled?
Life's old foul weeds blow up, and they are smelled
Above the violet and the columbine.
The taste of vinegar, and not of wine,
Is in my mouth. And so my fate is spelled.
Oh, this debasement! Even so from birth:
Corrupted childhood, and corrupted youth,
Out of a bitter, black ancestral stream.
So I must join the miserable of earth,
Be in self-loathing if I be in truth. . . .
Let me be false one moment more, and dream!

Sad sonnet, poor thing. The hand of Caliban, callused, sweaty and begrimed, apparent in every line. Yet a truth, maybe. Swamp light, slough mire, life of the common man, spirit of the common lot, me fit to be its sonneteer, fit only for this. However ill worded this sonnet was, yet the images of its words in my mind had power to darken me. I got up and went over to fix the fire. I did, and then stood and poured out, rolled, licked and twisted up another cigarette. I lit it and stood with my back against a rock flank of the fireplace, leaning against the rock, neck bowed, a-brooding. There they sat, fair saint and black dynamiter, reading the big one now, the long poem, the main job, the one I banked on. This was the "Poem on a Poor Boy," written at Orofino, Idaho, on November 22, 1912; with William Howard Taft still President and Woodrow Wilson coming up. A free land. That was a free poem they were reading, one truly free and not all from despond and self-loathing. They read it through, not noticing me. The last, the last page. I stood on.

Uncle Dan'l got up without looking at me and brought back his old copy of *Leaves of Grass* from a wall shelf. He showed a a page to Lily. She motioned me to come and see with them. I read these lines—

Sit awhile dear son.
Here are biscuits to eat and here is milk to drink,
But as soon as you sleep and renew yourself in sweet clothes, I
    kiss you with a good-by kiss and open the gate for your egress
    hence.

Long enough have you dreamed contemptible dreams,
Now I wash the gum from your eyes,
You must habit yourself to the dazzle of the light and of every
    moment of your life.

Long have you timidly waded holding a plank by the shore,
Now I will you to be a bold swimmer,
To jump off in the midst of the sea, rise again, nod to me, shout,
    and laughingly dash with your hair.

It was then as a spring breakup inside me. There is no telling it, no testifying what hell cracked and flooded away. There was no saying for my mouth to them, to fair and saintly Lily Hurd and to the black-maned giant with the face of a pickhandled Lincoln, and no saying for them to me. We looked through tears. It was all joy. I don't know why we had to weep.

18. The Fight

I WAS DEALT A FULL HOUSE. RUSS, BUD AND OLLIE Hicks were all in the roundup camp when I came to it early in the afternoon. They were in an argument, bunched on their horses up this way by the string of wagons and tents. A dozen or more other riders were back yonder at the corrals, working the beef. Russ Hicks stood out, tall in the saddle, proud and aglitter, as of old. He was haranguing Ollie, his voice ringing hard to me, like the sound of steel on rimrock. A pearl-handled gun butt caught the sun at his right hip. He was ordering Ollie to get out and go home and leave the riders here to do and say what they damned well pleased. There'd been some mighty change in Ollie Hicks. It was marked to me even at this distance. Bud was the same, squatting in the saddle, wearing plainest work duds, sitting by while Russ ran things with a high hand. Ollie was now bigger than both his brothers, but he bowed his head to Russ.

Well, I'd vowed to Dan'l Barton that I was not going to rest until I'd made a play to satisfy my soul with these men. Now it was a deal, I had the hand I'd asked for, and I needed to move in or crawl—crawl forever in my life. No excuse for a backout. There were small ranchers there among the riders to see to fair play.

"Gird ye ye loins, Jim Turner," I heard myself say.

Funny thing. Casting back, remembering a revival story of the Rev. Pearl Yates and the words with which he'd admonished himself before tearing into a saloon hell to clean it out bare-handed.

Preaching fever. Girding now to drive the coward, the Old Nick
out of my soul, to wipe out this dreaming and dreaming of stories
in which Russ Hicks was made to hang and burn, bleed and die at
my hand. I hoped it might not come to actual battle with him.
The play I had rigged up was a solid part of the hope. Now I kept
Montan reined up and thought the play over, while Russ Hicks
went on tongue-lashing Ollie.

The big game of people and locations on the land was moving
into what Black Dan Barton called a consolidation of the interests.
John J. Navarre had organized it, representing Grundy Johnson.
He had started it by selling his interest in Navarre & Hurd to the
banker, George B. M. Hoover. The consolidation seemed to be
working itself out now in harmony and peace. When it was done
Lily would have the money and be free to take Ramon to Portland on the bright chance for his recovery of strength of mind.
Her mother and father were dead. They had left her nothing. Black
Dan Barton would feel free to return to his own business in life,
the business of the revolution, his faith still.

There was more to it, a lot more. What counted for me at this
time and in this place was that Russ Hicks wanted no trouble
with any man, no risk of political or other scandal on his name,
while the Big Consolidation of the Interests was in progress.

The land and its growth. The coming of people. Locations.
Boundary lines. The game for locations on the land, for its growth.
Trees here. Forests of pine. Sawmill and logging railroad to tap
them. Big money needed. Big interests required. Able men wanted.
Opportunity for a Jack Hard, with his kind of ability and ambition,
opportunity for a Dan'l Barton, with his kind. Old rebel and Wobbly? Ex-con? What of it, if he can fill the bill?

Bright and early this morning I'd seen the work of Black Dan
Barton in this great project of men on the Lemolo pine forests.
I had my horse grained and saddled, and Lily had me fed before
the camp's first dingdong. We made quick farewells, and I was
three miles down and on the ridge of the high-bulging basalt hump
above the gorge of the Little Lemolo River before there was a
streak of daylight. There I let Montan blow, and swung down and
crawled to the rim for a sight of the job that Black Dan had come

from the Grays Harbor woods to do for the injured Ramon and his family.

The river was a roaring white ribbon two hundred feet down, between black walls. Under my eyes a shelf marked the bank of the river, well above flood marks. The daylight glimmered along the rails of a logging spur on the shelf. I could make out the ragged line, fifty feet or so below me, that marked the top of the giant rock slice that Black Dan Barton had blasted out of the canyon wall in one charge. It was a gamble. Jack Hard had everything in it. So did the Hurds. The firm had gone deep into debt to Grundy Johnson before the blast was fired. All bets were on what the old dynamiter knew about hard rock and blasting powder, and particularly about the hard rock of the Little Lemolo canyon.

He had driven a four-foot coyote hole along through the canyon wall, with stopes, side holes, at what he judged to be the right places. This tunnel, in which men worked squatting or on knees, had been loaded with seventy-five hundred kegs of black powder and thirty-five hundred boxes of giant, all for a single blast. And he made it. Navarre & Hurd made a clean win on the gamble. The blast sliced the rock wall down where Black Dan had ordered the blast to slice, and set the loosened and lifted rock over and down where he had ordered the blast to set it. The canyon gorge was thereby not ruinously dammed, and a steam shovel moved in and made the grade, with only cleanup blasting required.

The way was opened for the building of a railroad logging spur to the pine sections owned by Ramon and Black Dan, and to some twenty thousand acres of prime government pine in the upper basin of the Little Lemolo.

Salvation to Lily and Ramon. A big win for Jack Hard, and backing for a still greater play for him in this forest region. Black Dan Barton had no pride, but I was proud for him, there in the daybreak high above the white water of the Lemolo. I took my hat off to the Big Job he had done here. Then I climbed Montan and rode for the trail by which Lily and Ramon had come over the mountains from Bob Creek on that long-ago November morning. I rode on with good heart and high head, an apprentice poet whose ax-hewn lays and walking-plow chants had been blessed as shapes of promise.

I turned Montan off the old freighting road and down the tracks to the camp. I rode up to the Hicks men and spoke in a low and pleasant tone, reminding them who I was.

"This here is as good a place and time as I can ever hope for to settle things with you," I said. "My one want in such settlement is witnesses for fair play. There are plenty nigh. In a fair fight I'm ready to take you on one at a time, and I'm ready to take you on all three in a bunch." The blood pumped thick and hot to my neck, now that I'd come into this too far to haul back. "God damn you, choose up, you bastards!" The words came up hoarse and high.

"Take it easy, Jim Turner." Russ Hicks kept his voice as level, hard and cold as he would in making talk to a wild-tempered horse. "It's no use, kid. I've long expected you to show up, looking for trouble. I'm all set to put you in the pen like a shot. That's enough for me. I'm not fightin' you."

"You'll be runnin' from me, then," I said, passing over his bluff about the pen. "Fight or run, Mr. Hicks."

Some of the people over at the corrals were looking our way.

I don't remember too well most of the words said in that set-to, but these I do remember well. Saying them did my soul more good than almost anything else I've ever spoken. I repeated them. I looked dead-straight into the eyes of Russ Hicks and said them over.

"You'll fight, or you'll run," I said. "And this right soon."

He glanced over his shoulder. I held an unwinking look on him, but I could see some riders starting for us. Art Yardley was one, Walt Payne another. They knew me, surely. Russ faced me again. His face was tight with the temper he was holding back, his mouth a straight-edge line, little muscle knots bulging from jaws and chin. His eyes stared without light. Suddenly he said—

"You want more than a fight. What do you want?"

I said, "I want my name cleared down in Knox as only you Hickses can have it cleared. I want to bind you to it now. I want you to tell in front of witnesses what the three of you did to me in the Copper King Saloon and how you railroaded me to jail——"

"You be God-damned," he cut in on me, like the arrogant son of a bitch he could not help but be in his soul. "You're askin' for the state pen, I tell you. What's more, you'll spread scandal and shame over all of your folks here, your aunt, Sue Hurd—don't you know she's a widow and a wheel-chair cripple now?"

That caught me. Lily and Uncle Dan'l hadn't told me of that. Russ Hicks talked on at me, hard and fast.

"You've got a sweet horse, hobo. I'll give you three hundred gold, as he stands, not even a look at his teeth, and I'll throw in a straw-tail for you to ride into Oregon tonight and out of this country again. Say it's a deal, you'd better call it a deal, Jim Turner!"

He had me going, he really had me going. I'd told myself over and over that this thing I'd determined to do, the thing I was in the thick of now, would pile trouble and worry on many others, and shame, I reckoned. But the play I'd gambled on was lost—Russ Hicks had taken it from me, and now my brag had to be made good.

He was easing the gauntlet from his right hand. Now I had to go for him. Now I had to, or else freeze and back down and away as I had with Joe Hill. "Run or fight," I'd said to Russ Hicks. I had to hold to it, oh, I had to now! I strained to set Montan for a shotgun plunge at the palomino. Russ saw it as his hand came free of the gauntlet. So did Ollie Hicks see it. Then, suddenly:

"Oh, don't, Jim Turner! Oh, don't, Jim! You're right, we are all wrong, and I'll confess everything, if Russ won't, and I'll beg your forgiveness too, and God's forgiveness for the evil we done unto you, Jim Turner—"

"Ollie, shut up, for Christ's sake!" There was fury and fear together in this cry of Russ Hicks. "Keep quiet! Get out of here! You'll ruin us, you—you crazy religious fool!"

Walt Payne heard it all, and so did Art Yardley and some others. The riders pressed nigh as Ollie Hicks swung his horse over in front of Russ and close to me. He was bigger than Russ, as big as me, and his face was as a huge baby's face now, all screwed up and crying, the tears streaming.

"Jim Turner, I've prayed for this hour!" he moaned and blubbered on. "All these years I was haunted by the sermon you preached about the boy who was ruint by his sins, and then my own sins found me out, my ma, my own dear mother, she died, and grief for my sins it was that killed her!"

"Shut up about her!" Russ snarled at him.

"I'll shut up, I'll say no more, dear brother," Ollie cried and snuffled on. "All I want to say is to beseech your forgiveness, Jim Turner, and atone for the wrongs we done you. I will testify on them, I will kneel down here in the dirt and call all to hear me confess the evil I done to you, and how I repent it and would atone!"

Bud Hicks swung over and grabbed Ollie to hold him in the saddle.

"You win, hobo," Russ Hicks said, low and fast to me, spurring close. "Give us a week. Ride on out. Keep over in Oregon and in the clear till it's all fixed, all charges against you rubbed out. It's a promise. Let's shake. You need any money?"

"I don't need money and I don't need to shake," I said. "I'll take you at your word. But I want you and Bud to back up what Ollie said, that the three of you did me dirt, and you are sorry. I want that as much as I want to be cleared."

He grated it out, loud enough to be heard, "We played a dirty trick on you. I'm sorry. We'll do what we can to make it up. That goes for Bud."

"It goes for me," Bud said.

"You heard them," I said, standing in the stirrups and looking from one to one of the seven or so riders who had come up; nodding and wagging a hand at the four I knew. "You can witness that I'm to be made clear and free of the law here. I don't expect to make more of it, there's no need to stir up an old trouble and hurt other people. I'm pleased to settle it this way. So long, and I hope to see you later."

Something like that, something like that I said it, standing in my saddle stirrups and looking over the high head of my big red horse. I'd never felt so gloried up from anything, outside the writing of a poem. It seems a kind of fool bragging story, as I set it down. For I see and hear all that happened through the light and thunder of a moment, that moment when I stood high and knew that for once in my life I had me a triumph. It was the real one, for it was not just a win of a deal over the powerful Hicks men, but a triumph over the coward in the marrow, over the Old Nick in the soul of

Big Jim Turner. A moment, and I don't expect to know its like again.

There I faced the riders, the strong men of a rough country; the corrals, the spread of cattle, the hills rolling up for the mellow sun of the late September afternoon; and all was light.

The night was clouding down when I put Montan up at the Knox stockyards, in the feed shed for saddle horses. Then I hiked up the railroad tracks to the riverside plant of the Lemolo Lumber Company. It was still only a one-headrig sawmill and a box factory. I'd made it in all right, a few minutes before quitting time. The screams of the headsaw, resaw, edger, trimmer and planer knives working green pine died away at the order of a booming whistle as I hustled along. White lights shone up from where the red lights of the Notch used to shine. The sawmill and the lumbermen had done what the Knox churches and preachers had been unable to do in forty years—put Big Mag Hinote out of business. The saw-mill looked, sounded and smelled like home to me. A little cold twilight breeze was fragrant with the rousing smell of pine sawdust. Hurrying past a string of cars at a loading shed, I saw steam from a dry kiln in the outside lights. On down in backwater, behind a long hooked finger of rimrock, logs were cradled in booms that stretched almost up to the bridge that crossed the Snake to Oregon.

I ought to be over that bridge before daylight, I thought, and knew that I was a fool not to be riding over it now, and no dally-ing. Let Marshal Moss Eckert or a deputy sheriff pick me up to-night, and the lid would be blown off the bucket, with Russ Hicks able to do nothing on keeping his promise. But I had to risk it, I had to be here tonight, for a little time.

The people were stringing up the roadway from the plant and spreading on their homeward ways from Old Street. Sawmill men, box factory boys and girls. I spied Bess Clover with two others, in the flare of a hanging street light as it struck between two cot-tonwoods. I speeded up and spread my stride. The other two were a tall, yellow-haired young man and a short, fat Indian woman with a bandanna tied over her head. I was right behind them when the tall man tipped his rag of a hat and turned with the woman to cross over to a side street. I looked over. The corner there was the location of the old Copper King Saloon. Now a three-story frame boarding house stood there, fronted with a sign—ATKINS HOTEL.

Bess started on. Some people were stringing by. I softly called her name and said, "Wait." She stopped dead still for seconds, then turned to me as I came close. The rays of the light struck right on her face. She was wearing a red bandanna too. Under its color and in the brightness her face seemed so pale, thin, strained and weary. But her eyes were steady, strong, looking up to mine. So we stood there, gazing, eyes taking each other in. I was no sight to cheer her, I well knew. My mackinaw collar was turned up and my hat was pulled low. I half expected scorn from her, the word that she despised me, and I could feel the sullen smoke of this fear in my face, its heat in my eyes. Then the mood sank away. "What if she does?" I thought. "What the hell!" There she stood, Johnny Clover's kid, thin, tired, ill maybe, lumped in old work clothes, but with eyes steady, eyes without fear. Woman worker. Rebel girl. Sister, little sister, if she wanted it so, if that was how it had to be.

"Hello," I said, and then my throat was stone.

"Hello," said Bess Clover. "Why, Jim Turner! Come over here."

She was no way shaken and seemed little surprised. I tracked three or four steps with her around a cottonwood trunk. We stopped in its shadow, faced, and I took her hands and looked long, long, not saying anything.

Dream, dream. One more dream story. This, too. This now. I could be riding over the Snake River bridge yonder to a free trail in Oregon, and be dreaming this. Two in a story. Two in a theater play. Jolly Della Pringle and Her Merry Company. Poor girl, ragged boy, so forlorn on the stage of the old opera house up yonder; standing in the howling wind and freezing snow of a slum street, and the worst yet to come; for back in the shadows lurks the deathly villain, the false Lord Lonsdale; who now knows well that the ragged boy is the true Lord Lonsdale, and so is out to kill.

I told her, trying to make it a laugh and break this strain. Then I said I'd made a deal with Russ Hicks to clear me with the law, but I had to get on to Oregon and give him time to keep his promise. I couldn't risk being picked up by Moss Eckert now.

"But things can happen, Bess," I said. "I had to stop and see you for a minute. I've never been sure since that night in Portland if you'd even want to speak to me again."

"Jim, you were all wrong in your mind. So was Joe Hill."

"I reckon. But right now my concern is why you're back home here, killin' yourself as a wage slave."

"I'm not."

"I can help you. I've got some gold on me——"

"Don't you mention it! We're fixed now. We're all right."

"I met your brother Albert and Aunt Sue's oldest, Joe Hurd, in Salmon City. Albert ought to be made to help you out. I gave him a preachin' to but I confess it seemed to do no good."

"We'll get along without him, unless something happens to lose me my job."

"Something like me," I said. "I'd better be goin'."

"Don't you sull on me, Jim Turner!" All of a sudden she reached to the upturned collar of my mackinaw with both hands and snapped it down. Yet holding on, she stood close. "You always have," she said, soft and slow, somehow as to herself although her eyes searched my eyes and face. "Always, Jim Turner. Maybe I've always loved you. Easy hurt, you. To me you would brood, moon, dream, show sullen face. One moment you showed me love in your face, one moment of a snowin' day. You didn't tell me you loved me, you didn't ask me if I loved you, you left me, Jim Turner. Don't you want to go now?"

"No. This has to be settled," I said; and then I told her that I loved her truly.

We just stood there, looking at each other, she gave me one little slap on the cheek with her thin hand, and stood away, then went to talking. She told me about Aunt Sue and Wiley Hurd and then said where she'd come and meet me in an hour. Then she started on up Old Street for Shack Row, walking from shadow of cottonwood tree to cast of street light, from shadow to light, smaller and dimmer, smaller and dimmer in my sight. Little speck of life on the great earth. Lone, lone. I stood and put my hand up and held it where her hand had slapped me in love, love, which doth ever triumph in the end, says Jolly Della Pringle. Let me exult now and be proud. Ho-hidey-ho; and why so pale and wan, fond lover?

Why, thou knowest, wight, that under thy tatters thou art the true
Lord Lonsdale and all will come out in the wash——

"Oh, for God's sake," I said. "Hang on to yourself."

We might come through on it, with some luck, with everyday
sense; with Russ Hicks keeping his part of our bargain, we could
come through.

I rolled a smoke and lit it, then hit across the railroad yards for
the river. On the bench's lip I stood and looked down, right about
where I'd looked from in another dusk, watching Joe Hill and the
rebel hobos in their jungles camp. Logs were boomed there now.
Up to my left the bank bulged out and hooked around the backwater, with the bridge going on from it to the Oregon bank. Wide
water here below the bridge. Quiet water. Water at work, cradling
logs. No end to the uses men could find for a river. The river didn't
know or care. Love, birth, death. The time of man a brief candle
to the river; less—less than nothing to the river. Essie Clover had
looked on the river here many a time, and the river had looked
on her, unknowing. She was dead, and here was Bess. Wiley Hurd
had come to the river here in "the early days," and time was old,
old to the river ten thousand years before the early days. Wiley
Hurd was dead, and Fay Yardley, and here was I. Bess Clover
and Jim Turner. Life was a river. Its flowing force had pulled Bess
Clover out of her work and way and back here to take Ma Essie's
place in keeping the younger girls together and putting them through
school. Susan Hurd had been burned and crippled in trying to
save her husband from the fire that had exploded through their
big house last winter. Now she was able only to hobble about to
cook meals for Bess and the Clover girls.

I surely didn't want to hurt Aunt Sue, or to harm Bess, or to
make trouble for anybody. I'd ridden Montan hard past the Hoover
place, now built up and thriving, to keep from seeing Isabel and
Gabe Turner and to keep them from seeing me. Bad medicine,
me. Bad medicine for everybody I'd ever lived around. Now Bess.
I was afraid.

The bridge was a clear, free trail. I stood and looked over it and
felt a powerful pull from it to be riding there, to be on my way on
my big red horse, Montan. Riding on where the bridge went into

the darkness, riding on Portland-wise, for the new temple of books. There was power in me to write poems and stories. Now I was sure of it. My mood and thought kept turning on this as I headed up the road from the bridge, crossed the tracks, some with lines of boxcars on both sides of the road, then back to the cottonwoods of Old Street. I turned across for the business blocks at the old Copper King corner, and walked fast, head down, collar up, for the restaurant that Jenny Atkins had kept going, along with her new boarding house for sawmill workers. Jenny had been a Socialist comrade of Wiley Hurd's. She had made money and built up a business, but she held to the rebel faith. Jenny and Bess were friends.

The dim flow of light from the shaded electric bulb on the booth wall caught in the puffs and coils of Bess Clover's hair, under the turned-up side of her feathered hat. Her left hand, thin hand, worker's hand, fooled with the shining hair while she read into my poems.

" 'Grass is poetry,' " she read aloud, " 'a brook is music, and a willow by a brook is a poem and a song . . . for you and for me.' " She looked up sharply. "Was it really written for me, Jim?"

"Yes," I said, "though this is a copy from memory. A library girl got hold of the first copy. She kept it."

I told her about Ellen Crady.

"That's the girl for you," said Bess.

"Well, she's not mine. You are mine."

She went on reading. I could tell she was missing something she'd hoped to find, or wanted to find.

A waitress had cleared our supper dishes away and left us with some fresh coffee. I supped at mine now, and smoked. A green curtain was pulled over the entrance to the little booth. The plaster wall was a paler green. The end walls of the booth were painted pine. I hooked my chair around, leaned back to the corner, smoked, brooded at Bess Clover as she read the poetical works of James Birney Turner, and mused some on what she'd told me of her own doings before Ma Essie's death.

"Poems by me, rebel girl poems," she had said. "I think I tried them only on account of you, Big Jim. It was a kind of companionship. I put all I had into organizin' waitresses and kitchen workers and into speakin' and singin', agitatin' for the One Big Union. But I lacked strength. I wasn't let to go to the Lawrence strikes back East last year; when riots broke in the California hopfields, I was here, bound here—workin' ten hours a day for fifteen cents an hour at pickin' up box shooks and puttin' 'em down, pickin' 'em up and puttin' 'em down. But I'm thrivin' at it. I'm gainin' strength. I'll be all right, Jim."

She didn't look it. I wondered, seeing her now through the cigarette smoke, and it was more worry for her in me than about the pack of poetry and my writing of poems. I didn't need the library and the books for this. I could work here, once cleared, take care of her and the girls and Aunt Sue, and study and write at odd times as I'd always done. But that wasn't the thing, and I knew it. The thing to be settled with us was in what she said, her reading done.

"Strong lines and sweet lines, like the ones written by the poets of the books as their early poems," Bess Clover said. I could tell she was picking her words. She leaned toward me, her elbows on the table, hands up, fingers interlaced and working nervously. Her face was so tired, white, strained, but her eyes burned. Then she pulled herself back and broke out a smile. "There is power, there is power," she said. "It kind of beat me down. I feel like I want a cigarette. You don't care, do you?"

She rolled one like a charm from my makings. I made another one. We smoked together and supped a little more at the cooling coffee.

"I'll be honest on how I feel about the poems," Bess said, easily now. "I know you want me to be." She looked at the stack of paper and scrawls, drew a long breath, and went on. "I'll tell you what I kept lookin' for and didn't find, Jim. It was for a blaze, a flame, then a spark from your own life, your own labor, your own struggle, your own revolt, you Big Jim Turner—and I found only borrowed fire. What can this matter, what can it mean"— she waved her hand over the poems—"if they do not speak as a voice of the masses, of the people who are poor, weary and heavy-laden, your own people, Jim—mine and your own? These are all poems of self, self, self. You can be stronger, and give of your strength to others; surely you can be stronger."

"No," I said. "It's no use to preach to me, Bess. I sweat blood to write anything. It's not in me to pick up a faith or a cause and write a poem for it. I tried to, I truly tried to in 'Poem on a Poor Boy.' And it wrote itself out on me alone and my lone hope, with the masses left in the ditch."

"It has a power. You aren't mad for what I said, are you? You still love me, don't you?"

"Oh, Christ, yes! Go on. Let's straighten this out, Bess."

"Say it."

"I love you," I said; the strange words.

"Jim, let's write a poem on Ida Dorst. Remember her?" Bess dropped the cigarette butt on the saucer. It went right out. "The poor thing," she said. "You told me of the Grande Ronde. I've been there, organizin'. It's a real pretty country. La Grande is a lovely place. I stopped off there and started agitatin' with the girls in the railroad restaurant. I was jailed, then run out almost before I started. But I was with some women at the jail long enough to learn about Ida Dorst. She'd been taken sick in La Grande, and was sent from there to the state hospital, with what Miss Goldman calls the oldest occupational disease. It had hit her like lightnin' consumption, finished her in a few years. Couldn't you be inspired to write a poem on her, Jim? Or on the mothers of Lawrence who were clubbed by the police when they tried to send their children away from the terror of the textile strike? Won't you try, with me, Jim?"

"No," I said. "I feel like dirt to say it, Bess, but I won't try it in the way you want me to try it."

"But why? How can you lack this fire, this revolt?"

I said, " 'Here, lilac, with a branch of pine.' " I reached over and took her hands in my hands. Pretty soon we went out into Old Street.

We walked in silence up the line of cottonwoods, then crossed the street that ran between the depot and the main business part of town. This also led to the roadway over the tracks and down to the Snake River bridge. Across the street we walked into the same old ruts of the Shack Row road. Dead weeds stood and a gravel path ran crookedly along at our left, and the railroad fence and sidetracks were at our right. It was a late hour for the hard workers of Shack Row. Back from the gravel path the section houses were gaunt, black, monstrous shapes in the faint moonlight.

"Saddle moon," I said. "Yellow saddle moon."

"That's it," Bess said. "Pretty words, Jim, for such a rotten, foul old stretch of human life as this. Did I tell you that the Dorst family still lives here? Dorst hoboed with Joe Hill until he got caught in a Billy Sunday revival and hit the sawdust trail. So he came home in contrition and Luella took him in. Now he's a full section boss, a real king snipe. He preaches hangin' for the Wobblies and the chain gang for other sinners. Luella is so proud of him. They are the two best haters in Knox."

"Two of the people, two of the masses," I said. "Ramon Hurd goes about sayin', 'Love one another,' and 'Reap in mercy,' and is called out of his mind."

That was all we said. I heard the ever forlorn far whistle of a running locomotive. It sung the sadness of parting to me. I imagined that Bess heard it so with me, that she pressed closer and her hand held tighter to my arm. It seemed harder for me to breathe. I took a deep breath and looked from her, up at the saddle moon riding high over the hills, and around at the red and green circles of the switch-stand lamps on the tracks. We were past the section houses. Along over there at the left the shacks of the Row were ugly black blobs in the weeds and bush, and one was the home of the Clovers.

We stopped at her gate. We stood close. I felt my left hand touch her arm, then clasp it. I felt my right hand touch her face, and move to her breast and down and about her, as the honeybee moves down the flowering vine. So it happened with us and to us, and we went into her place together.

It was deep dark but coming on daybreak when I left, with the people in the shack-home stirring.

"I'll be back for you," I said, "as soon as Russ Hicks makes good on his promise and I can be free here."

We'd said seven farewells. "Hurry, Jim," Bess said now. "Hurry over the river. Daylight comes."

I was about a half hour making it on shank's mare to the stockyards, saddling and packing and riding back up Old Street. It was breaking day, all right, when I rode Montan into the depot street and wheeled him eastward. There ahead the street was clear to see, over the tracks and between the broken lines of boxcars.

The big red horse shied and snorted. In the same second two men on horseback loomed against the east, rearing out from behind a row of sidetrack cars. One hollered, "Halt! Name uh zuh law!" Then the caller was close, cutting his horse around Montan, poking a finger at a shield that shone from his coat, then slapping his hand down to a rifle in a saddle sheath. He kept on a-hollering, " 'm Dep'ty She'ff Madden. Jim Turner, y'un'er 'resht 'n' whashuh shay be use' 'gainst yuh." He hiccuped and belched and reeked of whisky. I only sat in the saddle, reining in on Montan, paying most attention to the second rider. Now he rode up to me. He was Russ Hicks.

"Shut up, Muley, and keep ready for your gun," he said. He pulled his palomino up slantwise on the road. Then his voice sounded on, each word like a rub of stone on stone. "That's a stolen horse. Light down."

"No, you don't," I said, so sick with my idiocy and with the old fear rising. "I don't light down," I managed to say. "And I've got a legal and good bill of sale on this horse."

"We've other evidence at the county jail. Muley, throw a rope on this stolen horse and put the manacles on the thief."

The drunken deputy had me blocked on the road back to town. He picked up the lariat that he'd carried loose on his saddle horn, but he only fumbled with it as I glowered at him. Maybe there was hell showing in my face to scare him. Anyhow, he kind of pleaded, "Now, don' make trouble, shon. I don' wanna haf to shoos-shoot yuh. You lishen Mr. Hicks, shon." Then he whined past me at Russ Hicks. "You go on an' reashun with'm, Mr. Hicks, like you tol' me you would do. Pleesh. Iffen you pleesh."

He was drunk but deadly. He was a killer from away back. Russ Hicks called him a boozing old bastard, and crowded yet closer to me, craning his head and staring with eyes of pure malignance in the breaking light.

"All right, Turner," he said. "I'll reason with you. I don't want

any shootin' out of this, no more scandal than you and Ollie pro-
voked yesterday. But I'm not lettin' any slick-ear hobo like you
beat my hand, either. I've got you foul. I rode in to the ranch
and telephoned the brands on that sorrel to Montana. I know
how to cinch you on him. So we are runnin' you in. If you raise
a yell on that old business I'll say you are lyin' to get even with
me for peggin' you as a horse thief. Don't think Ollie will help you.
That boy has gone crazy over religion. He is right now confined
under doctor's care. The men who witnessed your play yesterday
were convinced by me that I agreed with you only to quiet poor
Ollie. I'd already been tryin' to get him home because of his crazy
preachin'. You can see there's no use to buck me any longer,
can't you?"

I could. The only trouble of it for Russ Hicks was that he had
made it too tight and too strong on me. He was running a whizzer.
It was pure bluff. He aimed to scare me, scare me into a promise
to leave Idaho for good. Well, he scared me. He scared me too
much. I sat there frozen, hearing him, slack-jawed and knowing it,
seeing my crimes and the sentences for them bunched and stretched,
and me in a march of toiling convicts until I was old and gray,
until all sense was scared out of me. I had no thought of begging,
of trying to make a deal. All I had left was an instinct to strike
out like a wild man and run and run and run. And so I struck.

It was my left. It was a hook. It struck at Russ Hicks, geared
with the lick of my left foot on the flank of the red horse. That
Montan had lightning in his feet. He leaped from the lick as fast
as I struck, and this was as fast as I'd ever hooked that left anywhere. Just exactly what spot it hit and how I did not see or know,
but it turned Russ Hicks out of the saddle and set him down on
his neck. His horse lunged into a run. Russ Hicks's foot was hung
up in the stirrup, from the twist of his leg in that knockout fall—
the sickening twist of a broken leg. I saw that much over a shoulder
in the gallop of Montan across the sidetracks. I looked ahead,
zigzagging Montan and hunching low in fear of Muley Madden's
deadly gunfire. But no shots cracked after me. Again I peered
backward. The deputy had thrown his lariat at Russ Hicks's horse
and was pulling him to a stop. A couple of men were running up
from the cottonwoods in the now clear light. Then one reached

to pull Russ Hicks's boot from the stirrup. That was in my sight as Montan sloped down the road; and then I could see no more.

Then I was over the Snake River and on free land and open road. I loped Montan into the side trails of the hills, pointing for the Grande Ronde.

19. Poem on a Poor Boy

THIS IS FOR YOU, BESS. YESTERDAY LILY HURD FOUND me in the room which is my temple, the great room walled with books. She came up with Mary Wink and Ellen Crady to the long table. I was working to weave more of the simple truth into the pattern of the story of our September night, to make it truly yours in the telling as well as mine. For a while I'd been looking up at the poetry shelves, seeing you there, a book in your hands. This is now a well-worn fancy, yet ever fresh and bright. Then I imagined it was your hand on my shoulder. But it was Lily's. She was at last in Portland with Ramon, hopeful for his cure. I gathered up my work from the long table and we went out into the July afternoon. We sat on a cool stone seat under the inscriptions and in tree shade. I had a new writing of the Orofino poem along. I asked her to see what she thought of it now. Lily told me about you and Uncle Dan'l before she took up the poem.

It was a bad day for me, a brooding day. There was a fire wind, a hot wind from the east. It carried the smoke of burning forests. The sun was red in the dying breath of thousands of trees, its light was sickly, and the air bit my throat. I felt emptied out, a husk, a shell of a man. Nine months and more of mean living and lone labor I'd pulled out of myself and packed into the book of *Big Jim Turner*. It was a search of my life, up to and through the Orofino poem; from its earth, seed and roots to its promise. My dream was to bring the book to you. But now you are gone, gone away with Dan'l Barton in your faith, to fight for it. And I have left a poem and a tale. . . .

POEM ON A POOR BOY
By James Birney Turner

I write now in November, on my birthday's morning.
　　I remember another November,
　　and a birthday's nightfall.
Just turned seventeen, I stood in the lantern light
　　of a bunk tent, sure of myself as a man among men.
We were a construction outfit on the move in rains
　　of late fall, over the Idaho desert. Now,
　　before crossing the River Snake,
　　we had pitched tents for overnight.
I stood in the lantern light, swaying some with the surge
　　of tent roof and walls in the wind,
　　hearing the rain.

Strength of freedom was mine.
Winter, spring, summer and fall on the road,
　　with the camp men, the hobos,
　　the crop stiffs, the team hands,
　　with dynos, scissorbills, boomers,
　　gandy-dancers, shacks, snakes, snipes,
　　with punks, fuzzfaces, gaycats,
　　gunsels, roadkids,
　　with finks, dehorns, johns,
　　with timber beasts, sawdust savages, pinetops,
　　and with other breeds of working go-abouts.
Water boy, camp flunky and wagon greaser in the first months
　　of a poor boy's freedom. Then upward to a man's place
　　with the team hands of the camps. A wheel-scraper two-up,
　　then a set-in with Mormon-scraper and slip, four
　　on a Fresno scraper then; and at last
　　mule skinning from the seat of a dumper,
　　a three-up on a little red Stroud.
Now, on this camp move, a four-in-hand, two abreast,
　　wheelers and leaders, four lines,
　　and a buckskin slasher with a twine whang.
Prime for a poor boy, good for me.

Standing in the lantern light, 1 could see a long, free
   field for the running of my furrow.
Glory for me, a little gleam of glory.
I spraddled my legs, racked my hat back another notch,
   bit me off a chaw, hooked hands behind me, and
   looked so God-a'mighty proud.

There was music in the night camp, in the big tent.
Let the winds blow, and old Sunny Horn would yet
   have his guitar out, strumming and singing soft and
   low. This was glory to him, and enough glory..
Now old Sunny caught my bold eyes and sung to me.
   He sung—My mother called me to her death-bed side,
   these words she spake to me, iffen you don't quit
   yore roving ways, they'll take you to the penitentiaree,
   oh, yes, pore boy, they'll take you to the penitentiaree!
I let on not to hear. Sunny Horn was of the time of
   old, and his were the songs and the ways of old.
Not for me; not now, old-timer.

I looked ahead, seeing glory. I had a furrow to run.
   A lantern was well enough to light me on.
   Yonder away in the world all looked pretty good to me.
   Nothing to my name, I could yet spread my shoulders high and
   wide in a sheephide coat, look time in the eye, and tell—
   I'm coming on, coming with bells.

Why, yes, sure enough, I said, for this is America.
She's a great country, a good land, for all of the sin the
   Methodists see, for all of J. P. Morgan and the Gold Standard.
I stood there under the drumming of the rain on the tent,
   and I heard America singing in accord with the young
   heart; I saw her hardest face responsive to young hope,
   and I had faith that in her darkest and lowest fields
   a furrow could be plowed by lantern light, lined out
   on the flags of the American dream.

(Was the faith true then? Is it true now?
What turn of my plowing led to this abyss
   of sunless east and sunless west?

How is it that my lanterns are burned out,
   and my furrow flags down?
I dream of war and death, and why I know not.)

   I was telling . . .

He read a book, *Martin Eden,* by a lantern at the head of his
   bed of tarp and blankets on the ground. The wind drove
   rain through the tent roof there, in a slow drip on and
   about him. Tom Maguire cared only to shield his book. He
   was young, too, young and eager for more tomorrows.
In all the work camps there were young men of hard hands and
   tough minds who would read by lantern and candle to
   post themselves on their land and their world, and this
   was glory to America.
None too many of the readers, yet on every town job, in every
   wilderness camp, a few Tom Maguires, respected by their
   mates, called book-learned, scribes, and well posted.
O Sailor, too many forget, even now they forget,
   you having failed them!
Let me say for you here, Sailor, that for a good, long time
   you wrote with pure heart and clean hands as poet and
   prophet to tens of thousands like Tom Maguire. They packed
   your books in their balloons, toted them over long desert
   and timber roads to the camps, kept them through the
   hardest high-roading in the guts of Pullmans and on the
   decks of the cannonballs, carried them to county jails
   and county hospitals.
Men in Montana, up at the shift change from the bowels of the
   Big Red Hill, men in the Coeur d'Alenes free for the
   night from the sweating silver-lead stopes, men of the
   woods tracking in from ten hours of slinging rigging
   on the round stuff, harvest men, crop stiffs, bedding
   down by lantern light after dawn-to-dark slugging of
   wheat bundles in the hills of the Palouse, sailor men
   coming off stormy watch to fo'c'sle bunks and reading for a bell,
   page and print pitching with the winter rollers of the
   North Pacific, men of all the hard trades to be named, in
   from the job, bellying up to supper tables, scoffing

without words, then figuring how to put 'er in for a
  couple of hours before blackest sleep.
And a slew of them from all over using those hours to read
  story books by a man of their own blood, their own sweat,
  their own hunger, their own dreams, their own revolt.
The Tom Maguires were heard by their mates. Socialist votes
  piled high. A million votes have grown behind Eugene V. Debs.
  The ballot is our way to the Social Revolution, and we are on
  our way, said Tom Maguire. Capitalism is done for.
  Bryan and Roosevelt have stolen the platform of Socialism.
  Piece by piece, the Wage System is falling all over the world,
  and the end will be one people of the world, united in peace
  and order forever.
Standing in the lantern light under the storm-blown tent, I
  thought of this hope and faith of the Sailor and of Tom
  Maguire as furrow flags for my own plowing.

But there was Joe Saint, hunched on his blankets in a dim corner of
  the big tent. A hard-rock man, the dynamiter of our outfit,
  a silver-lead miner who was marked as a member of the revolu-
      tionary
  Industrial Workers of the World on the black-lists of the slave
  markets. A battle-loving bull of a man, misnamed Saint.
I heard him!
The employing class and the working class have nothing in common.
  It has to be a showdown war, and the sooner the
  quicker. One Big Union. Seize the machinery of production,
  and we've seized all.
Don't talk ballot to us! By the ballot the workers have
  always been betrayed. The place for the ballot box is under
  the bed. Socialism is a wet dream.
Yours for the Revolution, Fellow Worker Joe Saint.
He meant it to his soul. The time came when I saw Joe Saint
  beaten off a speaker's box, an American altar of free speech,
  and dragged to jail, trailing blood on the snow.
Direct Action. The Black Cat. The Wooden Shoe. Pie in the Sky.
  The Fighting Wobblies. John Brown. The Shays Rebellion.
  Sam Adams. The Boston Tea Party. An American Way.

There was rebellion in my blood and I owned some fighting temper.
　　The vision of blood-red furrow flags in tremendous storm
　　stirred my soul but did not move its faith.

The top man in my sight was "Jack Hard"—John Navarre.
He was another young one, though up in his twenties and old to
　　　　me, and
　　another reader and talker. Among the sixty-five men of the outfit
　　Jack Hard stood alone, and only the walking boss could tell
　　him what to do. On the job, he drove the twelve mules that
　　pulled the machine grader and wagon loader. He was the king-
　　　　jack
　　gambler of the Saturday and Sunday poker games. He had fought
　　a two-hour draw with Paddy the Devil. He had enemies and he
　　packed a gun, which he well knew how to use, having come up
　　to sergeant in one hitch with the United States Marines.
He was from Michigan. His people were people of the woods
　　from away back. His hopes were in the lands of the West.
Put politics and religions and other stuff of superstition and
　　revolution out of your mind, he said to me, Jack Hard of
　　twenty-eight years to Jim Turner of seventeen. It's all a
　　hangover from the Dark Ages, he said. It's the hell.
　　The land and the work have been the American glory, which
　　has risen and shone in spite of the preachers and politicians.
　　And now we have the machines to improve the work, to
　　improve the land, to increase the glory of America.
The work, the ruin of the work, the hope of the work, I'll
　　try to tell you how I see it, said Jack Hard—John Navarre.

There was the work in Michigan, he said, the work of fifty
　　years, the work of horses and men in the pine woods.
　　Man work and horse work up to the sawmills, and a lot
　　of muscle power doing the work there.
He said that one day he sat on a high Michigan hill,
　　thinking it out, while he looked four ways and nothing
　　but stumps, stumps, stumps in his sight.
Fifty million acres of pines had been turned to stumps in
　　the Lake States by that time. Forty trees to the acre
　　would sum up to two thousand million pine trees. Jack Hard

had looked over the stumps four ways from a Michigan hill
and strained to imagine the ax strokes, the saw pulls, the peavey
pries, the horse sweat, and all other items in the work of
the biggest logging job ever heard of, forgetting only
Paul Bunyan and Babe the Blue Ox.
In fifty years maybe two thousand million pines were cut down,
  limbed, bucked, skidded, loaded on sleighs and big-wheels,
    hauled
  to rollways on river banks, and rafted to the waterway
  sawmills of Michigan, Wisconsin and Minnesota.
In miles of yearly swaths the harvest took the pines. The
  forest primeval melted away in the heat of giant toil.
  All the while the forest grew again, on the treeless
  prairies, in the building of cities, towns and farms.
  The loggers went over hill after hill, ever westing on
  the trails.
On and on, from section to section, from river to river,
  from town to town, for fifty years.

Men wearing out at the work, boys growing up to the work.
A river of sweat streaming from men, boys and horses
  for six hundred months and more.
Enough backaches in the making of the big clearing to form
  one backache as long and wide as the Mississippi Valley,
  and maybe bigger.
Enough calluses out of the chopping, sawing and peavey pushing
  to raise up a callus mountain the size of Pike's Peak.
All of the horse sweat and man sweat, gathered in one puddle,
  would have made another Great Salt Lake,
    vowed Jack Hard, of the Michigan Navarres.
Enough muscle power was generated from meat and beans,
  oats and hay in the logging of Michigan, Wisconsin
  and Minnesota to have pulled all the railroad freight
  trains of America for seven years.
Jack Hard said he would bet on all that, or on any item of it,
  and he was careful with his bets.

There was death on the pine lands as well as life and labor.
Fire followed the pinetops as settlers moved in and burned

off the logged country for grazing and farming.
Fire killed the seed trees and wounded the soil.
A great green ocean of pine was drained into the building
    up of the Middle West, and then the land was left
    as a dead sea, a black desert,
    under summer palls of smoke.
Death rode on fiery winds to the people of the woods.
The Peshtigo Forest Fire took eleven hundred lives.

Twelve men were President, each in his turn, of the Lake
    States forests through the work of the Big Clearing.
Twelve Presidents of the pineries that were the one great
    good of the land from Lake Huron to the Black Hills
    thought no more of the forests than the land office
    jobs and the tax collections.
President Buchanan made no motion whatever on the need to
    cut here and keep there in the forest, as the clearing began.
President Lincoln left the homesteader free to burn at will.
The other Presidents of the pineries were no better and no
    worse, up to President Theodore Roosevelt. And even he
    did not raise the hand of authority to say, "Let there be
    light on the black burns, let the trees grow."
The Congress, the Cabinet, the bureau chiefs, the governors,
    the legislatures have all failed to raise hands against
    the man-caused fires that burn and burn, on and on, year
    after year through the stumps of fifty million acres
    in the Lake States.
So said the son of the Navarres, in hard, white anger.
    Some Presidents! he said. Some God-damned government!
He went on to say that the fires would not be stopped
    and the trees would not be let to grow until there was
    money in it.
Some man with a money head on him will rise in the smoke,
    seeing through it to the soil, seeing how to grow
    trees instead of grass and make her pay; savvying how
    to sell other men with money heads on the proposition;
    and then all making it their business to stop fires,
    to let light be on the land, and let the trees grow.
That's the System, said Jack Hard. That's how it Works.

He said meanwhile he'd come West to grow up with the
   country and to get away from burned-over lands of
   jackpine, popple and stump-farm starvation. He said
   he hungered to see some growing and building done.
The West had been spanned seven times by rail. Jack Hard
   called that building the country up, he called that growing her.
   And here was our River Snake job. It would spread water over
   a hundred thousand desert acres and make them bloom. It was
   a project that had started in somebody with a money head.
   More were coming, more were on their way.
I've got something in my own head, that Navarre man said to me.
   It is for a new kind of dirt-moving machine. I have
   still another notion for power logging in country
   that stands on end.
Idaho looks good to me, said Jack Hard. Spread her out flat
   and she's bigger than Texas. But I like her bunched up
   and sky-high. I sing up to the breaks of the River Snake,
   I dream of spraddling my legs on the peak of He Devil,
   looking down a canyon side for a mile and a half, and
   dreaming more. Let me blast the old basalt and grade
   out roads through the tall and deep places, let me
   log out the old timber and grow up the new. I'll do her,
   by Jesus, and do her right, if there's money in her!
I said it wasn't in me, I couldn't invent a machine if
   my life depended on it, and I had no head for money.
For fame, then, said John Navarre, Jack Hard. You have read
      poems,
   you talk about poems, and you are free to write poems.
Go to the books and keep to the books until you are
   able and fit to write a book of your own.
I told him I was too ignorant for that.
Read Walt Whitman, he said, that's all you need.

(Then it was me by myself, I alone.
I walked alone one afternoon to the north rim
   of the canyon the Snake River had dug through lava rock.
A day of clear sky and booming wind
   over a gray, snowless plain.

I walked and stood as a speck of lone life there,
Looking down five hundred feet to the river giant.
I looked into that dark depth and said
   what I had learned by heart.
The speck on the earth chanted to the giant in the earth—
"I listened to the Phantom by Ontario's shore,
I heard the voice arising, demanding bards, . . .
Of all races and eras these States with veins full
   of poetical stuff most need poets, and are
   to have the greatest, and use them the greatest."
In the red of the sagebrush desert sundown,
   winter sundown, I stood chanting.
I peered into the river crack of the desert, darkening,
   and seemed to hear and see a Phantom of mine own.
The high time, the great day for me.)
But that was to come, that was 'way ahead of the night
   I stood, hearing the horns of
   wind and drums of rain on the tent, eyes on tomorrow
   and more tomorrows, visions in lantern light.

Trifles in the night, trifles in thunder.
The main thing for me was to think that now I was seventeen
   and getting on, spreading out, rising high. It was enough
   to know for this time that tomorrow it would be strung-out
   wagons on the desert road again, winding over the wet
   rimrock and through the dripping sagebrush, and with me
   on a high seat, handling four horses, tooling four lines,
   swinging a buckskin slasher with a twine whang, popping
   it high, handling them easy, right and proud.

Now it is another November.
Long, long look the few years back to the time of seventeen,
   to a time that seemed so young and fine and fair,
   so fresh and brave and primed with hope for me and my kind.
The night plowing, the furrow running by lanterns,
   in rainy darkness, yet my seeing a way clear.
Now I have read Walt Whitman. I revere him and love him and
   know

him by heart, I have written poetry, I carry a pack of my
   own poems with me, and I know them by heart also.
Now I have used my birthday on a poem. In the twilight I read
   the lines through, and in the twilight I hang my head.

In Walt Whitman's day the American glory was as the virgin
   pines of the Lake States. Now it is smoke on a dark land.
Now I have turned in my gear and my tools and my time.
Now I only remember.

Postscript, July 27, 1914 . . .

HERE ENDS THE BOOK, AS THE NIGHT ENDS. THE
dawn rides a gray east wind down the gorge of the Columbia
River. The smoke of a hundred thousand dying trees clouds Portland town. Daybreak comes to me as gray-green glimmers through
my room's ceiling-high windows, to thread the murk above the
shaded bulb. I've been at sonnets again; for you, Bess, but you
will not want them. Mood of the smoke-fouled night. Spake Caliban.

Let me be plain now. Work is done, eight months and more of
it. Stacked on my bunk for wrapping and packing away are the
scrawled-in tablets of the book of *Big Jim Turner,* with this postscript for the last pages. Today I go on a journey, hoboing out
with eleven dollars and thirty-three cents for a road stake, the
leavings of last fall's three hundred and forty. On my early October
way I'd stopped by in the Grande Ronde and sold the big red
horse to Bush Brown for a song, a measly seventy-five. Bush and
Rusty had gone homesteading on their own, proud children. Well,
what the hell! I've come through. The book is rough-green, but I
must go. Write these words down, then sleep for a spell, arise and
take the tablets of the book to Mary Wink, the old friend of Lily
Hurd at the Free Public Library, a Home for Poor Poets. She will
store it for me there.

The black scrawls run on across the yellow page under the poor
pale light and my hard right hand. I have my left elbow up on the
green oilcloth of the table. My head rests on this left hand, for I
am some tired; weak and weary, Brother Poe.

(This is my basement room of the year of old, 1911. It was

rundown, except for new oilcloth and such, and was easy to get. I felt right at home in the place. The blob above the door has changed with the seepage of three years. The image of William Howard Taft is gone from it as from the White House. But it is my bust of Pallas still.)

Now, Bess, here's a poem. It is an exercise I call "Flawed Sonnet." I could speak it to you soon, on some night sister to our night on Old Street and Shack Row. But I'm afraid not. I expect to go north to Rud Neal and our soldier friends at Fort Fox. We have swapped letters. Rud has his mind on a fine cove for hand logging in the Queen Charlottes. His Haida wife wants a visit home. His brother and a cousin are due to be let out of the army in mid-August. There will be four of us going then, we plan and I hope, into the quiet mists of the waterways and the green peace of the forested islands. I am proud that Rud Neal wants me. We are a team at falling timber, born for it, brothers by trade.

Here's a sonnet, Bess—

> *All manhood shrinks from loathing of his soul*
> > *By his own self! Well, shrink—yet bear the stroke,*
> > *Man with the hoe, man collared in the yoke,*
> *Tiller and sower for a dribbled dole,*
> *Who begs a hundredth when he grasps the whole,*
> > *Fool of the gods, a mean immortal joke!*
> > *Aye, shudder, man-beast, as the thongs and oak*
> *Punish your spirit for the hope it stole!*
>
> *You may not quit this mire and toil of truth,*
> > *Your flesh will quiver with the memory yet:*
> > *Who, alone, did naught but what you must atone,*
> *Who, alone, did form then fail high dreams of youth,*
> > *Who, alone, sank in self-pity and regret,*
> > *Who, alone, was only fit to be alone. Alone.*

So, Bess, you like it not. No twitter and peep. No hymn praising the base-browed. Nothing of thee, Dr. Lang. I write what flows to my hand. If I could dwell where Israfel hath dwelt. Colorado. Have you heard the wings and song of Israfel over Colorado, Bess? Or seen Poe's spirit brooding there? Or the ghosts of past and gone Presidents of These States walking whitely in Ludlow's bloody streets? Are angels seen and poets heard and Presidents encountered in Colorado now? By you, Black Dan Barton? By you, Bess Clover?

(*Postscript,* be plain.) Lily Hurd told me why Bess had not answered my letters. My sermon to Albert Clover in Salmon City on his duty had worked in him at last and brought him home at Christmas, freeing Bess to follow Black Dan and fight beside him for their faith in the Colorado war.

War of the Rockefeller Baptists and the Haywood Wobblies.

Joe Hill is in Utah, organizing the copper miners. He may go to you, Bess, and to Black Dan, but I shall not. I will not go. Mr. Russell Hicks, lamed by me, yet has me outlawed in Idaho. There's Jack Hard, now in the rain forests, a king, a kaiser over a hundred thousand acres of big timber, in a new Grundy Johnson deal. He would use me well and pay me high, but he has a tree for a heart and sees men as vermin. No timber kaiser's thumb for the neck of Big Jim Turner, or other thumb! For me plain friends, good labor, quiet mists, green peace, Poesy.

Here, Bess, last song—

> *Never the depth, the depth you may not know,*
> *Where broods the inmost spirit of my heart.*
> *From there no sound of oath or song can start,*
> *Thereto no blade or balm of love can go.*
> *Even to love this life could never show*
> *(Lacking the hand of diabolic art)*
> *Its old damned self in every shape and part,*
> *A soul so scarred, so fearful and so low.*
>
> *This is departure. Now with love-bright hours*
> *Left in high starlight, I alone descend*
> *Into the pit, e'en from the morning bell.*
> *They are abandoned, our sun-seeking flowers,*
> *As I pass to the shadows without end,*
> *Where grow the cypress and the asphodel.*

Once upon a time there was a free man. Today I seek his way again. This day. July 27, 1914. Mark it well. Hobo's mark, northbound to Fort Fox and the Canadian coast. To peace, oh, peace! and poet's freedom.